# The Warrior Enchained

part 2 of the Terrillian series

## by Sharon Green

grass
stain
press

*a division of Greenery Press*

Cover illustration by Kenneth Waters.

Published in the United States by Greenery Press, 1447 Park Ave., Emeryville, CA 94608.

www.greenerypress.com

ISBN 1-890159-26-3

*ONE*

The day was sunny, bright and fresh after two days of rain. I stepped out of my house onto the Neighborhood lawn, still wondering if I'd been wise letting myself be talked into attending the Neighborhood party. After a week and a half of being back on Central, I still wasn't in a party mood.

The blue, blue sky stretched far and wide above me as I walked; a small breeze chased around here and there, stirring my hair; the lawn was cool and green and thick as far as the eye could see. I wore a dress of pale yellow that billowed around me to the ground, making me feel as if I were floating, and my neighbors turned where they stood or sat, smiling and waving and waiting for me to join them. The success of my assignment had been made public three days earlier, but the rain had kept me from being mobbed by admirers right from the beginning. I'd had to turn the call off to save my sanity, and that in itself was a new experience. But then, one of my rewards was that I saw everything in a new light.

"Terry, come sit over here," Leebril Conrad called, her face animated behind the alternating pink and orange diagonal stripes of her face makeup. "I'm so excited I may burst!"

"Not on a Neighborhood chair, if you please, Lee," Sam Raymond put in dryly. "Save it for your own furniture."

"Samprey Raymond, you stop teasing me!" Lee pouted as everyone within hearing laughed. "Just because you're Neighborhood Chairman doesn't mean you can tease everyone – isn't that right, Terry?"

A large number of eyes turned in my direction, and I could feel the sudden wall of expectation arising from each mind behind those eyes. I was supposed to say something monumental and historic, something legend would some day be built on.

"What suddenly makes me an expert on Neighborhood Chairmen?" I asked, watching Lee tug at the skirt of the Alderanean leisure suit she wore. She was short and plump and the brief leisure suit looked terrible on her, but she'd worn leisure suits before without caring how she looked – as long as she was dressed in the height of fashion.

"Notoriety makes the acclaimed an expert on everything," Sam grinned, stepping back to give me access to a chair if I wanted it. "If you plan on staying home for a while, I'll probably end up losing the Chairmanship to you."

"Not to me," I denied with a headshake. "I'm not Chairman material. And even if I were, tomorrow I'm off on another assignment, so your position is safe."

Sam echoed everyone else's disappointment at hearing the news, but he seemed relieved even as he protested his displeasure. It was the main reason I'd said what I had, even though I hadn't originally intended making an announcement of it. His original words had been lighthearted, but he'd been seriously worried.

"Terry, that's not fair!" Lee protested, getting to her feet once she was sure I wouldn't be sitting. "You only just got back from talking those savages into letting us build our complex on their silly planet! How can they give you another assignment so soon?"

"Possibly it happened because I asked for one." I shrugged, ignoring Lee's resentment. "I'm feeling very restless these days, and work is the best cure for that."

"It certainly is," Ted Rohman agreed, putting an arm around my shoulders. Tedlor Rohman was a newcomer to the Neighborhood, as tall and good-looking as Sam, but five or six years younger. "But don't forget, Terry, work is also the best thing to make us appreciate relaxation. I've been looking forward to asking you to a real, but you've left me very little time. You'll have to tell me what time to pick you up tonight."

"*You* pick her up?" Sam frowned, moving a step closer. "What makes you think she's going out with you? I intended asking Terry out myself tonight."

"Neighborhood Chairmen and diplomats don't have *every* privilege," Ray Ladiff interrupted the argument. "I've known Terry longer than both of you, and it so happens I was going to...."

"You're not a Mediator, Ray," Sam interrupted with a gesture of his hand. "Just working in Terry's department doesn't entitle you to special consideration. As far as knowing her the longest goes, longest doesn't mean best. I can remember...."

"That's right, longest doesn't mean best," Ted agreed, interrupting in turn. "It seems to me this can be taken care of by...."

His words trailed off as I moved out of hearing range, disgusted by the way the three of them were acting. They didn't want to take me out, they just wanted to be seen with me, showing everyone what big, important men they were. I could feel everything they felt when they looked at me, no matter how they tried to hide it.

"Terry, wait a minute," Lee called, hurrying after me. I stopped where I was until she reached me, and she gave me a broad, friendly smile and asked, "Aren't they disgusting? Can you imagine men fighting over a woman in this day and age?"

I looked back at the three men engrossed in calm conversation and saw, in a flash of memory, three other men facing one another in the rain. All three carried swords and all three had wanted me, and only one had walked away from the disagreement.

"I don't know if I can stand the excitement," I commented, again ignoring Lee. This time she was jealous, even though it was common knowledge that she'd already had all three men in her bed at least once each.

"Well, you can teach them all a lesson." She smiled, smoothing her straight orange hair. "If you come to the party I'm giving tonight, they'll all be left feeling foolish – especially if you stay over as my house guest until it's time for you to leave."

I looked at her easy smile, seeing nothing but warmth in it, wondering why I never realized before how shallow she was. Lee wanted me at her party and as her house guest, but only for the prestige my presence would bring. It was easy to feel that she didn't like me, that she resented my height, my slender build, my un-made-up face, my plain, long brown hair. The only thing she *did* like about me was my reputation as a Prime Xenomediator, a reputation she could use to advance her own cause.

"Lee, I'm crushed but I can't make it," I said, projecting the least amount of honesty and regret. "There are still dozens of things to be taken care of before I leave, not to mention all those reports on my new assignment. I'll be spending the rest of the day and night on them."

"That's too bad," she pouted. "I guess I was looking forward to having you come more than I should have." She hesitated briefly. "Well, you'll just have to promise to be my guest as soon as you're home again. You will promise, won't you, Terry?"

"Of course I promise," I assured her at once, patting her hand. "You can give me a homecoming party."

"How lovely!" she squealed, clapping her hands in delight. "No one has ever given you a homecoming party, and I'll be the first!"

She turned around and hurried away toward another group of our neighbors, anxious to pass on the word about how important she was going to be. I watched until she reached the nearest group, then turned away and headed back to my house. The party had definitely been a mistake, but now I knew it as a fact.

Once I got the front door closed I leaned against it, automatically clearing my mind of all the emotions that had been prodding at me. I took a deep breath and went upramp to my living quarters, heading directly for the bathroom. I'd already had one bath that day, but I felt the need for another. I'd been bathing a lot since I got back from Rimilia, but whatever I'd been trying to wash away still wasn't gone.

I dialed a hot bath, and by the time I was out of the long yellow dress, the tub was filled. I stepped into the water and sat down, letting my mind go back over the last two weeks and beyond. It was hard to think about, and the passage of time wasn't making it any easier.

I'd gone to Rimilia to help convince its natives to allow the Centran Amalgamation to build a complex on their planet, and everything had gone according to plan – with one unexpected addition. I'd fallen in love with the man I'd been sent to help, making the mistake of thinking he loved me, too. I'd given him everything within my power to give and he had given me his child – and then he had sent me back to the embassy we had on the planet, my assignment completed, my talents no longer needed. I was an empath, a Prime Xenomediator, and feelings are impossible to hide from an empath. Tammad, my beloved, the man I had been willing to give my life for, felt no regret or sense of loss when he sent me away from him. This I knew better than any other fact of my life, and the pain continued to plague me both asleep and awake.

I stirred in the warm bath water, thinking about transparenting the walls around me, then rejecting the idea. I no longer felt the need to reach out in some vague way, groping for something I couldn't explain even to myself. Empaths usually lived half-lives when on Central, their gifts and the very memory of those gifts suppressed until the need to use them came along again. Then, once they'd reached their destinations, the triggering word would be spoken to awaken them and let them do their jobs, the countertrigger coming only when the assignment was complete. This time, as a reward for the work I'd done for the Amalgamation, the countertrigger hadn't been spoken to me and I still retained my talent, although I'd been forbidden to tell anyone. I stirred again in the water, wondering just how much a reward I'd been given. All the people I'd thought of as friends had turned out to be something else entirely.

Abruptly I felt bored with sitting in a tub of water, and rose to my feet without even washing. I'd felt the same sort of impatience on Rimilia – the impatience to do rather than sit – and had been lucky enough to be able to take over Murdock McKenzie's transport back to Central. Murdock McKenzie was in charge of Central's Diplomacy Bureau – and considerably more, I was beginning to suspect – and he had decided he and his people could wait for the transport to return for them. I'd left the very next day after I'd been returned to the embassy, and as soon as I'd grounded at Tallion City Outer Port, had gone directly to the medical center. The tiny speck that was Tammad's child and mine now lay in stasis, waiting for me to decide what to do with it, and my body was protected again. I didn't plan on needing the protection, but I was protected.

I toweled the water off myself, then picked up the yellow dress and carried it back into the bedroom with me. It had come to me that I'd worn it only because Tammad wouldn't have approved of a shorter dress, and in spite of everything I was still dressing to please him. A man who beat me when I disobeyed him, who ignored my wishes when his own failed to coincide, who used me and then sent me away – and I was still trying to please him.

I took out a gray one-piece body suit and got into it, but didn't bother with shoes. I'd gotten so used to going barefoot on Rimilia that shoes now seemed a burden rather than an aid. I hadn't been lying to Lee when I said I had reports to go over, but somehow I wasn't in the mood for reading reports. I remembered the last time I'd had reports to read, reports on Rimilia, but it hadn't mattered then whether or not I was in the mood to read them. That barbarian had been there and he'd forced me to read them, just as he'd forced me to do everything his way.

I was still standing in the middle of the floor, dwelling on the past, when my visitor call sounded, telling me someone was in my entrance hall. I felt annoyed at being disturbed and almost decided against seeing who it was, but I really didn't want to read those reports. I wavered briefly, my annoyance against everything growing, then resolutely headed downramp.

Sandy Kemper looked around when I reached the hall, his long, thin face as serious as ever. He'd been standing and staring at a wall, and my appearance seemed to bring him out of introspection.

"Terry, how are you?" he asked, coming forward to look down at me. "I didn't have the nerve to come and see you when you first got back, but now that you're leaving again I couldn't stay away. Are you all right?"

His brown eyes were concerned, but more than that, his emotions agreed with his words. I was startled that he really was concerned about me, and the sarcastic retort I'd been about to speak died in my throat.

"I'm fine, Sandy," I assured him, dredging up something of a smile. "How have you been doing?"

"Possibly better, possibly worse," he sighed, returning my smile. "Murdock paid quite a bit of attention to me before he left for Rimilia. 'Sandros, I foresee a great deal of difficulty for you should you be unable to overcome your aversion to dissembling. The tree of Diplomacy is nurtured with evasions grown to look like certainties.' You know how he is."

"I certainly do," I laughed, hearing Murdock McKenzie's dry tones in Sandy's mimicry. "How's your quadriwagon behaving? Any more problems?"

The brown eyes came to me with pain in them, making me realize I'd said the wrong thing. Sandy blamed himself for what Tammad had done to me, but only after I'd blamed him first.

"Terry, I can't tell you how sorry I am!" he blurted, reaching out to take my hand. "What happened was all my fault, and the thought's been haunting me ever since! Is there anything I can do, anything I can say...?"

"Sandy, you can forget about it," I interrupted, resisting the urge to pull my hand away from him. "Once we were on Rimilia, Tammad admitted he knew I hadn't been given to him as a house-gift. He wanted to use me so he did; it was as simple as that. Nothing you could have said or done would have stopped him."

"But that's barbaric!" he gasped, his mind filled with shock. "To rape and beat a Prime – to subject her to indignities and cruelties... Aren't they going to punish him?"

"Of course they are," I said, suddenly giving in to the desire to take my hand back. "They're going to punish him by giving him everything he asks for, up to and including whatever he needs to make himself supreme leader of his people. Don't you remember, Sandy? It's called political expedience. Now if you'll excuse me, I have reports to go over before I leave for Alderan. Give my best to Murdock when you see him."

I turned away from Sandy and headed back upramp, pretending I didn't see or feel his unspoken protest or his outstretched hand. What had been done to me had been terrible, but only because I was a Prime – or at least so Sandy felt. Everyone on the planet had been conditioned to pity an empath, but Sandy's concern went deeper than most, surfacing as a need to hover nervously, hoping for some sort of notice. His touching my hand had produced a flash of intense desire in him, a heat I could almost feel from the echoing flash in his mind. Sandy ached to have me – but probably only because I was a Prime.

I went back into my bedroom and closed and locked the door, then paced back and forth to help myself calm down. The fifth time I passed the door I paused to stare at it, then went over and unlocked it again. There'd been no need to lock it in the first place, not against someone like Sandy. Sandy Kemper would no more come uninvited into my living quarters than – than Tammad had allowed a locked door to stand between us. He'd broken the door down immediately, striding angrily through the wreckage, then had –

I stopped the train of thought and put my hands to my head, appalled at what was happening to me. Could I actually be blaming men for rationally discussing their differences rather than spilling each other's blood, for accepting a refusal of disinterest rather than taking me against my will? The men of Central were civilized and sensible, not barbarians who needed to be criticized and sneered at! Then why was I –

I cut off that thought too, closing my eyes against the anger building inside me. It was all that barbarian's fault, all part of what he had done to me. Wrong looked right and right looked wrong, and everything had to be thought of and done according to *his* beliefs and preconceptions! He had forced *me*, a Prime, into fulfilling his every desire, obeying his every wish – and then had thrown me away, my usefulness over. I hated him, hated, everything about him – and hated myself for wishing he had kept me.

I went to my bed and sank down onto it, then stretched out beside the reports I'd left there. I was going to have to force myself to forget what had gone on during my time on Rimilia, and burying myself in work would be the first step toward doing that. I *was* a Prime, one of the best; even if *he* didn't want me, everyone else did.

I pulled the first report to me and thumbed through it quickly, verifying that it held nothing but details about Alderan. Everyone in the Amalgamation knew about Alderan, how it was one of the greatest fashion centers, one of the first planets settled by Central, one of the first to break away into independence. Its main claim to fame, of course, was being the home planet of the Kabras, but that need hardly be pointed out. Mediation assignments on Alderan invariably involved the Kabras, which never failed to amuse me. In my opinion, the doings of the largest group of professional soldiers in the Amalgamation should not require the services of a Mediator to settle its differences.

The second report described the disagreement one contingent of Kabras were currently involved in. They had hired themselves out to a merchant on the planet Defflore to protect his interests against a rival merchant – and incidentally take as much land and goods from the other merchant as possible – but the second merchant had also hired a contingent of Kabras equal to the first merchant's force. Such a situation had come to mean a standoff, as it would be foolish to expect two equal groups of Kabras to fight, and the only alternative at that point was for the two merchants to come to a peaceful understanding, or for one of them to hire an additional Kabra fighting force. The presence of the additional force would give the merchant who had it immediate victory –

after all, a fight between two unequal Kabra groups is a certainty in outcome without needing a single blow to be struck – and reparations could then be claimed against the defeated merchant. In this instance, however, neither merchant could spare the expense of an additional force, and the agreement between them was quickly concluded. Not quite as quickly concluded was the fulfillment of payment to the forces of the first merchant, the one who had begun all the difficulty. He insisted he had been expecting acquisitions from the efforts of the Kabras and would have paid them from those. Without the acquisitions he was totally unable to live up to his end of the bargain, and demanded that the Kabras remove themselves from his property and return to their home world. The Kabras, of course, refused to stir until their fees were paid in full.

I sighed deeply and put the report aside, then stretched the weariness out of my body. The Mediation would be dull and unimportant, but sending anyone but a Prime to Alderan would be considered an insult by the Kabras. I'd been to Alderan a number of times before, and had disliked being there each of the times. If any other assignment had been available I would have refused this one, but even Alderan was better than staying on Central. I looked again at the third folder – which gave details on my transportation and time of departure – then put it all aside and went into my kitchen to dial a meal from my chef. Going to bed early would take care of the rest of the night, and tomorrow I would be on my way – hopefully, to forgetfulness.

*TWO*

The skies were gray above stuffy, dead calm when I left the transport at Nidah Inner Port on Alderan. Unlike Central and most of the other worlds of the Amalgamation, all of Alderan's ports were inner ports, situated right inside the cities they were related to. That fact alone said something about the Kabras of Alderan, but the Kabras themselves were pleased with the arrangement – as though any civilized being could be pleased to have transports take off and land at their front doorstep. I shook my head over custom and the people who conform to it, then made my way across the open field to the landings building where arrangements were made for visitor accommodations. There wasn't a breath of air anywhere, not even on the field, and I was pleased I'd brought an entire wardrobe of Alderanian leisure suits and had had the foresight to wear one of them for the landing. The short skirt and low-cut bodice gave my body some relief from the oppressive humidity, but I could almost feel the perspiration on my face running my makeup.

The landings building was large, starkly undecorated, and totally without air-conditioning of any sort, a reminder that Kabras supposedly believed in living the austere life. I'd been vaguely impressed by the lacks on my first visit to Alderan, but had soon discovered that the vast majority of the Kabras paid more lip service than attention to the custom of austerity. Their own homes were luxurious to the point of decadence, a sure sign of how far they had come in the last three or four generations. Austerity was no longer necessary, and they'd grown mature enough to realize it.

I detached myself from the group of new arrivals I'd been walking with and went toward the pre-reservations desk, knowing arrangements would already have been made for me. I stopped in front of the young woman behind the desk, cleared my throat to get her attention, then suddenly discovered that her attention was unnecessary.

"Terrillian Reya," came a deep voice from behind my left shoulder. "Welcome back to Alderan."

I turned in the direction of the deep voice, already knowing whom I would see. Garth R'Hem Solohr stood there, tall and unselfconscious in the short Kabran kilt of officer blue, his long dark hair tied back with a small blue band, his chest bare beneath the regulation straps of office, his feet thonged into sturdy sandals. I had once told him how amusing it was to see a grown man's bare knees, trying to insult him out of his usual air of extreme superiority, but all he'd done was laugh and tell me he didn't mind seeing my knees at all. I felt the usual stab of annoyance at the way he looked at me, his mind full of sharp desire, his gray eyes filled with amusement, and found impatience coloring my tone.

"One of these days I'll be considered important enough to be met by someone of standing," I said into his grin, then turned to the girl behind the desk. "Has a visitor registration been made in the name of Terrillian Reya, Prime Xenomediator on assignment from Central?"

"But – but of course it has!" the girl protested, shocked out of her own air of superiority. "Colonel Solohr is here to see to your every need and desire – and the Colonel's family is one of the oldest and most respected on Alderan! How can you say...?"

"Now, now," Garth interrupted her. "The Prime is already aware of my exalted status and abilities. She merely feels it necessary to protest our acquaintanceship in the hopes of insulting me. The rudeness is simply her usual manner of behavior."

"Rudeness is not rudeness when truth is involved," I shot back, immediately feeling the girl's indignation. "Family position has nothing at all to do with individual actions. Have you arranged accommodations for me, or am I to be forced to sleep in the streets?"

"Never the streets, my dear Prime," Garth laughed, folding his arms across his chest. "If no other alternative presents itself, you can always share my accommodations."

"I would prefer the streets," I told him. "Would it be too much to ask you to see to my luggage?"

"The matter has already been taken care of," he informed me with a bow edged with sarcasm. "If you'll follow me, I'll show you to the transportation I've arranged."

"Certainly," I agreed with a pleasant nod. "I'd rather have you in front of me than behind me any day. Lead away."

The girl behind the desk was close to spluttering by then, something Garth was well aware of as he took my arm and led the way to the street. His amusement left me close to the teeth-grinding point myself. What would I have to say to him to dent that obnoxious air of superiority?

"This vehicle is ours," Garth said, leading the way across the crowded strollwalk to the sled at the curb. "If you find it unacceptable, I'll have it destroyed at once."

"And then make me walk," I nodded, climbing into the sled by the door held open for me by a uniformed Kabra of lower rank. "Or would you find it necessary to carry me?"

"Oh, carry you, of course," Garth laughed, settling himself beside me on the white fur cushion. "An opportunity wasted is an opportunity regretted."

The Kabra closed the door behind Garth, cutting off all outside noise, then climbed up to the front of the sled and guided it into the stream of sled traffic moving past us. Slide walks were disapproved of on Alderan, having been considered too effeminate by generations gone by. I wondered what they would have thought of the force-field enclosed, decro-powered sleds their descendants used to take themselves everywhere.

"You really shouldn't have embarrassed that girl like that," Garth said, leaning back to put his arm across the seat top behind me. "Whether or not you care for the idea, I do happen to be an important man on this planet. My ferrying you around is a greater compliment than you realize."

"The girl wasn't embarrassed," I murmured, looking out at the crowded streets and wondering why the emotional ocean wasn't as strong as it had been on my last visit. "She was awed at seeing you and scandalized over my lack of appreciation of the honor bestowed upon me. Her reaction was too generalized to be personal."

"But, of course," he said, his tone still humorous: "How could I have thought to describe an emotional reaction to *you*? Please forgive my stupidity."

"What, again?" I drawled, evoking a chuckle from him, but not really paying attention to the conversation. I was studying the people on the streets, those riding, those walking, those going in and out of the large, square-cut stone buildings rising all around. There was something like a mental curtain of sorts between me and them, one that could be pushed aside easily enough when I thought about it, but which fell into place again as soon as I turned my attention to something other than wanting to know what they were feeling. My gift had never worked that way before, and I didn't know why it had changed. Was it possible I disliked Kabran pretensions of superiority so much that I was beginning to block them out?

"I do seem to be something of a burden to you," Garth commented, his body relaxing in enjoyment of the cool air suddenly beginning to fill the sled. "A pity you'll be forced to put up with me again during your visit."

I turned my head to look at the self-satisfied smile on his face, knowing he also *felt* self-satisfied, and then my mind seemed to – *center* on his, so to speak. I became aware of something behind the self-satisfaction, something that wasn't quite as flippant and free-swinging as he wanted me to believe.

"It's strange you should use the word 'burden,'" I said, feeling my mind probe at him. "Bore, scatterbrain, obnoxious pain in the rump, yes. But, 'burden'?"

"Possibly I was trying to help you with your cataloguing of my virtues," he chuckled, unaffected by what I'd said. "If you feel the word inappropriate, by all means remove it from the list."

"The word wasn't my choice to begin with," I pursued. "Why would the famous Colonel Solohr consider himself in conjunction with the concept of burden, even to me? It seems an unconscious attempt at self-rebuke, possibly even the hint of resentment at your current assignment. Where would it be more fitting for you to be? Where would you prefer to be?"

"Don't you think you ought to save that for tomorrow's mediating?" he asked, the smile gone from his broad, handsome face, a stiffness entering his thoughts. "I'd never forgive myself if you became overtired."

"For some of us, thinking is nearly effortless," I commented, moving around to face him. "You were off-planet on campaign for a while, weren't you? What made you come back so soon? And why the dissatisfaction?"

"Terry, it really is unwise of you to continue with this," he said, the stiffness having reached his voice and eyes. "Insulting me isn't as impossible as you seem to think it is, and I doubt if you'd care for the consequences."

"Do you mean you'd challenge me?" I scoffed. "Just imagine yourself in front of your peers under *those* circumstances. They'd laugh themselves silly."

I turned away from him with a headshake, deciding I'd accomplished what I'd set out to do. His air of superiority had been nicely punctured, and was rapidly being replaced with annoyance and frustration. It couldn't have happened to a more deserving fellow.

The sled traffic was rather heavy, and we rode along in silence for a few minutes. There was no doubt Garth was unhappy and dissatisfied with something, but all I cared about was the fact that he no longer throbbed with desire when he looked at me. Garth had wanted me since the first time we'd met, but the desire was an automatic one, something combined out of his position and mine. The fact that I'd refused him and continued to refuse him fed his desire, but I had no interest in soothing his longings and satisfying his curiosity. His interest in women wasn't particularly unusual; I just didn't care to have that interest directed toward me.

"You certainly must feel secure in your position," he said at last, making a great effort to recapture his former attitudes. "It would scarcely be proper for me to challenge you, but Kabras have been known to be severe with women who offend them. Are you trying to force me to be severe with you?"

I turned to study him again. He was making good progress in throwing off the frustration I'd produced, even going so far as to try returning the annoyance.

"Are you trying to pretend to be so uncivilized as to threaten a Prime?" I asked in turn, arching my eyebrows in disbelief. "No one, on any world in the Amalgamation, would so much as slap my wrist and we both know it. Are you trying to impress me with your virility?"

"If I am, it isn't working very well," he laughed, the amusement real. "You seem to have no trouble resisting me. Why won't you even consider the idea of spending a night with me?"

"What, directness?" I gasped, pretending to be shocked.

"After I'd decided Kabran men didn't know the meaning of the word?"

"When all else fails," he shrugged, keeping his light gaze directly on me. "Has the stratagem succeeded?"

"Not in the least," I came back. "Did you really expect it to?"

"You should know the answer to that as well as I do," he observed, still staring at me. "Do you care to explain why I haven't succeeded?"

"No, I don't care to explain it," I smiled, a stiff, inflexible smile. "I have no need of explaining my actions to anyone, least of all you."

"I see." He nodded, keeping his eyes on me. "I'm too far beneath you to bother with."

"Exactly," I nodded, turning away from his smoldering anger. I much preferred having Garth R'Hem Solohr angry and distant rather than amused and near. I had sensed a boldness and restrained strength in him the moment we had first met, convincing me how much safer it would be to keep him at arm's length. It would be foolish to say I feared him – fear is such a strong emotion – but uneasiness is uncomfortable enough to make one avoid it. Perhaps I had now managed to avoid Garth as well.

A few moments later, Garth stirred and touched my arm.

"Your lodging at last," he announced, and I looked around to see the sled pulling into the circular drive that led to the best visitor's Residence in Nidah. It was so new I'd only stayed there once before, and I was pleased to see it again. The suites were large and well furnished, and the food was of better quality than anywhere else on Alderan. When we pulled up at its front entrance, a garishly costumed servant stepped forward to open the sled's door, saving the Kabra who had been driving from having to lower himself again. Garth stepped out, turned to offer me his hand, then directed the servant to see to the luggage in the compartment beneath the sled. The heat was wilting after the coolness of the sled, but directly behind the entrance's air curtain lay more cool air, supplied, so it was said, only for the comfort of off-planet visitors. Those Alderaneans standing and walking about the immense entrance foyer were far too good to notice how comfortable they were.

Garth made inquiries as to which suite had been reserved for me, all the while pretending not to see the marble and mirror surfaces all around us, the plush white carpeting, the silver fixtures. As soon as records had been checked and identities verified, we were led by a servant carrying my luggage to a lift which swept us eighteen stories in the air, then to a cream-colored door which opened on a green and blue suite. My luggage was left in a far room to be seen to by the Residence's maid staff, then the servant bowed and left us alone. Garth had stood himself to one side of the room, and once the servant was gone he bowed to me.

"Now, if you will excuse me, I have several personal matters to attend to," he said, his voice overly neutral. "I will, of course, return for you in the morning."

"Of course," I nodded, turning away from him to glance around the room. "Do have a pleasant evening without me."

"I wish you the same," he said, and then suddenly he was behind me, his hands on my arms forcing me to turn back to him. "You are an insolent, unbearably overweening woman. One day – "

He let the words trail off as he looked down at me, his emotions mixed, and then he showed a grin.

"One day you may learn that I truly am a Kabra," he murmured. He let me go, took my arm, slapped me hard on the wrist, then turned, strode to the door and was gone. I gasped at the sting of the slap, furious that he would dare to strike me, but he was already out of reach of any words I cared to say. I stood and stared at the door for a moment, rubbing my wrist, then went to the call to arrange for immediate maid service. I wasn't sure what Garth's gesture meant, but I knew I didn't want to be alone in case he came back. His mind pattern had very briefly become stranger than I had ever known it to be, but I had no interest in finding out why it had happened.

The next morning, when Garth came to call for me, he found me already in the entrance foyer, waiting for him. I wore a fresh leisure suit, completely different from the one of the day before, but the only thing different about him was the ceremonial sword he had added to the rest of his accouterments. He came up to me where I sat and bowed very slightly, his left hand resting on the sword hilt.

"Such exemplary promptness," he greeted me with amusement. "I thought it would be necessary to come to your suite before my duties as your protector might be begun."

"Yesterday a guide, today a protector," I remarked, getting to my feet. "Your career seems to be progressing in leaps and bounds. At this rate, by tomorrow you might even be a clerk in Central's Mediation department."

"Now, now, none of that," he scolded, adopting a fierce and dedicated look. "Your protector mustn't be distracted with attempts at insult. You wouldn't care to have him forget his duty at the wrong time."

"I've never been told what it is you're supposed to be protecting me from," I said, folding my arms. "Which of the two parties of the dissension is supposed to be the dangerous one?"

"Both parties of a dissension are dangerous." He grinned, taking my arm to lead me out. "My presence may be pure tradition and formality these days, but at one time it wouldn't have been. You can never tell who will decide you're biased."

"A Prime Xenomediator being biased!" I snorted, flinching at the heat as we passed through the entrance curtain. "There couldn't possibly be anyone foolish enough to believe that."

"You'd be surprised," be answered, opening the door to the sled at the curb. "Most people don't know how mediation works, and when you deal with ignorance, you also deal with fear and mistrust."

He climbed into the sled next to me, and we pulled away from the curb and down the driveway, undoubtedly heading for Mediation Hall. He'd made a good point about the way people think, and I was surprised to see such clear understanding from someone who couldn't feel the emotions firsthand. Most unawakened people knew little enough about their own emotions, let alone about the emotions of others.

Garth seemed content to let the ride pass in silence, and in just a few minutes we pulled up beside Mediation Hall, a large, grim, blocky building made of dark stone rectangles piled one on top of the other. I felt my usual shudder at the appearance of that building, sensing the flood of desperate emotions locked in the cold, dark stone. But, as I'd always done in the past, I forced them away from me and followed Garth out of the sled. A Hall guide waited just inside the front entrance, and five minutes later we were entering Mediation Chamber C.

The Chamber itself was familiar enough, being a large room containing a small table at its center, three chairs around the table, and four benches lined up about ten feet behind each of the two chairs that faced one another. The chief adversaries were already in the room, each standing with his own group of supporters, all of them turning toward the door when I entered. Murmurs arose from each of the groups, underlining uneasiness and suspicion from both sides, but the tenor of thoughts changed immediately when Garth stepped in behind me. The Deffloran merchant group began buzzing frantically, outrage in their gestures almost as clearly as in their thoughts; the Kabran contingent hummed contentedly, considering their claim already conceded to. I stepped aside to let Garth move forward ahead of me, then watched the contenders as their attention centered on him.

"Gentlemen," Garth announced, looking from one group to the other. "I am Colonel Garth R'Hem Solohr, assigned protector to the Prime Terrillian Reya. Should any of you attempt to harm her or interfere with her mission, that one must answer to me. Don't make the mistake of considering my commission an idle one. I assure you I take it seriously."

Garth stepped aside, letting the men see me again. All of their eyes were on me, the merchants with nervousness, the Kabras with faint annoyance mixed with uneasiness. None of them had ever been involved in Mediation before, and their hesitation was easy to feel.

"Gentlemen, please take your places," I said, walking forward to the third chair at the small table. The room was unbearably close, and everyone in it was sweating. Two men, one merchant and one Kabra, separated themselves from their groups to join me at the table, and the rest of the men, six per side, retired to the benches behind their respective representative. The Kabras were dressed as all Kabras are, but the main representative wore the same sort of ceremonial sword as Garth had.

When we were all settled at the table, I nodded to each of the men studying me.

"You will now be discussing the disagreement between you," I told them, settling myself more comfortably in the chair. " Speak to each other, not to me, and don't look to me for decisions of any sort. Whatever decisions are agreed upon will be agreed upon by you two. You need only introduce yourselves when you first begin. Please proceed."

The two men began glaring at each other as I closed my eyes, meshing in with the deep hostility they both felt. The Deffloran merchant stirred in his seat, probably tugging at the tight, high collar of his shirt. He and his contingent all wore the same sort of shirts, high collared and long sleeved, probably so that they might, when dealing, open the collars and roll up the sleeves. The gestures were meant to show their willingness to deal, but collars were unopened and sleeves unrolled that day. The merchants had taken their stand and had no intentions of abandoning it.

"I will begin," announced the Deffloran merchant, his voice high and stiff with resentment and defensiveness. "I am Raskar Alnid, a man who has been done out of his due! A man who stands to lose all he possesses because of the knife at his throat! A man who was cruelly threatened and robbed...."

"Gently," I cautioned, projecting peace and calm at both men without opening my eyes. The Kabra had been about to retort in anger, but both men's heat cooled when they felt my projection. The bands of fire red in their minds eased down to dull purple, still angered but well within their control. "Just the actual happenings, if you please," I added.

"The happenings are not difficult to relate." The man huffed, a faint, nearly unnoticed surprise behind his anger. He had intended pursuing his complaints and didn't quite understand why he wasn't doing so. "I engaged these – these – Kabras to aid me against my enemies and they accepted the commission then refused to uphold the contract. Therefore I, in the same manner, refuse to pay their outrageous demands."

"Our demands are not outrageous," the Kabran officer put in coldly. "We contracted to appear at a certain place and time and did so. We now seek no more than to collect our fee."

"For standing about like statues?" Raskar Alnid demanded. "For greeting the troops of my enemy as brothers? For refusing to face them as fighters and men, in defense of my claims and attempts?"

"Merely for appearing as we contracted to do, if you care to put it in that light!" snapped the officer, sharing the other's outrage. "Our bonds cover that, and battle against an equal Kabra force is specifically interdicted. With two forces, of equal ability, what sense is there in fighting? Both would be wiped out without any settlement of the original argument."

As soon as the attention of the two men left me and they began speaking to each other, I was able to move to the second phase of my purpose there. The Kabran officer felt deep conviction in what he was saying, and I passed that conviction on to the merchant, along with a sense of honor defended. The merchant felt the emotions and hesitated, then dropped the outrage that he'd been projecting so strongly.

"But Kabras are *fighters!*" he protested, not knowing I was passing on his bewilderment. "If you have no intentions of fighting, why do you accept commissions to appear?"

"We will fight any force other than our own people," the officer said, made uncomfortable by the lack of understanding. "Should we slay our brothers, nothing would be accomplished but our own destruction. Surely this was explained to you?"

"I was told only of Kabran traditions," the merchant sighed, feeling the officer's guilt. "I was led to believe I would be triumphant if I engaged your force. Why do you hire out to both sides of a disagreement?"

"Would you have us practice favoritism?" the officer asked, attempting to soothe the merchant's deep disappointment. "What if the commission we refused was yours, allowing your enemy a clear path to victory? Would you have more than you have now, or less?"

"The thought never occurred to me before," the merchant responded, frowning. "What am I to do now? I haven't got the amount contracted for, not without a victory."

"But you agree we honored our contract?" the other man pursued, but gently. At the merchant's defeated, reluctant nod, the officer added his own nod and a smile. "Then settlement should not be difficult. Our honor is more important than monetary considerations, and it was a recognition of honor we sought here, not gain. Are you able to meet half the agreed upon fee?"

"Half?" the merchant blurted, surprised. "You're willing to settle for half, without argument?"

"Certainly." The officer smiled. "Our expenses were far less than they would have been if we'd fought."

"Excellent," smiled the merchant, rubbing his hands together. "I'm sure we can work matters out now to our mutual satisfaction. Would you and your group care to join my cousins and myself at a meal? A tall, cold drink would work wonders right now."

"That sounds perfect," agreed the officer. "I know just the place, I'm sure you'll love it."

They were feeling very brotherly and satisfied, but I was feeling the least bit annoyed. All that traveling and bother for a ten minute dispute that could have been handled by the newest of Xenomediators! I stood up from my own chair, beginning to wonder what my alternative to returning to Central was, and the two men suddenly remembered that I was there. They both felt an instant of guilt at having forgotten my presence, but the merchant recovered first and spread some of his satisfaction in my direction.

"My dear young lady," he purred, reaching out with the intention of taking my hand. "How rude of us to have ignored you! After having wasted your trip, you must at least join us at our meal. We insist!"

"Thank you, no," I said at once, stepping away from him. "My trip accomplished the purpose it was meant to, so your offer is unnecessary. I'll be returning to my accommodations now."

"Then we shall see you there safely," the merchant announced, expansive in his relief, ignoring the fact that I hadn't let him touch me.

"That's my job," Garth interrupted, abruptly right next to me. "The Prime continues under my protection as long as she remains on the planet. No need to trouble yourself."

Garth was controlling himself outwardly, but inwardly he was more than annoyed. He didn't seem to care for the merchant, and something in his eyes must have sent the message to the Kabran officer.

"You're right, of course," he interrupted hastily, cutting off whatever the merchant had been about to say – against Garth's statement if his less friendly expression and abrupt flash of anger meant anything. "We'll just walk you two out to your vehicle and be on our way."

The officer had put a friendly smile on his face, but his left hand rested on his ceremonial sword, pointing up the sword Garth wore. The merchant looked from the officer's sword to Garth's, then nodded his head.

"Of course we'll abide by the lady's wishes," he said, pointedly not looking at Garth. "An escort to her vehicle, and then we'll be on our way."

Garth was only half pleased with that answer. He put himself next to me as I turned toward the door, leaving the merchant and Kabran officer to bring up the rear. I was so happy to get out of there, I didn't even bother checking for ruffled sensibilities.

The weather was still horribly hot and humid outside, but a thick cloudiness had descended that couldn't be appreciated from indoors. Our party went down the steps to the walk, people pressing around me as if I were some sort of celebrity; people were on .the walk, the thrum of their emotions close, my mind tugging so tenaciously at the question of where to go that the thrum barely touched me, and then –

"Terril!" a voice called, a deep, strong voice I never thought I'd hear again. I stopped short in the middle of the walk in disbelief. He couldn't be there on Alderan where I was, there was no reason for him to be there. It had to be my imagination playing tricks –

"Who in the name of sweet reason is *that*?" demanded the merchant Raskar Alnid. I still couldn't believe this was happening, but I slowly turned my head in the direction from which the voice had come – and there he was, striding toward me. I was aware of others behind him, men who were either hurrying to catch up to him or following easily with no effort, but I couldn't force my attention to them. All I could see was Tammad, impossibly tall and broad, longish, shaggy blond hair, startling bright blue eyes, his well-muscled body clothed in no more than the brown loincloth he usually wore, his immense sword sheathed at his side. I wondered briefly why he wasn't dressed in Alderanean clothing, but all I could do was stand there staring like an idiot until he reached me.

"Terril," he said again, automatically brushing aside the men who stood between us as if they were children. His mind held an excitement of sorts mixed in with other emotions, but they were all so completely covered by that iron calm of his that I couldn't see them clearly. "Terril, what do you do here?"

"What am *I* doing here?" I blurted, feeling a desperate need to sit down. "I'm supposed to be here. What are *you* doing here?"

"I come seeking you," he said, and an anger of sorts entered his mind and eyes. "With whose permission was the embassy on Rimilia left? By what right have my bands been removed from you?"

"What are you talking about?" I nearly screamed, feeling my mind tremble and whirl. I'd wanted so much to see him again, but the growing anger in him was building a wall between us. "I don't know what you mean! You sent me away from you, back to my own people, without the least sense of regret. *You* sent *me* away!"

"I did no more then keep my word," he answered, a coldness growing beside his anger at the accusation he thought he heard in my voice. "Many times I vowed to return you to your embassy when your efforts at the *Ratanan* were complete; what need to speak of intention to reclaim you once my word had been kept? I am *denday*, a leader of my people, and need not account for my actions."

I stared at him with my mouth open in shock, seeing the snap in his blue eyes, the fold of his massive arms across his chest, the solidness of his barefoot stance. Then that was why he hadn't felt any regret over sending me away – he intended coming after me. He was only keeping his word, not shutting me out of his life forever.

"You still want me?" I whispered, feeling that terrible weakness spread over me. "You're not – tired of me?"

"Have I not shown you how greatly I desire you?" he returned, softening. He saw the wide-eyed way I looked at him and a smile began to grow. "With bands or without, you remain mine, *wenda*. Do not doubt this."

"Tammad," I choked, unable to say anything but his name, and then his arms were around me, holding me to him. I wanted to cry as I had never cried before, with joy impossible to contain, but just clinging to him was all the fulfillment the world contained. I could feel the surprise and astonishment surrounding us, but ignored feelings to glory in the strong desire coming from the man who held me.

"Your unexpected departure from Rimilia has cost me much time," Tammad murmured after a brief moment. "We must return immediately, for there is considerable work yet to be done. You cannot aid me if you are not by my side."

"Aid you?" I echoed, lifting my face from his chest to stare up at him with a smile. "You mean in caring for your house and needs when we get back to your city. Oh,

Tammad, I can't wait to learn everything Gilor has to teach me! I'll do everything for you, be everything to you...."

"No, Terril, no," he laughed, cutting off the flow of words pouring out of me. "There is no need for you to do that which any *wenda* might do. There is work to be done which only you might see to, the reading of men, the deciphering of their needs, the binding of their loyalty. It is for this reason you must stay beside me."

All my happiness suddenly faded. I stared at him in silence for a moment, then stepped back out of the clasp of his arms.

"Then it's a Prime you want beside you," I said without any inflection to my voice, looking at the amusement in his light eyes. "You want me because of what I can do and what I am."

"It is my furs which have felt the greatest lack of a woman called Prime," he chuckled, reaching out to touch my arm. "There are no others who may take your place, *wenda*, a thing clearly shown me in your absence."

"Because I'm an empath," I choked. "Any female empath would do you, as long as she could handle your work and keep your body satisfied. Well, you'd better start looking for another one, because this empath never wants to see you again!"

I whirled away from the startlement he showed, savagely pushed my way through the people behind me, rounded the sled at the curb, and began running across the street. Sleds hissed to abrupt and unexpected stops all around me, nearly running me down, but I ignored them and the shouts of their drivers as well. The hurt I felt was worse than what I'd felt when Tammad had sent me away, simply because I'd known then how badly I fit into his society, how useless I was in it. It was a legitimate reason for rejecting me, something I could understand even if acceptance was hard. But now.... All he wanted me for was my talent, something he could use to advance his cause, to secure the ends he had in mind. He hadn't come looking for me because he wanted *me* – there was still work for a Prime to do and he had to get her back. My eyes filled with tears and I stumbled, nearly going down before regaining my balance. An open parkland stood behind the throngs of people and I ran toward it, leaving jostled, exclaiming, insulted people in my wake – and not caring.

The parkland stretched wide through the thirty-foot entrance between tall trees, and I just turned to my left and kept running, looking for some place thick and private to hide myself in. He was just like all the rest, wanting me for nothing but my talent, nothing but the prestige I could bring him. I sobbed as I ran, tears streaming down my cheeks, breath rasping through my throat, heart hammering from exertion and crying, but I didn't want to stop. I wanted to run forever from all of them and never stop to be hurt again.

The parkland was just that – wide open stretches of grass with occasional bushes, tall trees bordering it, stone benches scattered here and there beside short, pebbled walks. I ran as far as I could, finding nothing of the hideaway I needed so badly, at last forced to a stop by shuddering lungs and strengthless legs. I fell to my knees in the short, velvet grass and put my face in my hands, almost to the point of letting the pain and loneliness wail from my mind to everyone in range. Letting go would have been so easy – but there was too much shame beside the pain to broadcast it all over. I'd been a fool, and it was enough that I knew it.

No more than a minute or two passed before I heard the sound of running behind me. *He* was there, trailing a lot of other mind traces, his confusion and flickering emotions nearly drowning the others out. I tried to get to my feet to run again, but his hand was suddenly on my arm, pulling me around to face him.

"*Wenda,* why did you run?" he demanded, ignoring the way I fought desperately to pull away from him. "Speak to me of what has disturbed you so that I may understand it."

I couldn't answer him. All I could do was pant and struggle in an effort to free myself. The tears rolled down my cheeks with nothing to stop them, and then Garth was there, standing close enough to take the barbarian's attention.

"This woman is under my protection," he said in a calm, deadly voice, his mind furious with anger – and faintly frightened. "Let her go right now, or face me with that weapon you wear."

"The woman is my belonging," Tammad answered, looking down at Garth with an abrupt calm that his mind echoed. "Though she wears no bands, I have not unbanded her. Are you mistaken in thinking her unclaimed, or do you challenge me for possession of her?"

"What are you talking about?" Garth demanded, confused. "That woman is a Prime of the Centran Amalgamation, not something to be owned. I don't know where you came from, but you'd better let her go."

"Tammad, he doesn't want her for himself," another voice interrupted, belonging to a stranger who was one of those following after the big barbarian. He wore the uniform of a transport captain, and he'd stopped beside Tammad, not far from Garth. "He's a – a – warrior of this planet, trying to protect the Prime. He's not trying to take her from you, he's just trying to keep her safe."

"I see," Tammad nodded, staring deep into Garth's eyes. "He has no feeling for the woman, he merely protects her. Know then, warrior of this world I stand upon, I have paid more than *dinga* for this woman between my hands. I shall not harm her, but neither shall I release her. I mean to return her to my world as soon as possible, therefore have I little time to spend in talk. Are you able to stand aside knowing she goes with he to whom she rightfully belongs, or does your honor forbid this?"

Garth shook his head. "I still don't understand most of what you said, but your final question comes through clearly enough. Your answer is, no, I can't just stand aside and let you take her. Not as long as it isn't what *she* wants."

"A man rarely knows the true desires of a woman," Tammad sighed. "Though I do not wish to take your life, I nevertheless give you honor for the honor you show. I shall face you as soon as I have seen to the temporary disposition of my *wenda.*"

He'd been looking around as he talked, one hand still clamped tight to my arm, but apparently he quickly found whatever he was looking for. He moved toward me, turning me around, then continued past where I'd been standing, drawing me along with him. The best I can say is that I didn't go willingly; tear-stained, and struggling, I still ended up going toward a large, barred and screened structure that held many different kinds of birds. The thing stood flat on the ground and was built with very simple lines, probably to keep the container from detracting from the appearance of the contents. I was pulled right up to it, the barbarian having no more trouble with me than he ever did, and then he opened the door and thrust me inside.

Wings exploded in all directions around me, feathers of many brilliant colors floating under screams of fear and outrage. I threw my arms over my head and tried to back away from the panic my presence was causing, but the door had been closed again behind me. Soft bodies tried to escape but flew directly at me instead, in fear. My back pressed against the bars, I slid to my knees, my arms still over my head, my mind in as much of a turmoil as those tiny minds around me. I could almost feel the bands the barbarian had been talking about, the five small-linked, bronze-colored chains he had used to mark me as his, one each on my ankles and wrists, the fifth about my throat. I didn't want to wear his bands again, not anymore, but he would take me back to Rimilia and force me to wear them, with no one to stop him or free me from him! The sobbing started again, heaving my chest and hurting it, and I clawed my way around to face the bars I'd been leaning against, ready to scream out my desperation. I don't want to go back! I started to scream, but no one was paying any attention to me with the greater attraction they had in front of them.

Tammad stood surrounded by the men who had accompanied him, Garth stood with his back to Tammad's group, facing the Kabran officers and the merchants from the dispute, both groups obviously trying to talk the two men out of the fight they intended having. I wiped my eyes with the back of one hand, more miserable than I would have thought possible, then tried to slide my fingers through the mesh covering the bars of the birdcage. The catch that kept the door closed was a simple one, but the mesh was so small and fine I couldn't slide even one finger through it. My hand trembled from the way my ragged breathing shook my body, but I kept trying to force my fingers through the mesh, only distantly noticing the abrupt calm settling on the birds behind me. The fluttering and screaming had stopped completely, the feathery minds were relaxed and happy, a chirping and trilling had started up again. I was too upset to know what it meant and I didn't even care when great big raindrops began pattering down on me, slowly at first, then faster and faster. The rain had no trouble getting through the mesh, but I couldn't! I had to get out of there, but I couldn't!

And then, through the thickening rain, I saw all the men on the grass draw back – except for the two who stood staring at each other. Garth had looked so big and strong to me when I'd first arrived, and compared to the other men he was – but not when compared to Tammad. The barbarian and his men towered over all the others, standing tall and confident and feeling and thinking the same way. Tammad drew his blade quickly and with ease, holding it in a sure grip with the point lowered toward the ground. Garth drew his smaller sword more slowly, and it came to me that his fear wasn't gone but was now under control. He wasn't about to let it distract him from the upcoming fight, any more than Tammad was letting unconcern distract him. The barbarian had no doubts about who would win, but the conviction had no chance of turning him cocky or careless.

I raised dripping wet fists to beat at the bars and mesh of the cage, then struck at them once only, but with the force of frustration and a screaming rage behind the blow. Those men had no *right* fighting over me, but they were doing it anyway, one to reclaim a needed possession, the other to defend a point of honor. Neither one was thinking about me, and I hated them both! They were contending over a Prime of the Centran Amalgamation, a thing of definite and specific value. I hadn't attained the status of human being to either of them, and I probably never would.

Tammad and Garth raised their swords to what were probably defensive positions, then slowly began to close with each other. They circled warily, each watching the other closely, then Garth struck at his big opponent, more a testing stroke than an actual attempt to reach him. Tammad knocked the advancing point aside and replied almost casually, but Garth found himself defending frantically, just short of having his arm sliced open. They returned briefly to circling, exchanged attacks again and then a third time, and I realized then that although Garth had been able to keep himself from being hurt, his mind had turned numb with a deeper fear, a deeper understanding of his mortality. Tammad's calm determination hadn't changed, but Garth was no longer as he had been.

I suppose they kept at it for no more than ten or fifteen minutes, but the time somehow seemed endless. The rain poured down on me and on everyone else, drenching everyone and everything, leading me to wonder if rain would always be an aspect of Tammad's entry into my life. There always seemed to be wetness for me when he was around, if not from the skies or my tears, then from other parts of me. One minute he and Garth were still at it, and the next Garth had slipped during an advance and had gone down to the sodden grass. Tammad had him then, an undeniable victory, but for some reason the barbarian didn't press his advantage. He lowered his sword and stared briefly at the man who was slowly trying to get to his feet again, then he stepped forward and said something to his erstwhile opponent. Garth looked up and shook his head, his mind sick and resigned, then Tammad said something else. The surprise in Garth's mind was so strong I could feel it like a blow. Tammad stepped even closer then crouched down, his sword still in his hand but seemingly forgotten, and then the two men began to talk.

The conversation lasted longer than the fight had. I was sitting on the sodden ground, my back against the bars of the cage next to the door, my eyes on the bright plumage of the birds huddled in the tree at the other side of the cage, when the birds began to stir uneasily and I heard a step behind me. I still didn't have to turn to know who it was; there was only one man in the entire Amalgamation who could throw such deep calm on himself and make it feel natural.

"Come, Terril, it is time to depart," he told my rounded back, his hand thumbing open the door catch. Some of the birds began fluttering wetly, fearfully, but they weren't the quarry being pursued.

"I won't come with you," I said into the downpour, my voice weak and ineffective even in my own ears. "I'd rather stay locked in here than come with you."

"I have not the time," he said, reaching in to grab my arm and pull me out of the cage. "Once we have departed this place to return to Rimilia, we shall speak of that which disturbs you."

He pulled me along beside him through the rain, moving obliquely to join the other men who had been with him. One of them helped a limping Garth, who must have twisted his ankle when he went down. The merchants and Kabran officers were nowhere to be seen, nor was anyone else left in the park. I moved alone through the rain, all around me a delegation of those who did as they pleased. Only I was denied that right, I, who should have had it before any of them.

The barbarian's fingers were tight on my arm, making my mind seethe in a fury as useless as struggle would have been.

When we reached the park entrance where I had come in, two sleds were at the curb waiting for us. Tammad hesitated very briefly, then sent Garth to ride with those in the second sled before forcing me into the first one. I didn't understand why Garth was going with us, but more than that I didn't understand why Tammad had sent him to the second sled. He couldn't have felt Garth's vast reluctance to look me in the eye, the deep well of guilt he worked frantically to control – or his infinite relief when he saw he would not be riding in the same vehicle with me. I moved over as far as possible on the sled seat, seeing the water that dripped from me soak down into the seat cushions, ignoring the amusement coming from the other men in the sled. They were warriors, Tammad's *l'lendaa*, and anything he did was perfectly right and proper to them. He was their leader, their *denday*, and kidnapping women was nothing new to them.

The sleds left the curb together and merged into the thinned stream of traffic, sliding past the suddenly emptied streets. No more than a handful of people were left afoot in the rain, and that handful hadn't remained out of choice. Cold air began to fill the inside of the sled until Tammad spoke to the driver, then the cold air cut off and we were left with the stuffiness and damp. Even as sopping wet as I was, the stuffiness wasn't very welcome.

The ride to the port didn't take very long. I suppose I kept expecting officials of some sort to stop the sled and take me away from the unpleasant dream, escort me back to my accommodations, then assure me that everything would be fine. Instead, the two sleds stopped beside a small, official-looking transport, I was pulled back out into the rain, and then the transport's ramp was right in front of me. I hung back against the fingers digging into my arm, more than reluctant to go up that ramp, feeling the hurry in the minds all around me, but sharing none of it. My mouth opened to scream for help any help, but another big hand grabbed my other arm and I was half-carried, half dragged up the ramp and inside.

I wasn't released until we stood in the middle of the transport's common area, a section usually containing table to eat at and couches to socialize on. Yellow and brown carpeting still covered the metal of the deck plates, but the tables and couches had been replaced with pillows of all colors and a few small hand tables. Why it had been done was obvious, but how Tammad had gotten an official transport for his own use was beyond me.

"Return us to Rimilia immediately," Tammad told a man who had followed us with the others into the transport, a man with captain's insignia on his tunic. He was the same man who had spoken to Tammad in the park, explaining Garth's position, and he nodded and began to turn away, then hesitantly turned back to the big barbarian.

"Tammad, are you sure this is all right?" he asked with concern. "Murdock McKenzie told me to do as you ordered and advise you if you needed advice, but this whole thing is beginning to bother me. The woman's a Prime, and she doesn't seem to want to go with you."

"I *don't* want to go with him!" I told the man as forcefully as I could. "Call the Port officials and tell them to make him let me go!"

"The woman is mine," Tammad rumbled calmly, ignoring what I'd said in the same way that he ignored the captain's increased indecision. "Was she reluctant to accompany me when first I approached her? What was done to cause the change you see?"

"I – don't know," the man admitted, his tone heavy. "First she was glad to see you, then she was running away. I don't know what happened."

"It is difficult for any man to know the mind of a woman," Tammad smiled, and the power of his personality was so strong that the captain found himself smiling in return. "It is fortunate that upon Rimilia, all things are as men will them. Are you now able to return us there?"

"Certainly." The captain nodded, still smiling. "I'll get immediate clearance for departure."

This time he kept going when he turned away, pretending not to hear my shout of "Wait!" as he strode toward the corridor that would take him to the command deck. I was furious all over again, furious that the captain refused to hear me – and furious at Tammad's amusement. He looked down at me where I stood beside him, his blue eyes nearly twinkling, and reached a hand out to touch my hair.

"It is now time to delve into the question of what disturbs you, *hama*," he murmured. "But first we must dry ourselves from the rain we passed through."

"I don't want to dry myself!" I snapped, knocking his hand away from the sopping strings of my hair. "And don't you dare use that word to me! I am not your *hama!*"

"Not my beloved?" he echoed, surprised and amused. "If you are not my beloved, then what might you be to me?"

"Nothing but a tool," I answered harshly, feeling the stab of pain again. "A tool you can use to get what you want. If I hadn't been a Prime, would you have left everything on Rimilia to come chasing after me?"

He started to answer immediately, undoubtedly in the affirmative, but I could sense the hesitation in his mind. If he hadn't needed me to complete his plans on Rimilia, the thought of coming after me would never have entered his head. I turned away fast to hide my grief, and suddenly came face-to-face with Garth. He stood off to one side of the common area, leaning against a wall to ease his twisted ankle, and the accusation in my stare must have been stronger than I thought. He flinched visibly, as though I'd struck him, and then Tammad's hand was on my arm again.

"Had you not been a Prime, I would not have had to release you to begin with," he said, pulling me around to face him again. "Would any have asked my word to release you had you been a *wenda* of no consequence? Would your people have denied me whatever woman I fancied?"

He stared down at me fiercely, willing me, with his anger, to believe what he said. It was a good show – for someone who couldn't tell what he really felt.

"No, my people wouldn't have denied you," I ground out, shaking my head at him. "But that doesn't change the fact that you *wouldn't* have come after me if I weren't a Prime. Well, you've wasted your time after all. I won't help you ever again and you have *my* word on that. And if I've learned anything from you, it's how to keep my word."

A tremor of frustration ran through him, the sort of impatient anger I'd learned to know so well, an emotion that rarely ever reached his face. He took a breath to immediately calm the feeling, then drew me closer to him.

"You are mistaken in all you have said," he told me softly, letting his calm patience flow toward me. "You are indeed my beloved, the woman I have ever sought, and I shall not release you. Perhaps some day I will find the means to make you believe this."

"And while I wait for that day, you think I can be talked into helping you anyway." I ignored the fluttering inside me he had so purposefully produced. "If that's what you're counting on, you might as well forget it. You can't fool me that way a second time."

His face and eyes lost their soft, patient look and a breath of vexation hissed out between his teeth.

"Truly, I had forgotten how stubborn a female you are," he muttered, fighting to cool the anger inside him. "First I will see us both dry, then we may discuss this thing further. I will know what has made your mistrust so great."

With his hand still on my arm, he headed for one of the cabins around the periphery of the common area, naturally pulling me along with him. I wasn't feeling nearly as brave as my words had suggested, but what else could I have done? He had made a fool of me once; could I have let him do it a second time?

The cabin we entered was no different from any other transport cabin. The large bed was bolted to the deck, as were the two chairs. The drawers of a dresser grew out of a wall, and the floor was covered with a tan and green carpet. Tammad closed the door behind us, finally let my arm go, and walked toward a wall cabinet which usually held towels, beginning to remove his *haddin* as he went. Beneath the swordbelt, his brown body-cloth was as wet as my suit, and it didn't take him long to get rid of it. He unstrapped his leather wrist bands, put them on the chair with his swordbelt, then reached for a towel.

"There is at times great comfort to be found in off-worlder possessions," he said, appreciating the softness of the large towel against his skin. "We on Rimilia have not such cloth as this. Why have you not yet begun to remove your clothing?"

"I told you, I don't want to," I muttered, turning away from the sight of him. His bare body was as magnificent as I remembered it, tall and broad, muscles moving silkily beneath the tan of his skin. His blond hair, darkened by the rain, was as shaggy as ever, but on him it was as appealing as custom styling would be on a man of Central. I couldn't bear to look at him, let alone imagine his hands on me, but a minute later imagination was unnecessary.

"Have you forgotten so soon?" he murmured, his hand suddenly on my neck beneath my hair. "Must I fetch a switch to remind you of the obedience due him to whom you belong? Remove the clothing and dry yourself."

"I don't *want* to!" I screamed without turning to look at him, then pulled away from his hand and ran to the far corner of the cabin to throw myself to my knees on the carpeting. My head bent to my hands as the sobs shook me again in abject desolation. I didn't *want* to take my clothing off, and it didn't take him long to understand why.

"Do you truly believe your clothing will keep me from you?" he asked from very near, having followed me across the cabin. His amusement was back, and a strange, unexplained elation. "You have said you do not care for me. If this is so, why do you strive to keep me from you? You have known my use many times before, and surely must have grown used to it."

"I hate you," I choked out, really meaning it. I could feel him standing behind me, tall and strong and impossible to deny. I'd wanted him so desperately, had so much wanted to be his, but all he wanted was a Prime.

Then I felt his hands on me again and I screamed, "No! Don't touch me!" but it didn't do any good. The scream would have stopped a man from Central, but the barbarian had nothing in common with men from Central. His hands loosened my clothing and slowly pulled it off me, while he ignored the fact that my eyes were closed tight, refusing to look at him. I lay on the carpeting in the corner, curled into a ball, shivering less from the coolness of the air-recirculation system than from what he had done. He had refused to allow me my way, refused to consider my desires above his; he wanted me because I was a Prime, but he refused to treat me as one. I hated him, I knew I hated him, but that didn't stop the shivering.

"We must take all the wetness from you," he said, suddenly covering me with a towel. "I do not wish to see you fall ill again. Why do you continue to doubt my words when I have assured you of their truth?"

His hands were moving around on me above the towel, supposedly drying me, in reality setting me on fire. I hadn't felt his hands in so long a time, as I was sure he was aware.

"Please don't touch me," I whimpered, finally forcing my eyes open to see him crouched so close above me. "Please don't touch me."

"Your flesh is as cold as death," he said, using one hand to push my hair away from my face. "Beneath your clothing, you appear more slender than you were upon Rimilia. Are there none upon your world who concern themselves with your well-being? For one of such great importance, you seem ill cared for."

"Why are you doing this to me?" I whispered, pulling the towel up to my chin. "I won't help you, I swear I won't help you!"

"Then we need not concern ourselves with the matter," he murmured, stroking my face very gently. "You will be no more than another woman upon Rimilia, though one of great beauty and desirability, a true *rella wenda*. Men will envy my ownership of you for that reason, as they have done in the past."

"You're lying!" I cried, feeling the tears beginning to roll down my cheeks. "All you want me for is my talent, and what that talent can do for your cause!"

"There are other uses a woman may be put to." He smiled. "It has been long since I had you in my furs."

"No!" I whispered, shaking my head so hard the tears flew off my cheeks. My hands were clamped tight to the towel at my chin, but the towel was pulled away and then he was lying down beside me, taking me in his arms. I beat at him with my fists and struggled to get away, but when his lips touched mine I whimpered in defeat. He didn't care how hard I beat at him, how hard I struggled. His body was muscled in metal, his mind hard with determination, his desire so strong it was impossible to ignore. I moaned at the heat coming from his flesh, feeling it seep deeply into mine, and then he was above me, beginning to enter me, and a madness took me. I screamed and struggled and almost got away, then wailed out loud when one surge made his possession too deep to refute.

"I will not cause you pain." He tried to soothe my frantic writhing, holding me to him with those massive arms. "You have my word, *hama,* I will not cause you pain."

I tried to speak, but could do no more than gurgle and choke. I was being flooded with such intense feelings of desire and need that I couldn't tell whether they were coming from me or him. And then his hips began to move, thrusting hard, sending lightning through me, nearly drowning out the sudden thrum of the transport's engines. I cried out in protest over the pending takeoff, finding the cry smothered beneath his demanding lips, then thunder came to match the lightning in my body and all protest was gone forever.

## THREE

The common area was spacious enough under most circumstances, but Tammad's large blond *l'lendaa* seemed to fill it more than six people ought to. They sprawled on the carpeting, leaning against the cushions, laughing with each other as they helped themselves to the food and drink brought them by the transport's steward. Garth sat to my right, watching them with frowning interest, paying almost no attention to the food he shoveled into his mouth. He seemed determined to continue in my company, and much of his distress was gone since the last time I'd seen him. He and Tammad had had a long talk before the meal was served, which probably accounted for his new attitude.

I sat beside the barbarian on the carpet, holding a pillow rather than leaning on it. The sense of satisfaction from the man beside me was so great that it set my teeth on edge. He had promised not to give me pain and he had kept that promise, at least on a physical level. Mentally I was furious, miserable, frantic, fearful – and more confused than I had ever been. Not knowing what to do or how to think had turned me sullen and unresponsive – until the barbarian put his hands on me. He had used me twice in his cabin, once on the carpet and once on the bed, and all I could remember was moaning helplessly and kissing the light-haired chest I was held against. Afterward I could have kicked myself for being such a willing victim, but the barbarian's amusement was punishment enough. He knew I couldn't resist him, and that seemed to settle whatever doubts he might have had.

I moved in annoyance on the carpeting, unhappy with the *imad* and *caldin* the barbarian had made me wear. The blouselike *imad* and full-skirted *caldin* were both pink in color, made of a thin, formless material that both hung on me and clung to me at the same time. Tammad's *l'lendaa* had murmured in appreciation when they'd seen me in the outfit, and even Garth had been startled enough to stop and stare, but I've hated pink long enough not to care what other people think about it. Pink is too vulnerable a color for my taste, but the barbarian was back in charge, of me and everything else.

"Terril, the food was put before you so that you might eat," the barbarian said, undoubtedly having noticed the untouched serving on the small table near me. "Do you now take the plate and do so."

"I don't like regim in cream sauce," I muttered, keeping my eyes on the bright orange pillow in my lap. Bright orange and pink. Maybe I'd get lucky and the barbarian would get violently ill.

"It matters not what the dish might be," he persisted, a faint annoyance tinging the edges of his thoughts. "The Garth R'Hem Solohr informs me you have eaten no more than once this day, if that. Take the food and eat."

"It really isn't bad, Terry," Garth put in, trying to sound encouraging. "I'm not crazy about regim either, but I've tasted a lot worse. Try some and see for yourself."

"I said I don't want it," I repeated for both their benefits, beginning to hate even the sound of their voices. "I don't want it, I don't want it, I don't want it!"

I was so close to throwing a screaming fit I don't know why I didn't, but passing up an opportunity often means you don't get another chance at it. The annoyance in Tammad's thoughts spread from the edges inward, giving him all the encouragement he needed. He twisted where he sat, grabbed both of my arms, upended me across his lap, then used his hand instead of a switch. He put enough strength into the swats to let me know what was happening, kept it up until I began twisting and crying out in spite of my embarrassment, then put me back where I'd been sitting. Garth and the *l'endaa* laughed, making my face burn so red I could feel it more strongly than what the barbarian had done to me. I was furious with them all, but there was nothing I could do to stop them.

"Now do you take the plate," the overgrown monster directed, his voice as calm as it had been, his mind set in that no-more-nonsense mold. I unclenched my fists and reached the plate slowly over to me, ignoring the tears of frustration and misery that rolled down my cheeks. How was I supposed to fight a man his size, how was I supposed to refuse him? All he wanted was the use of my talent, but I couldn't even turn and walk away.

"Don't cry, Terry," Garth chuckled, wiping at the tears on my right cheek with one finger. "Once you're finished eating, you'll feel better. And it looks like you've also learned a very valuable lesson: despite the way you act with everyone else, Tammad isn't someone you can stand up to."

I turned my head to look at him, seeing and feeling the immense satisfaction he was filled with. If the barbarian had threatened my life Garth would have defended and protected me, but as long as I'd only been punished, Garth couldn't have been more pleased. He was reveling in feelings of masculinity by proxy, glorying in the embarrassment I'd been given. Right then I hated him more than I ever had, and the hatred found expression in words.

"Well, I guess that makes two of us who can't stand up to him, doesn't it, Garth?" My voice was hoarse but filled with venom. Garth felt a deep-down stab of pain that paled his cheeks and blanked his mind. He stared at me no more than three seconds, then rose painfully to his feet and hobbled away toward a cabin. Tammad felt a very strong urge to go after him, did not act on it, then waited till Garth had disappeared into a cabin before speaking.

"It is ever true that a woman will attack with words rather than use a more merciful weapon," he growled, then reached over and turned my face toward him, his anger as clear in his blue eyes as it was in his mind. "You are not to speak to that man in such a manner again," he said, holding my face tightly between his fingers. "You have no concept of what occurs between men, therefore are you forbidden to make mention of the matter. Eat what was given you, and do not forget my words."

He let go of my face and turned back to his own food, the thrill of anger still sharp in his mind. I poked at the regim, then ate it mechanically. The dish was as bad as I'd thought it would be, but its taste really didn't matter. It would have been horrible no matter what it tasted like.

I shifted around on the carpeting again, uncomfortable and unhappy, resisting the urge to turn and stare at the barbarian in tight-lipped resentment. What was supposed to be so special about being a man and talking about men's things? I had every right to say anything I cared to to Garth, even if the barbarian *didn't* like it. Garth acknowledged my position as Prime even if Tammad refused to, and that gave me the right. Tammad wasn't concerned about excluding me from so-called men's discussions; he was afraid I would alienate Garth and negate his attempts to make use of the Kabra. I didn't know how he intended using Garth, but Tammad wasn't one to waste whatever talent came past him. Ever since the swordfight in the park, Garth had become an important part of the barbarian's plans. Just how important and exactly what those plans were remained to be seen.

After getting poked in the ribs and frowned at a couple of times for picking at my food, I decided I might as well get it over with and began swallowing as fast as possible to avoid tasting the stuff. I was almost all finished when the captain of the transport and two of his men showed up, but the three men weren't alone. They each had a woman in tow by the arm, a piece of well-worn luggage held in their free hands, their scowls showing how disapproving they were, especially at the grins the women were wearing. The three females wore cheap, gaudy day-suits, cheaper jewelry, and the wrong sort of makeup. Their faces looked as though they belonged on a stage, and I soon found I wasn't far wrong. The captain dragged his captive in front of Tammad, then shook her slightly as though showing evidence of guilt.

"Look what we found on the cargo deck," he growled, obviously expecting the barbarian to understand what was going on. "Turn your back for more than a minute, and your ship is suddenly swarming with trippers."

"Trippers?" Tammad echoed, examining the woman in detail with his eyes. She had very blond hair, as did the other two, but also had the brown eyes that they did. They weren't natural blonds, not the way Tammad and his *l'lendaa* were, but the barbarian didn't seem to know that. His mind hummed faintly as his eyes moved over the suit-hugged curves of her body, and the captain finally realized his meaning wasn't getting through.

"Trippers are travelers who either can't or won't pay their way off the planet they're on," the captain explained, looking the woman over with less interest than Tammad had shown. "They hide on a private ship until the ship is on its way, then come forward demanding their rights under the distressed travelers' law – the one that says all travelers on your vessel have to be taken care of whether they can pay for the trip or not. The law wasn't meant to protect people like these three, but they don't mind taking advantage of it. It gets them where they want to go without costing them anything, and being women, they can't be forced to work out their fare. It would put them in 'too compromising' a position."

"I see." Tammad nodded, not missing the way the three women were laughing at the captain's anger. His mind hummed again, but in a different key, and he added, "Perhaps they should have been told that this vessel concerns itself with Rimilian law, not that of the Amalgamation."

The captain and his men suddenly grew wide, happy grins, and the women, noticing the abrupt change, found their own amusement deflating. The one in front of Tammad glanced back at her friends, then gave her attention to the captain again.

"We don't care *whose* law you're working under," she told the captain with brash belligerence. "It's too late to turn back to Alderan, so you've got to take us with you. And if you try not feeding us or getting too fast with the handwork, we'll report you as soon as we set foot on your planet of destination. As a matter of fact, we just might report you anyway – if you don't get smart real fast and come up with some sweet, pretty apologies for rousting us around. How about it, girls? Should we yell compromise?"

The other two laughed and agreed with enthusiasm, really enjoying the needling they were doing. Not one of them was worried about what would happen – as if they'd done the same thing many times before without anything unpleasant developing. I put my plate back on the small table without bothering about the rest of the regim. The barbarian wasn't likely to notice, and I didn't want to miss whatever was going to happen.

"Apologies, huh?" the captain snorted, his mind full of glee and satisfaction. "If we don't treat you like something special, we get reported, do we? Well, go ahead and start reporting. The authority you'll be talking to is sitting right there."

He pointed to Tammad, and the woman stared at the barbarian thoughtfully. She still wasn't worried, especially when she caught the way she was being inspected.

"Well, well," she drawled, deliberately standing straighter and sticking her chest out. "So you're the authority we'll be complaining to. How about it, handsome? Are you going to be listening to his side of the story – or ours?"

The woman was being deliberately provocative, trading on the promise of her body for favoritism over the captain. I could see she considered the barbarian attractive, but I could also see she had no intentions of delivering on the promise she was making.

"You speak of a story," the barbarian mused, leaning his broad body back on his cushions to stare up at the woman. "What is this story you wish me to hear?"

"It's simple but tragic," the woman sighed, trying to project honest heartache. The emotion was as false as her hair color, and everyone but Tammad seemed to know it. "My friends and I are an exotic dance team, working as many worlds as possible in order to pick up enough Earning Pluses to pay for an operation for a fourth friend of ours. She used to dance with us until – the accident. Without the operation, the doctors say she'll never walk again."

The woman paused to put her hand briefly to her face, supposedly in a spasm of grief, in reality to cut off a laugh at her own corny story. The captain groaned and tried to interrupt, undoubtedly thinking Tammad was buying every word, then groaned again when the barbarian gestured him to silence.

"I try not to think about that too much," the woman said, gazing sadly at her victim. "Thinking about it is too painful. Well, at any rate, there we were, trying to earn E.P.s for our friend, when this – this – ruffian you call a captain comes over to us with some of – his friends. He says he has a special job of dancing for us that will bring us more than what we need, but we have to go with him. My friends and I would do anything to help out our other friend so we do go with him – but once we get here we find out he's lying. Not only is there no special job, but the transport takes off! Then he and his friends come down to where they left us, and tell us that if we don't start being nice to them, they'll turn us in as trippers! Well, my friends and I don't do things like that, so we refuse – and the next thing we know, we're being dragged in front of you. Now, we're just girls so we can't fight them, but you – is a big, strong man like you going to let them treat us like that?"

Tammad continued to stare at her as she batted her eyelashes at him, his expression thoughtful but unaccusing. She had picked up on his backwoods accent and was trying to take him for everything he had, without once considering whether or not the try would be safe. It came to me suddenly that she had never dealt with a barbarian before, and didn't know she was dealing with one now. I stirred where I sat, half tempted to warn her, half tempted to let her find out the hard way, but the decision about what to do really wasn't mine to make. The woman and her friends had voluntarily walked into a trap for innocents, and without their knowing it, the trap had already closed on their legs.

"My congratulations, Captain," the barbarian drawled at last, keeping his eyes on the woman in front of him. "I had not realized you would be so thoughtful as to provide us with entertainment. As you were brought here to dance, *wenda*, I suggest that you do so."

The captain's grin came back, stronger than before, but the woman next to him and her friends were instantly furious.

"What do you mean, dance?" the first one demanded, putting her fists on too-curvy hips. "We're not here to entertain a bunch of yokels! If you didn't buy my story that's too – bad, but there's still nothing you can do about it! We're here and you have to take care of us!"

Tammad, a lion among sheep, an outstanding warrior even on a world of warriors, rose to his feet to stand in front of the woman, a silly female who looked up at him with a dumbfounded expression. Somehow, Tammad's *l'lendaa* were also on their feet, three of them around the second woman, the other three around the third, all of them much larger than any of the women had expected them to be. The captain and his crewmen looked at each other, withdrew half a step from the women they'd been escorting, then quietly put down the luggage they'd been holding.

"If I had my guess," the captain muttered to the woman nearest him, "I'd say you were about to be taken care of. Don't ever claim you didn't ask for it."

"Hey, wait!" the woman protested faintly, reaching for the captain without taking her eyes off Tammad. Her reach and protest did as much good as mine had done; the captain and his men were already most of the way to the passage that led to the control deck.

"Do you dance well?" the barbarian asked the woman in front of him, staring down at her over folded arms. His voice was no more than mildly curious, and that gave the woman enough false encouragement to try bluster.

"We're the best!" she tried, raising her chin in his direction and putting her fists back on her hips. "When you want to see the best, you have to pay for it and pay high!"

"Does she speak the truth, Terril?" he asked in that same casual way, keeping his eyes on the woman. I'm sure he was trying to catch me off-guard and thereby set a precedent; it was his bad luck it didn't work.

"If I were in your employ, I would explain the difference between opinion and fact," I said, keeping my voice as casual as his had been. "Since I'm not in your employ, you can go jump in a lake."

I didn't quite look at him when I said that, but I wouldn't have taken the words back even if I could have. The flash of annoyed anger he experienced was something I'd have to get used to – that and a lot more – otherwise I was wasting my time refusing to help him. He could make me obey him – he'd certainly done it often enough – but I couldn't let him force me to work for him.

*"Wendaa,"* he muttered under his breath, making it sound like a curse. I could feel how close he was to the limit of his patience, but the silly female in front of him couldn't.

"What are you asking *her* opinion for?" she demanded, jerking her chin at me. "She don't even know how to dress. If you want to know how good we are, ask anybody who ever saw us."

"There is no need to ask anyone at all," Tammad answered, his tone losing its mildness. "You were instructed to dance for us and you will do so. Should you refuse to obey, you will be punished."

"Punished?" the woman echoed, shocked. "What are you talking about? You can't...."

"Renny, wait," a second woman called, one who hadn't felt shock at the threat. "Renny, tell them we'll do it."

"Are you crazy?" the first woman exploded, turning on the second. "I'm not about to …"

"The L.M. Special," the second woman interrupted again, stepping closer to her friend. "How about the L.M. Special? It's been months since the last time we did it, and it'd be perfect for them."

"I'll say it would," the first one muttered, turning to glare at Tammad. "Okay, big boy, we'll dance for you. It'll only take a minute to get the costumes out."

The three women picked up their luggage and walked to the opposite side of the lounge area, two of them experiencing a "just wait!" sense of satisfaction and anticipation, the third somewhat nervous but determined not to show it. They all began opening their multi-colored day suits, and even though their backs were turned, the seven *l'lendaa* watching them inwardly began to hum. The women had plans of some sort, the men had plans of their own, and I didn't need to be put out an airlock to know I'd be much happier somewhere else.

"Where do you go?" Tammad's voice came from behind me, stopping me no more than two or three steps on my way. "I have not given you permission to depart."

Permission! I stood where I was for a minute, facing away from him, finding it impossible to unclench my fists. Primes don't need *anyone's* permission to do *anything!*

"I don't like group orgies," I finally choked out over my shoulder. "From the tenor of your thoughts, I would have thought you'd be pleased to get rid of me. You know, fifth wheels and all that."

He seemed disconcerted then suddenly inwardly amused, chuckling.

"Truly, I had forgotten how easily my inner feelings might be read," he said, and then his big hand was stroking my hair. "Nevertheless, your interpretation is incorrect. I do indeed wish you to remain, for I would have my *wenda* know something of dancing with which to give me pleasure. As you are to be no more than my belonging, it is your duty to learn that which will please me."

His mind was under its usual full control, but way back and deep down there was something covered over, something he didn't want me to see. I might have refused to guess about his motives if I hadn't known the situation, but I knew the situation only too well. I turned around to face him, and had no trouble meeting his eyes.

"You don't want my ownership," I told him, finding I had accepted the truth of the statement. "You want the ownership of a Prime. Having another woman around means less than nothing to you. You should have led me on a little longer, gotten me good and hooked, and only then lowered the boom. As it is, you're wasting your time *and* mine – which, contrary to your own opinions, is considerably more valuable than yours."

At the very least I expected him to be annoyed, possibly even angry. I watched carefully for either of those reactions or any other, but none of them surfaced. The calm continued in his mind as though he had expected the sort of answer I'd given, no more than a faint weariness backdropping the way he sighed.

"Men and women speak the same words, yet those words, spoken by a woman, are not the words of a man." He spoke very gently, almost as though what he'd said was supposed to make sense and be important. I didn't react to the nonsense, and he shook his head. "Perhaps some day we will find ourselves able to exchange words and make them our own. For now I wish you to remain here, learning what you might, in order to be able to please a man. You have not yet learned how little you know in this respect."

He touched my hair again then turned and went back to where he'd been sitting, totally unconcerned about my wishes in the matter. I had no desire at all to stay, but there was little point in walking out; if he really wanted me there, he wasn't above following and dragging me back. Instead of going back to him I sat down where I was, on the fringes of the eager and expectant group of *l'lendaa*. I wasn't one of them, had no wish to be one of them, and wanted my choice of position to make that abundantly clear.

If I'd thought the barbarian and his men would notice the way I was trying to insult them, I must have forgotten what *l'lendaa* were like. They paid no attention to anyone but the three women, who had changed from the day suits they'd been wearing to gaudy, almost nonexistent stage costumes. The outfits were very short and brief, barely more than multicolored lightning flashes at four cardinal points, and I'm sure none of the *l'lendaa* were able to notice the fine network of wires covering all three bodies, not with the largesse shown them. The costumes accented what the girls were naturally endowed with, and I was undoubtedly the only one to wonder what the wires were for.

The first girl took a tiny micro-recorder from her bag, turned it on, then went to stand with the other two, who were already in position in the middle of the floor. The three women formed a triangle, two in front of the six *l'lendaa*, one in front of Tammad, all three facing outward, left hands on hips, right arms straight up. When the opening strains of music began, their heads came up and their bodies grew poised, their stance graceful in the very high-heeled shoes they wore. The next minute they were moving slowly to the blary music, swaying sensuously, stepping about broadly and suggestively, swinging their bodies and bumping their hips. The Rimilian men laughed and shouted, entertained by the novel sort of movement and pleased by it, watching closely and appreciatively as the triangle became a circle to allow the women to shift about. All the men were danced to by all of the women, giving them a good time, but I didn't share their enthusiasm. Despite Tammad's belief to the contrary, I knew certain audience-appreciation dances too, most of them more subtly sensual than the out-and-out brassiness that the blondes were exhibiting. The dances I knew undoubtedly would have pleased Tammad, but he wasn't going to know anything about them. I'd decided a long time earlier that I wasn't about to be forced to dance for a barbarian.

The dancing went on for a good fifteen minutes, the men continuing in their vocal appreciation, their desire growing so high it was hard to believe the three women didn't feel it as strongly as I did. The *l'lendaa* sat cross-legged in their places, laughing and occasionally reaching for the dancers, laughing even harder when the girls moved out of groping range. Tammad was enjoying himself as much as the others were, but he alone showed no desire to touch the women. He sat leaning back on his pillows, his face covered with a grin, his mind pleased but somewhat distracted. I had the feeling he was visualizing something other than the women in front of him, and I didn't want to know what that something was. I would *not* be dancing for any barbarian!

The end of the dance was as much of a shock to me as it was to the men. One minute the women were bumping and twisting madly, apparently enjoying the men's enthusiastic shouts of encouragement, and the next minute they had stopped dead, two in front of the six *l'lendaa,* one in front of Tammad. I could feel that something was about to happen, and abruptly it did – without seeing anything coming from the women, the men were suddenly covered with a foul-smelling sticky substance, brown-colored and nauseating, coating them as though it materialized out of thin air. Even I didn't entirely understand what was happening – after all, set route induction fields are hardly in my province – but at least I finally understood what all those wires were for. Some dancers used the fields for effect in their routines, causing magical showers of glitter or flower substance to float gently down on their audiences. These dancers were obviously prepared to supply something other than audience delight, causing me to wonder what sort of audiences they were used to.

"Have a good taste of the L.M. routine!" the woman in front of Tammad shouted, not only to him but to all of the men. "The L.M. stands for Loud Mouth!" She and the others were laughing at the men's outrage, continuing the spreading of the field even as their victims struggled to their feet. The *l'lendaa* were disgusted and offended as well as outraged, but I couldn't help but find a certain poetic justice in their predicament. If you spend your life demanding things of others, you sometimes get more than you asked for.

"Stop that at once!" Tammad shouted, reaching through the haze of unseen spray to grab the woman nearest him by the arms. He didn't know what was causing his problem, but he wasn't simple enough not to know the women were responsible. As soon as he drew her to him the coating stopped, and he gestured his men to close with the other two women as well. All three women struggled, surprised and outraged that the men would dare to touch them like that, and then Tammad saw the wires on the woman he held. He couldn't have known what the wires were for, but logic said they were the unknown in the equation, and Tammad was no stranger to logic. He began ripping them off the woman, causing the other *l'lendaa* to do the same, and the fury and outrage from both males and females was enough to give me a headache. I sat where I'd been sitting, on the outskirts of the battle, and tried to block out as much of the mental noise as possible.

In a matter of seconds, the women were no longer wired for mess. They were screaming as if they were birds whose feathers were being pulled out, but the screams still had no real sense of personal fear in them. If they knew nothing else, they knew that women in the Amalgamation were safe no matter what they did. I'm sure the smell they'd caused to be was turning their stomachs, but that was nothing more than to be expected. I put a heavily veiled wall between me and the others, and just watched to see what would happen.

"Just look what you did to our equipment!" the woman near Tammad screamed, so wild with anger her voice shook. "You jerks are going to pay for this, I swear you'll pay!"

"*You* feel anger toward *us?*" Tammad demanded, his emotions so strong they surged through his attempts at control. He held the woman between his hands, and it seemed all he could do to keep from crushing her or tearing her apart. "You dared to soil us as you did, and yet *you* feel anger? It was not we who came in search of you, *wenda,* nor was it we who forced our presence upon those who sought us not! Had you merely danced for us, you would have been freed at journey's end to return to the *darayse* you are accustomed to; now you will be punished and held as long as we wish."

The woman was reverting to feelings of shock, but that didn't stop her from being thrust toward the other two women. She stumbled from the push, but was kept from going down by two of the *l'lendaa,* who took her in tow the same way the other women were being held. All three were then started out of the common area amid screams and struggles, their minds beginning to be more than worried, and Tammad watched them disappear into three of the cabins before turning in my direction.

"I'm glad you insisted that I watch that," I said as he stared at me, still angry. "It never would have occurred to me to please a man in that particular way. It seems I *don't* know as much as I thought I did."

"You are amused," he rumbled, his mind quivering with near-illness at the sticky mess all over him. "You undoubtedly knew what would occur, yet saw no reason to warn me. Had you given warning, there would have been little amusement."

"That odor allows for very little amusement altogether," I said, close to a shudder from the repulsion in his mind. "Under other circumstances, I might at least have felt sorry for you."

"I have no need for your pity," he rasped, his light eyes growing hard. "There will be a reckoning for this."

He turned away then and strode toward his cabin, anger and frustration anti a tinge of hurt boiling around in his mind. It came as a shock that he would feel hurt, but then the shock turned to frustrated anger. No one but a barbarian would kidnap a woman, then feel disappointment when she refused to be loyal to him.

"What in Darvin's name happened here?" a voice came, and I turned my head to see Garth standing in the doorway to his cabin, his nose wrinkled in disgust. Tammad was already gone into his own cabin, so he had to be addressing me.

"That expert on women you're so friendly with demanded a show from some trippers the captain found," I explained. "The women gave him a show he'll never forget."

"That has to be grub slime," he said, hobbling farther into the common area. "I haven't smelled that smell since the time I went drinking in the dives around the port. One of the strip dancers used the stuff to discourage someone who tried to put his hands on her at the wrong time. How did a strip dancer get *here?*"

"Three strip dancers, if that's what they are," I corrected, shifting to look up at him. "I couldn't really say one way or the other. I don't often spend my time in port dives."

"Of course." He nodded, looking down at me with less than friendliness. "Doing something like that would be too far beneath you. And you did say they were trippers. I'll have to ask you to excuse my slowness."

"Don't I always?" I came back, getting satisfaction from the flash of anger I felt in him. His sarcasm had been meant to annoy me, but his plans had backfired. He wavered a moment, trying to decide whether or not to be angry out loud, then decided against it. He moved forward again instead, and lowered himself to the carpeting in front of me.

"What does – *darayse* – mean?" he asked, stumbling over the unfamiliar word. His gray eyes were serious, as though the question held personal importance.

"It means non-man," I supplied, wondering why he wanted to know. "The concept is the antithesis of *l'lenda,* who is a warrior and a man in the Rimilian society. It means coward and fool and anything else derogatory you'd care to call a male. If you saw the party, why did you ask about it?"

"I didn't see all of it," he denied with a headshake. "I heard the uproar and started out to see what was going on, but this ankle kept me from getting to the door until everything was just about over. Tammad thinks you knew what was going to happen, but I'm convinced you didn't. Why didn't you deny his accusation?"

He was still looking at me in that very serious way, his mind echoing the look in his eyes. I dint know what business it was of his, and didn't mind saying so.

"Since when do I have to excuse my actions to you?" I demanded, letting the heat come through in my tone. "I couldn't care less what that barbarian believes, and you can include yourself in on that!"

"What will he do if he does come to believe it?" Garth persisted, unaffected by my anger. "You know him better than I do; you must know what his reckoning will consist of."

His gray eyes did not leave me, and I couldn't stand it. I closed my own eyes and turned my head away, wrapping my arms around myself as if against a chill.

"He'll beat me," I said harshly, suddenly fighting to keep the bitterness and hurt from flowing out of my mind. "Does that please you, Garth? Does it make you feel proud to be a male? Well, I don't care if he does beat me. I simply and completely don't care!"

Garth cringed as a portion of my bleakness touched him, his mind recoiling from the strength of mine. Most non-empaths never feel any emotions but their own, making them particularly vulnerable to outside projections. If an empath's range was greater than the mere twenty-five feet it was, we never would have been allowed to survive. I savagely cut off the flow, disgusted with myself for having let it happen, and suddenly Garth's arm was around me.

"Terry, take it easy," he soothed. "He won't really hurt you, I'm sure he won't. He told me he loves you and wants to be with you forever."

"Oh, sure," I nodded, keeping my eyes closed even as the tears began to form. "He wants me so desperately he's even willing to let me work for him. That's what I call true love."

"Work for him?" he echoed with a frown. "What do you mean?"

"He's in love with my abilities as an empath," I whispered, feeling tears roll down my cheeks. "He doesn't want *me*, Garth, he wants the sort of help I gave him during my assignment on his world. I fell in love with him then, and I'm sure that was part of his plans. The only thing that wasn't I part of his plans was my finding out the truth."

Garth's arm was around me, holding me close to his chest, but even the wave of pained sympathy that came from him was no comfort. I just let the tears roll out of my eyes, making no attempt to atop them, feeling the great contrast between the pushing and turning in Garth's mind and the deep, thick silence he chose to show me.

After a few minutes of the silence, Garth stirred and said, "What do you really want to do now, Terry? Do you want to stay with him, or would you leave if you could?"

"Do you think I ran from him just for the exercise?" I sniffled, feeling very tired on the inside. "Of course I would leave, but do you really think he'll let me go? He's convinced he can get me to do as he wishes."

"And you think he can't?" he asked surprised. "From what I've seen, he'll have very little trouble getting anything he wants."

"He can't force me to work for him," I denied, looking up at him. "He knows I lose control when he beats me, so he can't beat me when he needs my ability. There's nothing else he can do but try to convince me with words, and I'm all through listening to his words."

"How many times has he beaten you?" Garth frowned, his mind definitely disturbed. "I never thought Tammad was the sort to beat a woman."

"Tammad is the sort to do anything he damned well pleases," I snorted. "And he's beaten me every time he cared to, except for the one time I used a projection on him and lied about my range." I moved against the arm he still had around me and added, "And you'd be wise to remember not to touch me from now on. The mighty *l'lenda* doesn't like having other men touch his woman – not unless it happens to be his own idea."

"I don't like the sound of any of this," Garth growled, slowly moving his arm away. "From what he said, I thought – well, never mind what I thought. I've just decided that if this is the price I have to pay for it, the price is too high."

"What did he offer you, Garth?" I asked, trying to keep my tone soft and without too much curiosity. If the barbarian's plans included Garth, and they certainly seemed to, I wanted to know about it.

"He – offered me a place in his world," Garth answered after a brief hesitation, his mind almost embarrassed. "He described it as a place where a man is free to be a man, free to do what he yearns to. I'm tired of being a fancy-dress play soldier, but I won't buy a new life with the misery of innocent women. He seems to want me with him for some reason; if that's true, then the only way he'll get me is if he lets you go."

Garth sat next to me, glaring off into the distance, seeing nothing of what was around him. It wasn't particularly surprising that he would bargain his dream in return for my freedom; that was the sort of man Garth was. High idealed, high principled – and totally uninvolved in any human way. He wasn't about to do something to help *me*, he was adhering to beliefs he felt very strongly about. He would have done the same no matter who was involved, me or any other helpless woman. On behalf of all helpless women I was disgusted, but I couldn't afford to reject the offer. If he managed to get me free, he could be as high-principled as he liked about it.

We lapsed into another silence after that, but it didn't take long before faint sounds began intruding into my distraction. Automatically my mind reached for the source of the sounds, but once I had them I was sorry I'd tried. The three women, each in a separate cabin, were so hysterical over what was being done to them that I cringed away, unable to cope with even the fringes of their desperate hysteria. I didn't know the details of what the *l'lendaa* were doing, and I didn't want to know. I just rose quickly to my feet, passed a surprised Garth, and hurried to one of the cabins on the far side of the common area. The locks had been removed from all of the doors, but I didn't need a lock to keep the smell and hysteria out. I closed the door behind me, went over to the bed, then tried to get some rest.

I didn't know I had fallen asleep until I woke up. The cabin light, which I hadn't turned down, showed me one of the three trippers standing right next to the bed. It had been her hand on my shoulder which had awakened me, and I blinked at the changes in her. The heavy stage make-up was gone from her face, leaving her younger-looking and almost vulnerable. Her short hair, which had been puffed up and out, was neatly combed down around her face. Her gaudy costume and tasteless day suit were both gone, having been replaced with an adapted towel. The very large light blue towel had been slit in its center to allow it to be slipped over her head, a cord around her waist drawing it closed as if it were a sleeveless *imad*. The thing fell nearly to her knees, making it considerably more modest than the costume she'd worn, but the girl blushed when I looked at her, and bristled.

"That big one says he wants you," she told me sullenly, glaring out of angry brown eyes. "Can you understand me?"

"It's difficult, but I *am* making the effort," I told her, raising myself to a sitting position. "I take it the big one you're referring to is Tammad."

"You talk like me!" she said in surprise, momentarily forgetting her anger. "I thought you were one of them!"

"Not through choice, I assure you," I grimaced. "Unlike you, I wouldn't have come within parsecs of this vessel if I hadn't been kidnapped. Have you learned yet how big a mistake you've made?"

"I still don't really understand what's going on," the girl complained, allowing the confusion and hurt she'd submerged to surface. "That bunch is different from any men we've ever met! Oh, sure, lots of guys will try to get it on with us, but all you have to do is turn your back to freeze them. These guys don't even ask – it's like if they want us they'll take us without asking! And what they did to us – do you know they made *us* clean them up, right after they – they – "

She swallowed, trying to make room for the words to come out, but the bright red in her cheeks kept it from happening. I caught a brief flash of replay in her mind, the vividness of it leaving no doubt as to what had happened.

"You were switched," I finished for her, feeling a good part of her embarrassment. "It hurt more than anything ever done to you, but it was worse than simply being hurt because it was humiliating. They're strong enough to tear you apart, but all they'll do is punish you because you're not in their league."

"Sure," she nodded, totally depressed. "We're not in anybody's league. But we found that out a long time ago. Come on, you'd better get up or he'll be in here himself."

She turned away from the bed and left the cabin, wrapped up in a private disappointment that didn't seem to have anything to do with what had gone on earlier. I got to my feet and followed her, wondering what she could have meant, and saw her walking over to her friends, who were sitting in the common area not far from Tammad and his warriors. The other two were wearing the same sort of towel arrangement she had on, and once she was part of the group again I could see she was the one I had thought of as the third, the one who had been somewhat unsure about spraying the men. She spoke to the other two as she sat down near them, but they didn't answer or look up from their laps. Her mind was calm reason compared to theirs, and I could see they weren't far from being terrified.

"Terril, come here," the barbarian called, gesturing to me from what seemed to be his permanent place among the pillows, which had been completely cleaned up. Garth was also in the same spot he had been in earlier, so walking over and sitting down put me between them again.

"Now that you are rested from your long sleep I would have you do a thing for me," the barbarian said, keeping his voice low. His pretty blue eyes were serious, and his broad, handsome face was concerned. "The *wendaa* who tended my warriors – they do not seem quite right. I would have you read them and tell me what must be done to see to them."

He sat there watching me, truthfully concerned but also covertly pleased that he'd found a way to commit me to the first step along the path he was determined I would take. The request he had made wasn't an idle one, therefore he had every right to expect my cooperation; the one thing he didn't expect was the way I chose to cooperate.

Instead of interpreting what I read as I had done on Rimilia, I gathered the sullen depression, the shock, the fear, the confusion and near-terror coming from the women and fed them all to Tammad, just as I'd done during the mediation on Alderan, amplifying the emotion for clearer understanding by a non-empath. The barbarian paled as the unexpected load struck him, his eyes widening as he flinched, and then his control was fighting back, pushing all unwanted thought out of his mind. I could have held the picture even against his resistance, but there was no sense in letting him know that. As soon as he resisted I let it all go, then tent a smile toward him.

"Is that what you wanted to know?" I asked very sweetly, being abrasive on purpose. I was braced for a violent response, but he was still unsteady enough from what I had done to let Garth get the first words in.

"What are you two doing?" the Kabran demanded, frowning at Tammad's dazed expression. "And speaking of those women, what was done to them? I haven't heard a word out of them since your men turned them loose."

"They are – frightened and unhappy," Tammad answered in a husky voice, obviously trying to interpret what he had been made to feel. "It seems they are unused to being punished for that which they do." Then he straightened up with a sigh and his eyes, filled with a strange expression, came back to me. "Is this what you are ever concerned with, *hama*?" he asked very gently. "The fears and hurts and disappointments of others? Is there no joy for you to read and share, no happiness and delight? Where is the pleasure in your own world, when all about you touch you with pain?"

The soothing, sympathetic thoughts coming from his mind were so strong that all I could do was sit there and try to swallow down the burning in my throat. He was the only one who had ever known without being told how hard it was for awakened empaths to fend off the waves of emotion coming at them. Likes and dislikes, preferences and faint aversions, these were all pale shadows next to the burning bright red and orange of overwhelming hate or lust, the black-green of gut-eating envy, the ghost-white of stark terror, the ice blue of deep fear, the bloated gold of greed. Deep love was a light velvet brown, happiness a pale pink, delight a bouncy yellow, laughter a bubbling sparkle of silver. What chance did the lighter emotions have against the stronger, what chance did an empath have of avoiding them? I faintly remembered children disappearing from the creche for the gifted where I had been raised. We had all been told that those children had gone elsewhere to study and live, but none of us had ever seen them again. Were they the ones who hadn't been strong enough to shoulder the load, the ones who had been crushed in the trying? What made an empath strong enough – and what made that strength fail?

"You have the nerve to ask about her pleasure?" Garth sputtered at the barbarian after a minute of silent courage, obviously not knowing what Tammad was referring to. "How much pleasure can she have, being kidnapped and threatened, beaten and bullied? You've already done enough to her; why don't you try being a man about it and let her go?"

Tammad was surprised by the sudden outburst, surprised and puzzled. He shifted his stare to Garth and considered the other man in silence for a moment, then slowly nodded his head.

"It is as I discovered earlier," he murmured, his tone even and calm. "Men of your worlds have been taught a strangeness when dealing with their women. Tell me what terrible things have been done to this woman, and tell me also what action would prove my manhood."

"What was done to her is obvious enough," Garth came back stiffly, knowing there was a hidden trap but not knowing where it lay. "Is she on board this vessel willingly? Is she to be released when the journey is over? You know the true answers to those questions as well as I do."

"Indeed." Tammad nodded, still totally unruffled. "The woman has not accompanied me willingly, nor will I release her when we have reached Rimilia. Have I not said what reasons I have for doing such things?"

"You – said you love her," Garth grudged, far from being convinced. "But if you really loved her you would let her go, give her a chance to think things over and come back on her own. This way you're trying to force her love."

"You would have me release the woman, believing as she does that I care only for her ability and what use I might make of it?" the barbarian countered, his light eyes sharp. "What woman of pride would return to me under circumstances such as those? Even should she recall the love she once felt for me, how might she return and profess it?"

"You could – follow after her and court her," Garth said, but his mind was full of embarrassment at the suggestion. It was impossible imagining the giant barbarian courting any woman, and even Garth could see that.

"Follow after and coax her attention as the men of your worlds," Tammad said, refraining from showing any of the scorn in his mind. "Is the fate of my world to await the whim of a courted *wenda*? Even had I the time to spend on such an undertaking, what would the woman think of the man who came begging her favor? Should she wish to indulge her humor the fate of the man would be humiliating, calling for the deepest self-abasement possible. Is this a thing to offer a woman, a man who has forgotten his manhood?"

"It doesn't always work like that," Garth muttered, rubbing his face with one broad hand. "What you're saying is that it's better to carry the woman off than to try to convince her. It may be easier, but that doesn't necessarily mean better. And once you do carry her off, how do you get her to see things your way? Beat her, the way you beat Terry?"

Garth was using anger to bolster his position and Tammad seemed to know it. He unfolded his large body and leaned back on his pillows, then shook his head at Garth.

"A man speaks best to a woman when he holds her in his arms," he said, as though explaining the matter in words of one syllable. "She then knows the truth of his feelings, clear beyond any doubt. Should she be completely uninterested, her body will so inform his, giving him also the truth of the matter. If he is wise he will then release her, for she is not his true love. What led you to believe I have ever beaten this woman beside me?"

"Why, she told me so." Garth blinked in surprise, turning his head to look at me. I knew he was looking at me because I could feel his eyes even though I had turned my head away. Her body will tell his if she's uninterested, Tammad had said. I knew what my body had told him, but that wasn't the truth. What the body wanted and what the mind wanted were two different things.

"Do you believe the woman is incapable of speaking other than the truth?" the barbarian asked Garth, still without accusation. "It is true I did indeed beat her once, yet the thing was not a doing to boast of and build one's manhood upon. The woman gave me deep insult, yet punishment would have been a more fitting response. A switching teaches what a beating does not – it builds a basis for respect and obedience rather than for hate and a need for revenge. A switching is little more than what was given her earlier."

"But that was nothing," Garth protested, and then his hand was on my arm, demanding my attention. "Is that all he ever did to you, Terry? That and nothing more?"

I raised my eyes to study his face, but looking at him didn't tell me anything I didn't already know. Garth had switched sides again, and for reasons that seemed to be totally irresistible to certain men.

"How would you like that little bit of nothing done to you, Garth?" I asked, wasting my breath because I was in the mood for it. "How would you like to be taken in a man's arms and made love to even if it wasn't what you wanted? You stood and faced him with swords once. Could I do that? He beat you, Garth, but he didn't laugh at you. If I tried it, he would laugh. I can't even lift a sword."

I got to my feet then and walked away from them, blocking out whatever their reactions to my speech were. I didn't want to know what they were thinking and feeling, I only cared about what I was feeling. Even if nobody else cared, at least I cared.

I went back to the cabin I had napped in, closed the door behind me, then sat down on the bed with my back to the closed door. I was hoping for enough peace and quiet for a good session of uninterrupted brooding, but without a door lock there wasn't much chance of it. No more than a minute later the door opened again, admitting guess who.

"Do you truly wish you might face me with swords?" the barbarian asked, a definite disturbed note underlying his usual calm. "I had not considered the possibility."

"Of course not," I answered without turning. "I'm nothing but a woman." He didn't reply to that, but just stood there waiting, and after a minute I understood what he was waiting for. "I know well enough I could never face you with swords," I said, lowering my head. "Even if I *could* lift one."

"I would not have laughed," he said, finally coming closer to stroke my hair. "To draw sword against another is not a matter for laughter. Why do you refuse to hear my words, *l'lenda wenda?* That I have need of your abilities does not mean I have no desire for you in your own self. How may I convince you of this?"

"You can't," I said, shaking my head against his hand. "If I let myself believe you I'd just be leaving myself open to be hurt again, and I can't do that. The pain would be less if I did face you with swords."

"I would never find myself able to raise sword to you," he whispered, sitting down next to me to draw me close. "And yet, as great as my love is for you, my need is nearly as great. My people – *our* people – have need of the talent you possess, and you must not deny me. Turn your face from me in all other things if you must, but do not deny me in this."

My cheek was against that broad, bare chest, feeling his warmth and the vital life in him. His brawny arms were around me, holding me gently yet possessively, his mind speaking to mine of the desperation he felt. I felt a crushing need to cry like a child, sobbing wildly, but the time for tears was long past. When pain goes deep enough, nothing soothes it.

"I can do nothing else but deny you," I whispered back, falling easily and naturally into the Rimilian language. "Tammad, *hamak* of my soul, I would give up anything and everything I possess for you, even unto my life, but you, through your own words, show your love for your people greater than your love for me. You would allow me to turn from you completely, if only I would aid your people. I cannot fault you for this love that takes you from me, nor am I able to fight it. I simply cannot allow myself to be placed second, not knowing when another love might place me third or fourth or lower still. Should I attempt such a life, I would wither and die. I have not the stuff of sacrifice within me."

"Terril," he sobbed, crushing me to him, his mind searching frantically for a way to deny what I'd said. A terrible ache had come to claim him, one almost as bad as mine, but he was the one who had set up the rules. His own words proved what mine could not, and the search for denial was a waste of time. I had never seen this giant of a man cry before, but there was no shame in him for what he was doing. In his culture tears were reserved for very special times, times when nothing else will serve. His sense of loss was nearly inconsolable and I moaned with the pain of it, far too close and – personally involved to fend it off. His arms crushed me, his mind crushed me, I tried to contain it all, but I couldn't. The raw power of his body and mind overwhelmed me completely, sending me tumbling down into gray and yellow-shot black.

## FOUR

"Take it easy, Terry," a voice came through the thinning fog, supposedly calm and soothing but laced with enough worry and fretting to make my head throb. I motioned at the voice behind the fog, trying to wave it away; the gesture didn't work, but at least the worry eased up. "Tammad, she's coming to," the voice persisted. "You can tell that doctor he can take his time now."

"I have told him how close he stands to the end of his life," a second voice growled, farther away but suddenly coming closer. "Should he not appear in the next moment, he will learn that my words were not idle."

The first voice, Garth's voice, muttered something that was half agreement, half deep-throated snarl, and I opened my eyes to see the two of them standing over me, staring down at where I lay on the bed. Tammad was furious with what was mostly self-directed anger, and Garth was puzzled.

"You two are giving me a headache," I muttered, trying to smooth the pain creases out of my forehead. "If you can't turn that off, you'll have to leave."

"Turn what off?" Garth demanded, increasing instead of decreasing the puzzlement. "And what's going on here? What happened to you?"

"Nothing," I muttered, starting to sit up, and then I winced at the soreness of my ribs. Nothing was cracked or even close to being seriously damaged, but Garth saw me flinch and whirled angrily on Tammad.

"What have you done to her now?" he demanded. "Another mere nothing to be overlooked?"

"It would be useless to deny the guilt," the big barbarian answered, his voice calm but his mind in a turmoil. "I have once again done the opposite of what I wished to do with this woman, though the why of it is beyond me. I have never before had such difficulty with *wendaa*."

"What's going on here?" another voice demanded before Garth could say anything. The voice belonged to a portly man of middle years, who was breathing hard from the pace he had been moving at when he came in. He wore the uniform of a ship's officer, but I had never seen him before. The two men turned to him, and Garth looked him up and down.

"Well, I'm glad to see you've finally made it," he said grimly. "Do you think you might examine this woman before going back to your collection of dip-reals?"

The man flushed, guilt flaring in his mind, and I just couldn't take any more. I lay back on the bed again and tried to see what I could do about blocking them all out. Tammad was angry at himself for hurting me, Garth was angry because things weren't going quite the way he had expected, and the man, who was undoubtedly the ship's doctor they had sent for, was smarting under Garth's accusation. So-called dip-reals were made only for men, supplying highly erotic fantasy females for men who couldn't or didn't care to pair up with real women. Accusing a man of using dip-reals was an insult, but Garth had very little to worry about. The portly man couldn't have stood up to the Kabra even if he'd wanted to.

The doctor stood glaring at Garth for a minute, then turned away from him and walked over to the bed I was on. His anger grew clearer the closer he came, pushing at the thin shield I had somehow formed in my mind. I say I had formed the shield, but that isn't entirely accurate. In some manner the shield had formed itself, needing only my lack of active resistance to grow immediately where it was needed. As the doctor's anger touched it it thickened, taking up the burden of his emotions without passing it on to me. I knew I could release it any time I cared to, but I would also have enjoyed knowing where it came from. I had never been able to do that before, and had never heard of anyone else able to do it.

"What's bothering you, young lady?" the man asked, his expression working to be concerned. It felt strange not to be experiencing his thoughts directly, but my mind needed time to come back from the buffeting it had taken.

"Nothing's bothering me," I told him. "All I need is to be left alone for a while."

"That isn't true," Garth insisted, coming to stand closer to the bed. "When she tried to move a minute ago, I could see she was in pain. Pain from what I don't know, but there was definitely pain."

"The fault was mine," Tammad put in, coming to stand next to Garth. His tone and expression were calm, but I doubted that his mind matched them. "I – embraced the woman, forgetting how slight she is. I may have done her serious harm."

"Well, there's only one way to find out," the doctor sighed, turning his head toward the other men. "If you two will step outside, I'll examine her."

Garth nodded and began to turn away, but it was immediately evident that Tammad had no intentions of going with him.

"I will remain during this – examination," the barbarian announced, his light eyes openly mistrusting the doctor's intentions. "The woman is mine, and I do not care to leave her with strangers."

"Then I won't examine her," the doctor shrugged, seemingly unimpressed with his antagonist. "I won't make any woman take her clothes off in front of an audience."

"The man's right, Tammad," Garth put in, coming back to where he'd been. "You don't want to embarrass Terry, do you? If you insist on staying when she has to undress, she'll be embarrassed."

"I see no need for the removal of her clothing," the barbarian maintained, folding his arms across his chest as he continued to look at the doctor. "You may see to her as she is."

"Is that so?" the doctor came back, his belligerence evident in the thrust of his fleshy chin. "That's not the way I conduct an examination. If you know so much about it, do it yourself."

"Come on, Tammad, let the man do his job," Garth urged, moving closer to put a hand on the barbarian's shoulder. "If we stayed, we'd just be in the way. This way we'll find out what's wrong with Terry, and we'll still be right outside the door. You have my word he won't do anything you'd find unacceptable."

"You are willing to give your word on the matter?" Tammad asked, turning to look at the Kabra. When Garth nodded he nodded as well, and added, "I know little of the doings of the men of your worlds. Perhaps, in this way, I shall learn the sooner. Very well."

He turned then and led the way out of the cabin, Garth following along and talking to him in low tones. When the door closed behind them, the doctor turned back to me.

"About time," he muttered, his eyes on me. "If you'll remove that blouse-like garment, we'll be able to begin."

"There's nothing to begin," I told him, moving myself carefully into a sitting position. The shield made me feel as if I were wrapped in layer after layer of transparent cloth, but it didn't stop me from noticing that the soreness in my ribs was already fading. In another few minutes it should be gone completely. The major damage had been done to my mind, and even that wasn't as bad as it could have been. The headache was already gone, and I had to smother the urge to peek out from behind the shield.

"Now what's the problem?" the doctor demanded in exasperation, the frown on his round face making him look severe. "Did you people get me down here just to give me a hard time?"

"I wasn't the one who called you," I pointed out. "I told you earlier I wasn't interested in your services. If you're still here it isn't my fault."

"Those two oversized men out there are the reason I'm still here," he hissed, pointing back toward the closed door. "Do you know what that blond one said to me?"

"I can imagine," I nodded. "If you have to examine someone, examine them. You don't have my permission to tend me."

"I give up!" the doctor exploded, throwing his hands up and turning toward the door. When he got there he threw the door open and said to the two surprised faces he saw, "There's nothing I can do. The woman refuses to allow me to examine her, so there's nothing I can do. May I return to my sick bay now?"

"Just a minute." Garth frowned, coming back into the cabin past the doctor. Tammad followed him, also wearing a frown, and the two of them stopped near the bed to look down at me. "Terry, this is ridiculous," Garth said. "You have to let the doctor examine you."

"No, I don't," I answered with a headshake. "Even if there was something wrong with me, which there isn't, I still have the right to refuse."

"You have no such right," Tammad said, interrupting whatever Garth had been about to say. His eyes were hard and displeased, and I could feel the shield thickening to keep his thoughts from me. "You will allow this man called doctor to see to you, for it is my will that you do so."

"That's already been settled," I told him, calmer than I thought I'd be. "You and I are nothing to each other, not even friends. Your will means as little to me as mine means to you. As a Prime of the Centran Amalgamation, I demand that you leave me in peace until this trip is over. Once it is, this transport can take me wherever I have to go."

I folded my legs under me, watching the barbarian's face, peripherally aware of the way Garth and the doctor stirred uneasily to either side of him. He had unconsciously straightened himself to his full height, and his arms folded across his chest as his head nodded slowly.

"It is as I have always believed," he said, his musing tone apparently directed toward the other two men. "Speak to her, each man of your worlds tells me, convince her gently to do as you wish. Do not demand that she obey you, petition her agreement. So have I attempted to do, and now do you see the results before you. My words, clumsily formulated, gave a meaning to my thoughts which I had not intended. My forbearance, shown to the woman against my better judgment, gave her the belief that she might defy me in safety. All these things might easily have been avoided, had I simply commanded her obedience. Is there reason to continue with such foolishness?"

"Tammad, it isn't foolishness," Garth tried, running an anxious hand through his hair. "You can't deny the fact that the woman's a Prime. You just have to be a little more patient." Then his eyes turned to me and they were just about pleading. "Terry, you've got to understand that this isn't a situation where you can afford to be stubborn. After the doctor examines you, you, Tammad and I will sit down and try to straighten out the rest of this mess. It's the only thing we can do."

"Why, because you say so?" I countered. "First I do everything I'm told to do, and then as a reward I get to listen to why things will continue that way? Sorry, Garth, but I've already stated my position. I suggest the rest of you try adapting to me for a change."

"Terry, please ..." Garth started, but Tammad's hand on his shoulder stopped the words.

"It is easier to do battle with the wind and the rain," he told a Garth who was beginning to grow red-faced. "It is not possible to reason with one who refuses to hear you. Do not ask the woman. Tell her."

"Damned if I won't," Garth muttered, straightening the way Tammad had. "Terry, you've had every chance and then some, but you refuse to be reasonable; now we'll do it without resorting to reason. Doctor, I want this woman examined. Now."

"Are you out of your mind?" the doctor gasped, paling at the order while I bristled. "You said yourself she's a Prime. Do you expect me to disregard the desires of a Prime? If we were on Central, you'd be mobbed for the suggestion!"

"And yet, we do not now stand upon your world of Central," Tammad put in when Garth hesitated. "That we do not do so is a great relief to me, for had the woman been truly hurt, her care would be left to her discretion alone. You have been told to see to her. Do so."

This time it was the doctor's turn to hesitate, and Tammad wasn't pleased. He moved closer to the man, towering over him, his broad, tanned, nearly bare body a striking contrast to the statement of confinement of the doctor s uniform. The smaller man looked up at him, licking his lips nervously, feeling the entire weight of those hard, light blue eyes.

"I am in command here," the barbarian said very softly, so softly the doctor shivered. "Do not doubt my word on this. See to the woman."

"B – b – but her clothing," the man stammered, pale and likely to stay so. "How can I – With you and that other man here – ? She won't – "

"Terril, remove your clothing," the barbarian directed, interrupting the limping flow of words from the doctor by moving those light eyes to me. The relative calm I'd felt the entire time was touched with shock that he'd dare suggest such a thing, and then the shield was gone, disappearing in the flare of outrage that exploded from my mind. The doctor's thoughts trembled with deep, uncontrollable fear, Garth's mind quivered with indecision; only Tammad's thoughts were as calm and decisive as ever. My fists clenched against the frothing madness that tried to claim me, and I found it almost impossible to speak coherently.

"You dare tell me I – In front of – After what you – Never! I swear it! Never!"

I was trying to verbalize every thought and feeling I had, suddenly rushing at me from every corner of my mind. I was well nigh insane from the frustration of it, from everything that had happened, from everything that was about to happen. I scrabbled about on the bed, pulled the *caldin* out of my way and got to my knees, then threw myself at the barbarian, beating at him with my fists as I screamed incoherently. I felt the shock in his mind even as his arms came up in reflex protection, keeping me from battering at his face as I so wanted to do. Garth and the doctor were also shocked, so shocked that they stood rooted in place; only Tammad reacted with the reflexes of a cat, catching my arms and forcing me back. I struggled and kicked to keep from being pinned to the bed, but then Garth was helping the barbarian, holding my legs down, and the doctor was at a wall, inserting his key, pressing buttons, removing what a slot in the wall spat out at him. I screamed again, trying to get free, and then a touch of ice at the base of my neck ended it all.

Deep quiet all around, peace and silence and, best of all, no other minds to impose themselves on mine. I took a deep breath and stirred on the bed, then opened my eyes to see that I was still in the same cabin I'd been in earlier. I put a hand to my head and rubbed fretfully, trying to keep a frown from forming. I remembered everything that had happened before the doctor knocked me out; the one thing I couldn't understand was *why* it had happened.

I sat up on the wrinkled linen, closed my eyes and put my fingers over them, then carefully examined my mind. The screaming rage I'd felt was gone, flushed out and away like dirty water down a drain. The rage had come so suddenly that I'd been entirely unprepared for it, finding myself buried under the avalanche even before I knew it was on the way. There was no denying how deeply upset I'd been, but a few minutes of thought passed before another, more probable reason for the blow-up occurred to me. I'd been using that shield, the one that had protected me from everyone else's emotions; could it be it had protected me too far? Not having to receive other people's emotions may have encouraged my own to run wild, if for no other purpose than to fill the void that felt so unnatural when I was awakened. I took a shuddering breath, feeling my heart beat faster at thought of the shield. I'd used it so casually, without once considering possible consequences, without considering careful experimentation before actual use. Anything could have happened, anything at all, and the thought frightened me more than anything about my talent ever had. It was something entirely new, and it would be a long time before I tried using it again.

"You have returned to yourself," came Tammad's voice, and I pulled my fingers away from my eyes to see him standing in the now-opened doorway. His mind was under its usual strong control, and I'd been so deeply immersed in my own concerns that I wouldn't have known he was there if he hadn't spoken. "How do you fare?"

"Oh, I'm just fine and dandy," I answered, staring straight at him. "What's the matter, did you stop by because you were afraid I'd be unable to strip for the rest of your men? I know how unfair it is, asking me to do it just for two of them. The rest would undoubtedly be insulted."

"I see you have indeed returned to yourself." He nodded, coming farther into the cabin and closing the door behind him. "Once again you feel yourself unjustly treated."

"Why, whatever would make you say that?" I wondered aloud, expecting the flash of anger I felt in him. "Just because you've turned my entire life into an insane asylum? Just because you feel you have the right to direct every breath I take? Just because one minute everything is over between us, and the next we're right back where we started? Don't be silly."

I laughed lightly, knowing it would annoy him, but the annoyance he felt never reached his face. He stood there tall and magnificent, broad and strong and handsome and more desirable than any man of all the worlds of the Amalgamation, his mind showing nothing but agreement with what I'd said.

"You have spoken the words I, myself, meant to say," he put in at once, then folded those massive arms. "Perhaps with more sharpness than I care for, yet the words are not untrue.

The fault for this – insanity – as you call, it is indeed mine, for I committed the folly of believing other men were perhaps wiser than I. I shall not do the same again."

"What are you talking about?" I snapped, fed up with round-abouts and hidden meanings. "If you have something to say, say it!"

"There, my point has just been proven," he said. Then he came very close to stare down at me. "When you were yet my belonging on Rimilia, what would have been done to you had you had the temerity to speak to me in such a way? And above that, would you have spoken to me so?"

I stared up at hard, unamused blue eyes and shaggy blond hair, wondering exactly why it was that I *had* spoken to him as I had. It was hard not remembering what he was like, but for some reason the thought hadn't stayed with me.

"Maybe I'm more interested in suicide these days," I shrugged, looking down at the wrinkled *caldin* I wore and smoothing at the creases. My voice had been somewhat faint, which brought a chuckle to his mind.

"You still have not answered my first question," he persisted, looking at me in a way I could feel. "Had we been upon Rimilia, what would have been done to you?"

"You would have beaten me," I mumbled after a minute, keeping my head down, knowing when I really was beaten. If men like Garth couldn't stand up to him, what chance did I have?

"Nothing quite so dramatic, as you very well know," he corrected, his voice not giving an inch. "You would have been switched for the insolence, punished to teach you to curb your tongue. Is this not true?"

I nodded reluctantly without saying anything, still looking at my lap, by then convinced I'd never be able to look up again. Feeling brave when I was all alone or just talking to Garth wasn't hard to do; with Tammad standing over me, giant-sized and without a hesitation in his mind, it was just about impossible.

"The men of your worlds will accept insolence from their *wendaa,* thinking they achieve peace by doing so," he said, still in that same, remorseless voice. "They plead and coax to attain their goal, forgetting their manhood in their frantic search for a manner in which to appease their females. They forget that appeasement is not necessary with one who obeys you to keep from punishment. You were taught to obey me, *wenda;* was the condition as confining as you first believed it would be, as damaging to your sense of dignity?"

I hesitated even longer over that one, remembering how wonderful my time with him had been, once we began really working together. I had done everything he asked, had lived to please him – but I had been in love with him then, really in love. I'd had no doubts, no worries, no insecurities over what he was after – but that was all behind us.

"It's not the same now," I muttered, wishing I had the courage to look up at him. "I couldn't do it again, not the way it was."

"You will find that it is more than possible to do again," he said, and his hand finally came to touch my hair. "Once we are upon Rimilia, among our people, you will recall what others have allowed you to forget. You will recall that it is I to whom you belong, not the *darayse* of your worlds. Once we have returned to our home, we will again find happiness."

"Going back to your old attitudes won't change anything," I told him, terribly aware of the gentleness of his touch. "You speak of *our* people and *our* home, but that's not what they are and we both know it. The good time you remember was when we worked *together,* not when I was your obedient servant. Forcing me to obey you won't bring those times back."

"Such remains to be seen," he answered, sitting down behind me on the bed. "I may do no less than make the attempt." His hands came to my arms and I was gently turned sideways, then lowered to my back to lie across the bed. He sat beside me, looking down at me, the hum in his mind growing stronger the longer he stared. I didn't want to lie there in front of him like the living sacrifice in a pagan ritual, but sitting up again was out of the question. He didn't want me sitting up, and his thoughts made that abundantly clear. He continued to stare silently for a moment, then his hands came first to my left wrist and then to my right, untying the thin leather ties holding the sleeves of the *imad* closed. After my wrists his hands went to my waist, opening the leather ties there, turning the *imad* into even less of a covering than it had been. I could feel my breathing increase to match my heartbeat, both uncontrollable as my mind floundered around, trying to think of something to do to stop him. He had no right to open my clothing like that, he had no right!

"Remove the *imad*," he said, a faint grin on his face for the wide-eyed, frantic expression I could feel possessing me. "I would look at the woman who is my belonging."

He made no attempt to remove the *imad* himself, undoubtedly demonstrating his right to command me – and demanding an example of how well I would obey. I hesitated a very long moment, trying to tell myself I didn't have to do it, watching his mind closely to see how he took my hesitation. I intended refusing if I could get away with it, but it didn't take long to see that refusal wasn't going to be allowed. His faint grin faded to nothing as his thoughts took on a tinge of anger, the muscles in his wide shoulders beginning to tighten at the same time. I swallowed at the instantly growing hardness of his thoughts and began to sit up to do as I'd been told, but his hand came to my throat to press me back down again.

"Remove the *imad* without rising," he said, his voice nearly a growl, his hand heavy on my throat. "You have not been given permission to rise."

I swallowed a second time against the pressure of his hand, wilting under the weight of his stare. As soon as he removed his hand I hurried to squirm out of the *imad,* pulling it off over my head and out from beneath me as quickly as I could. I had never in my entire life thought of myself as a coward – until the moment I had first been taught what a true barbarian was like.

"And now the *caldin*," he said when I held the *imad* in my hand, his fingers making brief, easy work of the sash knot. I dropped the *imad* and pushed the *caldin* down past my hips, then kicked it off onto the floor. I was nearly frantic in my rush to obey, and the laughter in his thoughts came as crashingly as a flood of freezing water.

"And just so quickly will you obey in future," he grinned, reaching across me to take the *imad* and throw it after the *caldin*. "Even should every *l'lenda* who follows me be about, you will not hesitate nor disobey. Your body, though at present too slim, will not displease them. It certainly does not displease me."

I closed my eyes and put an arm over them, the burning red of humiliation covering me completely. I knew how pleased he was with the way I looked but I could tell he was even more pleased with the way he had made me obey him.

What he'd said about stripping me in front of his men was meant to add to my humiliation, not to be taken as a serious threat. On Rimilia the concept would not *be* a threat, merely a matter of things-as-they-were. Men and women bathed together without shame, and women bathed while men stood guarding them. Despite everyone else's views, I had never quite gotten to the point of nonchalance over the matter, and Tammad knew it.

"How lovely a woman is in the sight of a man," my tormentor continued, suddenly putting his hand on my thigh. I gasped and tried to pull away, but his fingers tightened, holding my flesh prisoner. "The softness of her body is a constant delight, designed to stir him beyond all control. Your body stirs me like no other, Terril mine. Open your eyes and look upon he to whom you belong."

Slowly, reluctantly, I moved my arm away from my face and opened my eyes, blinking back the bright spots dancing in my vision. Haloed in the midst of them was Tammad, a man who never worried about appeasing a woman.

"Woman, you are mine!" he said, his expression and thoughts fierce. "No man of my world may claim you without facing me with swords; no man of your worlds may deny me for they are nearly all *darayse*. Once we found happiness together, and I mean to see it so again. Think only of achieving such happiness, for in no other way will you find peace. There are none to take you from me, as you now so obviously hope, none to return you to your former life. You are mine and will remain so."

"You forget about my government," I said in a rush, hurrying to get the words out before my throat closed up. "There aren't so many Primes around that they'll give one up without a fuss. What if they send troops after you and – and – sh-shoot you down?"

I stumbled over the words as I said them, but not because of what Tammad's reaction might be. The possibility of the giant barbarian being shot down was not as remote as it might be, and no one deserved that, not even him.

"Your government wishes to deal with me," he answered, scorn in his mind for the entire transaction. "Once before they granted me your body, to be used as I wished the while you used your talent. Think you they will deny me now, when I have the leadership they wished me to have? Prime or no, you are no more than *wenda* to them, Terril. One benefit accruing to a man who is victorious is the *wenda* of his choice. You are my choice."

"That isn't true!" I cried, looking up at him where he sat so close above me. "Last time they made you promise to return me! This time they won't let you take me at all!"

"My word was given only for *your* comfort," he said, sadness in his tone. "The Murdock McKenzie , and through him, the Rathmore Hellman, knew I meant to keep you and they did not attempt to dissuade me. It was no more than misunderstanding that the Murdock McKenzie allowed your departure before I might arrive to reclaim you. Because of your words to him, it was his belief that I had tired of you. When he learned that this was not so, he brought this vessel for my use. Though he stands as father to you, *hama*, he will not refuse my wishes."

"I won't believe it's all so one way," I said, shaking my head against the certainty in him. "My people won't give me up without an argument on no more than your sayso. I'm worth more to them than a simple item of trade to sweeten a bargain. I'm a Prime – and I'm one of them."

He sighed as he looked down at me, his mind unangered by my arguments, his light eyes serious and sympathetic. He wasn't bothered by what I'd said simply because he was convinced it wasn't true.

"For your sake do I wish there would be need to do battle with your people for you," he said, leaning down beside me to put his arms around me. "I would gladly face whatever battle there was, yet there will be no battle. When this occurs, do not despair, *hama*. Recall the fact of my love, and know that you go to people who *will* make you one of them. Those who live by constant bargaining may know no loyalty – for, in the presence of loyalty, bargaining comes a poor second."

I stared at the understanding in his face for a moment then turned my head away, knowing he was letting me keep my hopes of rescue after all, just to show me how wrong I was.

He was absolutely certain that my people would let him walk off with me, but I couldn't believe that. I was a native of Central and would not be abandoned, not after all the years I'd worked for the Amalgamation. No group, not even a government, could be that insensitive.

I intended spending a good deal of time listing in my mind all the reasons why the barbarian was wrong, but it didn't work out that way. One minute I was thinking defensive thoughts and the next, almost to my shock, my body was registering gentle tease-kisses and feather-light caresses. I turned my head back to look at the barbarian, trying to understand what he was doing. Out and out rape was his usual style, without finesse and without exception, but suddenly he seemed to be in a teasing mood, his shaggy blond head bent over me almost casually, with passion nowhere to be felt.

"What are you doing?" I asked, stirring uncomfortably at the way his fingers trailed slowly up and down my thighs, backdropping the touch of his lips near my breasts.

"I merely amuse myself," he answered in distraction, seemingly lost in thought over something else entirely. He wasn't paying attention to what he was doing, as though he were engaged in the equivalent of doodling or some such. I didn't care much for his concept of self-amusement, but it was certainly better than rape.

Or so I thought to begin with. After another few moments of it, I was considerably less certain. He lay beside me across the bed, his right arm beneath me and holding me to him, his left hand free to move all over my body, tracing, trailing, tickling and teasing. Not once in all the movement had he touched me intimately, not once had his lips pressed themselves to my breasts, and yet, despite these lacks, my flesh had begun to burn and quiver; the movements of my discomfort growing sharper and more demanding. I didn't understand what was happening, but I didn't have to understand it to dislike it. I stood it for as long as I could, then simply *had* to say something.

"Can I – get up now?" I tried, hoping he'd miss the unevenness of my voice. "I'm – tired of staying in bed."

"No," he answered in the same distraction, not even slowing the rhythm of his movements. His mind was still directed elsewhere, his body uninterested in what his hands and lips were doing. I could feel the heat of his closeness, underscored by the strange, male smell of him, increased by his constant touch on my body. I closed my eyes and swallowed a moan, then tried to pretend I was elsewhere.

In less time than it takes to form the thought, I discovered pretense was impossible. I was being held by a man I'd had sex with many times, a man who usually overwhelmed me with his desire, a man who had taught my body to feel the same desire. He was doing no more than playing with a toy now, but the toy was growing frantic for the way he usually touched her, for the way he drew instant fire from her. I moved against him deliberately, hoping for a forceful response, hoping to direct the movement of his hand, feeling the sweat break out all over me when the ploy failed. His broad hand moved across my belly, stroked down the top of my right thigh, rose slowly on the inside of the same thigh – then shifted to stroke down the top of my left thigh. I shivered and pressed to him again, intending to meet the hand that now rose on the inside of the thigh, spreading my knees and moving my hips downward – but the hand was suddenly gone from where it had been, moving, instead, over my right side. I moaned in frustration and disappointment, aching and sweating, at a loss to know what to do.

"Tammad, please!" I gasped out at last, putting a hand to the broad, tanned chest I was being held against. "Rape me if you have to, but don't torture me any longer. I can't bear it."

"I have no interest in raping a woman," he answered, finally moving calm blue eyes to my face. "A man, in his need, will use the woman he desires, hoping to cause her to desire him as well. Should it prove impossible to kindle this desire, his interest in the woman must necessarily fade, even if only for a short while. There is little pleasure in feeling desire for one who has no desire for you."

"B – but you can't mean that!" I stuttered, literally horrified. "You can't continue making me feel this way and not do anything about it! I'll explode! I'll die!"

"Your need does seem much upon you," he agreed, running a finger down between my breasts to wipe the sweat away. "In times past I gladly saw to such need, yet found little gratitude for the effort. Was I not reviled for having intruded upon your weakness, for having done – ungentlemanly – things? As it is restraint you seem to prefer, I have decided to attempt such restraint. You will undoubtedly be much the happier."

He turned his attention back to my body then, and suddenly his tongue was on me, licking at a drop of sweat. I choked on the shock that flashed through my body, trying to scream and cry out and argue all at once. I had never been that badly in need before, not without his doing something about it.

"Please, please!" I begged, writhing in his arm against his body. "You can't leave me like this, please, you can't!"

"But I do not desire you," he said very simply, his mind confirming the words as those sober blue eyes returned to me. "The restraint I have imposed upon myself disallows this. I am not a woman, able to perform at any time. Restraint robs a man of ability."

"Restraint be damned!" I screamed, struggling against the way he held me. "Throw it off! Don't let it rule you any longer!"

"What reason have I to throw it off?" he asked, raising one eyebrow. "What reason have I to fight it?"

"I'll give you a reason," I growled, and pulled so hard I broke his grip, then threw my arms around his neck. His surprise raised both his eyebrows, and then I was too close to see his eyebrows any longer. I kissed him, as hard and demandingly as he had ever kissed me, pressing my body against his to increase the pleasure of contact. He didn't resist me or try to push me away, but the feeling I wanted didn't surface in him, and I knew it almost immediately. I kept our lips together for another minute, then finally backed away.

"What am I doing wrong?" I demanded, kneeling in front of him, watching his mind as the faint pleasure he had gotten out of the kiss flickered and died. "Why aren't you feeling anything?"

"Perhaps the time is wrong," he shrugged, shifting from his elbow to lie flat on his back. "Perhaps it is no more than the fact that I am uncomfortable in my *haddin*. It is rather warm in this place."

"Your *haddin*," I mumbled, desperately seizing on anything that could be the reason for his coldness. I quickly turned to the brown body-cloth wrapped around his loins and began tugging at it, looking for the end that would unwrap it. He grunted when my frustration made me pull the wrong end too hard, then reached down to start the unwrapping for me.

"I had best assist you before your desire unmans me," he muttered, but I knew he wasn't laughing at me because his mind showed no laughter. Once he had gotten the end loose I finished the unwrapping, then threw the *haddin* after my *imad* and *caldin*. He had helped further by raising his hips to let me remove the *haddin*, but once that was done he lay still again without showing the least amount of interest in me. He looked somewhat foolish with his legs hanging so far off the bed, but I wasn't in a position to appreciate anything having to do with foolishness.

"Now what do I do?" I asked, shaking my hair away from my face. "Do you need anything else to make you more comfortable? How about a pillow for your head?"

"How will a pillow for my head bring me desire for a woman?" he asked, watching as I bit at my lip. "Only a woman may bring me desire for a woman."

"Well, I'm a woman," I pointed out eagerly, moving a little closer to him. "Don't I do anything to make you desire me? You said you were pleased with my body."

"Perhaps the sight would do more had you not grown so thin," he sighed, moving his hand toward me then changing his mind and taking it back. "No, the effort is too great."

"Please try!" I begged, leaning forward to put my hands on his chest. "I'll help you if you'll just tell me what to do!"

"I find myself easily accepting the fact that you have no knowledge of how to excite and please a man," he said, looking up into my anxious eyes. "What man of your worlds would demand that you please him, you who stands so much higher than he? I suspect all women are treated so, begged for their favor then praised for no more than the use of their bodies. Had I realized this sooner, I would not have accustomed you to no more than acceptance of my use."

"What are you talking about?" I asked, finding it impossible to follow what he had said. If he was making comparisons again, I didn't *want* to know what he was talking about. Every time he made comparisons, a little more of my self-esteem was chipped away.

"It is nothing of immediate concern," he said, and suddenly he was looking at me differently. His hands came to my arms and he pulled me close, so close he almost could have kissed me. "Should you truly wish my desire, you must say so now," he rapped, staring at me so sternly I wanted to cringe. "I have no wish to be aroused and then spurned, pushed to one side as though I were a rag. Do you desire me, woman? Will you raise my need and then see to it?"

Numbly, woodenly, I nodded, not really knowing what he was talking about but too desperate to disagree. When he told me what I had to do to arouse him, I almost cried; I had never done anything like that before and I was sure I'd do something wrong or be sick or maybe even faint. I'd never really fainted before either, but I could see that the longer I associated with the barbarian, the better my chances would become.

It was silly to be timid with a body I knew so well – or thought I knew so well – but I discovered I wasn't as aggressive as some people considered me. It's one thing to let a man know where you stand with words, quite another to be the one to begin the exercises. I put my hand out and touched his thigh, lightly, almost without contact, suddenly more shy than I'd been during my very first sexual experience. He lay quietly watching me, his mind totally unanticipating, totally lacking in active cooperation. If I didn't raise his interest nothing would happen, but I wasn't sure I *could* raise his interest. If I were clumsy he would probably give up entirely, and how could I not be clumsy when compared to the other women he'd known? No woman of his world would even consider refusing him, even if it had been her option to refuse. He could have any woman he wanted, as often as he liked, all of them eager to please him and knowing how to do it. I looked at him in misery, finding I had already given up even though I didn't want to give up, and something of my problem must have touched his understanding. He hesitated very briefly, somehow seemingly considering options, and then his hands were on my arms again, pulling me close. His lips touched mine with less demand than he normally showed, but his mind warmed toward mine, telling me without words that he wanted me and approved of me. The need I had felt till then had been purely physical, but being held in his arms like that extended the need to a psychological one – and satisfied that part of it. He held me gently, with loving approval, and I suddenly knew I wouldn't fail him or disappoint him. I needed to give him pleasure but I also *wanted* to, more than I'd ever wanted to do anything. The feeling built higher and higher until I couldn't stand it any longer, until I had to pull from his lips and arms and begin kissing him all over.

His body was rough and hard, covered with light hair that was nearly lost against the tan of his skin. I pressed my lips to him with high desire, inhaling deeply of the musky odor of him, the pleasant leather-and-metal-and-animal smell that clung like a faint aura of definition, expressing this one man without confusion or mistake. I also tasted him as I went, knowing his clean, warm flavor as well as I knew the strength of his thoughts, the touch of his hands. I became aware of the deep slowness of his breathing and realized that it was a forced slowness, a contrived match to the shallow-growing disinterest his mind was attempting to maintain. I laughed to myself and ran my tongue down his belly, feeling the shudder in his flesh as I did so, feeling the agonizing flare of heat in my own body as I finally reached the goal he had ordered me to. I touched and kissed and ran my tongue all about, taken by a frenzy that was a driving obsession, blind and deaf to everything but what I was doing to him and what that very doing was doing to me. He may have shouted and closed his hand around my calf, nearly crushing it in reflex action, nearly rising off the bed; I may have thrown my arms around his thighs to keep from being bucked out of place, to keep from being deprived of obtaining my obsession's demands; the sole fact that came to me clearly was the fact of his immediate response, the fact of his uncontrollable desire, undeniable and simultaneous in both body and mind. His mind again attempted control of his body, presenting demands for slowness and patience, repeating the need for denial of immediate response. Again and again the attempt was made but the body, awash in a flood of liquid lightning and drowned in delight, proved deaf to the demands. Sensation alone ruled the body I clung to, the body I tasted to its very soul; when the explosion came it was unexpected and violent, seemingly designed to drive me away. I cried out and began to retreat, suddenly confused and unsure, the pleasure he projected battering me down, subtracting his need from the equation we'd formed and leaving only mine. I cried out again but this time with my mind, sending him my body's flames as I had refused to do earlier, as I had been too proud to do earlier. His projection changed tone and pitch immediately, reverting to raging desire, a renewal of need so strong it frightened me. He snarled and threw me to my back, taking possession of my body so quickly I had no time to express my fright, only to gasp and melt in his arms, his beyond question and doubt. I had what I'd begged for, what I'd wheedled and worked for; all that was left to do was accept.

## FIVE

He stirred in the bed beside me, his mind coming instantly awake the way an animal's does, no pauses to question location or self, no sense of disorientation whatsoever. He picked up the thread of consciousness so quickly it was almost as though he had never let it go, even through hours of sleep. He shifted gently and put his arms around me, one below my body, one above, immediately spreading his hands out. If I hadn't already been awake I would have returned to awareness thinking we had spent our sleep time like that, pressed together in mutual pleasure. I stirred to the stroking of his fingers, feeling the deep pleasure in his mind, feeling the relief he felt at being able to acknowledge that pleasure. He hadn't been able to do that the last time he'd touched me, and why he had held himself back was perfectly clear.

"I feel you are awake, *hama*," he murmured, putting his lips to my hair. "Is this not so?"

"Yes, I'm awake," I agreed, not moving any more than I had to. When I didn't add anything, he moved even closer.

"The night was filled with much pleasure for us," he pursued, pulling me tightly against him. "I have not had such deep response from you since before we parted. You cannot deny the significance of the thing."

"So you proved you've made me as lustful for your body as you seem to be for mine," I shrugged, keeping my tone light and uncaring. "Do you mean you intend making me rape you from now on?"

"I mean nothing of the sort," he answered from behind me, annoyance beginning to push his pleasure aside. "It is clear to me, and should be equally as clear to you, that your desire for me is as it was. Speaking words to the contrary will do naught to alter this."

"I thought you didn't care what I said," I observed, feeling his annoyance increase. "I thought you were taking me to Rimilia even if I had to go kicking and screaming all the way. Wasn't that little charade you devised before last sleep period meant to make life in the furs more pleasant for you? I can't very well deny it worked, because it did. In future, I'll probably find it impossible not to respond exactly as you wish."

"That was not my sole consideration," he objected, suddenly moving his hands so he could shift me around to face him. The light in the cabin was dim, but I've never needed external light to see him. His mind and personality were an inner blaze of light, growing stronger whenever he became angry. "I primarily wished you to know the depth of frustration possible when the one you desire feels no desire for you," he said, staring down into my eyes. "It is also necessary that you learn to please a man to a greater extent than you have so far attained. Much pleasure is lost to ignorance when it need not be so."

"Well, there's no denying I learned *something*," I muttered, looking down from his eyes to stare at his chest. "I never had the least urge to do that before, but it wasn't as bad as I thought it would be. Did you really enjoy it as much as you seemed to?"

"It was magnificent." He laughed softly, gathering me close to him. "As your expertise grows, it will become even more magnificent. I have not had sufficient opportunity to school you in such things, which shows how great a fool I am. I should undoubtedly have made the opportunity."

"You were too concerned with other things of greater importance," I said into his chest, rubbing my cheek against it. "Even if I went with you, nothing would change. You're part of something that goes beyond personal preference, beyond pleasure and desire. What do you intend doing with Garth?"

"He will aid my people and become one of them," he answered after a very brief hesitation, his mind closing into a guarded mold I'd seen before. "His assistance will secure for him a life he now seeks in vain. He, like you, will find acceptance among my people."

"But not if he doesn't do things for them," I pointed out, keeping my eyes down. "If he just tries to live among them, doing nothing special, he'll just be an outsider to be ignored and forgotten. No one will care about him or care whether he stays or goes."

"This is not true," he denied, beginning to feel a faint upset. "My people concern themselves with strangers among them, ever seeking to make them less of a stranger and more of a brother. One does not build a strong community by denying others entrance to it nor disallowing their assistance."

"No one welcomes a stranger without demanding an entrance price," I maintained. "If they can't pay the price they become outcasts, unwanted and uncared about. I wonder how long you'll even remember me. once you have someone else to do your work. Will you, think of me from time to time, and at least wonder what I'm doing?"

He was quiet for a moment, ripples of disturbance touching his mind, and then his hands were at my face, lifting it so that I must look at him.

"You speak as though you believe you will not accompany me," he said, his voice soft but his eyes directly on me. "However this thought came to you, it is untrue. You will indeed accompany me – wherever I go."

"As nothing more than your woman?" I smiled, then shook my head. "You'd probably starve to death waiting for me to learn how to cook. And you don't even really want me that way. You told me so before we slept."

"I said no such words!" he growled, working automatically to keep his distress from growing. "Never would I have said such words!"

"You didn't have to put it into, words," I answered, losing the smile. "You mind is the strongest I've ever seen anywhere, and last sleep period you did something I didn't think was possible. You hid your feelings from me, so completely I didn't even know you were doing it. I know how great an effort you had to make, and I also know you wished you didn't have to make that effort. With an ordinary woman, the effort would be unnecessary."

"It is possible one might indeed be loath to make such an effort," he agreed, keeping his eyes directly on me. "However, should one prefer a woman who is far from ordinary, one will make the effort gladly. I have no interest in ordinary *wendaa;* my desire is solely for you. Perhaps I had best prove this."

He immediately lowered his lips to mine then, cutting off all further discussion. His desire leapt as quickly into being as it usually did, igniting my own desire, but I felt the need to make an effort of my own. It was impossible not to do and act exactly as he wished, but that time I refused to let our minds merge, refused to allow him entrance to my deepest feelings. My body was his completely, the pool he plumbed to the furthest depths, the vessel he filled with the wine of desire; my mind was encased by a trembling will, as weak as a thought, as strong as desperation. When he was through with me he held me in his arms, his body only partially satisfied, his mind filled with frustration. He tried to hide that frustration the way he'd hidden his desire, but the sour emotions are always harder to handle.

"The experiment didn't work out too well, did it?" I asked, feeling like an intruder in his arms. "The deep unending love you claim to feel for me seems to be based on *what* I am, not *who* I am. How long would your love continue if I never let our minds merge again?"

"I do not have the words to speak what I feel." He groped, the frustration increasing. "Why do you feel it necessary to withhold yourself from me? Why do you seek to be what you are not?"

"I want to be wanted for the kind of person I am, not for what I can do," I whispered, close to tears. "Is that so wrong? Am I being totally unreasonable pointing out that all you're interested in is what I can do for you, even in bed? You don't really want *me,* and we both know it."

"This is not the truth," he sighed, holding me close to comfort the tears he could undoubtedly feel on his chest. "I am able to think of no way to prove this to you, yet to me it is patently untrue. Perhaps one day I will find the means to prove my words, yet at this moment I am unable to do so. You must take the words and cause yourself to believe them, for they are all I have."

He projected calm belief as he held me, obviously trying to convince me that way, but his emotions were too well under his control for them to make the sort of impression he was hoping for. I didn't spend too much time crying, but the tears I did shed weren't wasted; every farewell deserves at least a few tears. After a few minutes Tammad stirred, then kissed me before getting up and reaching for his *haddin*.

"Do you now dress yourself," he directed, looking down at me as he wrapped the cloth around himself. "You will eat well this day, and then, perhaps, matters will seem less insoluble to you."

"You expect food to solve all our problems?" I asked, sitting up to wrap my arms around my knees. "Even a nine-course banquet wouldn't stand much of a chance."

"We will at least make the attempt," he chuckled, moving over to the light dial. Turning the dial brightened the cabin and let me see his grin, but it also showed me the well-worn *imad* and *caldin*, lying crumpled on the floor where they had been thrown. I sighed over the determination in his mind, got out of bed, then threw the dirty clothing into the wall cleaner before going to wash. I didn't want to put those things on again, but it was that or walk around naked until I had my own things back. Naked would have been bad enough all by itself, but with the barbarian around it was impossible. He kept his eyes on me constantly until the cleaned clothing was returned by the wall recess and put on, and only then led the way out of the cabin to the common area. If he was trying to show how much he wanted me, he could have chosen a less unnerving way of making the attempt. All he did with his try was make me too aware of his determination.

I suppose I expected the common area to be empty, but as soon as the cabin door opened I found I was wrong. All six of Tammad's *l'lendaa* were there, sitting where they'd been the last time I'd seen them, none of them aware of being watched by Garth, who was also in his usual place. The main point of interest for Garth seemed to be the three female trippers, who now sat among the six men, laughing in delight as they fed their giant captors by hand. When one of the men ignored the bit of food being offered him and snapped instead at the hand holding it, the woman involved shrieked in mock fear, setting off further laughter in everyone else. It was an unexpectedly jolly and intimate grouping, and Garth was filled with vast confusion. When Tammad spoke to him, he started guiltily.

"What?" he asked, turning his head to look up at the barbarian. "I'm sorry, I didn't hear what you said."

"I merely asked after your sleep," Tammad answered, lowering himself to the carpeting without showing any of the amusement he felt. "Was it adequate to your needs?"

"I suppose so," Garth muttered, reaching for the cup of hot kimla sitting on the small table at his elbow. He sipped at the kimla then sat staring at it, just as though there were nothing else in the room worthy of his attention. I sat myself on the carpeting beside Tammad, not too near, not too far, hoping I might be forgotten. I didn't have much of an appetite, and wasn't in the mood for an argument.

"You seem uncertain in your answer," Tammad observed, still talking to Garth. "Do you perhaps feel a lack unshared by those about you?"

"Aside from the fact that I seem to be the only one who slept alone, not at all," Garth answered, watching his cup until he drank from it. "Maybe I ought to borrow some of the crew's dip-reals."

"Ah, you feel yourself badly used," Tammad nodded. "Or perhaps it would be more apt to say, badly unused."

"Are you laughing at me?" Garth demanded, raising furious eyes toward a Tammad who was grinning faintly. "You *are* laughing at me!"

"I merely find amusement in a discomfort *l'lendaa* rarely know," the barbarian soothed him, leaning back against his pillows. "If you wished a woman, why did you not take one?"

"Just like that?" Garth asked, sarcasm strong in his voice. "Sure, why not. Come on, Terry, it's my turn."

I continued to sit where I was, knowing Garth wasn't serious, knowing he had no intentions himself of getting up. But I wouldn't have minded leaving at that, since I had the very strong conviction that Tammad had set himself to teach Garth a lesson, one that I would not particularly care for.

"This woman is mine," Tammad told him mildly, merely stating a fact that called for no argument. "Should her use be given to another the decision would also be mine. Your request was not serious, I know, yet you addressed yourself to her. Why did you not address me?"

"Because you're not my type," Garth snorted, sending Tammad a sour look. "Do you really expect me to take this discussion seriously?"

"Perhaps not," Tammad conceded. "Perhaps it is impossible to teach a man of your worlds freedom. Why did you not take one of the other females to your bed? My warriors are not that badly in need, and are aware that you are my guest."

"Why – I don't know." Garth faltered, suddenly finding more sobriety in the discussion. "Was I supposed to just walk over and pick one? What if she refused to go with me? And don't you remember how they were acting? What if the one I picked had hysterics?"

"There seem to be a great many reasons why it was best for you to remain alone in your bed," the barbarian said, not conceding the point in the slightest. "Had my warriors been equally concerned with questions such as those, they too would have slept alone. And perhaps the females would not be as pleased as they appear to be."

"And that's another thing I don't understand," Garth complained, turning his head to look at the other group again. "Suddenly those three can't do enough for your men, and they're practically singing while they do it. Unless I've gone stark, raving mad, those women were raped during the sleep period, and by two men each. Now, I've seen women who were raped before, and *none* of them looked like those three. They were more like what those three looked like before the sleep period."

The bewilderment in Garth's voice was painful to hear, almost as painful as feeling it in his mind. He turned tragic eyes to Tammad, who gave him understanding without pity.

"Perhaps the reason for this is clear once it is explained," he said, then gestured toward the other group. "Perhaps asking them would assist you."

Garth, embarrassed, hesitated. "How could I – " then stopped in confusion before turning his desperation toward me. "Terry, tell me what they're feeling," he pleaded, his face as flushed as if he'd been running. "I can't just go over there and ask them, but you don't have to."

"I don't know how many times I have to say it," I observed, ignoring his desperation. "I'm not here to make life easier for you mighty males, even in passing. If you want to go through channels to get an answer, be my guest. I'm sure the captain knows the right frequency to reach Central central."

His embarrassment faded immediately to angry annoyance, echoing the annoyance that came more strongly from Tammad. The barbarian hadn't really wanted me to read the women for Garth, but he didn't care for the way I had refused. He had the distinct impression I'd meant the words for him as well – and he was right.

"It seems you have now discovered why one does not plead with a woman," he said as Garth began drawing himself up. "Yet this discovery is only incidental, to the purpose of our discussion. We have as yet to discover the reason for the behavior which disturbs you. Let us question one of the three together."

Garth let his anger at me drain off reluctantly, then turned his attention back to Tammad. The barbarian had gotten the attention of one of his men, and had pointed out the girl he had chosen for his victim. The *l'lenda* took the girl's arm, spoke to her quietly, then gestured toward Tammad, causing the girl to lose most of the laughter that had filled her. She hesitated very briefly, as though gathering her nerve, before getting to her feet. By the time she was standing in front of us, her defensiveness was a mile high and a yard thick. I recognized her as the one Tammad had sent to wake me the day-period before, and wondered why he kept singling her out.

"My companion wishes to speak with you," Tammad told her, nodding toward Garth. His voice had been very gentle and encouraging, but that hadn't done much to affect the girl's stiffness. She turned her head to Garth, waiting without speaking, defying him with her eyes no matter what he wanted.

"I have a question," Garth said, his voice as gentle and confident as Tammad's had been. He wasn't feeling any less distress than he had been, but he'd been embarrassed once over the distress and didn't want it to happen again. "You and your friends seem a good deal happier than you seemed before the sleep period. I won't pretend I don't know what happened to you three between then and now, so my question should be obvious. *Why* are you so much happier?"

The girl drew herself up, her face tinged with pink, her body trying to look dignified even in the altered towel she still wore. It didn't seem possible for her defensiveness to increase, but she proved it was more than possible.

"We were hard up and got taken care of!" she snapped, her shoulders tensing to the scrape in her voice. "Chalk it up to that!"

"Now, look …!" Garth began, his own voice beginning to be angry and offended, but Tammad interrupted before a shouting match could start.

"Why do you speak so, *wenda*?" he asked, his tone still mild but his voice sharpening just enough for her to notice. "A question was asked you; we await a civil answer."

The girl's head snapped around to allow her to stare at Tammad, but whatever she'd been prepared to say to him was swallowed when she met his gaze. She bit her lip trying to sustain her anger, and in some small measure succeeded.

"A civil answer won't do him any good," she muttered, not quite up to using the same tone on Tammad that she had used on Garth. "One like him already has all the answers – about everything. Besides, he wouldn't understand."

"Why don't you try giving me a chance to understand?" Garth put in, his voice calm again. "If all my answers are wrong, how will I ever find out if no one tells me?"

Her face screwed up into a stubborn, resentful mold, showing as clearly as her mind that she was just short of refusing, but a quick glance at Tammad showed her that he was still watching her with the same look he'd used earlier. It was a look I was well familiar with, one he usually used on me, and she couldn't stand up to it any more than I could.

"You won't understand," she muttered again, but to Garth, looking down at the way her fingers twisted at her waist. "It sounds stupid when you put it into words." Then her head came up, and she looked at Garth defiantly. "Sure, they did whatever they wanted to us last sleep period, but not like any other man ever did. They didn't ask, and after it they didn't treat us any different than they did before. They – just didn't ask."

"You were right," Garth said, shaking his head in bewilderment. "I don't understand. What has asking got to do with it?"

"All men ask," she said, looking and sounding disgusted. "It's not the asking that gets you, it's what goes along with the asking. If you answer yes, you're a tramp, if you answer no, you're a dip-teaser. With most men, no matter what you do is wrong. With these guys – they wanted it and they took it. They didn't give us a chance to say yes or no, and they made us like it. After it was over, they still liked what they saw. We never had that before."

She was staring at Garth, trying to see if he did understand after all, but Garth was staring down at his folded legs, his mind working furiously. He thought in silence for a minute or two, then raised his head again.

"This – difference in attitude you're talking about," he said, meeting her eyes. "Would you try it with me to see if *I* could do it?"

"No," she answered immediately, disgust back in her voice. "You asked."

"So I did," he sighed, shaking his head but at himself. "Thank you for answering my question so completely."

The woman hesitated, wondering if he would say anything else, then shrugged and turned away when it was clear that he wouldn't. When she was back among her group again, Garth turned to me.

"So that's what I was doing wrong all that while," he said, a strange. calm-but-excited feeling in him. "I was asking."

"Don't be an idiot," I snorted, very aware of Tammad, behind my arm, looking at us. "You can't really believe all women think like that. Garth, no one alive is that innocent."

Garth flushed just the way I wanted him to, and the confusion rolled back over him. I shook my head in derision to increase his confusion, feeling Tammad's annoyance flare when he realized what I was doing.

"One must use sense when listening to the words of a *wenda*," the barbarian put in to Garth, sounding considerably more casual than he was feeling. "The *wenda* who spoke before us resolved the matter in her own way, which is but one way of many. It may seem different to other *wendaa*, yet it may also seem the same, as each *wenda* is not equally willing to speak of the thing. A woman's denial is often meant as a gesture, to salve her pride and protect her willfulness, a thing the truth would not accomplish."

Garth breathed an "Ahhh" of satisfaction, his mind and eyes filling with instant amusement, especially when I turned on the barbarian in a fury.

"You think you're so smart!" I hissed at Tammad, feeling – actually *feeling* – the way he was laughing at me. "When it comes to women you think you know it all, don't you? You think you can roll over anything or anyone you please, especially if they're female! Well, the one thing I really want to see is the day you meet a woman you can't push around or browbeat into listening to you! That's the day that overblown ego of yours will explode in your face and free all that hot air you're filled with! You'll probably end up being no more than two feet tall!"

I began getting to my feet to storm back to my cabin, furious with both of them, when a big hand grabbed my *caldin* sash and pulled me back down to the carpeting. I sprawled on my left side, closer to Tammad, and looked up to see the deep amusement those blue eyes still retained.

"As the time of my come-uppance has not yet arrived, you would do well to recall that you have not been given permission to leave," be said, his voice just short of its usual chuckle. "I will see what food there is within you, so that you may be more attractive to him who claims you when I am no longer able to defend my right to you."

"Maybe I'll be the one to claim you then," Garth put in, leaning forward to grin down at me. "I don't know as much about women as he does, but I intend learning all I can. By the time he can't control you any longer, I should be able to take over – if I haven't found anyone of my own by then."

"I have no worries on that score," I told Garth angrily and with bitterness, sitting up again with my back toward Tammad. "By the time you've learned to ignore a woman's wishes the way he does, to beat her and bully her the way he does, you won't want me around any longer. Every time you look at me you'll know how wrong you are, and how quickly you turned your back on what's right. I'll bring back memories that are too painful, Garth, and every time you look at me you'll know what's right. You just won't want to admit it."

Garth's grin had disappeared entirely by the time I was through, his light eyes a somber reflection of his thoughts. He didn't mind seeing me embarrassed and pushed around a little, especially if he could help, but turning mild revenge into a way of life was something else again. Tammad had been trained to it from childhood, but Garth had been taught different values, ones the barbarian would not find as easy to overcome as he thought they would be. Tammad was trying to turn Garth into a barbarian, but I was fighting to keep him civilized and sensible. One barbarian in a woman's life is more than enough.

"And yet, right and wrong are not simple entities," Tammad put in. "To each of us, that which we desire is right, that which hinders us, wrong. A woman, however, will consider that which she feels *should be* desirable as right, where a man is able to see the reality of the desire. My Terril has been taught that all those about her owe her deference and obedience, for her talent sets her above those others. She strives to maintain this state of affairs, yet finds happiness only when she is made to obey my wishes, whatever they may be. Is she, then, one whose words it is wise to give heed to, one who clearly sees her own needs and the needs of others? A man listens to the words of all; a wise man hears the true from the false."

"And an intelligent man uses his eyes and common sense," I added immediately, not liking the way Garth's distress and confusion eased in Tammad's direction. "He talks glibly enough of happiness, but how happy do I look to *you*? Am I glowing and in love with the whole universe, am I laughing over nothing and constantly humming to myself? If I'm all that happy, why does he have to keep me a prisoner?"

"Your happiness would return if you allowed it to do so," Tammad growled, his eyes undoubtedly hard where he sat behind me. "A stubborn, female foolishness keeps you from what once was yours, before the foolishness occurred to you. Am I to bow to foolishness and release you, thereby adding to the foolishness? Once we have reached Rimilia, things will be as they were."

"Things will *never* be as they were!" I flared, twisting around to glare at him. "As soon as you find out I'm not kidding about not working for you, your intense interest will dissolve and turn elsewhere. You won't know if I make it back to my own people and you won't even care. If another man takes me prisoner instead, well so what? I'm nothing but a woman, a mere *wenda,* and that's what women are for, to give men a good time. What difference does it make which men and women are involved?"

He stared at my anger in silence for a moment, the hardness in his light eyes tinged with disturbance, and then he shook his head.

"Would that I had your ability," he murmured. "It seems impossible to me that you truly believe this, that I would cease to care what befell you."

"You haven't begun caring about me yet," I pointed out, finding it impossible to keep the bitterness out of my voice. "When I stopped to think about it, I discovered that everything you did was designed to make life easier for yourself. You protected me because you needed me, not because I meant anything to you. You let me fall in love with you because I was easier to control that way and gave you less trouble. You returned me to the embassy not because it was what I wanted, but because you had given your word to do so. You could have saved me a lot of grief by explaining what you were doing, but it was too much trouble explaining a *l'lenda*'s actions to a mere *wenda.* You simply did not care enough about me. And you don't care enough about me now to keep from embarrassing me in front of strangers. If you want to know how I really feel, you now have it all."

I was looking at him defensively, half expecting him to punish me for having spoken to him like that, half wondering what he was really thinking. I'd learned to be wary of touching his mind too deeply, knowing how he disliked it, which was why he'd been able to fool me so completely the sleep period before. His surface emotions were mostly vast confusion, swirling around a tinge of outraged denial, but his control was too good for me to believe that denial. Garth's mind was even more troubled than it had been, but he wasn't prepared to put his distress into words. Tammad, though, was a different matter.

"It is beyond me how you are able to believe these untruths," he said, shaking his head again. "The sole thing which occurs to me is that you are interpreting through mistake rather than describing from reality. That you now find yourself embarrassed is no more than the fruits of your own doing, the results of your attempts to disobey me. Should you again begin to obey me, the embarrassment will be no more. As you will find when we have reached Rimilia."

I opened my mouth to continue the argument, especially to demand why I had to obey him, but changed my mind and turned away without saying the words. Arguing with a barbarian is a waste of time, not to mention breath and effort. Getting to Rimilia wouldn't change a thing, especially when my government found out what he was trying to do. Truths would be proven on Rimilia, all right, but not the truths he was expecting. A minute later the steward showed up with our food, giving us something else to concern ourselves with, but not something to divert our thoughts. Through the silence of eating,e the twisting of Garth's uncertainties was very clear, especially as he had no food to partially divert him. He drank fresh kimla and worried at his problems, never noticing that Tammad wasn't enjoying his meal any more than I was. The barbarian was too distracted to do more than make sure I ate as he wanted me to, but I no longer cared what he forced me to do. He would only have to be tolerated until we reached Rimilia, and then I would be free to go about my business again – without the stupid ideas I'd somehow managed to pick up. A Prime has no business thinking about spending her life with a barbarian, no matter how romantically attractive the notion appears to be. I'd made a mistake, but it was not a mistake I'd be making again.


## SIX


Two more ship days went by before we reached Rimilia, but they weren't pleasant ones – at least not for me. When I tried to continue working on Garth, the barbarian got so annoyed he banished me to my cabin. He wanted to work on Garth himself, and didn't enjoy having me there to counter his nonsense. He and Garth spent hours at a time sitting and talking, sometimes one of them engaging in a monologue, sometimes the other doing it. I had no real idea what they were talking about, but the longer it went on, the straighter Garth stood, the more he squared his shoulders, the higher he held his head. Not all of it could have been heap-big-male propaganda, they had to have been discussing Tammad's plans for him as well; whatever it was, it seemed to bolster and encourage him, filling him out the way a month's worth of good meals will fill out a starving man's body. Garth had obviously been starving for something, but it hadn't been for food.

Being kept in a cabin had been boring in the extreme, but nothing I'd said or done had succeeded in getting the barbarian to change his mind. The three trippers had taken to dancing for their men friends any time the *l'lendaa* had wanted them to, and dance time was the sole exception made to my incarceration. I was told to watch carefully so that I might learn, an order that almost made me bare my teeth. I retaliated by closing my eyes tight when the girls danced; pretending I didn't know what they were doing because I couldn't see them. Tammad grew annoyed when he discovered what I was doing, but Garth's amusement kept him from punishing me. Garth had regained his equilibrium but on a higher plane, so high that nothing I said seemed to disturb him. His new attitudes bothered me, equally as much as the way he began looking at me.

When landing time finally came around, the transport's common area seemed to be filled with more long faces than happy ones. I, myself, was furious over the fact that the barbarian had refused to return my own clothes to me, insisting that I continue to wear the *imad* and *caldin* he had given me. He, on the other hand, was none too pleased himself after two sleep periods and a number of fun breaks when he failed to make me share my emotions while he used me. I'd had to use every ounce of control I possess, but I wasn't a Prime for nothing. I'd kept him from entering my mind the way he entered my body, and his *l'lendaa* had taken to staying as far away from him as the cramped quarters permitted. He had stalked around the common area like a wild beast looking for a victim, keeping himself from snarling only through extreme effort of will. I'd half expected him to complain to me, but he hadn't been *that* foolish.

Unlike me, the three trippers had been given their clothes back in preparation for letting them go. Two of them stood with five of the *l'lendaa,* talking quietly and shyly, their minds filled with sadness and regret, but firm in their decision to continue on their way. They were still somewhat awed by the big male warriors, and knew better than to believe that the fun would continue past the trip. *L'lendaa* may be good in bed and good for a woman's ego, but living with them on a full-time basis is another matter entirely.

The third tripper stood off to one side of the group by herself, her head down, her mind filled with hopeless tears that never reached her eyes. She was the one Tammad had singled out twice, but Tammad hadn't been the only one with his eye on her. The sixth *l'lenda*, a tall, husky blond named Hannas – but not the same Hannas I had once met – had taken an immediate liking to her, which apparently was mutual. Hannas and his cabin-mate Dirral had shared her use, but it had been Hannas who she had spent each sleep-period with, falling asleep next to him and waking up in his arms. I had overheard Hannas telling Tammad about it, and that's where Hannas was right then, talking to Tammad and stating certain facts. What those facts were I didn't know, but Hannas was determined and Tammad was unsure. In spite of being unsure, Tammad nodded to Hannas, then clapped him on the back. The two of them were agreed on something, even if the agreement wasn't totally wholehearted on Tammad's part. The men were wearing their swords again, and the steward had disappeared permanently.

"Well, it looks like we're there," Garth muttered in my ear as the engines faded from a noticeable throb to nothing. "Shouldn't we be standing by the exit port, eagerly awaiting our first view of the promised land?"

"Maybe it's promised to you," I muttered back, "but as far as I'm concerned, it's a broken promise. If you're all that nervous, why did you come?"

"If there was nothing to be nervous about, I *wouldn't* have come," he countered, flickering an annoyed glance in my direction. "And from now on stay out of my mind. I don't like being constantly poked and pried at."

I stared at him for a second then looked away, more hurt than I would have admitted. Garth's nervousness was obvious to anyone with eyes, empath or not. I hadn't probed him because I hadn't had to, but it would have been a waste of time saying so. Most people don't think about being probed, but once one of them gets the idea in his head, he decides he's under constant observation.

"Look, I didn't mean that," he apologized almost immediately. "I *am* nervous, and I'm sure everyone can see it. If poking around in my emotions does anything for you, feel free to indulge at any time."

His tone of voice was trying for lighthearted, but the rest of him wasn't making it. At another time he might have had my sympathy, but right then I had my own problems.

"I have better ways of wasting my time than bothering with emotional infants," I shot back. "If you think I'd spend any time on you, you flatter yourself."

"I can see I asked for that," he sighed, surprising me by not being angry. Then he squeezed my arm gently. "Don't worry, Terry. Things will work out well for both of us. Tammad won't let it happen any other way."

"You sound as though you think he's a god or something," I snorted, pulling my arm loose from his easy grip. "I hate to disillusion you, but he isn't even a civilized, rational man. He's nothing but a barbarian, and you'll be sorry you ever involved yourself with him."

"That's possible," he agreed, "but I'm betting it doesn't happen that way. I'm betting everything goes the way it's supposed to and everyone lives happily ever after."

"I can't afford to bet," I whispered, watching as everyone began moving toward the corridor that led to the exit port. "I can't afford to bet on fairy tales coming true because I can't afford to lose. If you can, good luck to you."

Garth was about to say something else, but the words were lost when Tammad came over to join us.

"It is now time to disembark," he said, standing in front of me but looking at Garth. "Do not feel hesitant or uneasy, brother. You enter our world as one who is needed, not as one who must prove his worth. Your worth will prove itself many times over."

"It's strange, but I don't have to force myself to believe that," Garth answered with a smile. "I believe I can feel posterity waiting for me, and I'm anxious to get started. After you."

Garth gestured toward the corridor, and Tammad, with a grin, preceded him out of the common area – with his hand wrapped around my arm. Garth had been invited to join the general departure, but Terrillian wasn't good enough to be invited; she was nothing more than a *wenda,* to be taken wherever her owner decided he wanted her to go. I was angry enough to beat at the barbarian with one fist and use words I had seldom used before, but Tammad couldn't have cared less. He ignored me the way someone else would ignore a recalcitrant child, and willy-nilly I soon found myself down off the ramp and onto thick green grass. The transport had landed not far from the embassy, in an open field that held more than four dozen *camtahh* about a quarter of a mile away. Planetary time was past middle of the afternoon, but it was still easy to see that the day had been a beautiful one. Small insects hummed and buzzed in the warmth, and birds happily soared around the soft breeze that whispered of evening to come. The six *l'lendaa* stood around the three female trippers, and as we came up to them, one of the men pointed toward the embassy.

"It is there where you will find assistance in returning to your people," he said, looking the women over in a final sort of way. "Should you ever wish to return to us, have word sent to our city and we will come for you. As you are not women of our world, we have been told the choice must be yours."

The *l'lenda* made it plain how little he liked that idea, which got two of the women flustered all over again. They'd been feeling a small amount of regret over leaving, but the relief the concept brought them far outweighed the regret. The third woman wasn't allowing herself to feel anything, but the forced numbness was an ineffective shield against her pain. Once she was out of sight of the men, she would let herself cry forever.

One final round of good-byes was said, and then the women, carrying their luggage, started off for the embassy – or at least two of them did. When the third tried to leave with them, she found a large, immovable hand on her shoulder.

"You go in the wrong direction, *wenda*," Hannas told her, looking down at her bowed head. "The *camtahh* of my people lie in the opposite direction."

The girl, her head still down, wanted to answer in words, but the burning in her throat refused to allow that. She shook her head, a defeated, miserable gesture, filled with the knowledge that fairy tales never come true. If she went with him even her memories would probably be lost. I felt sick to my stomach from the vast helplessness welling out of her, but the steel fingers on my arm kept me from turning away and moving out of range. I swallowed down the urge to try the shield again, but didn't know how long I'd be able to resist the temptation. Concentrating on how everyone's hair moved gently in the breeze wasn't enough of a distraction.

"Woman, you are not faced with a request," Hannas persisted, his voice and expression turning stern. "The others may go or stay as they wish, but you will not be given that choice. I find I desire you, and have decided to take you with me when I return to my people. Had I brought my bands with me, you would not have been left this long in doubt."

"I don't know what you're talking about," the girl whispered, raising wildly confused eyes to his face. "There was nobody to stop you from doing whatever you pleased on the transport, but we're on a planet now. You can't just decide to take me with you whether I want to or not. It's against the law."

"Should you speak of Amalgamation law," Tammad put in, drawing her eyes to him, "you err in thinking of Rimilia as an Amalgamation planet. The laws of Rimilia hold sway here, and all those who visit the planet must abide by them. Hannas may take any woman he wishes, so long as she is not the belonging of another. Are you the belonging of another?"

"But, that's crazy!" the girl blurted, shaking her head as she ignored Tammad's question. "Sure, I'd like to go with him, but what if it doesn't work out? I don't know anything about him, and he – he knows even less about me. What if he – decides he doesn't want me after all?"

The girl's voice was quivering, true fear staring out of her eyes, but it was Hannas rather than Tammad who answered her question. He took her gently by the arms and turned her to face him, then smoothed back her short blond hair.

"In time we will know all there is to know of one another," he told her softly, staring down into her widened eyes. "At the moment, you need only know that I am a man who desires you and will have you. Will you walk with me to my *camtah, wenda,* or must I carry you?"

"You wouldn't carry me," she whispered, still wide-eyed with shock. Even after everything she'd said about being asked, she still failed to realize that the attitude carried over into everything *l'lendaa* did. Men were given the option of refusal as men were able to back up that refusal with a sword; women couldn't, therefore the option was never offered them.

Hannas sighed, knowing when words were useless, then bent and threw her up on his shoulder, making her drop her suitcase. The girl, suddenly frightened, squawked and struggled, causing the other two women, who had stopped to watch, to pale and back away. They'd been told they were being released, but with men like those a woman can never be sure. The other *l'lendaa* laughed as they watched Hannas striding away toward the tents in the distance, a squirming, protesting bundle of girl over his shoulder, then a couple of them turned to look speculatively toward the other two women. The women, having learned what was good for them, turned and began running toward the embassy, stumbling and breaking stride every time their suitcases threw them off pace. They were filled with pure panic, and it didn't ease much when they saw the ground cars filled with people coming from the embassy. The ground cars were going in the wrong direction, and the women were smart enough to know that the people in them might not be able to do any more than they could – which was just about what their friend had accomplished. They moved as fast as they could toward the embassy, refraining from looking back in case they saw something they really didn't want to see.

"That must be your welcoming committee," Garth observed to Tammad, watching the ground cars get closer. "Quite a turnout for a world with no more than a single embassy."

"They have reason to be concerned over my health and doings," Tammad murmured back, the dryness in his voice like sandpaper. "I had no doubt they would greet us, yet their numbers have grown since my departure. Perhaps I will find the discussions to come of interest after all."

Neither one of them had anything to add to that, so we all stood in silence as we waited for the two ground cars to reach us. I squinted against the lowering sun, trying to make out who the cars contained, unconsciously breathing deep of the fresh, clean air around us. If nothing else can be said for Rimilia, at least the quality of its air is superior.

The first ground car stopped within five feet of us; the second stopping just behind it, and by then I knew who some of the passengers were. The first car, driven by Denny Ambler, who was resident diplomat at the embassy, contained three other diplomats and Murdock McKenzie, head of the XenoDiplomacy Bureau on Central. I stirred uncomfortably in Tammad's grip as I watched Murdock struggle his way out of the car, forcing his twisted body to move the way he wanted it to. Murdock had his mind under its usual tight control, but I hadn't missed his reaction when he saw the way Tammad was holding me. He realized immediately that something was wrong between us, and his regret and relief were mixed exactly half and half. Considering the fact that he was the one who had given Tammad a transport to use, his reaction was rather unexpected. I couldn't help getting the feeling that Murdock was playing with inner wheels again, probing deep in an attempt to make things turn out the way he wanted them to: He and Tammad were very much alike, but Murdock had been playing the game a good deal longer than the barbarian. If experience counted for anything, Murdock would not be the loser in any showdown between them.

The second ground car held two more members of the XD Bureau, but it also held a surprise. Aside from the very beautiful, dark-haired woman who was helped out to the grass by one of the diplomats, the fourth passenger turned out to be Lenham Phillips, a fellow member of my XenoMediation Bureau and a fellow empath. Len wasn't bad for an empath below Prime grade, but he looked nervous and not too pleased about being where he was. I remembered the last time I'd seen Len, at the real he'd tried trapping me into completing, and hoped his displeasure would grow considerably greater before it was eased. It was the least he deserved.

"Ah, Tammad, I see you've found her," Murdock said when he was finally standing in front of us. "Terrillian, my dear, you seem tired."

"Sick and tired is more like it," I muttered, glancing briefly at Tammad. "Murdock, will you please be so kind as to tell this – this – beast to release my arm? I think the circulation has stopped."

Murdock kept silent as a folding chair was placed behind him, then he began lowering his thin, twisted body into it. No sweat appeared on his forehead below the hairline of his neat, gray hair, but I was more than close enough to feel how near a thing it was. Bending that way was endlessly painful for him, but his legs weren't able to support him for more than a short while. I slid quickly into his mind and eased as much of the pain as I could, but wasn't quite as deft as I'd hoped I could be. His hard, gray eyes snapped to me as he settled himself, but it was impossible telling whether he was grateful or furious. His mind was discipline incarnate, more rigidly controlled even than Tammad's, and the first hint I had was when he smiled his narrow, tight-lipped smile at me.

"My dear Terrillian, I'm sure Tammad realizes that there is very little need to hold you so closely beside him," he said in his sleek, even way. "Where on this world might you run to where he could not follow? Perhaps you have misbehaved again, and he seeks to punish you. Has our Prime been disobedient, my friend?"

The hard, gray eyes turned to Tammad, who smiled faintly before answering. "It is indeed as the Murdock McKenzie suggests," he said, smiling. "The woman is forever disobedient, yet we have now returned to my world where her disobedience will be seen to. Your assistance was invaluable in my quest, and you have my thanks."

"Which is no small thing," Murdock nodded, the wintry smile warming not at all when the barbarian's hand left my arm. I rubbed at the fingermarks left in my flesh, pleased that Murdock was doing so well. If matters continued in that same vein, I would be free in no time.

"I see others have joined you here," Tammad observed, looking around to those who stood a distance away from the conversation. One of those was Denny, who stood looking off toward the line of tents Hannas was making his way toward, very obviously not meeting Tammad's eye. Something had happened to the friendship between Denny and the barbarian, but I couldn't imagine what it could be.

"Others you will be interested in," Murdock agreed, toying with the cane he held. "I thought about the difficulty you had with Terrillian here, added the possibility that you might fail to find her again, and took the liberty of making a few arrangements which should please you. Reven, bring the others over here."

The man Reven, who had been standing beside Murdock's chair, nodded once then turned toward Len and the dark-haired woman. His gesture brought the two of them toward him, and in a minute they had joined the group.

"Tammad, I would like you to meet Lenham Phillips, a very capable empath," Murdock purred, watching as Len and Tammad exchanged nods. "Lenham has been told how important your work is to the Amalgamation and will prove to be considerably more reliable than a stubborn young girl. Despite the fact that he is not quite as large as you and your men, it should not prove difficult disguising him as one of your people. His blond hair and blue eyes are, of course, assets in this situation."

"I see." Tammad nodded, looking Len over as his mind began to hum. Len picked up the hum with a frown, recognizing the calculation in Tammad's thoughts but not knowing how deep it went. It would be awhile before he learned the barbarian well enough to probe him.

"Our other newcomer should also take your fancy," Murdock continued, watching Tammad's approval of Len with approval of his own. "I would like to present Gaynor King, a most accomplished young woman. Gaynor is on loan to us from Central's Professional Friendship Bureau, which was established to provide companions for Amalgamation heads of state when they visit Central. She does not normally work off-planet, but Rathmore Hellman saw fit to make an exception in this case. She will, of course, return to Central when Lenham does."

Tammad's eyes were already on Gaynor King, openly rating her and obviously liking what he saw. From twenty feet away she was a very attractive woman; from five feet away she was startlingly beautiful. Her glossy black hair was short but beautifully styled, setting off her smooth, pale complexion and green eyes. She was two or three inches taller than I, and even Tammad wouldn't have called her underfleshed. Her build was slender but very round, emphasizing her large breasts and curvy hips. The very stylish, electric-blue day suit she wore showed well-molded, attractive legs, a point the barbarian was careful not to miss. Gay King posed in front of him, breathing desirability in and out as if it were air, her mind cool and very nearly bored. She was used to being looked at by men, and seemed to be somewhat in contempt of them – an attitude which didn't show in her face.

"This woman is more than acceptable," Tammad murmured, apparently not noticing that I had slowly drifted closer to Murdock's chair, on the left. Len and Gay King stood to Murdock's right, and only Len's mind had registered my movement. "I ask you to convey my thanks to the Rathmore Hellman, also assuring him of my satisfaction. I will be sure to seek for a fitting return gift."

"That is generous of you but quite unnecessary," Murdock said with the same narrow-faced, wintry smile he always showed. "You have so far attained our highest expectations, and deserve whatever we might provide in return. Do your plans yet extend beyond those we discussed before your recent journey?"

"Only in small part," Tammad answered, speaking to Murdock as though they stood eye to eye, equal to equal. "Unification of the twenty-five cities has already begun, and our requirements before the building of the complex will be given you as soon as they are compiled. It is now necessary to consider a manner of contacting the out-lying peoples, those our cities cannot speak for. Such a thing has never before been done."

"I am confident you will see to the matter as ably as you have already seen to previous difficulties," Murdock assured him, beginning to lever himself out of the chair. I gave him the same non-physical assistance I had earlier, felt his brief flash of gratitude, then stepped behind him. "I must leave Rimilia soon to see to Bureau matters on Central, but I will return as soon as I may. Would your companion there care to share my transport to Central? There is room for him as well as for the two women who recently passed us going to the embassy."

Murdock's eyes had gone to Garth, but there had been no curiosity or demands in his tone of voice. He very much wanted to know where Garth fit in, but he knew better than to demand information from Tammad.

"My companion has agreed to accompany me to my city," Tammad answered smoothly, sounding as though the visit couldn't be more casual – but not thinking the same. "It has occurred to me to wonder how off-worlders will be treated among my people, and my friend will assist me in determining the truth of the matter. Should there be difficulty ahead of us, it would be wise to know of it as soon as possible."

"Wise, indeed," Murdock nodded, his suspicious nature considerably mollified. He wasn't dismissing the question of Garth, but he wasn't considering it a priority any longer. "I will be sure to send word to you when I return, to learn the results of your experiment. As always, you have my good wishes."

Murdock nodded in farewell, undoubtedly adding his wintry smile, then turned slowly to be facing his ground car again. His hand came toward my arm as I turned with him, to guide me to his car, I thought, but another hand reached his shoulder before his hand reached my arm.

"Perhaps the Murdock McKenzie has forgotten," Tammad's voice came softly from right behind us. "The *wenda* he takes with him is mine."

A sense of frustrated annoyance flashed briefly in Murdock's mind, a fitting companion to the concern I, myself, felt. We both turned halfway back to the barbarian, but only Murdock was able to smile.

"My friend, I must ask your indulgence," he said, leaning on his cane. "You now have no real need of Terrillian, while Central has a sudden urgency which only her talents might see to. Rathmore has asked me to bring her with me when I return – and would count her presence as the gift you mentioned earlier."

"A gift which I was told was unnecessary," Tammad countered, his voice still soft and overly mild, his light eyes calm but determined. "Yet, even that has no bearing. One does not tell another what gift to give, nor does one seek to deny a bargain already struck. Are you prepared to return the value given by me for the possession of this woman?"

"No!" Murdock said immediately. "No, I do not wish to return what was paid for her. I'm sure you are well aware of the fact that I *cannot* return what was paid for her. Is there no compromise we might find – a temporary loan, so to speak? You would find us very grateful, a state not without its benefits."

"The gratitude of the Murdock McKenzie is a thing to covet," Tammad allowed with a sober nod which encouraged Murdock to the point of returning his smile. "However," the barbarian added, and suddenly his big hand was wrapped around my left wrist, "in this instance I must decline the honor. A woman belongs with him who has chosen and banded her, him to whom she was given. Is there any here who will challenge me for possession of this woman?"

His voice was loud enough to reach everyone in Murdock's party, and every man there heard him. Almost as one they stared at Tammad, appalled at the size of him, at the musculature showing beneath his tanned skin, at the confidence fairly oozing from every inch of his giant body. Very quickly their eyes left him again, their minds trembling with the fear that Tammad might decide he'd been challenged, their bodies tense, their movements jerky. The only exception to that general reaction was Denny, who looked away to hide the amusement he felt. It suddenly came to me that Denny was hiding his friendship with the barbarian, keeping it a secret between just the two of them. Tammad had a secret ally among the strangers he dealt with, a valuable asset any way you looked at it.

"I see there are no challenges," Tammad said after a minute, taking his eyes away from the rest of the men to bring them back to Murdock. "I will return to my people now, to continue the plans already begun. I wish the Murdock McKenzie a safe journey home."

"Wait!" I cried as he began to turn away, my wrist still held in his hand. Murdock was furiously silent, his fist clenched in frustrated rage, his mind seething in impotence. There was nothing he could do to stop the barbarian, and I was desperate.

"Yes?" Tammad inquired, turning back to me to raise one eyebrow. "There is something you wish to say?"

"Yes," I agreed with a grim nod, wishing my voice wouldn't quaver. "If you want a challenge for possession of me, you've got one. I don't want to go with you."

He blinked at me in silence for a moment, his mind groping for meaning, and then he said, "The challenge comes from you? From a *wenda*?"

At that the five *l'lendaa* still with him began laughing, roaring out their amusement at the thought. A woman challenging a *denday* like Tammad was the biggest joke they'd ever heard.

"Yes, it comes from me," I ground out over the laughter, clenching my teeth at the ridicule. "Are you too good to accept a challenge from me?"

"In what way would you see to such a challenge?" he asked, his tone soft and reasonable and free of the ridicule his men showed. His mind was under rigid control, hiding whatever traces of amusement or annoyance he might be feeling, carefully centering on nothing more than our conversation. "How might I face you, *hama,* without exposing you to either danger or embarrassment? As I care for you, I would not have you exposed to either thing."

"You *don't* care for me!" I choked, suddenly losing control to such an extent that I tried pulling my wrist loose. "You only want to use me the way you use everyone else! And I don't *care* how I face you, just as long as I have a chance to get free! One way or another I've got to be free of you!"

I was trembling so strongly with the emotions I felt that my whole body shook, sending echoes of the tremors through my mind. I stared at the barbarian wildly, more determined than I had ever been, and slowly, resolutely, he nodded his head.

"Very well," he sighed, drawing me forward a good five feet before letting my wrist go. "As your need is so strong, I may do nothing other than see to it. I will face you with daggers."

Daggers! I felt numb as he turned away from me, leaving me rooted to the spot. He planned on playing fair, I could see that in his mind, but I knew nothing of daggers, not to speak of fighting with them! I didn't even want to touch one of the things, but there was nothing else I could do.

The barbarian spoke quietly to his men for a minute, took the dagger one of them proffered, then turned back to me. I watched him come closer, my eyes glued to the weapon in his hand, and then he was right in front of me, closing my fingers around the hilt of the blade he had brought.

"You are now armed," he said, drawing the dagger he wore in the back of his swordbelt. "As am I. We may now begin."

He took a step away from me and went into a slight crouch, his arms held ready in front of him, his weight balanced on both feet. The lowering sun gleamed off the blade in his fist, a blade that suddenly seemed completely a part of him. I stood in the thick grass where I'd been put, feeling the breeze stir my hair, tightening my fingers around the dagger I'd been given. He towered over me, he was a trained warrior, and he undoubtedly didn't even need the weapon he held, but maybe I could still –

"Hai!" he cried, suddenly jumping at me, the dagger raised high and coming down at me. I screamed and stumbled back away from him, the grass tangling my bare feet, the dagger I'd had falling from my grasp as I frantically tried to get away from the wild man coming at me. I tripped and fell, plunging headlong into the grass, quickly burying my head in my arms as I screamed again. I was trembling violently, panic ready to come flooding out of me, already beginning to cry. He was going to hurt me, I knew he was going to hurt me, and there was nothing I could do to stop him.

"*Hama*, are you all right?" he demanded, his hands, not his dagger, coming to my arms. Gently he turned me over, rolling me toward him, and through my tears and terror I could see and feel his anger. "The thing has proven itself as foolish as I knew it to be," he snapped, his anger growing higher the longer he looked at me. "Your challenge has been met and answered, and I will now return to my people – *with* my *wenda*! On your feet, woman!"

Roughly, he pulled me erect, then turned and headed toward the line of *camtahh* in the distance. Garth moving off with him on his right. I stumbled along behind him, still crying, still too overwhelmed to protest in words. I turned my head back to look pleadingly at Murdock, sobbing as the tears rolled down my cheeks, but there was nothing Murdock could do and he knew it. And yet he took a step after us, as though intent on following, his mind in such a whirling frenzy that he barely registered the increasing pain he felt from being erect so long. He took another step, raised his cane off the ground – and was caught just in time by two of the XD men before he crumpled to the ground. The two men hurried him toward the ground car, so intent on getting him back to the embassy that they totally ignored Tammad's *l'lendaa*. The *l'lendaa,* two escorting Len and two escorting Gay King, firmly urged their charges after Tammad and me; the fifth, after retrieving his dagger from where I'd dropped it, calmly brought up the rear. None of them looked back, and Tammad didn't either.

By the time we reached the *camtahh* and the people waiting for us, I was exhausted. I'd been dragged the entire distance by one wrist, refused a slower pace, refused a rest break of any sort. I was gasping from the lack of air in my lungs and stumbling from the weakness in my limbs, but Tammad had refused to notice my difficulty and Garth had decided not to mention it. I hadn't mentioned it either, but only because I'd known that mentioning it would have wasted what little breath I had. I was being punished, and I didn't have to wonder for what. The more Tammad thought about what had happened, the angrier he got.

"*Aldana, denday, aldana!*" "Welcome home!" came from all around us, a cacophony of greeting in every mind and on every pair of lips. The men came forward with the women right behind them, and it wasn't difficult seeing that the group was the same which had accompanied Tammad to the *Ratanan,* the Great Meeting. Fifty warriors, more than half of them with women, still trailed after their leader, following where he took them, asking no questions.

"We have heard something of the happenings on your journey, Tammad." Faddan grinned, limping closer with everyone else. There was still a bandage around his thigh covering the wound he had gotten during the fight with the savages at the *Ratanan,* but that didn't mean he was going to allow himself to be left behind when Tammad decided there were places to go and things to do. Faddan was a true *l'lenda,* contemptuous of wounds and unwilling to allow them to slow him down.

"Aye," Loddar laughed, with Kennan chuckling at his side. "Hannas was somewhat preoccupied with other matters, yet he paused briefly to speak with us. Should you need to go in search of Terril again, I would be pleased to accompany you."

"And I!" agreed Loddar and Kennan together, the others around them laughing further agreement. I wiped at the sweat covering my forehead and face and tried to collapse onto the grass where we'd stopped, but one jerk on my wrist and I was standing straight again. Or as straight as I could manage after a quarter-mile run.

"There will be no further searches for Terril," my tormentor said, looking at me with grim satisfaction. "She will remain with him to whom she belongs, and no further disobedience will be tolerated. Has my pavilion been erected?"

"It stands there, *denday,*" Loddar answered, indicating a place in the middle of the other tents. All of the *l'lendaa* were examining me with their eyes, understanding that Tammad's anger wasn't for them. They were curious about what I'd done, but they weren't about to ask their leader for details, not when he was in such a touchy mood.

"Good," Tammad said, and then we were off again, heading for the pavilion that was the *denday's* tent during the *Ratanan.* If they hadn't come straight from the *Ratanan,* Tammad's *camtah* would have been just like everyone else's.

If I'd had to go a step farther than the pavilion, I probably would have fallen down dead. As soon as we were through the tent flaps and my wrist was finally released, I fell straight down to the furred carpeting covering the floor and didn't move. The hanging that divided the pavilion in two was stretched across the width of it, but even if sleeping furs were arranged and waiting behind that hanging, I couldn't have gotten to them. I let my eyes close as I concentrated on gulping in as much air as possible, paying no attention whatsoever to anyone else in the pavilion.

"I think it'll be a while before she makes any more trouble," Garth's voice came, his attention clearly on me. "What were your men talking about when they came to meet us?"

"They merely discussed the journey recently completed," Tammad answered, a sudden thoughtfulness to his voice. "Amid this woman's distractions, I had forgotten you are unable to speak our language. The *l'lendaa* who accompanied me were given your tongue at the embassy, before our departure, by use of that termed 'learning machine.' A pity I cannot have you acquire our tongue as easily."

"I think that would create more problems than it would solve," Garth agreed with a sigh. "It looks like I'll be acquiring your language the old-fashioned way."

"There are enough of those about us to see to the matter," Tammad said, moving around the pavilion. "Until your lessons have begun you may have an interpreter, perhaps even this female here. After they have begun, there will be no speech for you other than in the language you are attempting to learn. In such a way will your comprehension be sooner in the coming."

"Ouch," Garth said wryly, the prospect less than appealing to him. "If I don't learn, I don't talk to anyone but myself. I don't think I'm going to be enjoying the next few weeks."

"I have no doubt that you will learn quickly," Tammad chuckled, finally ceasing his wandering. "Take your ease here while I see to the quartering of our other guests, and also to the preparation of a meal. We will retire early this darkness, for we leave early on the morrow."

Garth grunted his thanks and Tammad left, too wrapped up in his newly made plans to think about me any longer. I rolled over onto my back and opened my eyes to stare at the tent ceiling, still too played out to think of anything but how miserable I felt.

"Your face is dirty," Garth observed from the spot he'd chosen to sit down on, a few feet to my right. "I don't think I've ever seen a Prime with a dirty face before."

"Don't speak to me," I muttered, still staring up at the ceiling. "Not even to ask the time of day."

"Why not?" he countered, stirring where he sat. "Are you afraid I'll tell you what a stupid, infantile thing you did? Well, you're too late because that's exactly what I am telling you."

"It's none of your business what I do!" I snapped, jerking my head around to glare at him. "At least I *tried*, which is more than I can say for the rest of you big, brave men!"

"Oh, sure you tried," he snorted sarcastically. "You tried to make Tammad look like a damned fool and nearly succeeded! The only reason he faced you like that was because he cares for you and doesn't want to see you unhappy. Haven't you any idea what it means for a warrior to face an untrained woman half his size? Whatever he does, he looks and feels like an idiot! If he had any sense, he would have put you over his knee again and whacked you till you howled!"

His light eyes were furious with me, his voice harder with determination than I'd ever heard it before. I tried to keep the tears from welling out of my eyes again, but it was a lost cause. I was too tired to have the control I needed, and hurting too much inside to try for it. I rolled away from him and curled up, resting my cheek against the fur floor covering, letting the tears come any damned way they wanted to. It was quiet for a minute or two, then Garth was sitting right behind me.

"Your wrist is bruised," he said in a much quieter voice. "I'm not surprised, but I honestly don't think he did it on purpose. Terry, why don't you try meeting him half way? If you give him a chance to make you happy, I know he can do it."

Happy. The tears increased to sobs, making it very difficult to speak. I let it go on for a short while, then managed to force the words out.

"I need an honest answer from you Garth," I husked, turning to my back again to look up at him. "Will you give me an honest answer?"

"If I can," he agreed quietly, looking down at me. "What's your question?"

"If a woman you loved challenged you with weapons, would you agree to face her?" I demanded. "According to what you said you would be more likely to grow angry and punish her for trying to make you hurt her. But if a woman you needed desperately for other purposes tried the same thing, wouldn't you be even more likely to agree against your better judgment just to make her happy, just to coddle her into a good enough mood to do what you needed her to do? Even if it made you look foolish?"

"I see what you're leading up to, but you're wrong," he answered immediately, his expression concerned. "Tammad *did* punish you for getting him involved in that fiasco – even I had trouble keeping up with him, and I wasn't being dragged along by one wrist."

"Sure he punished me." I nodded, closing my eyes again. "After he realized he'd made a tactical mistake. There isn't another woman on this world he would have taken that from, not the way his mind works. He doesn't want anything from me but my talent, and everything he does makes me more and more convinced of it."

I couldn't see Garth's face, but that doesn't mean his emotions were closed off, too. He felt a pang of guilty realization when I said my piece, privately agreeing with my conclusions but not about to say so out loud. He wanted to believe Tammad's reasons for kidnapping me were noble and romantic, not mercenary and emotionless, but things weren't working out well for him. Well, he wasn't the only one they weren't working out for.

"Do you know what it's like being wanted for nothing more than what you can do?" I asked, watching the colors appear and disappear against my closed eyelids. "It's like a slap or a kick, but a lot less honest. It makes you want to run and run from wherever you happen to be and never go back. I thought he wanted me and I was the happiest woman in the universe. Then I found out he just wanted to use me and something broke inside. I swore I wouldn't help him and I'll keep that vow. Why won't he let me go?"

"Perhaps because he no longer cares to press the matter of your assistance, yet still desires you," Tammad's voice came instead of Garth's, startling me. His calm was as deep as it had ever been, and I hadn't been aware of his return. "It is now no more than your own fears and misconceptions which keep you from me, *hama*. I will not long allow such a state to continue."

"You're just being stubborn!" I cried, twisting around in the fur to look at him where he stood by the pavilion entrance. "Anyone with any sense could see that it was over between us! I can never again believe anything you say, and nothing will change that! It won't get any better just because you want it to!"

"Perhaps you are mistaken," he said, grinning faintly as he folded those massive arms across his chest. "Am I not *denday*, and is my word not law? It remains to be seen what my will is able to accomplish. At the moment my will concerns you, and I have returned to assign you your duties."

"What duties?" I frowned, narrowing my eyes at him. "How many times do I have to say I won't work for you?"

"You will work if it should be your wish to eat," he came back dryly, staring down at me. "When last you were upon my world, your meals were earned with your talent. As you no longer care to exercise that talent, other duties have been found for you. You will assist the other women in the preparation of our provender, hopefully learning that which requires no great talent – merely some manner of intelligence and diligent effort."

"And if it doesn't happen to be my desire to eat?" I shot back, feeling his ridicule as strongly as the throb in my right wrist. "If I tell you to go to hell with your jobs and your meals, what then?"

"Do you need to ask?" he said softly, crouching down in front of me to stare at me more closely. "In one manner or another you will obey me, *wenda*, do not believe otherwise. Do you rise to your feet and follow me now, else we shall see the strength of your will – compared to the strength of my arm."

The look of determination in his blue eyes was steady and solid, as steady as the calm still possessing his mind. He had undoubtedly decided to bore me to death with menial chores, and then simply wait for me to beg him to change his mind and let me do things his way. Well, if that was what he was up to, he had a long wait ahead of him.

"As long as I have to be here, one job is as bad as another." I shrugged, then forced myself to my feet. "If it's cooking you want, then you've got it. As long as I don't have to share the meal with you."

The flash of anger was too strong for him to cover up entirely, but his expression never changed – as though I couldn't tell he was angry if it didn't show in his face. He had a habit of behaving that way sometimes, acting as though he believed I couldn't tell what he was feeling if there were no external signs of it. He knew better than that, of course, but only intellectually. Emotionally he was just as badly prepared to cope with an empath as any other untalented person.

"There is one other thing before we go," he said, reaching to his swordbelt without getting out of his crouch. "On this world, *wendaa* are banded, and you have too long gone without my bands. Stand as you are."

I looked down to see him holding two of the small-linked, bronze-colored chains his people called *wenda* bands, and as I watched he closed first one and then the other on my ankles. The chains weren't locked, but they didn't have to be. It took the strength of a man to get them open again, the sort of strength no woman could exert. I stiffened as he closed them on me, but didn't bother trying to protest. His satisfaction was a palpable thing, so strong I could see it in his eyes when he stood straight again.

"Should you be wondering, you will not be banded further this time," he informed me, looking down at me as he folded his arms again. "Should you wish the third, fourth and fifth bands, you will discover you must earn them, as any other *wenda* must. When I find myself pleased with you, I will consider banding you further."

"That goes without saying," I nodded, "but you haven't told me what I must do to be banded less. That's the part I'm interested in."

The great mass of satisfaction he'd been feeling was suddenly punctured, causing an explosion of frustration to light his mind. His eyes darkened with the thunder of his anger, and his hands came to my arms so fast and hard that I gasped.

"I am pleased to see you feel free to find amusement at my expense," he growled, lifting me off the floor toward him. "Did you find less pleasure in my company, you would undoubtedly feel less pleasure in taunting me so, for you would fear my wrath. Though my wishes are of little concern to you, *wenda*, I suggest you consider my wrath. There are those who deem it a thing to be avoided at all costs."

"Tammad, don't let her get you angry," Garth urged, suddenly right beside the barbarian. My eyes wide and staring, I wasn't up to saying anything yet, but Garth took care of that lack. "Don't you see she's doing it on purpose, to force you into turning her loose? If *she* doesn't know what to say to people to get them to do as she wishes, no one does! If you really don't want her, let he go now, but if you do – then fight for her!"

The barbarian stared at me another long minute, his mind shifting through emotional sets and responses so quickly I blinked, theft he put me down again and nodded his head.

"It is as the Garth R'Hem Solohr says," he agreed, the calm flowing back over him so completely it was as if he stood under a falls of the stuff. "To win the *wenda* of his choice, a man must sometimes do battle with the *wenda* herself. This woman's weapons are not mine, yet I will not refuse to wield them. I will not fall to anger again."

"Good." Garth smiled, clapping him gently on the shoulder. "If she won't believe what you say, make her believe what you do. Words can be argued against; actions can't."

"And it is more than time for those actions to begin." The barbarian nodded, wrapping his hand around my arm. "Come, *wenda*. Your work awaits you."

It's more than tiring to be dragged around all over the place, but that was still the way I was taken out of the pavilion and over to the large fire half-a-dozen of the women were working at. Startled, the women stopped what they were doing when Tammad came up to them, but he raised a hand to gesture them back to calm.

"As you *wendaa* labor to provide for those without women," he said to them in their own language, "I bring you another pair of hands to assist in your efforts. You will find her unskilled in even the simplest of chores, yet must she be taught to do as other *wendaa* do – for she has no other value. School her in the hardest of labors – so that she may prove her worth as a woman."

His bland gaze shifted to me as the women giggled, pleased to be given the chance to help their *denday* discipline his *wenda,* but I didn't react to his speech or to the women's amusement, at least not the way he expected me to.

"I have no worth," I informed him with the same calm he showed to me. "I am worthless and ignorant, useless in all things a *l'lenda* might find of interest. No one other than a fool would retain ownership of me under such circumstances."

The women's amusement disappeared in abrupt shock, but the anger I was expecting from Tammad – and already half cringed away from – never materialized. His calm remained unruffled with no effort on his part, and even slightly amused.

"It is a *l'lenda*'s place to say what worth a woman may have," he informed me in turn, the ghost of a grin on his face. "Your helplessness in the furs is some small asset, yet do I demand to see more. Work hard and learn well, *wenda,* and think upon how you might add to my pleasure in the furs. I will not accept refusal from you in either area."

He chucked me under the chin and then turned and strode away, off to see to more important matters than the doings of women. I stuck my tongue out at his retreating back, making a face at the same time, then turned around to find all six of the women staring at me.

"Terril, have you lost your wits?" one of them hissed at me, looking around quickly to see if any of the *l'lendaa* had noticed what I'd done. "That Tammad punishes you is clear to all, yet there are worse punishments than being made to do that which you so clearly dislike. That he found amusement rather than anger in your words was your good fortune; it would not be the same were he to learn of insolence shown toward his authority."

"Your *denday* is well aware of my feelings toward him," I told her. "The sooner I am free of his bands, the sooner will life hold meaning again. I will give him no pleasure that is not forced from me, and will obey him no more than I must "

"A great deal of pleasure must then be forced from you in the furs," purred another, a tall slinky blond who would have given a lot to take my place. "Helplessness in a man's arms comes from the *wenda* herself, brought about by her feelings for the *l'lenda.* Should she be the sort to allow a man her soul, her words to the contrary are a fool's boasting."

"I cannot help that over which I have no control!" I snapped at her, feeling the women's renewed amusement in the red on my cheeks. "Should you one day find yourself in that beast's arms, speak to me then of helplessness and a fool's boasting!"

"Let us not argue over such matters," the first woman said, overriding the flush of anger on the second woman's cheeks. "Is it not the same for all of us, no matter which *l'lenda* holds us? Is there one among us who is able to deny their least demand? Is there one among us who would have it other than as it is?" The other women looked at one another and laughed, shaking their heads, and the first woman smiled at me. "Terril, we do not know you, yet do we know of the desire Tammad feels for you, for our *l'lendaa* have spoken of it. Do not seek to deny him, for such an action would be futile. Join us, and learn from us, and soon the happiness of obedience will be yours as it is ours."

The others murmured their agreement to what the first had said, their minds confirming the words, and I had to hide the sickness I felt. I could never be conditioned the way they were even if I wanted to be; I was too used to freedom, and they didn't know it well enough to judge what was best. We could speak to each other of needs and desires, but each spoke of something the other was incapable of comprehending.

"I thank you for your offer of assistance and will do my best to learn from you," I told all the women, looking down from the first one's smile. "Should you fail to teach me some aspect of your way of life, the failure will not be yours."

"Nor will be the punishment," said the first woman briskly, putting her hand to my chin to raise my face to hers. "Therefore let us begin now, that the punishment may be longer in the coming. I am Bisah, and I will concern myself with your instruction."

They all went back to tending the large animal they were about to put over the fire, and Bisah kept me right beside her, explaining what she anal the others were doing. The small breeze that ruffled the air could barely be felt beside the blaze of the fire, but none of the women complained about the sweat covering them. They worked quickly and efficiently, seasoning the skinned animal, burying vegetables under the fire, mixing a basting oil, and the like, ignoring everything but what their hands were concerned with. My attention kept drifting from Bisah's voice to the end of the lovely day around us, my eyes finding it impossible to search out the sight of the embassy with all the *camtahh* standing around. The mere sight of it would have helped, letting me know there was more than barbarians on that world, but even that comfort was denied me.

Bisah didn't notice how far my attention had strayed, but the second woman, the one I had argued with, had formed a near-instant dislike for me and was not above trying to make trouble for me. Her burst of triumph brought my attention to her, and I found her just turning around from the fire, apparently looking for a *l'lenda* to complain to. I could feel the whininess and helplessness she was preparing to use while she told about my disobedience to Tammad's orders, and a deep anger welled to the surface in my mind. Without stopping to think about it I hurled a bolt of hesitation at her, cutting off her words more effectively than with a gag, then added a good dose of fear to the hesitation. I heard a gasp from her as her mind seized the fear and built on it, adding personal slants to the general emotion I had given her. It was impossible for me to know what framework her mind built, but the speed with which she turned back to the fire showed she was probably picturing herself being punished right along with me, for some reason only she herself would know. Her pale face and wide-eyed look turned in my direction, but her mind said she wasn't really seeing me. I watched her trembling hands go back to what they'd been doing with some small sense of wonder of my own; I'd never really thought of using my abilities in just that way before, and hadn't realized how much could be accomplished. If I hadn't been angry, I would not have tried it even then. It was obvious I'd have to think about what else might be done along the same lines.

In a very short while, the prepared animal was placed on the spit over the fire by four of the women. It took four of them to lift the thing, but the spit was arranged to be turned by two, an opposing handle on each side of the rod. Bisah chose the youngest of the other five females to turn the handle on the far side, and unsurprisingly designated me for the near side.

"It will undoubtedly be difficult for you at first, Terril," she said, "yet it is the sort of action which will draw the anger from you. Also, consider the ache which comes to your back and arms, and know it as the punishment given you by Tammad. When you at last find full approval in his eyes, you will no longer need to concern yourself with aches. You will again be his *rella wenda,* concerned only with pleasure."

Her smile and nod of friendliness were genuine, but I had the sudden suspicion that she worked more in Tammad's cause than in mine. As far as she knew I was nothing more than her *denday's rella wenda* – the local equivalent of a fancy lady – but she felt no resentment over that arrangement. If Tammad wanted a *rella wenda* instead of a work-ing *wenda,* he had earned the right to have one – or so his people believed. If I got away with having to do no more than keep his body satisfied, that was my good fortune and no more than a by-product. The important part was Tammad's pleasure, and as long as that was assured, everything else was fine. I grabbed my handle and began turning it, surprising the girl on the other end, making sure nothing of my thoughts showed on my face where Bisah could see them. I wasn't anyone's fancy lady, least of all a barbarian's, and nothing they could do to me would change that. I might be tired of living in the shadow of being a Prime, but I wasn't about to exchange that for living in the shadow of a man.

Once Bisah was satisfied that the animal was being turned at the proper rate, she and the other four unoccupied women went about their business elsewhere. The young girl and I turned the spit and turned it, watching the animal rotate slowly over the fire – until I discovered it was getting harder and harder to turn the thing. My arms and shoulder and back were beginning to protest my efforts a lot sooner than I'd thought they would, and I began to wonder how long I was expected to keep that up. It would be quite a while before the animal was done, but I was sure to be done considerably sooner.

"Your face is dirty and you're sweating," a voice came suddenly from behind me, startling me, "but I don't think I've ever seen you look better. How long has it been, Terry?"

"Not long enough," I answered, glancing over my shoulder at Len, who stood to my left and somewhat behind me. "And I didn't know there was a law against having a dirty face. From the number of people who have mentioned it to me, I'm assuming the Peacemen have already been called. I'll just have to plead ignorance."

"The same old Terry," Len said, stepping forward to where we could see each other without my having to turn my head. The jacket to his leisure suit was gone, leaving him in trousers and shirt with his shirtsleeves rolled part way up his forearms against the heat. His face was expressionless but his mind was angry, something he didn't try to hide. "If I didn't find such pleasure in looking at you, Terry, I would probably never come within sight of you again. You flaunt your untouchability and take advantage of it by hurting people and then walking away. The practice doesn't make for a very pleasant personality."

"You should talk!" I huffed, examining his tall, blond-haired and blue-eyed good looks with displeasure. "Was it me who tried to trap someone into completing an illegal real? Was I the one who took advantage of trust and friendship? Was I the one who…."

"You were the one who refused to have me in any way but on my knees!" he snapped, interrupting my tirade with a strong flash of anger and resentment. "Did you expect me to crawl to you, begging your favor, the way the rest of them did? I wasn't raised to that any more than you were, Terry, and if yon wanted no part of me you had business saying so! Leading me on just to torture me was lousy – and no different from what I tried to do to you in return."

"Why, I never led you on!" I sputtered, so filled with outrage at the accusation that I let go of the spit handle, forgetting about it until it hit my arm on the return arc. "I treated you no different from the way I treated the rest of the men I knew, and probably a bit better because of the bond we shared! You have no right saying I led you on!"

"You really believe that." He frowned, staring at me as his mind probed toward mine, I allowed the probe to go as deep as it was able, then thrust it from me when he'd seen I wasn't trying to hide anything. He winced somewhat from the strength of my thrust, but his anger had cooled to a considerable degree.

"I believe it because it happens to be the truth," I informed him, holding myself as straight as the spit-turning allowed. "Any belief you had to the contrary was your own doing, born of an overactive imagination. I have never asked a man to crawl to me for my favor, and I never will. All I ask is the same courtesy in return, an attitude some men find unreasonable."

"But I don't happen to be one of those," he said, shaking his head. "I don't know what made me believe I was right about you, but it wouldn't have happened if we were allowed to be awakened all the time. I'll offer my apologies if you're willing to accept them – or I'll just walk away if you're not. I wronged you and I'm sorry – and I'd like to make it up to you if I can."

I stared at him as I turned the spit, seeing the sober expression he wore, feeling the truth of the words he'd uttered. Len and I had been the victims of a misunderstanding, and prolonging the argument would have accomplished nothing.

"On this world, there's very little choice in places to walk to," I said, glancing at him before returning my attention to the animal on the spit. "There's no sense in holding grudges over past happenings, but you'll forgive me if I fail to offer you renewed brotherly love. I find myself somewhat down on men these days."

"I can feel that," he said, the soberness of his tone tinged with curiosity rather than personal. affront. "I was told I'd be taking your place here, but things didn't work out that way. What was that business with challenges and owning all about?"

"It's a long story," I answered, deciding to use both hands on the spit to see if it helped. "Suffice it to say that your new employer still has hopes of having his very own Prime to see to his needs, both political and physical. The Prime in question doesn't agree."

"I see," Len murmured, his thoughts suddenly blurred in the only way he could shield them. "I can't say I blame him, but doesn't he know he can't get away with it? I've never seen Murdock McKenzie so furiously out of control; he'll do something, and it won't be a mere gesture."

"Out of control or not, there's a limit to what anyone can do," I muttered, turning the spit harder as my anger grew. "They need Tammad to get what they want, and Tammad couldn't be more aware of it. And if I were you, I'd try for a more effective shield or do something about my reactions. If you think I can't tell you'd like to have me in the same position, you're out of your mind. Men!"

The scorn in my voice didn't half match what was in my mind, and Len didn't miss either. His mental eyes considered my emotions calmly and from a distance for a moment, then a faint grin lit his handsome face.

"Terry, I really am sorry about the misunderstanding we had, but we're now in the middle of a new misunderstanding that's no one's fault but yours. You've discovered that I'd like to have complete, undisputed possession of you and you blame me for it, but that's only because you're a woman. A man sees nothing wrong in wanting a desirable woman, and refrains from taking her only because of legal and social restrictions. If Tammad has found a way around those restrictions, more power to him. And the same to me."

"You're disgusting!" I snapped, shaking my head to get the sweat-soaked hair out of my eyes. "Just like the rest of the barbarians on this world! No matter what you think, you have no right doing anything to me against my will!"

"Right is viewed differently by different people." He shrugged, his grin widening. "I can tell from your thoughts that you've been taught a lesson about how some men decide what their rights are on their own. I'm looking forward to seeing Gay King learn that same lesson and from a master."

"What's the matter, Len, did she refuse you too?" I pounced immediately, getting a good deal of satisfaction from the thought. "It's a shame but more power to her."

"Stop feeling so smug," he laughed, really amused. "Gay is a stunningly beautiful woman, as attractive to men as you are, and I nearly fell all over myself when we were first introduced. I could have been ready for her any time, but she kept me at arm's length and I didn't think it wise pursuing the matter with Murdock McKenzie there. And then I was awakened."

"And you found out she was too shy and sensitive to be touched," I summed up, wiping the sweat off my forehead with my arm. I was just about ready to drop – but not in front of Len.

"Hardly too shy and sensitive." He laughed again, folding his arms. "Gay doesn't think much of men, and she enjoys using her body to turn them into sweating, trembling puppets. In a way she's the same sort of spoiled brat you are, and needs someone who can't be complained about to the Peacemen. I don't think she'll enjoy her visit here – or, if she gets lucky, it'll be the best time she's ever had."

I stared at him, seeing the casual satisfaction in his mind, realizing he understood the situation he was in and intended taking advantage of it. Len had had the same sort of upbringing I'd had, and somehow it had prepared him for the sort of life Tammad offered, a life where men were free to do whatever they pleased to women. On Central, Len could have had almost any woman he wanted, but with the one provision that she also wanted him. On Rimilia that provision no longer applied, and I shuddered with the feeling of defenselessness that rolled over me. Wasn't I a person, too? Didn't I have the right to refuse any man I didn't want?

"Don't feel that way, Terry," he said very softly, sending me a touch of gentleness as I discovered that my eyes had left him to study the ground at my bare feet. "I know you're not in a very comfortable position, but don't you see that I'm the same position on Central? On our own world, desirable women can have any man they want, whenever they want them, and the men have no way of complaining if they're made to suffer. Here it's the other way around and the women have no recourse, but I don't see many of them suffering. They enjoy being used a lot more than men enjoy not being used."

"I don't come from this world," I whispered, refusing to meet his eyes. "It isn't fair forcing me to live their way."

"Of course it isn't fair," he agreed, still gently. "But it also isn't unfair. It just is. It's my turn to be accommodated, your turn to be taken advantage of. If I struggled through it on Central, you can do the same here."

I was about to say I didn't want to struggle through anything, but was interrupted by the appearance of Gay King. She still wore the stylish leisure suit she'd had on earlier, but it looked considerably more wilted than it should have. She dabbed at the light sheen of sweat on her brow, then her finger flicked imperiously in my direction.

"You there, how much longer until our food is ready?" she asked, her voice too lazy to be considered demanding. She knew who I was, but she wasn't the type to be impressed.

"I haven't the faintest idea," I informed her, trying again to stand straighter. "Maybe you'll be told when it becomes your turn at the spit."

"Don't be silly," she sneered, moving her eyes around the camp in obvious disapproval. "I wasn't brought here to turn spits. I'll leave that to those of you who are more obviously suited to it."

Fury rose in me at her insolence, and I was just about to snap an answer, but once again I was interrupted. Tammad appeared out of nowhere beside the woman, and looked down at the cooking animal.

"I see the *krayea* is barely begun," he observed, needing no more than a glance to tell how far along the animal was. "As there is considerable time left before we may eat, I believe I will look more closely at the newest gift given me by the Amalgamation. Come to my pavilion with me, woman."

He was looking down at Gay King, rating her again with his eyes and liking what he was seeing. Gay was well aware of his inspection, but wasn't terribly impressed by it.

"I can't possibly join you until I have something to eat," she stated, still looking around at the camp. "And while you're at it, see if you can find something light and cold in the way of wine. There are certain standards due my position, and I see no reason to disregard them."

"Perhaps you mistake what position is yours," Tammad answered with his usual calm, then his fist was suddenly in Gay's short black hair; causing her to pale and gasp with shock. "It is your position to obey my will, my position to command you. It seems necessary to teach this truth to each female of your worlds, and I grow weary of it. My pavilion is this way."

He turned Gay around by the fistful of hair he held, and led her stumbling toward his, *camtah*. The woman was considerably deflated by what was being done to her, but I could see she wasn't the sort to stay deflated long. As angry as I was — at both of them — when the idea came I didn't hesitate an instant. I sent a strong sense of disinterest at Gay, trying to make the emotion soak down into her mind, hoping it would surface again and again during the hours to come. If it worked, I wouldn't give much for the pleasure either of them would feel, not having to work around an obstacle like that. Tammad was a beast, but he preferred honest response from the woman he used.

"That was a dirty trick," Len said, most of his amusement gone as he turned back to look at me. "I can understand why you did it, but I don't particularly approve — or understand how you did it. I was under the impression we weren't able to — hey, let go of that handle!"

Startled by the sudden sharpness of his words, I looked down at the handle I held to see the blood Len had already seen. As if on cue, I also suddenly felt the sharp stab of pain in my hands, where the blood was coming from, a pain I had only been partially aware of earlier. I stared at the blood very briefly, then continued to turn the spit as I'd been doing.

"Aside from my talent, I'm not worth much on this world," I told Len, feeling the incredulity he felt that I refused to stop what I was doing. "If I have to be here, I'll pull my own weight. I was given a job and I'll do it."

"You stubborn —" He choked, staring at me in bright anger. "You're not trying to do a job, you're trying to punish everyone for having given it to you by hurting yourself! Get away from that handle and let someone else take over!"

"No!" I spat, holding the handle tighter even against the burning, blazing pain I felt. "Think of it any way you like, but leave me alone!"

"The hell I will!" he snarled, looking around angrily until he saw Loddar, one of Tammad's *l'lendaa*. He gestured to Loddar, calling him over, then switched to Rimilian speech when the man reached him.

"You must call Tammad at once," he told the frowning *l'lenda*. "This woman is injuring herself, yet refuses to leave the spit."

"It is unnecessary to call Tammad," Loddar answered, pulling me away from the spit by one arm and gesturing toward a woman not far from us. The woman hurried over to take my place, first wiping my blood off the handle with her *caldin*, and the thing was done no matter how hard I struggled against Loddar's fingers.

"I am much of a fool," Len said, looking into Loddar's eyes and undoubtedly feeling the faint contempt Loddar was keeping from his face. "I have been considering myself a free man, yet I am not even free enough to stop a woman from hurting herself. If I were in your position, I would be feeling the contempt you do a good deal more strongly."

"Freedom is not an easy thing," Loddar told him, his smile filled with understanding. "For some, it is necessary to grow into the state, and it is Tammad's will that we assist you. If you are willing."

"I am more than willing," Len grinned, bolstered by the lack of critical judgment from the *l'lenda*. "Now what are we to do with this woman?"

"We will see to her," Loddar said, turning from Len to take my hands in his. I tried to close my hands to keep them from being looked at, but the pain was too great and I was too wild with rage to use pain control. Len reached over and held my wrists while Loddar pried my fingers open, then my brother empath waited while the *l'lenda* finished his examination.

"The injury is not serious," Loddar finally pronounced, raising his eyes to mine with a good deal of disapproval. "'Her hands are not the hands of a woman well used to hard labor, and should not have been subjected to such overuse. They will heal quickly, yet Tammad will not be pleased."

"You are mistaken," I told Loddar, my resentment of his treatment of me clear in every word I spoke. "I was ordered to see to the *krayea* by no one other than your *denday*, and that is what I shall do till he recalls my presence and commands differently. Release me so that I may return to my work!"

"Woman, you speak foolishly," Loddar said, shaking his large, shaggy blond head at me. "It was not Tammad's intention to see you harmed, therefore is it unnecessary to see his pleasure interrupted to keep you from it. Should you wish a greater portion of his attention, I suggest you labor toward that end when in his furs. For now you will come with me."

He let go of my hands to take my arm again, and then he, too, was dragging me in the direction he wanted me to go. I was so furious I was nearly speechless, and Len's very obvious amusement as he followed us didn't help at all. I seriously considered telling Loddar he was an idiot for thinking I cared who Tammad took to his furs, but finally decided I'd be wasting my breath. At least *I* knew I didn't care anything about that big barbarian, and one day I'd prove it.

Loddar dragged me to a tent not far from Tammad's pavilion, pushed me down on the edge of the verandah, then began rummaging through a sack of his things lying on the ground beside the verandah. I sat there wincing at the brightness of the setting sun, cradling my aching hands against me, ignoring Len where he stood staring down at me, and most of all wishing I were somewhere else. My hair was stringy with sweat, my shoulders, back and arms ached, my hands hurt with a stabbing pain, and I was beginning to hate everyone around me. I was vaguely aware of Garth coming over to Len to find out what was going on as Loddar turned to me with a silk-lined leather pouch of the salve he intended putting on my hands, and that's when I became aware of what was going on in Tammad's pavilion.

Many people have remarked, usually nervously, how empaths almost seem able to read minds as well as emotions. They point out the interpreting we do as an excellent example of the contention, asking how it's possible for an empath to know people's intentions and actions merely from knowing what emotions they're experiencing. During the period when I was still answering the contention, I usually cited the example of gestures among untalented people. If an untalented person saw someone else taste something and then grimace, did it take telepathy to know that the second person had disliked what he'd tasted? If that same untalented person saw a third person rubbing his hands together and grinning, did it take telepathy to know the third person was anticipating something extremely pleasant? Emotions are gestures of the mind, each nuance reflecting and defining a different action or reaction. A trained empath can usually tell what's going on between two people even if he or she can't see them, and Tammad's pavilion was much too close to where I was sitting.

"Give me your hands, Terril," Loddar directed, crouching down in front of me with the leather pouch. "This salve will heal the sores upon your palms, so that you will be able to use your hands come the new sun."

His mind, like every other *l'lenda's,* was prepared to accept nothing but obedience, but I wasn't about to just sit there and become an uninvited guest at Tammad's party.

"I cannot stay here," I said, looking up at his dark outline-form where he crouched in front of the. sun. "Should you wish to see to my hands, you may follow me to another place, farther away, where my thoughts may be my own."

I began to get to my feet to leave there, but Loddar's hand was suddenly on my shoulder, pushing me back down.

"I have no need to follow you," he said, shaking his head. "Perhaps Terril has forgotten that the *darayse* of her land do not dwell in ours. Give me your hand, *wenda,* for Tammad would wish me to see to your injury."

"I don't *care* what Tammad would want! I snapped, pushing at his hand, not caring that he didn't understand the language I'd switched to. "Get out of my way, you bully, and leave me alone!"

"I do not know the words you speak, *wenda,*" he answered, with a frown, "yet do I feel that were I to know them, I would not care for them. I have shown you the patience due from a man toward another man's *wenda,* yet does my patience grow exceedingly thin. Do you now obey me, else shall I see my will done in another manner."

"And what of my will?" I demanded, not having been able to budge his hand an inch. "Is my will nothing, a mere scream in the wind, a candle in the forest's darkness? Am I of so little value and worth that my will means nothing?"

He frowned at my question, confusion muddling his thoughts, and for an instant I thought he was going to answer me, but abruptly the intention was rejected. He shook his head with a sigh, let go of my shoulder, then pushed me flat on my back.

"Though there are not the words, a man does what he must," he muttered, reaching to his swordbelt, and then his hands were at my ankles, chaining them together with a bronze-colored clip that held to one link of each of the ankle bands I wore. I yelled incoherently and tried to struggle free, but he ignored my struggles and pulled me upright again to take my right wrist and tie it to the metal upright of his tent's verandah with a piece of leather. My left wrist was added to the upright just below my right one, and then the salve touched my palms, soothing the pain and hurt as if by magic. Loddar smoothed the salve all over with two fingers, checked to make sure I couldn't pull loose from the upright, then stood straight and walked away, wiping his hand on his *haddin.* He had already tagged me as a settled problem in his mind, but the problem wasn't settled as far as *I* was concerned. I pulled at the leather without doing any good, but I had to get out of there!

"I admire efficiency of effort, don't you?" Len's voice came, filled with amusement – I turned my head to see that he was talking to Garth, who stood next to him looking down at me. "Why do the job and leave the woman free to ruin it, thereby requiring that it be done again? Tie her up before starting, and you only have to do it once."

"I think I like that," Garth said, beginning a slow grin as he stared at me. "Yes, I definitely like that."

"Will one of you please get me out of this?" I said to them, gritting my teeth against their amusement. "You've had your fun by now, or at least you should have, so why not try being adult?"

"Are you asking us to go against the wishes of one of our hosts, Terry?" Len asked, stepping closer with Garth right beside him. "I don't think that would make us very good guests."

"Not to mention the fact that I'd hate getting that monster mad at me," Garth put in in a drawl. "He's almost as big as Tammad, and might even top him by a few pounds. He may be older than I am, but I doubt if he's any slower."

"Garth, Len, please!" I whispered, suddenly frightened by what I saw in their minds. They were having fun teasing me, but neither one saw the teasing as a prelude to untying me. They were going to leave me like that, and their minds were firm with the decision.

"What's the matter, Terry, don't you like the show?" Len asked very softly, his blue eyes bright even in the near-evening dimness. "You've got a front-row seat, and you should be a big enough girl to appreciate it. Why walk out when it's just getting good?"

"What are you talking about?" Garth asked him as I closed my eyes and pulled futilely at the leather which held me, forced to the sight by his words, against my will. "I don't see any show going on."

"Ah, but Terry and I do," Len chuckled in answer. "Tammad has Gay King in his pavilion, and he's beginning to teach her what men are all about."

"That big brunette?" Garth laughed is disbelief – but still in delight. "How do you know?"

"Aside from the fact that I saw him take her in there, their emotions are so clear and strong I might as well be inside and watching," Len told him. "And I'm sure Terry's getting it even more clearly than I am – aren't you, Terry?"

I tried to ignore his question, knowing he was only trying to direct my attention, but my try failed while his didn't. I tried to get my feet under me and failed again, accomplishing nothing more than scrabbling around against the upright.

"I wish *I* could tell what was going on," Garth said, sounding frustrated. "I've seen ones like that brunette before, and no matter how sexy they look, they're usually cold as ice."

"This one's due for some warming," Len laughed, and then there were small scuffling sounds. "Sit down and make yourself comfortable, and listen to this."

Another set of scuffling sounds came while Len rapidly rechecked his data, and by the time Garth was settled, Len was ready.

"As I said, Tammad took Gay to his tent," Len began with a good deal of relish. "What I didn't say was that he took her there dragged along by the hair. The woman was slightly shocked at being treated like that, but she didn't start out at the top of her profession. She's had her share of less-than-usual requests, so by the time she was inside and turned loose, she was back to her old attitudes."

"Which can be seen in her eyes, if you know enough to look for them," Garth put in.

"Exactly," Len agreed. "She started giving Tammad some speech she had used so often she'd memorized it, but Tammad cut her off right in the beginning with some sort of order, most probably to keep quiet and get out of her clothes. She cut off the speech feeling very put out and began to get out of her clothes, but the speed her mind was running at probably made her move too fast. Tammad spoke again, an addition to his first, order rather than a new one, and her mind closed down with outrage, but she obeyed. The appreciation in Tammad's mind said she moved very slowly, showing him just what be wanted. After that she started posing."

"I can see it," Garth said with a low whistle, his voice growing husky. "I can also feel it."

"You just think you can," Len told him with a strained chuckle. "You ought to feel what it's like through Tammad's mind. The man was looking at every part of her, examining each individual line, anticipating what touching her would be like but in no hurry to get on with it. He knew he'd have all the time he'd want or need, and he wasn't about to ruin it by hurrying."

"I wonder what they use here in place of flesh and blood," Garth said, decidedly more uncomfortable. "I don't know how long I'd be able to hold myself back."

"Gay didn't think Tammad would last long at all," Len breathed harder. "She was trying to force him into using her and getting it over with so she could start manipulating him, but her simple, savage little plans haven't worked out. She's still posing, he still hasn't touched her, and she's thinking about starting to get desperate."

"Why desperate?" Garth asked. "She can't be feeling embarrassed?"

"Not embarrassed," Len laughed, perking up a little. "She's beginning to react to the posing herself in spite of the fact that she's done it so often. The posing is usually her own idea, started when she wants to start it, lasting as long as she cares to let it. This time Tammad picked up on it at once and began directing her. She's been moving according to his directions, holding each pose as long as *he* wants it held, doing everything to someone else's taste rather than her own. It's making her feel – oh, oh, look out!"

"What?" Garth demanded as I cringed. "What's happening?"

"He's got her close enough to touch," Len said hoarsely, and then he groaned. "Lord, but her skin is soft! I've never felt a woman that soft, but he's not impressed! He's reacting, but it's still well within his control!"

"Do you mean you can actually feel her skin like that?" Garth demanded. "That's got to be more than just emotions."

"I can tell from what she feels like to him," Len explained, getting a better grip on himself. "The level of pleasure a man feels corresponds to previous levels set by tactile sensation. I know what a woman would have to feel like to feel like that to me, and I've never felt a woman that soft."

"Maybe you're not looking at it from the proper angle," Garth said, a comment I didn't understand any more than Len did, but before Len could question him Garth added, "Never mind. What are they doing now?"

"He's touching her," Len said, and the double, first-hand, second-hand narrative made me shiver against the upright. I could feel his hands on her, feel the calm she was seeing and not understanding, feel her confusion and distress as her body began reacting to being touched like that. She was used to being in control of the men who used her, used to watching their panting, sweating and moaning without being more than surface-involved herself. Gay King was already beyond being surface-involved, and she was beginning to be frightened.

"He's touching her while he makes her hold a pose," Len said, and the words sent a flash of intense heat through the two men beside me. "He's not showing her a damned thing more than interest, but his hands are starting to stir the fires in her. He won't let her move out of the pose no matter what she says, and it's making her feel – I don't know how to describe it."

I shivered again, but made sure my eyes stayed closed. Len didn't know how to describe Gay's feelings, but I knew exactly how she felt. She found herself in the possession of a man who would not accept refusal of any kind from her, a man who would take what he wanted, and she was discovering that her body was reacting to him automatically and beyond her control. Her body was getting her ready for his invasion, a protection she needed with a man like that. Her mind hadn't recognized what she was faced with, but her body had.

"He's got her," Len said, his voice dripping with satisfaction. "She really wants him now, but he's still taking his time and intends to continue taking it. In another minute she'll be yelling."

"Or begging," Garth said, his voice and mind strange. "Never in my entire life have I had a woman beg me. Have you?"

"No," Len answered, and then I jumped when his hand touched my leg just above the knee. My struggling and fighting had pushed the *caldin* up onto my thighs, but I hadn't realized it till then. My eyes flew open to see Len staring at me, and Garth was staring too.

"No, I've never had a woman beg me," Len said, "but I know the woman I'd like to start the practice with. And you're close to being ready, aren't you, Terry?"

"Don't," I whispered, trying to edge away closer to the upright I was tied to. Their eyes were terrible, and their minds – wanted me. They both stared at me hungrily, their bodies aching and demanding, their thoughts overfilled with a scene they wanted to be a part of. "Don't," I repeated in the same whisper. "Please, you can't."

"I've never felt the pull this badly before," Garth said, sliding away from Len along the ground and closer to me. "I find I'm having trouble keeping my hands off you, Terry. Why should that be?"

"It's because there's nothing to stop you," Len said, answering the question for me as I trembled against the upright. "She's sitting there tied to a post, her ankles chained together, on a planet where men make the choice. She can scream and cry and plead, but she can't order you away from her and expect to be backed up by the laws of this society. She's helpless and you know it."

"Yes," Garth breathed, raising his hand to the side of my *imad,* where it gaped open. His fingers and palm slid inside, decisively, touching my breast as he had never even touched my arm before. I whimpered and threw my head back, straining at the leather on my wrists, so close to projecting my frenzy that I was stiff with the effort of holding it in. Len touched my thigh and Garth touched my breast, and Tammad held another woman in his arms, a woman who kissed him and writhed against him, offering everything she could give, begging him to take it. He touched her deep and laughed at the way she cried, then ordered her to pleasure his body. The weeping woman hurried to obey, desperate to please him to the point of using her. She knew he was going to use her, knew it without doubt, but didn't know how long it would be before he decided he'd toyed with her enough. I could see the decision in his mind, the decision that he would use her, the curiosity over how good she would be, and nearly screamed out loud. She had no right being there, just as Len and Garth had no right being near me!

"Get away from me!" I spat at the two men touching me, startling part of the rut out of their minds. 'I'm *not* helpless, and you have no damned right touching me! I don't belong on this world and neither do you, and I won't be treated as if I do belong here! Get away from me, do you hear, get away from me!"

My tirade reached to them the way begging wouldn't have, shadowing their minds and making them draw back. They sat and stared wordlessly at me for a moment, the same bitterness in some strange way filling both of them, and then Len rose to his feet.

"I still can't escape the conditioning," be muttered, running a weary hand through his blond hair. "But neither can you, friend. What say we take a walk together and see if there are any spare body parts to be found around here. I think we're both missing a couple."

"At one time I would have disagreed with that comment," Garth sighed, also rising to his feet. "Right now I can see it would be a waste of breath. Let's go that way."

They rounded the side of the *camtah* and walked away from the glowing red ball of the setting sun, heading toward the already deepening shadows. I wanted to call them back and demand that they untie me, but I could see from their minds that they would not come back under any circumstances. They felt ashamed and self-betrayed, just as though they hadn't done the right thing by leaving me alone. I heard a sobbing scream come from Tammad's pavilion at the same moment I felt it, knowing that Gay had been foolish enough to try demanding release from Tammad. As punishment he had started her all over again from the posing, and the scream had come the first time he'd touched her. I knew if I tried to stand any more of that I'd go insane, as every minute that passed made it worse. Slowly, fearfully, I let the shield in my mind shut them out, then rested my head against the upright below my wrists and closed my eyes. I was very much afraid to be behind that shield, but I was too tired to struggle any longer with Tammad and his play time. I hated that beast, hated him with good reason; sitting behind my shield, very much afraid, I began listing all my good reasons.

I awoke with a start, realizing I had fallen asleep, wondering how it was possible to fall asleep in such an uncomfortable position. My back and neck ached more than they had earlier, and I stirred in discomfort, only then realizing how numb my wrists had grown. The entire situation was outrageous, but what else might one expect on that planet?

"Your awakening is precisely on time," Tammad's voice came, and I jumped to realize how close he was. He stood over me in what had become full darkness, partially illuminated by a nearby campfire. Only part of his expression was visible, but seeing that part made me wonder why I hadn't noticed his approach. The barbarian was controlling his anger with a great deal of difficulty, something rare for him, and then I remembered about the shield. I wasn't sure I really ought to drop it, and once it was gone I regretted its loss. Fury and frustration blazed from him so strongly I winced, something he noticed when he crouched in front of me.

"Why are you so angry?" I asked, drawing back as much as I could. "And why do I have to be awake?"

The bulk of my anger is not your concern," he answered, making no effort to control himself. "A part of it, however, is very much your concern. Why was it necessary for you to be tied so?"

"Since it was Loddar's idea, why don't you ask him?" I came back, but faintly. I couldn't see where what I had done, had been so wrong, but I didn't want that entire mass of anger aimed at me.

"I have already done so," he said, keeping those eyes directly on me. "I would now hear how you view the matter."

"I don't see how there can be more than one way of viewing it," I sniffed, raising my chin higher. "I told Loddar I didn't care to spend my time in this particular location, but he couldn't have cared less. It wouldn't have done him any harm to let me go elsewhere, but he couldn't be bothered with the wishes of a mere *wenda*. I've come to expect nothing else from *l'lendaa*."

"I see." He nodded, continuing to stare at me. "Loddar failed to grant you your whim, therefore was he at fault."

"Hardly a whim," I corrected sharply, though why I wasted good insult is a mystery. "I believe I've told you before that I don't enjoy being part of an orgy, even a part no one realizes is there. This *camtah* is much too close to your pavilion – or hadn't you understood that?"

"The thought occurred to me when first I left my *camtah*," he said, a strange tightening touching his mind. "Had I not stopped here to find you asleep, surely would I have thought – "

"Thought what?" I asked, frowning at him. His feelings had changed focus again, but they were so muddied and mixed that I couldn't separate them.

"The matter need not be discussed," he said, closing the subject. "We need discuss only one thing, which is the matter of your behavior. Should I ever again find you bound due to lack of obedience, there will be immediate punishment for you – no matter the reason for the disobedience. I will have food sent to you, and you are to finish all you are given."

Abruptly he stood straight again, and then he was gone, striding off into the darkness, taking his anger and touchy temper farther away than right under my mental nose. I started to protest that he hadn't untied me, but he was out of sight – and hailing range – before I could put the thought into words. I pulled at the leather again in frustration, hurting my wrists in the process, but the gesture was as futile as the cursing I did under my breath.

No more than fifteen minutes passed before two large figures moved out of the darkness toward me, one of them carrying something. It wasn't difficult telling they were Loddar and Kennan, two *l'lendaa* I knew better than I cared to. Kennan had claimed Loddar's oldest daughter, but that hadn't stopped him from giving *me* a hard time when I'd been on the planet the last time. Loddar was hardly a very young man, but as Garth had observed, he was a considerable distance from being feeble. He was *l'lenda,* and being *l'lenda* meant being something special.

"How are your hands, *wenda*?" Loddar asked as he came up to me, Kennan by his side. "The salve should have already brought you considerable relief."

"My relief would be greater were you to be so kind as to untie my wrists and ankles," I answered, peering up at his shadow form. "Should the task not be beyond you, I would count it a great favor."

Keeping the asperity out of my tone was impossible, equally as impossible as missing the flash of annoyance in Loddar and the flash of amusement in Kerman.

"Again her tongue has sharpened to match a sword's edge," Kennan chuckled, then gestured with the bowl he held. "Had I known this, it would not have been necessary to have her meal cut small. It would have been possible for her to eat it as it was."

"Were she mine, the sharpness would be quickly dulled," Loddar growled, even more annoyed that Kerman found the situation funny. "And what of Tammad? Should he return here and hear her speak so, will his humor be improved?"

"It is difficult to see how it might be darkened," Kerman winced inwardly, probably matching the feeling with a grimace. "Should the off-worlders bring forth another gift, it will undoubtedly provoke war between their people and ours. How is it possible for a *wenda* to behave so?"

"I have heard all off-worlder *wendaa* are of the same sort," Loddar sighed, stepping onto the verandah before sitting down. "To invite a man's interest, to beg his touch, and then to find distraction when taken in his arms – it is little wonder off-worlders are *darayse,* with *wendaa* such as those."

"It is fortunate that Terril, at least, is able to give Tammad satisfaction," Kennan said, crouching down in front of me with the bowl he held. "She will require whatever strength she possesses this darkness, therefore would I see this *krayea* within her. I shall remove the leather from her so that, she may...."

"No," Loddar interrupted, from where he sat, less than a foot from me. "Even were her hands to already have healed, I would not allow her free of the leather before Tammad returns for her. Should we encourage her disrespect by allowing her her will, we ourselves would pay through an increase in Tammad's fury."

"Such an increase could mean no less than blood spilled," Kerman muttered, reaching out to brush the disarranged hair from my face. "It is as Loddar says, Terril. You must obey completely and in silence, else shall we all pay dearly. You are not unfamiliar with the *denday's* anger."

"Would that I were unfamiliar with your *denday*," I came back, tossing my head against what his hand had done. "Also, please accept the same thought for yourself."

"A mannerly response," he replied with a grin, the firelight touching half his face. "Now, should we achieve silence, you may even prove acceptable. Here."

His words preceded his dipping his fingers into the bowl he held, coming up with a small chunk of meat, and thrusting it into my mouth. I was so outraged I didn't know what to do, and for obvious reasons couldn't say much.

"Ah, silence at last," Loddar chuckled, finally pulled out of his bad mood by the furious sounds I was trying to make round the bite of *krayea*. "Should the squeakings also be seen to, I foresee great possibilities for the darkness."

"You cannot treat me so!" I garbled around the mouthful, trying to get rid of it by chewing and swallowing. Kerman's mind was alert and his body ready, showing he was prepared to return the bite to me if I should try spitting it out. It was bad enough having his fingers on it once; if he'd touched it again after it had been in my mouth to force it on me a second time, I probably would have thrown up.

"A pity Tammad allowed you to travel from him," Loddar observed, staring at me. "To permit a *wenda* to forget the obedience due *l'lendaa* brings naught save difficulty – for both. We treat you in accordance with Tammad's wishes, for it is he to whom you belong. Must you be taught this in another way, *wenda*?"

I returned his stare without saying anything, feeling the sort of calm in him I recognized easily. Most of Tammad's *l'lendaa* had it, the feeling of calm unmuddied by frustration and denial; they denied themselves nothing, and frustration could always be seen to by a sword or switch, depending on who was trying to frustrate them. I hated that emotion, always finding it a blank wall to pound on, something without gaps I might touch it by. My wrists hurt and my legs were cramped, and I couldn't have emulated that calm through anything less than a threat to my life.

"I hate you," I told him as evenly as I could manage, including Kennan in the statement. "I hate each of you, but most do I hate him to whom I belong."

"Ah, *wenda,* your unhappiness distresses me," Loddar sighed, putting a gentle hand to my face. "I know not why this unhappiness should have come upon you, but you must trust Tammad to see to it. He will not long allow it to continue."

Kennan put another piece of *krayea* in my mouth, ending the conversation, but that didn't matter. Saying that Tammad himself was the cause of my unhappiness would not have done anything to change the situation.

Kennan continued feeding me until all of the *krayea* and vegetables were gone, then he bid Loddar good night and walked away into the darkness. Loddar continued to sit where he was, his mind distracted and far away, both of us waiting for the return of my owner. Thought of Tammad brought anger and bitterness again, but curiosity soon pushed the other emotions aside. What had Loddar and Kennan said about Tammad's dissatisfaction with Gay King? That she had drawn his interest, begged to be taken – and then had lost interest herself? I couldn't understand what would have made her act that way, not after being flooded with the frenziedness of her emotions – until I remembered what I had done.

I'd been the one to plant disinterest in her mind, and it had surfaced at just the right time.

I stirred against the upright and laughed softly, picturing what it must have been like for the barbarian. He'd gotten her wild and had made her serve him, forcing her to feel an intense need for him – but once he allowed himself to feel the same need, she suddenly became turned off, untouched by need and even by interest. I could imagine her yawning into his desire, her body cool and unresponsive, a flesh doll to be used by a male who had grown bored with doing it to himself. I laughed again at the height of frustration he must have felt, a frustration he couldn't possibly have been used to.

And then I stopped laughing and stirred again, remembering how angry he had been – and how he'd suspected that what had happened had been through my doing. If I hadn't been asleep when he'd come storming out of his pavilion – the thought made me shiver, even if it was unfinished. He wouldn't have been likely to see the humor in the situation, and he would have taken his frustration out on me.

But his frustration would still be taken out on me. Loddar and Kennan and the other *l'lendaa* couldn't wait until Tammad got around to using me – after all, didn't they all know how easily the barbarian got whatever he wanted from me? I sat straighter at the upright and raised my chin, knowing how wrong they were. Tammad *hadn't* gotten what he'd wanted from me, not for some time, and I had no intentions of changing that. If that made life difficult for his *l'lendaa*, it was just too bad. I hadn't sought *them* out, and I wasn't holding *them* prisoner.

After another few minutes Loddar stirred and got to his feet, recognizing Tammad's figure coming toward us. There weren't too many people still walking around the camp, but Tammad would have been hard to miss even in a crowd. His mind was still bent out of shape by the fury of the emotions he had experienced, but a good deal of his usual calm was back, at least on the surface.

"Loddar, you need not have remained awake," he said as he came up to us, only glancing at me. "The woman is safe in the midst of our camp, and would not have been able to stray of her own accord."

"It was no inconvenience, *denday,*" Loddar assured him with warmth. "I remained only to inform you that your wishes have been seen to."

"And perhaps to speak of why the woman was left bound?" Tammad said, folding his arms as he switched his stare to me. "It would be foolish to overlook any insult given you, Loddar. Others would not be as charitable."

"There was no insult, Tammad," Loddar replied, his tone remaining warm. "You have told us Terril is an off-worlder *wenda,* and therefore is her manner more understandable. Not excusable, you understand; merely understandable. She has been left bound to teach her that proper words are not enough. Obedience and respect go deeper than mere words."

"She must indeed be made to feel these things," the barbarian agreed, giving approval to Loddar's actions. "Only in obedience will she find happiness."

Loddar grunted to complete the agreement, but I didn't say a word. I could feel their surprise at my silence, but I just didn't care. I was tired of wasting my breath protesting fantasies.

"I will take her now," Tammad said, unfolding his arms as he stepped nearer to me. "I wish you a good rest, Loddar."

"I will not return the sentiment, *denday*," Loddar chuckled, turning toward his *camtah*. "Had I brought my *wenda* with me, I, too, would find little interest in rest."

Tammad grinned as Loddar disappeared into his *camtah,* the dying flames of the fire turning the grin into something ghastly. I waited patiently until the leather was removed from my wrists and the clip taken from my ankle bands, but being untied didn't mean I was free. Tammad crouched and lifted me in his arms, then headed toward his pavilion.

"If you'd give me a minute; I'd be able to walk," I said, feeling more annoyed than I cared to show. "Or are you afraid you'd lose me in the dark if you gave me the chance to run?"

"Should you run, you will find yourself no match for those who follow," he answered, undisturbed by my comment. "It pleases me to carry you, therefore do I do so."

To hell with what pleases you, I thought, looking at his face. His eyes were straight ahead, watching where we were going, paying no attention to me where I lay against his chest. I hurt just about all over, but that was nothing unusual on that planet. Then I found that I wanted to put my head against his shoulder, and had to sharply bring myself up short. It would be easy to give in and let him have everything he wanted, but living with. myself afterward would be considerably harder.

The pavilion was only dimly lit when we entered, but dim is considerably brighter than darkness. The barbarian let the thin fold of material fall closed behind him, then headed for the drape which usually closed off sleeping furs from view. Behind the drape the sleeping furs were all arranged, and in another moment I was put down on the smaller set. Tammad paused in his crouch to examine my hands, then stood straight to open his swordbelt.

"Do not attempt to remove your clothing yourself," he said, putting his sword and dagger on the far side of his furs. "It was foolish of you to overuse your hands so, and you are not to do so again. Do you understand?"

"Certainly." I looked away from him toward the wall bisected by the drape. "Anything you say."

"You have no intentions of arguing?" he asked, his mind suspicious. "Are you not prepared to make your injury the result of my actions?"

"Would it do me any good?" I asked in turn, still staring at the soft material of the pavilion wall. "If it won't, why should I bother?"

"I see," he said, the suspicion disappearing as his mind solved the problem. "You attempt to burden me with silent guilt, that which cannot be argued against. I have heard of such a thing from various men of your worlds, when they spoke of the doings of their *wendaa*. It is not a thing done by *wendaa* of this world, for they know it would avail them naught. Continue with the practice if it pleases you."

His unconcern – true, not feigned – was enough to set my teeth on edge with its callousness. He didn't care one way or the other whether I blamed him for something, as long as he didn't blame himself. He accepted the consequences of what he did without feeling guilt, no matter what those consequences were. I clenched my fists gently over the grease Loddar had put on my palms, feeling more upset with everything that happened. There was no reaching that barbarian on any level I was used to, and I was running out of ideas.

"Now we may see to your clothing," the barbarian said, bringing his hands and attention to my *imad*. I knew from the way he stressed the word "your" that his *haddin* must be gone, but didn't turn my head to look. I didn't care that he was slowly opening the *imad* ties before moving on to the *caldin* sash; I would *not* give him what he wanted.

"Lie back and raise your hips," he directed after pulling the *imad* off over my head and tossing it away. I did as he said and had the *caldin* taken as well, then had a quizzical expression sent toward me. "Why do you gaze at me so strangely?" he asked, reaching out to smooth my hair. "Your silence is strange as well, and quite different from your usual manner."

"Why bother asking?" I shrugged from my place in the furs, ignoring the big hand that touched my hair so gently. "Silent accusation doesn't bother you – remember?"

"I do indeed," he nodded, looking down at me. "Yet do I feel your silence as one demanding answers to questions as yet unasked. Should you wish the answers, you cannot leave I them unasked."

"I don't have any questions," I began, shaking my head, then changed my mind. "No, as a matter of fact I do have one. Are these the furs you put *her* on?"

"Ah, now do I begin to see." He grinned. "The reason for your coldness and lack of interest is the previous presence of another *wenda*, one who threatens your position by my side. Should you wish to take her from my thoughts, *wenda*, coldness is not the manner in which this might be done."

"She's welcome to her place in your thoughts," I answered. "She can even have whatever my relation to you is supposed to be. All I want to know is whether or not she used these furs – because if she did, I won't sleep in them. I may have nothing on this planet to call my own, but I'd rather have less than nothing than use anything *she* used first!"

He blinked down at my anger in confusion, finding my response different from the one he had expected. He was used to having women fight to get at him, not fight to get away from him. And the fact that all I was interested in was the furs really threw him. He stared at me thoughtfully for a minute or two, then reached out for a strand of my hair.

"The black-haired *wenda* was used in the front of the pavilion, without furs," he said, keeping those blue eyes directly on me. "You now know where she was used; do you also wish to know how she was used?"

"That I already know," I said, lying back down and turning my face from him. "As fond as you seem to be of posing, you should have been an artist."

"It continually amazes me how little may be kept from you," he said, and I could hear the amusement back in his voice. "Perhaps I should require this posing of you as well, to compare the delights offered by you both."

"I offer nothing," I rasped, turning on my side to be farther away from his amusement. "And I also leave the posing to professionals. Competition of that sort has never interested me."

"It would not be unpleasant to compare my gifts from your Amalgamation," he murmured, putting a hand on my side to stroke my hip. "The Gaynor King knows much of that which interests a man, yet you, too, strove to please before you returned to your people. Do you fear you will now be less pleasing than she?"

"You're absolutely right," I nodded against my arm, trying to ignore the hand that had moved to my thigh. "I'm way out of her league and couldn't possibly hope to come anywhere near her expertise. Where she's a professional, I'm a rank amateur."

"And yet not unskilled in denying a man," he said, annoyance suddenly flaring in his mind. "I see you have now taken to agreeing with my words in such a way that argument is as impossible as true agreement. And I now also understand Loddar's comment upon words and the lack of true obedience behind them. There is as yet no true obedience within you – but there will be."

His hand came to my right arm to push my shoulders back down to the furs, but his leg kept my hips turned to the left, as they had been. I looked up into the anger in his light eyes, feeling his determination, suddenly remembering he wasn't a man who could be controlled. He shifted slightly to put his hands to either side of my head in the furs, and stared down directly into my eyes.

"Pose," he ordered, a flat-voiced command that totally rejected refusal. He was so close above me I could almost feel his body heat, making it impossible to look away from his stare.

"I – I – don't know how," I whispered, feeling a weakness roll over my resolve. "Please don't force me to...."

"Silence," he said, knowing it was unnecessary to raise his voice. "This darkness I will have naught save obedience from you, naught save absolute and complete deference to my will. Begin now."

Wide-eyed, I shrunk down into the furs as far as I could, trying to avoid something he would not let me avoid. I struggled a long time against obeying him, but only on the inside; outside I did everything he demanded, everything he commanded. The positions he ordered me into increased the ache in my tired muscles, but he refused to let me protest. He sat very close to my straining body, his mind throbbing with pleasure, his eyes bright and hard and possessive. The further I went, the more I cringed away from his thoughts, knowing what sight of me was doing to him – and fearing it. His need was usually intense, but that night it was a raging river, threatening to overflow its banks at any time. I trembled as he stared at me, drinking me in, feeling his body's demands grow stronger and stronger – and then he touched me. I was so frightened of the flood awaiting me I should have screamed, but the sudden explosion of pain-need brought by the touch hit me so hard I gasped and moaned at the same time, disbelieving what was happening. The barbarian laughed softly and moved even closer to me then, knowing he had me completely. He proved the fact to me too long after that, making sure I knew it in every part of me, making sure I was able to deny him nothing. He took whatever he wanted, demanded and was obeyed, filled his cup of pleasure to the top and overflowing. It was a very long time before we slept, but my eventual dreams were filled with tears.

## SEVEN

Sunrise found us already on our way, our line spread out along the road in a casual manner, no one worried by thoughts of what we might come across. Tammad's *l'lendaa* sat their *seetarr* with confidence, tall and strong and assured, knowing there was very little on the planet that might stand up to them. The *seetarr* they rode were equally imposing, very large beasts all of black, stiff, bristly manes and tails, shiny, short-haired coats, minds more alert than most beasts of burden. Tammad's big male had remembered me immediately, and his enormous head had reached down to poke at me as soon as I was close enough, his deep rumble an attempt to soothe the disturbance he could feel in me. I'd stroked his nose to show appreciation for the attempt, but my mood had stayed the way it was. At that point it would have taken considerably more than a *seetar's* interest to comfort me.

I'd awakened in the dark of predawn that morning feeling absolutely terrible, and it hadn't taken long to dredge up a reason for the feeling. The night before the barbarian had gotten everything he'd wanted from me, up to and including the sharing of my emotions. After everything I'd said, after all the resolves I'd made – I'd still given him whatever he'd wanted. I'd hated and despised myself then and had tried to slip out of the furs to leave the tent, but my first movement had awakened Tammad, ending all thoughts of escape. The barbarian had been filled with satisfaction, and had taken me in his arms to kiss me, only then discovering the silent tears that wet my cheeks. He wiped them away with a gentle apology for any pain he might have given me, but it hadn't been the way he'd lost himself the night before that had caused the tears. It was true he had hurt me then, but I had hurt me more.

After a fast breakfast and a stowing of gear, we were ready to go. I was ordered up behind Tammad and Gay King rode behind Loddar, but Garth and Len were given *seetarr* of their own. Len, reaching the mind of his mount, relaxed at once, but Garth took considerably longer to get comfortable. Len sat proudly in the blue *haddin* he'd been given to replace his own clothes, Garth retained his kilt with a sense of accomplishment, and Gay King wore a comfortable one-piece jumper of pale green from the luggage she'd been allowed to keep. I wore a fresh *imad* and *caldin* supplied by the barbarian – of the same pink as the first outfit. Tammad enjoyed seeing me in pink, and couldn't understand why the gift had darkened my already bleak silence even further.

The day grew warm and beautiful, the sun rising to bring life back into the land, the air like silken perfume, the blue sky, the green trees – absolutely horrible. Everything and everyone around me was happy and satisfied, pleased with the world and glad to be alive; I was the only dark spot in the sunshine, and it was very frustrating. I simply did not want to be where I was, but could see no way out of the trap. As long as Tammad was satisfied with me – and there was no denying *that* – then I was stuck and stuck good. I'd even tried casually wandering away that morning, but Kennan and Loddar and a couple of other *l'lendaa* just happened to turn up directly in my path. I knew they'd been watching me after seeing their *denday*'s expansive satisfaction, but I hadn't realized just how closely until they turned me back toward the *camtahh* with wide grins and a smack on the bottom from Loddar. I was half hoping they'd tell on me – *anything* to dent the barbarian's satisfaction – but no such luck. They liked the frame of mind Tammad was in and weren't about to do anything to change it.

Riding along the road that way quickly grew very boring. I sat behind Tammad on his *seetar,* my fingers in his swordbelt to keep me from sliding off, seeing nothing past that big body but the limited view to either side of him, which wasn't very appealing. My mind, looking for distraction, stumbled into Garth's, who rode a short distance away from us up ahead. I couldn't see him, but I could certainly feel the frantic way his mind was working, probably in an effort to distract him from his worries and uncertainties. Len had started out riding next to him, but not much time had passed before my brother empath had moved out of range to spare himself the mental clamor. I could feel Len about fifty feet back, chatting with two of the *l'lendaa,* happy as a child on a trip day in Tallion City.

I don't know exactly when the idea touched me, but suddenly I knew the true meaning of temptation. While growing up I had never been allowed to experiment with my talent, and there had been enough weak empaths around to make sure I followed the rules. I had been stronger than my guardians and teachers almost from the first, but they didn't have to be able to stop me – only tell that I was doing something wrong. They'd waited until the first time I broke Rule One – the rule covering experimentation – and then had put me in a Silent Room. I was only in there a couple of hours, but being in a shielded area at such a young age seemed the equivalent of full sensory deprivation to me. I'd started to cry and then had kept on crying until they'd let me out, then had eagerly promised never to break Rule One again. It was a lot of years since I'd even considered it, but the realization finally came that my teachers were too far behind me to catch me again.

My body was lulled by the smooth stride of Tammad's *seetar,* but my mind was fully alert. I reached out to Garth's mind again and watched him, waiting until the gamut of emotions crossed uncertainty. I grabbed the uncertainty and held onto it, increased it enough to make it stand out from the other emotions, then held it in the front of his mind where he'd be sure to notice it. No more than seconds went by before he was supporting the emotion himself, his mind darting around looking for a reason for the feeling. I didn't want dear sweet Garth to suffer when no reason appeared, so I supplied a reason: the *seetar* he rode. Reaching the *seetar* was easier than reaching Garth, and all it took was the suggestion that the male beast might be getting too old for riding to make it toss its head and snort and suddenly pick up speed. I hadn't transmitted a picture – merely a string of emotional responses with doubt heading the list – but the *seetar* hadn't had any trouble understanding my meaning. I transmitted; the *seetar* reacted – and Garth shifted from uncertainty to panic.

"Hey, slow down there!" his voice came, a tightness in it saying he was trying not to show fear. "Take it easy, boy, take it easy!"

"Are you in difficulty?" Tammad called ahead to him, his mind suddenly ready to move forward quickly. "Do you require assistance?"

"No, I think it's all right now," his answer floated back, obvious determination in it. "I'll just have to keep a closer watch on this fellow."

"Very well," Tammad agreed, his mind wavering in uncertainty. He was probably trying to decide whether or not to have someone ride next to Garth, but he quickly decided against it. Under normal circumstances Garth would have resented the gesture of protection, but at that point Garth wasn't resenting anything. He was too busy centering all his attention on the animal he rode, too distracted to think or worry about anything else. It would be a considerable time before he rid himself of the uncertainty, but at least nothing else was bothering him.

It occurred to me then to check on Len, to see if he'd noticed anything, but a quick scan showed nothing but faint curiosity over what was going on with Garth. Len was apparently too far back to detect my experimentation, but there was no sense in taking further chances. Circumstances dictated that Len himself would be my next subject, to make sure he continued to miss what was happening.

Len had returned to satisfied conversation with the *l'lenda* on his right, the second *l'lenda,* on his left, paying only occasional attention to what was being said. Len's mind wasn't shifting around through emotions, but it didn't have to be. Len was an empath, considerably more sensitive than the people around him, and considerably more open to suggestion. I watched passively a considerable time, but every time the *l'lenda* on the left turned his attention to the conversation, I deftly made Len more aware of it. Shortly after I started with Len, I also began on the *l'lenda,* brushing his mind with amusement and laughter, heightening the emotions when he turned his attention to the conversation. After another short while I began with the *l'lenda* on the right, who was in a happy, lighthearted mood, probably because he was finally starting home. Subtly, cloudlike, I increased the happiness and lightheartedness to joviality and amusement, carefully working around Len's awareness, never imposing or changing, only heightening. Len was aware of every change and shift, of course, but my efforts weren't gross enough to bring themselves to his attention. He wasn't *expecting* anything to be going on, so he simply didn't notice it.

By the time Len began wondering why his companions were amused, I had already finished with those a bit farther away from him. They, too, shared an amusement, and I could feel Len's frown as he shifted from mind to mind, trying to figure out what was so funny. Len being Len, the conclusion I wanted him to draw didn't surface for quite some time. Len was tall and strong, not quite as large as the *l'lendaa,* but as close to them as an Amalgamation man was likely to be. He looked bigger and stronger yet in the *haddin* and swordbelt he'd been given, broad-shouldered and deep-chested and very handsome – but he wasn't used to dressing in that fashion. A man who is used to being covered all over with cloth can't help but feel *some* doubt when he strips to a body cloth, even if he's pleased to do it. When the thought finally came that possibly *he* was the source of amusement – shown by an increase in doubt and a decrease in self-assurance and confidence – I immediately puffed on the feeling, making it stronger without letting him see the boost. His mind followed the trail I'd begun, reinforcing the emotions unconsciously and automatically, letting me withdraw as his suspicion became a certainty. As an empath, Len should have known better than to believe that something was true because he was sure it was true, but Len was also a human being with human frailty. When be reached the point of being afraid it was true, he was already convinced.

I watched the silence Len lapsed into for a while then withdrew completely, satisfied with the way he was engrossing himself more and more with private thoughts. His sensing ability was drawn in close around his mind like a shield, unwilling to touch the minds around him for fear of what he would find, and that was just the way I wanted him. If he wasn't watching he couldn't pick up what I was doing, and he and Garth both were considerably more attractive as they were than as they had been the day before. The last thing they were currently concerned with was helpless females.

I rested for the next few minutes, letting my mind gather strength again, then went on to the next subject on my list. Loddar rode not ten feet away from us, on the left and somewhat behind, Kennan riding next to him. He'd started out feeling proud that Tammad had asked him to take care of Gay King, but pride goeth before a fall – of resistance if nothing else. Gay had been indignant over the "crude method of transportation" and had tried to balk at being included as a rider, but *l'lendaa* are infamous for their lack of indulgence of female whimsy. Gay had been lifted off the ground and seated on Loddar's saddle fur, and once his *seetar* began moving she'd quickly circled his waist with her arms, frightened at the thought of falling off.

Now, many an Amalgamation man would have had no problem ignoring a beautiful woman clinging to him for hours, pressing her breasts into his bare back, breathing on his skin, but Loddar wasn't an Amalgamation man, he was a Rimilian. He had enjoyed the sight of Gay from the first moment he saw her, and a Rimilian male's enjoyment isn't a cerebral thing. After hours of riding her behind him he had taken to trying to distract his mind and senses, cursing the fact that he would not allow himself to ask for her use. If his own woman had been traveling with them, he would have had a considerably easier time.

As it was, working on his desires was child's play. His emotions were hooked so directly into his physical reactions that stimulating one meant an immediate stimulation of the second. Fifteen minutes of work had him suffering intensely, his body stiff and rigidly under control, sweat on his brow, a trembling in his hands. He wasn't about to shame himself by showing how he felt, but that didn't mean he wasn't feeling it. A vivid picture of Gay King stripped naked clung to his mind, sending flashes of intense desire through his body, causing even more sweat to break out on him. I made sure the picture would stay with him for some time, then moved on to Kennan.

By the time we stopped to have lunch, I had reached almost everyone in our party. The men were withdrawn and either silent or snarling, the women were jealous, surly and uncooperative, and the male guests were feeling their alienness and out-of-placeness. I hadn't bothered with Gay King – who couldn't have cared less about anything but her own comfort – or Tammad, who was having trouble understanding why his people were acting the way they were, but I hadn't forgotten about them. I was trying to think of something really fitting for Gay, but right after we were back on the road it was Tammad's turn.

The barbarian hadn't been pleased with the way his men had behaved toward him and each other during lunch, having had to stop three arguments that were just about to become sword matters. His mind had been a blur of deep thoughts and planning during the morning's ride, but distractions during the afternoon kept pulling him away from it. The more his annoyance grew, the more I slipped in a "what's the use?" feeling of defeat and wasted time, working as carefully as I had with Len. Len would have been angry to find out my manipulations, but Len's anger couldn't hold a candle to Tammad's. The barbarian had very deep drives to do and win, and I became curious to see how far I could drive him from his original purposes. If I drove him far enough, he just might turn around and take me back to the embassy.

It was still early afternoon when we stopped to make camp, and by then Tammad's depression had grown so heavy it was like a black cloud pressing down on his mind, spreading and gathering force every minute. For a long while he had tried fighting it, tried convincing himself he was wrong to feel that way, but depression is insidious and hard to fight. He had begun to probe deep within himself, probably reexamining his purposes and aims, and had almost forgotten I was there.

Once all the tents had been put up, Tammad sat down in the grass in front of his pavilion to continue his soul-searching. Garth and Len showed up and quietly seated themselves not far from him, needing support and encouragement that they weren't consciously aware of, ignorant of the fact that they weren't about to get it. I sat in the grass a small distance away from them, watching clinically, seeing the depression the other two men had also developed. I wondered how far I could go maintaining them in their attitudes before they tried suicide, then wondered if it would be possible to keep them from suicide once they decided on it. I was sure I could, but I really had no intentions of allowing the experiment to go that far. There's a strange sense of power in controlling the people around you, a power that would be lost if the people themselves were lost.

I had just noticed a frowning lack of understanding in Len, an emotion that had popped up suddenly, when Gay abruptly returned from the walk she had been taking. Her mind showed boredom and annoyance, boredom over having nothing to do, annoyance that people weren't fussing over her and pampering her. She stopped a few steps behind the three men sitting in silence, stared at them for a moment, then stepped forward to take her place in the middle of the line they'd made.

"I have never in my life experienced such boredom," she announced as she folded gracefully to the ground. "I was told this trip would be an adventure, but so far it's more flop than fun. Aren't any of you going to *do* anything?"

"What did you have in mind?" Len asked sardonically. "Right now I can't even muster interest in the thought of raping Terry."

"Maybe she's volunteering to take Terry's place," Garth put in after talking a deep breath. Their comments offended me at once, but I was more annoyed at their attempts to throw off the depression. "For my own part, I'll have to go along with Tammad: accept no substitutes."

"Why don't you try raising Tammad's interest again?" Len suggested, finally turning to look at the fury in Gay's eyes. "That would give you something to do, and at the same time save Terry the effort. I understand she needs to conserve her strength for the part you're not up to."

"You repulsive mind-crawler!" Gay snarled. "The least you can be sure of is that you'll never find out *personally* what part I am and am not up to! And as far as that – that – backward female you call Terry is concerned, she'll never see the day she can best me at *anything*! Do you hear me, you silly little moist-eyed wimp? You belong in a place like this, serving your betters! Even the sight of you makes me sick!"

She was practically frothing as she looked at me, up on her knees with her fists clenched, spitting hatred and fury from mind and mouth alike. As furious as she was, I wasn't far behind, and I stormed erect even as Tammad, Len and Garth roused themselves far enough to get ready to break up a fight.

"So I make you sick, do I?" I spat back, clenching my own fists as I glared at her. "So I'm a wimp, am I? Well, wimp this!"

Gay herself had told me exactly what she deserved, and I didn't hesitate feeding it to her. I sent waves of nausea rolling at her, the sort of feeling accompanied by dizziness and sweating and uncontrollable heaves. The emotion describing the feeling was a complex one, but I had it put together and on its way in a matter of seconds. I was so angry I didn't care what I did to her, but I was so angry I also didn't pay attention to the spread of the wave. Gay went instantly pale and began to bend forward in helpless paroxysm, but even before she began, Len was already retching, emptying himself of everything he'd ingested, Garth and Tammad not far behind him. I hadn't thought I'd spread the effect to include all of them, but then again I really didn't care. They all thought of me as something to be ignored when not being used, and I was sick of it and them. People began hurrying over from all over the camp, anxious, concerned people ready to help. I watched the four victims of my anger for another minute, partially blocking out the sickness and disgust coming from their minds as their bodies spasmed, then turned and walked away.

Late afternoon should be a lazy, quiet time, but I was feeling too exhilarated and happy to want a quiet time. I walked to the part of the camp where the *seetarr* were tied and found a tree to lean against, then sent a triumphant gaze to the blue sky floating above the leaves. I had beaten them all, made them all feel as small and helpless as I usually did – or at least as I used to feel. I had lashed out at them in anger and I had made them *know* I was stronger, made them know what it was like to be pushed around! And I could do more, I knew I could do more, all I had to do was practice.

I sat down at the base of the tree and wrapped my arms around my knees, thinking about what I wanted to practice at. Considering the way most people made decisions, controlling their minds wasn't nearly as good as controlling their emotions. Very few people can be honestly objective about a decision, especially if one side of the decision "feels" wrong. Side A may be the only practical way of doing whatever they want to do, but side B can be more pleasant, adventurous, financially rewarding, more easily achieved, or shorter in duration. The lure of side B usually overcomes the benefits in side A, and all because of emotional reasons. Making one thing appear more attractive than another was child's play, so easy that it took almost no effort. I could – And then I stopped, immediately returning to the concept of effort. It had always been an effort for me to project, something that drained my energy in no time at all. I sat back against the tree again and examined my physical resources, very much surprised that I wasn't flat on the ground from exhaustion. Thinking about it showed how tired I really was, but the tiredness was a far cry from being completely drained. I was growing in strength as well as in ability, and all I had to do was sit and rest for a while to bring myself back to where I'd –

"There she is," a voice came, a rough voice under strict control. "Sitting and enjoying the view after making us lose half our insides. A good job well done."

I jerked my head around at the sharp bitterness in Garth's voice, seeing him standing with Len and Tammad less than ten feet away. I was only just beginning to be able to detect their emotions, undoubtedly due to the way I'd drained much of my strength. Len and Garth looked terrible, the emotions coming from them matching perfectly, but Tammad only looked angry; as soon as he got closer, though, I changed that description to furious. They stopped about a foot away and stared down at me, and I felt a sudden need to say something.

"I really didn't mean to include you three in on that," I told them, resting my head back against the tree as I looked up at them. "You *ought* to be more careful of the company you keep."

"That's very amusing," Len said, trying to stand straighter. "You have a great sense of humor, Terry – and don't feel the slightest trace of guilt."

"I don't see a need for guilt," I answered, the hardness in all their thoughts beginning to make me uneasy. "It was an accident that the wave caught you three, not something done on purpose. Why should I feel guilty?"

"How about for the way you've been manipulating people all day?" Len demanded, his handsome face twisting in anger. "Well, well, now I can see the guilt, but only a small flash, not very impressive. You're not sorry about what you did, only sorry that you got caught."

"I don't know what you're talking about!" I snapped, moving my back away from the tree. "And with a talent like yours, I doubt if you know, either!"

"That was unnecessary, Terry," Garth put in as Len reddened and stiffened in insult. "Len's talent may not be as strong as yours, but he's strong enough to know when people have been twisted around. When we stopped to think about it, we found that almost all of us have been touched – even Tammad."

My eyes were immediately and irresistibly drawn to the barbarian, who stood to the left of the others, his arms folded across his chest, his fury still under his control but also still growing. He hadn't said a word yet, but that didn't mean he was unconcerned.

"Well, why shouldn't I touch you?" I stormed, glaring at all of them as I got to my feet. "You three get a lot of fun out of pushing me around, but you don't like it as much when I start pushing back, do you? If you three can do what you like with me, I can do the same with you!"

"No," Tammad said, the single word overriding the protest coming from the other two. "The picture you show with your words is a false one, a thing designed to justify evil, and I will not accept it."

He unfolded his arms and moved closer to me, the anger coming from him strong enough to make the other two men retreat a step. I retreated too, back up against the tree, but he was still much too close.

"You feel yourself badly treated," be said, his words as harsh as his eyes were hard. "And yet, that which was done to you was done with your full knowledge, allowing you to resist as best you might. We, ourselves, were not accorded this privilege, instead being attacked in cowardly fashion, from a direction invisible to us. This was not the treatment received by you at our hands."

"You sound so damned sanctimonious," I said, frightened but unable to hold the words back. "Do you really think it makes any difference whether or not I can see what you're doing to me? How am I supposed to stop you, any of you? I'm as helpless as a child against your strength, just as you're helpless against my talent. It's an even trade, damn it, an even trade!"

"No," he said again, this time shaking his head. "Should we give you discomfort or pain, it is an unfortunate occurrence in our attempts to aid you to happiness. The same does not hold true for your attempts. You seek only to avenge that which need not have been, had you only been willing to heed and believe in that which was told you. When I took you as my woman, I wished only to share the happiness brought me by your presence. I now find there is no longer happiness to share."

"That isn't true," I whispered, my voice ragged because of my attempts to hold the tears back. "You weren't trying to *share* happiness with me, you were trying to force it on me. And I don't care if you don't like this side of me. If you want the dagger, you have to take both edges."

"But one need not be cut on either edge," he said as Len stirred and got ready to come closer. "Your displeasure was with me. It should not have reached out to give pain to others. It is primarily this for which you will be punished."

"No!" I cried as he wrapped his hand around my arm, cutting off whatever Len had been about to say, cutting into Garth's exclamation of surprise. Pulling against his grip was worse than useless, as the effort caused him to tighten his hold. I cried out again as he pulled me back toward his. pavilion, finding it as impossible to touch his mind as it was to deny the strength of his body. I was too tired from the projection to reach him, his anger too thick to work through. I was dragged stumbling and struggling back to his pavilion, amid knots of angry, glowering people, pulled inside, then roughly relieved of the *imad* and *caldin*. I ranted even as I shivered in the warm air, trying to tell him how wrong he was, but one look at the switch took all the words away. I backed away across the fur as he came closer, shaking my head, too well aware of how determined he was, then backed into the drape which divided the pavilion. Drowning in panic, I jerked the drape up and half fell behind it, trying to find a way out, but there was none. He found me again even as I tried to scramble past him, began beating me even as I begged him not to. I didn't want to be punished, it wasn't fair that he punish me when nobody punished him, but that didn't stop the beating. He switched me until I cried, until I projected my pain and fear, until I tried frantically to make him believe I was sorry. At that point I *was* sorry, desperately sorry, and he finally seemed to be satisfied. He left me crying hysterically in my furs, straightened the drape, then sat himself down in the front half of the pavilion.

It was a long time before the sobbing quieted down enough to let me do more than know how much I ached. Even the warm, gentle furs touching me hurt, but I found that the beating had somehow clarified and illuminated exactly what I'd done so that *I* understood it. As a child I hadn't understood what experimenting with people meant, but as an adult I should have known better than to let the poison get a hold on me. Sure I could control people and sure it was easy – as long as no one found out about what I was doing. The anger of the other people in the camp was a really frightening thing, and I'd forgotten all about that part of it until I'd been dragged through it. The switching seemed to have rubbed my nose in the truth – the truth that I might have been hit with rocks and fists for what I had done instead of just getting switched. I shivered as the thrill of fear increased, sending me a picture of my body lying on the ground instead of in warm, comfortable furs, broken and bloody and lifeless instead of throbbing painfully from a beating given in punishment. Whether he knew it or not, Tammad had saved my life again, and I stirred in the furs, wanting to go to him, but I couldn't go to him and pride had nothing to do with it. Where the barbarian was concerned I had very little pride left, and if I went to him I would beg him to hold me and comfort me – a luxury I couldn't afford to indulge in. He still wanted nothing more than my talent, and I couldn't live with that. If I went to him I would begin wanting to please him again, and that would be the end of me.

I was left alone so long I fell asleep, and when I awakened the evening meal was ready – along with the rest of my punishment. Garth, Len and Gay had joined Tammad in the front of his pavilion, and I was made to serve and apologize to each of Tammad's guests individually – without my *imad* and *caldin*. I was told to begin with Gay and I did so, burning with embarrassment, but I should have been watching her emotions rather than my own. I was expecting nothing more than scorn and humiliation from her, but when I extended her bowl of food and opened my mouth to apologize, she shrank back in fear before a single word was spoken. Her green eyes were wide and terror-filled, her skin was pale, and her mind was on the verge of being paralyzed with fear. It was clear she hadn't come into the pavilion voluntarily, and I did some shrinking back myself from the deep revulsion and horror she projected. Len turned to her with concern on his face, his mind trying to soothe hers, but before he could break through the emotional barrier she had erected she jumped to her feet, looked around wildly, then raced out of the tent.

"I don't think I blame her," Garth said with a sigh as I stared at the tent flap, feeling worse than I had earlier. "She hadn't realized that Terry was a Prime, or she wouldn't have said what she did. She's always been afraid of empaths, but on Central they're neutralized – and very few of them are Primes. Insulting Len didn't bother her, but Terry – who is female as well as being a Prime – is another story. Apparently she doesn't trust other females as far as she can spit."

"I see," Tammad said, and his quiet anger made me cringe. "Though she is mistaken in fearing one who has been taught regret through punishment, words alone will not convince her of her error. Actions are necessary to so convince her, and actions she will have. Continue with your serving, *wenda*."

With his last words I turned to find all their eyes on me, their minds nothing like Gay's had been. Len and Garth, who sat to Tammad's left, were eagerly anticipating my service and apology. Their eyes moved over me in a way that instantly made my entire body burn red with humiliation, a reaction that the barbarian found pleasantly satisfying. I took a tighter grip on the bowl I held and moved toward Len, but he looked up at me and made a gesture.

"If you please, Terry, I prefer having my apologies tendered from knee height," he said, grinning. "They seem more sincere that way."

I immediately looked in outrage toward Tammad, positive he'd never give his support to so barbarous a concept, but the sudden amusement in his mind and eyes clearly showed he liked the idea. Bitterly, I waited for him to add his own gesture to Len's, but the second gesture never came, making the situation even worse. It was Len I was to obey, a man of my own world, a man who was taking great pleasure in ordering a woman around for the first time in his life. Miserably and still with bitterness I lowered myself to my knees, making sure I avoided Len's gaze completely.

"I am ordered to ask you to accept my apologies along with your meal," I said in a monotone, extending the bowl with my eyes on my knees. "I shouldn't have done what I did and I'm sorry."

For a long moment Len didn't say anything, then his hand came to my chin and raised my face toward his.

"If you really are sorry, I think you can make that apology a little more personal," he said quietly, his mind calm with the decision to accept nothing but what satisfied him completely. "Make me believe what you say, Terry, or I won't accept it."

I swallowed hard, shocked to discover that the calm was well on the way to becoming a part of him. There was no more than a vestige left in him of concern over gentlemanly conduct, of worry over being pleasing and acceptable to women. His mind had been encouraged to shape itself to match those around it, and the process was nearly complete.

"Len, please," I whispered, mortified at the way his mind considered me. "You *know* how I…"

"No," he interrupted, slowly shaking his head. "I don't want to know. I want to hear it."

I swallowed again, terribly aware of being naked in front of him, hating the idea of what I had to do.

"Len, I really am sorry," I whispered, wishing he would let my chin go. "I was wrong to try experimenting with people, and I was even more wrong not to care what I did to them. It never occurred to me how foolish and dangerous it was – and that I was forcing you to share that danger. Even if you don't forgive me, I won't stop being sorry."

I had put it all into words, and the look in his light eyes showed he knew it. He nodded slowly, as though in answer to a question I hadn't been allowed to hear, then turned his head toward the barbarian.

"It seems you were right," he said with something of a smile. "Punishment does encourage a woman to think more clearly. Do I have your permission to take a liberty?"

Tammad nodded, curious as to what Len was going to do, but he didn't stay curious long. As soon as Len had the permission he wanted, his hand left my chin to move strongly between my thighs.

"Don't drop that bowl, Terry!" Len ordered sternly as I gasped and straightened, trying to escape the unexpected invasion of his touch. "And settle back down again, just the way you were. I have a story to tell you I don't think you've heard before."

His eyes and mind revealed an anger he hadn't allowed himself to feel earlier, one that forced me to obey totally against my will. I slowly settled down on my heels again, biting my lip against the way he was touching me, feeling as though my hands were chained to the bowl I held. I stared at him wide-eyed, almost afraid of what he would say, miserable that he had allowed himself to change so far that he didn't care whether or not I wanted to be touched like that. *He* wanted to touch me like that, and that was all that was important to him.

"Do you remember Williams Enright?" he asked, watching my eyes as he spoke. "Bill was a good friend of mine before he died, and I spent a lot of time at his house, sharing his hobby. Bill was a history buff, and he got me involved in it too, the tracking down of ancient volumes, buying private diaries of obscure periods, authenticating letters describing historical events that didn't jibe with generally accepted knowledge, that sort of thing. Bill knew I was an empath, of course, but he also knew what it meant to be unawakened, so when he gave me a wrapped-up gift just before I left on one of my assignments I was puzzled, but once I was keyed awake and began reading the gift, I understood completely.

"The gift was a personal diary from the period before Central took charge of all empaths, their raising, training – and conditioning. We all know there was trouble between the general populace and those hell-sent, twisted spawn-of-darkness empaths, but none of us knew any of the details – until I read that diary."

Len paused, as though he wanted to sigh, but the churning in his mind didn't allow it.

"The writer of the diary was an obscure Neighborhood Chairman whose name I forget," he continued. "His Neighborhood wasn't all that far from Tallion City, and the diary was boring squared – until some of his people captured four empaths, two male, two female. The empaths had been trying to reach State House where they'd have a chance to be protected, but they never made it. Somehow – and no reason was given – they were discovered to be empaths, and that was the end of the line for them.

"The diary describes days of argument and disagreement, but only over what was to be done with the scum; no one suggested turning them loose or even turning them over to the Peacemen. The Neighborhood Chairman held out for doing things his way, and finally everyone came around and agreed to go along with it. They took the two male empaths and castrated them, then dug a large hole underneath one of the houses and put them in it, chaining them to rings set in the ground and welding them into the chains. The females were chained in the same way to the opposite wall, and then the male members of the Neighborhood began visiting them. They were raped for hours, days, until they were half-dead from the number of men who took them, until both of them were incontrovertibly pregnant. They were all carefully kept alive until the women's pregnancies were over and they'd delivered their babies – and then those babies were killed, hacked to pieces in their mothers' arms. The next day the men showed up to start the rounds all over again, but they were wasting their time. The women were stark, staring mad, one of them catatonic, and the men had managed to commit suicide by hanging themselves in their chains. The Neighborhood people were disappointed, but all they could do was cut the throats of the women, bury all four bodies, and fondly remember a good job well done. They didn't like either of the dagger's edges, you see, so they sheathed the dagger in their own way."

I knelt rock-still with my eyes closed, sure I was going to be sick. Len had sent his own feelings along with the story, and it was all too much. I had never been so shocked and sickened in my life, which had surely been his purpose.

"The same thing could have happened to you, Terry," he persisted, his voice grating at my ears. "Invaded men do invading of their own, and usually not as gently as I'm doing. You're a Prime; do you think you could stop men from doing that to you?"

I shook my head spasmodically, shuddering, nearly spilling the stew out of the bowl. I'd die if it happened, but I could never stop it.

"I hope you really have learned your lesson," he said, finally taking his hand away from me. "Once you get over the shock of hearing that story, don't let yourself begin believing it could never happen *here* and to you. My share of the pogrom would be the easy share; yours wouldn't."

I felt his hand at the bowl, trying to take it away from me, but I was clutching it so tightly he couldn't do it. My eyes were still closed tight and my breathing was so hard and ragged I was nearly sobbing, feeling even more frightened than I'd felt when a predator of that world had launched itself at me. Len was gently trying to pry my fingers loose when I suddenly let go, leaped to my feet, and ran to Tammad. I didn't realize that his arms were open and waiting for me until I was already huddled against him, held tight to his chest as I shuddered and cried. I hadn't wanted to go to him that way but Len had given me no choice, sending me to Tammad's arms as surely as though he had dragged me there by main force. Satisfaction was all around me, mostly from Tammad but also from Garth and Len, who shouldn't have cared as much. I didn't understand what was happening, but I found myself choking out over and over again, "I'm sorry, I didn't mean it, please, I'm sorry!" and Tammad murmuring back that he knew and it was all right. It wasn't all right, but I was too miserable to argue the point.

When I was finally over most of the hysterics, I was sent to apologize to Garth in the same way I had apologized to Len. I couldn't believe Garth would make me do it after what I'd gone through, but his mind was as firmly determined as Len's had been. I knelt in front of him, sniffled out my apology, then gave him what had by then most probably become ice-cold stew. He took the bowl reluctantly, told me he didn't think much of my apology, then sent me back to Tammad, who looked at me with sober disappointment before asking for his own bowl. I brought the bowl with brand-new tears glistening in my eyes, but none of them seemed interested in my tears any longer. They sat and talked as they ate, ignoring me completely, not even noticing when I crept to the drape and huddled against it and the tent wall. Their minds said they didn't think much of me, and I really couldn't blame them. After what I had done, I didn't think much of me either.

They took their time finishing their meal, Len and Garth asking questions about Rimilia, Tammad answering them. They'd all purposely overlooked the fact that I hadn't eaten anything, and I was very grateful. One word from Tammad and I would have stuffed down whatever they gave me, but it would undoubtedly have come right back up again. I lay curled up in a ball in the corner made by the drape and the wall, glad to be left alone for a while but wishing they would hurry up and finish. I had to talk to Tammad alone, to try explaining to him why I'd done what I had. I really didn't understand it yet myself, but it had to do with being lonely and feeling unwanted and not fitting in anywhere. I didn't know what good explaining would do, especially after the way I'd run to him, but I wanted him to understand why I couldn't stay. He was trying to build a bright, new world, and didn't need anyone around who would bring it crashing down on his head. Even if he didn't particularly care about me, I could no longer deny what I felt for him.

The meal wound down the way all meals do, but just as they were standing up to part company another visitor arrived. I grabbed the drape and held it in front of me as Loddar came in, nodding to Len and Garth as he stopped in front of Tammad.

"*Denday,* you sent for me?" Loddar asked, his mind faintly curious. "Is there a service I might do for you?"

"Indeed," the barbarian smiled, putting a hand on the *l'lenda's* shoulder. "I am told, Loddar, that your ride this day was a most uncomfortable one, due entirely to the efforts of another. You were also told this?"

"Aye, *denday,*" he nodded, a sour annoyance immediately touching him. "Though any man is at times familiar with such feelings, increasing them when there is no opportunity for relief is a low act, fit only for one who has not the courage to attack openly. Had the *wenda* been mine, her punishment would have been more complete."

"Then perhaps you would care to complete her punishment," the barbarian said, turning to look at me and drawing Loddar's eyes with him. "Her use is yours for this darkness, Loddar, in payment for what was done to you."

Loddar's eyes gleamed as his mind filled with satisfaction to come, paying no attention to the way I shook my head and shrank back farther behind the drape. Tammad knew how I hated being given to other *l'lendaa,* but he was doing it anyway just to add to my misery. I could see he was trying to make the lesson as unforgettable as possible, but for me it was already beyond unforgettable. I squirmed the rest of the way behind the drape and crawled away from it, looking for my clothes before remembering they were still in a heap in the front of the pavilion. There was nothing left to do but crawl into my furs and pull them over my head and pretend no one would find me like that; I didn't want to be just sitting there when Loddar came after me.

It didn't take very long for Loddar to do the expected, but not all of what he did came under the same heading. Five minutes after I had buried myself in furs, two hands touched me through them, the mind behind the hands chuckling in amusement. Loddar was just making sure I was in the pile of furs before taking the next step, and that was the part that came as a surprise. Instead of pulling me out of the furs and giving me my clothes, he lifted me, furs and all, and threw me over his shoulder. I howled and beat at his back, knowing he was going to take me out of there with nothing but the furs around me, and that's just what he did. Tammad, Garth and Len grinned as I was carried past them clutching the bottom fur to my chin, but their grins turned to out and out laughter when the top fur was pulled away from me entirely! I lay on one fur over Loddar's broad shoulder, my hands holding to it with a death grip, his left arm circling my knees – but nothing else covering me! I howled even louder at the laughter coming from the people we passed and struggled to get loose, but what chance did I have against a *l'lenda*? And even if I did get loose, where would I go without clothes? Loddar laughed heartily at my frantic yelp when his big hand slowly stroked my bottom, but it was only the beginning of his exacting payment in full. His usual broad stride had become no more than a stroll, to allow everyone in camp to see what he carried, but we reached his *camtah* sooner than I thought we would. When he bent under the verandah to carry me inside I discovered I wasn't ready – not for anything and especially not for paying a debt – but that didn't make much difference on Rimilia. Loddar threw me on top of his own furs, quickly removed his swordbelt and *haddin,* and was down beside me before I had fought my way loose from the covering fur he had stood himself on. As he took me in his arms he let himself remember and acknowledge the raging need I had aroused in him earlier that day, his body and mind bursting into a flame so strong it nearly lit the darkness we lay in. I whimpered and tried to send him my fear, but his lips cut off the whimper and his mind refused to hear the fear. My body still ached from the beating Tammad had given me, but that didn't make any difference to him either. He crushed me to him, running his hands all over me, then put me beneath him to take everything I owed – and then some.

# EIGHT

I was awakened by the touch of hands on my body, but not awakened so far that I could do anything other than react. My mind told me I was a woman and a man wanted me, and my body quickly readied itself to receive him. The man wasn't long in coming to me, and he took such deep possession of my body that I moaned and clutched at his back, ecstasy shooting through me and turning me weak. I moaned again and floated to the heights with him, lost in the clouds and soaring high until he brought us both back to solid ground. It took a minute or two before my thoughts sorted themselves out, and then a series of shocks brought me fully awake.

The man who had just taken me was Loddar, not Tammad as I had somehow believed. I pushed my hair back from my face and half sat up, mortified at the way Loddar was chuckling. He had glanced at and nodded to the third figure in the *camtah*, but I couldn't bring myself to look at him. Tammad must have come in either before or during my use, and the calm approval in his mind was more than I could stand. He had just seen me being used by another man *and the thought didn't bother him!* He was pleased and happy and even his voice showed it.

"I now have no need to ask how the darkness passed for you, Loddar." He chuckled, solid and calm in his crouch. "Is there need to – extend her punishment yet further?"

"Unfortunately no, *denday.*" Loddar laughed, moving around to replace his *haddin* and swordbelt. "It would be pleasant to have it otherwise, but she does not merit further punishment."

"I have brought her *imad* and *caldin*," the barbarian said, tossing a light bundle onto the *camtah* floor. "They were somehow overlooked when you took her from my *camtah.*"

"Indeed," Loddar answered, grinning. "Now that she has proven satisfactory, she may have them. Had she not proven satisfactory, I would have returned her as I took her, though running before me and the switch I carried. Her ownership was pleasant, *denday,* temporary though it was."

"I am pleased to have it so, Loddar," Tammad said, and his mind told me he *was* pleased. "There is now only one further thing required of her, and I have come to see it done properly. Loddar awaits an apology, *wenda,* such as those given to Garth and Lenham. See that your attempt pleases him nearly as much as your use."

I raised my eyes in the dimness to look at him, searching for even the slightest hint that he intended easing up on me, but there was nothing, not even a shadow. I had never before been blamed that totally for something I'd done, most especially not into the day following the incident. I didn't know how long he would go on with it, and the thought was unsettling. Wasn't the fact that I felt badly about it enough? I could see he wasn't going to try to fool me about his feelings any longer, but did he have to make the reversal so complete?

I lowered my eyes again and slowly got to my knees, shuffling forward until I knelt in front of Loddar. The *l'lenda* had his *haddin* and swordbelt on, and he stood with arms folded across his chest as he looked down at me. I stared at his shadowy feet in silence for a moment, struggling with the humiliation of needing to apologize, then plunged ahead to get it over with.

"Loddar, I ask your forgiveness for what was done to you," I said, fighting to fill my voice with regret. "I have shamed myself with my actions more completely than those actions have shamed others. It is my hope that my – my – use recompensed you in some small way for the discomfort you were made to feel."

I kept my eyes on his feet as I ended it, wondering about the calculation I could feel in his thoughts. He hadn't missed the way I'd stumbled over the most humiliating part of the speech, and he didn't let it pass without comment.

"The thought comes to me, *wenda,* that your concern with shame is touched little by the concept of honor, a concept which once seemed understood by you," he said, a musing quality in his voice. "Have you merely strayed from the path, or are you no more than another *wenda* after all?"

I looked up at him quickly, seeing the sober way he stared down at me, feeling my cheeks redden from his criticism. There had once been a time when I'd thought about more than my own comfort and considerations, and Loddar remembered that time, comparing the present with it in an unfavorable light. His comment did make me feel ashamed, but there was nothing I wanted to say in answer to it. I looked down again, lowering my head, feeling my spirits lower to match. He wasn't the first to say he was disappointed in me, and he would hardly be the last.

"Are there to be no further words from you?" Loddar asked, his voice mild. "Perhaps at this time such is best. The future often finds words for us that we would not have used had we spoken earlier. Should you wish her now, *denday,* you may take her. I have no further use for her."

"Very well, Loddar," Tammad said, rising out of his crouch. "Dress yourself and bring your furs, *wenda.* There are things to be folded before my pack *seetar* may be loaded. Do not dawdle, for we must soon be on our way."

I looked up at him sharply, but he had already turned and started through the *camtah* opening, Loddar moving along behind him. Once they were both gone I took my clothes from where Tammad had dropped them and got dressed, then separated my furs from Loddar's. Folding them took only a minute, and I was just about to leave the *camtah* when I hesitated, thought for a minute, then turned back and folded Loddar's furs as well. I didn't really understand why I did it, but somehow it seemed appropriate.

Outside it was just beginning to get light, the warmth of the day to come still cooled by the last of the night breezes. I took my furs and walked over to the pile of things beside Tammad's pack *seetar,* knelt in front of the pile and began folding. Len and Garth were standing a short distance away, but I was able to ignore them until they came to stand right beside me.

"It's going to be another beautiful day," Len observed, taking an extra deep breath of the fresh morning air. "A beautiful day after a beautiful night."

"A beautiful day, yes," Garth agreed with a chuckle. "The night, however, was more incredible than beautiful. Beautiful is too mild a word."

"I know what you mean." Len laughed, and I heard a sound as though he had clapped Garth on the shoulder. "It's amazing what a new outlook will do for a man – not to mention what it does to a woman. I don't know if you could tell about yours, but mine started out feeling superior and impatient, for all the world like a woman of Central."

"As if it were an ordeal she had decided to suffer through just to get finished with," Garth agreed. "I couldn't read her emotions, but her feelings were plain enough in the way she acted. It didn't take long to change her tune, though."

"Only because you probably refused to accept it, just the way I did," Len said. "You couldn't even speak her language, but you still managed to make yourself understood. Women need to be put in their place fast and kept there – isn't that right, Terry?"

They both began chuckling at that, their mood mellow after a night of tension release, but their comments didn't bother me one way or the other. I just kept folding and stacking the things in front of me, approaching the bottom of the pile with satisfying rapidity.

"Don't be angry, Terry," Garth put in, the amusement in his voice softened but still there. "Len wasn't serious about that comment, he was just trying to get a rise out of you. We're not used to seeing you this quiet."

"She *isn't* angry," Len said, his voice considerably more sober than it had been. "She feels – no, she won't let me resolve the mixture. Terry, are you sure you're all right? I don't like seeing you like this."

"I'm fine, thank you," I answered, watching my hands finally reach the bottom with Tammad's sleeping furs. I hesitated the barest fraction of an instant before touching them, but realized immediately that being idiotic wouldn't get the job done. I started them fast, still watching my hands, and added to Len, "I'm sorry if you two are disappointed in me again."

I could sense the disapproval in Garth's mind, but Len jumped in before the Kabra could say anything.

"Terry, don't be stupid!" my brother empath said harshly, pulling me up to face him. "Expecting people to be disappointed in you is a way of giving up! I know the punishment you got wasn't easy for you, but it wasn't bad enough to make you give up!"

His blue eyes were as hard as his mind was angry, but I didn't know what he had to be angry about. I met the hardness in his eyes very briefly, then looked down.

"Expecting disappointment isn't giving up when you can feel that disappointment." I shrugged. "You can't lie to me about how you feel, Len, and neither can anyone else here. Are you trying to deny that that's what you felt?"

"Yesterday, no," he said with a headshake, loosening his grip on my arms but not letting go. "Today's a different story. And while we're discussing yesterday's disappointments, I want to mention the one you thought you felt in Tammad, when he said he no longer got pleasure from your presence. I know you couldn't have read him accurately through that flash of hurt you felt, so let me tell you what I got. He was trying to bring you back down to earth, Terry, to make you sorry for what you did. He wasn't telling the truth about how he felt."

Garth was silent but expectant behind me, Len was silent but attentive in front of me, and all around us people bustled about preparing the day's first meal and getting ready to break camp. A small flight of birds passed across the sky to my left, happy and free in their own special way, visualizing nesting places just left and fat bugs just eaten and endless sky to fly in before darkness fell again. The first rays of the sun were growing longer and more golden, less and less of the red of anger showing in them. I stared at Len's chest, wondering why it looked so much broader without a shirt covering it, and nodded my head.

"It was good of you to tell me that, Len," I said. "Please accept my thanks."

"Damn it, you don't believe me," he growled, tightening his grip again to shake me. "Can't you see I'm not lying to you, Terry? Can't you see I'm telling the truth?"

"Hold it a minute, Len," Garth interrupted, his voice quiet and concerned. "Maybe she – felt – what went on last night in the pavilion and is making the same mistake we made. Tell her what we found out – about all of last night." "I shouldn't have to," Len sighed, his fingers relaxing again. "She isn't as new to this world as we are. Look, Terry, once Loddar took you to his tent last night, the first thing Tammad did was send for Gay King and tell her she was spending the night with him. Garth and I both immediately assumed that he'd gotten rid of you to leave a clear road for Gay, and I suppose he saw it in our faces. He asked us what was bothering us and finally talked us into voicing our nasty suspicions."

"Terry, he laughed," Garth said. "He laughed as if he were really enjoying himself, but when he saw we weren't sharing the fun he tried to explain. And the first thing he said was that we were still looking at things like off-worlders."

"The men of Rimilia do as they please without having to make excuses," Len said, taking his turn. "Gay was given to Tammad as a gift, and according to the way he looks at things, he has the right to use her any time he pleases. The only reason he gave you to Loddar was that you owed Loddar some exercise and he wanted to see you pay up. If you hadn't owed Loddar anything, he might have given you to one of us or even kept you there while he played Gayms, but the choice would have been his."

"And his choice doesn't affect the way be feels about you," Garth said, reaching out to touch my face. "He asked two of his men to let us use their women for a few reasons, but one of them was to show us that using a woman doesn't commit you to anything beyond the general sense of responsibility all men feel toward women. On Alderan a man is supposed to at least pretend be feels true love for any woman he beds; here it isn't necessary."

They stopped their alternating duet and stared down at me, but I couldn't understand what they were so obviously waiting for. Len had been right in thinking I knew what the prevailing attitude on Rimilia was, but I didn't see what difference it made.

"Well?" Len demanded, frowning. "Aren't you going to say anything?"

"What would you like me to say?" I asked, standing still between his hands.

"Anything!" he burst out, frustration burning in his mind. "Argument or agreement, I don't care which, as long as you show me you're still alive inside! You haven't reacted to anything we said one way or the other; I don't like the way your mind doesn't seem to care."

"Just what is it I'm supposed to care about?" I asked, beginning to feel annoyed. "What difference will my caring make when it comes to what happens to me? Will caring get me back to Central or even to the embassy? Will caring change the way these barbarians think? Nothing makes them change, they make everyone else change. If you don't believe it, see if you can find a mirror. I doubt if you'll recognize what you see."

They were both staring at me again, this time with whirling emotions fighting within, the usual prelude to the beginnings of an argument. Before any words could come pouring forth, though, the conversation was broken up by higher authority.

"Terril, come here," Tammad called, and we all turned our heads to see him standing in front of his pavilion with Gay King. Gay was wrapped around his left arm, her body pressed tightly to it, her mind a nauseating mixture of extreme satisfaction and smug accomplishment. She was looking at me with a very superior smile, no more than a faint ghost-shadow left of the fear she had felt. Len and Garth stepped back away from me, freeing me to answer the summons, so I walked over to the cozy pair. Refusing to do so would have been a waste of time.

"Terril, you have an unfinished matter to attend to with the Gaynor King," I was told when I stopped in front of the barbarian. "Do you now see to this matter – in the same manner you have heretofore used."

He stared down at me with his usual calm expression, his mind under the same easy, calm control. I could feel Gay's superior smile spread into a smirk, but I didn't bother looking at her. Tammad had told me I had to apologize to her, from my knees, the same way I'd done with the men, and she knew it. The only thing she didn't know was what my answer would be.

"I won't do it," I told the barbarian, surprising myself almost as much as I surprised him. "I'm sorry if you don't like that answer, but I simply won't do it."

"You have not been given the choice of refusing," he answered, keeping the surprise from showing on his face the way Gay's fury showed on hers. "You will do as you have been bidden to do, and that at once. I have little patience left for you, *wenda*."

"There's always a choice." I shrugged, looking away from those beautiful blue eyes as I ignored the rest of what he'd said. "If you're willing to pay the price for it, the choice is always yours."

"And you have chosen to pay the price," he said, and then his hand came to my face to turn it back to him. His expression was odd, as odd as the emotions trying to crowd past his control. "You will pay the price you have chosen, *wenda,* but the coin will not buy what you seek. Come darkness you will be switched again and afterward made to obey me. Should you obey me sooner the switching will be lighter, yet the punishment will not be avoided. I will be obeyed, *wenda;* in this you have no choice."

He let go of my face and walked away with Gay, her fury somewhat mollified, by the promise he'd made me. I walked away myself, back toward where the *seetarr* were tied, slipping in among the huge animals and immediately shielding my mind. The next minute Len and Garth appeared, just as I knew they would, their heads turning back and forth as they looked for me, Len undoubtedly also probing with his mind. They walked a short distance beyond where I crouched, stood looking around with frustration plain on their faces, then turned and went back in the direction from which they'd come. I stood straight and waited a brief time, cracked the shield carefully to make sure my pursuers were gone, then left the *seetarr* to find a tree to sit beneath. Some of the *seetarr,* Tammad's saddle male in particular, snorted and sent questioning nudges with their minds, but all I did was reassure them automatically then drop them from consideration.

The grass was comfortable under the tree I chose, soft and thick like a fur carpet. I sat down facing away from the camp and leaned back against the tree trunk, wishing they would forget about me long enough to leave without me, knowing the wish was a waste of thought. Even if the barbarian had been willing to give up – and his mind said be wasn't – Len and Garth would refuse to leave until I had been found. They'd fallen into an odd sort of protective mold, one that was an offshoot of the usual care and protection shown toward a Prime. They couldn't – and didn't want to – take me out of the situation I was in, so they'd decided to try talking me into accepting that situation. They were determined to talk me to death if necessary, and I couldn't stand any more of it. They were happy in the places they'd found, but my place wasn't the same.

I put my head back against the tree and closed my eyes, determined not to get all melodramatic and weepy but finding the actuality hard to come by. I refused to think about what would happen that night, but that didn't mean I had nothing else to think about. I kept picturing a man happy over seeing a woman used by another man, a woman who was supposed to be his beloved. I'd been right in not believing what I'd been told, but I didn't want to be right – as if that made any difference. Nothing I wanted mattered on that world, and that was the way it would stay.

"Here, *wenda*, this is for you," a voice came, startling me. My eyes opened to see Loddar crouched beside me, a bowl in his hands, a deep calm in his eyes and mind. "You must eat this quickly, Terril, for it is nearly time to depart. As you will ride with me this day, I have sought you out."

I didn't stare at him for more than a moment, mainly due to the fact that his announcement wasn't terribly surprising. I found I'd been half expecting it, which was also not very surprising. I leaned off the tree and began getting to my feet to go back to the camp, but Loddar's free hand came to my shoulder to push me back down.

"I will first see the contents of this within you," he said, gesturing with the bowl he held. "We will return to the camp when you have finished."

"I do not wish the food," I told him, making no effort to take the bowl. "I thank you for the thought, yet there was no need."

"There is considerable need," he answered, his eyes moving over me critically. "Tammad, like myself, has little liking for *wendaa* with no flesh to their bones. Should you feel the need to refuse once more, I will call the *wendaa* of the camp, who are familiar with the manner in which small, stubborn children are fed. Is this what you wish?"

I hesitated very briefly, knowing he was serious, then shook my head. Having the women feed me would be worse than doing it on my own, even if I did get sick. I took the bowl he held out, used the short-handled wooden scoop inside the bowl, and quickly swallowed down the smooth, sweet, thickened cereal grain he had brought. It didn't make me sick the way I'd thought it would and it did fill something of the hollow inside me, but it wasn't nearly as satisfying as it had been the first time I'd tasted it. When the bowl was empty I held it out toward Loddar, but he just shook his head.

"You may carry your own bowl back to camp," he said, rising out of his crouch. "Once it is cleaned I will pack it away. Hurry now, for it is nearly time to depart."

He strode off back toward the camp with me following, but there was very little camp to go back to. All of the tents had been folded and put on pack *seetar*, and the last odds and ends were being put away. I washed the bowl and scoop I carried in a bucket of water just before the water was dumped out, then gave the still-damp things to Loddar to put away. After that the *l'lenda* disappeared for a minute, then came back leading his saddle *seetar*. It was the work of no more than another few minutes to get the beast saddled, and by then everyone seemed ready to be on their way. Looking around it was difficult believing more than fifty people had camped on the spot, but that was because the clearing had been left as clean as it had been when we'd gotten there. Civilized people know less about caring for the countryside around them, but civilized people are easier to get along with – and understand.

The sun seemed to be waiting for us to be on our way, and once we were it grew brighter and stronger, making the air curl around us in waves of heat. The higher the sun climbed, the warmer it got, soon covering Loddar's body with a sheen of sweat. I rode with my arms wrapped around his waist, my *imad* soaking up the sweat his body continued to produce. Holding onto him like that hadn't been my idea, but my wishes to the contrary hadn't altered anything. I'd begun the ride with my fingers tucked in Loddar's swordbelt, and then Tammad had come to ride beside us for a while, for no apparent reason other than to chat with Loddar. Gay King sat behind him on his *seetar,* her breasts pressed hard into his back, her arms as far around his waist as they would go, her cheek also against the skin of his back, her eyes closed in pleasure. I knew the pleasure she felt was real, but I couldn't decide on the reason for it. It might have stemmed from the way she clung to the barbarian, but it might also have come from her greatly elevated position. Not only was she now riding behind the leader of the party, she also wore two shiny new bronze chains, one on each of her ankles. Tammad had obviously decided to band her before trouble developed, and it was clear she didn't react to banding the way I did. I looked in her direction for no more than seconds after they joined us, then looked away and didn't look back.

As soon as Tammad had ridden off again, I became aware of the annoyance Loddar had been feeling but not reacting to while his *denday* was there. The annoyance grew greater with the next few minutes that passed, and finally Loddar straightened with a soft growl.

"*Wenda,* put your arms about my waist," he ordered, keeping his eyes straight ahead.

"For what reason am I to do this?" I asked, doing no more than responding automatically. I was too depressed to care one way or the other, but the command was unusual enough to seep part way through the lethargy.

"You are to do so for you have been told to do so!" he snapped, sending his annoyance toward me, but then he reconsidered and shook his head. "You are not the cause of my anger, therefore shall I not speak to you so. I will, however, say only this in answer to your question: it is expected that young warriors will at times be foolish where *wendaa* are concerned, yet the amusement felt at such an occurrence fades when the foolishness persists. A man should know which actions bring jealousy and which bring pain. Now, obey me."

I didn't understand a word he had said, but the decision in his mind was too strong to be ignored. I put my arms around him as I'd been ordered to do, eventually finding it easier to rest my cheek on him as well. The next time Tammad came by he didn't stop, and the annoyance in Loddar's mind faded to grim satisfaction.

By the time midday arrived, we were looking for a place to camp. The temperature had risen so high even the *seetarr* were having trouble breathing, and the dust of the road plastered itself to us as if we were mud people. No one seemed terribly surprised by the strange turn of events, but no one liked them, either. The only benefit to the heat had been the fact that Len and Garth had found the strength and resolve to come by no more than once each. I had managed to have my eyes closed each of the times, and

Loddar had been short enough with Len to make his visit a very brief one. Garth, not yet able to speak Loddar's language, didn't even stop, and I felt Loddar's amusement when Garth rode away. He had been saved from having to be short a second time, but he hadn't seemed to mind being short the first time.

When he found a clearing large enough to hold us, we stopped immediately and began setting up camp. Loddar put his *camtah* up in its usual position in relation to Tammad's pavilion, then led his *seetarr* away to be tied in the shade. When he came back he carried a large skin of water, which he put down near his *camtah*'s verandah. I'd just been hanging around, having nothing to do and not really interested in finding anything, but Loddar changed all that.

"I have been without my *wenda* for too long a time," he said, frowning at his *camtah* before turning back to me. "My furs need airing, my *camtah* needs cleaning and washing, my possessions need straightening and polishing and washing. Such things cannot be put off forever."

"Why do you tell me this?" I asked, looking up at him. I would have been happier off in the shade with the *seetarr*, but I couldn't get up the initiative to walk over there.

"I have informed you of this need so that you might see to it," he said, a considerable amount of patience in his voice. "I must attend a gathering called by the *denday*, but I will return at intervals to see what progress you make. Should I be displeased with the progress, you, too, will be displeased. Do you understand?"

"How might I fail to understand?" I shrugged, looking away from him toward the *camtah*. I didn't need to ask what his authority was – on that world his being *l'lenda* was authority for anything.

"Good," he said, a neutral satisfaction in his voice. "What worn *haddinn* of mine you find you are to set to one side, to be washed later at the stream. The stream is a distance from here, therefore will the *wendaa* of the camp be taken there once only, in small groups, to bathe and see to their washing. You will be told when you are to accompany the *l'lendaa* who will guard you."

I nodded to let him know I had his orders recorded in blood, then stood staring at the *camtah* while he walked away. I was tempted to do some walking away myself, but the trouble that that would bring was more than I could handle just then. I wasn't silly enough to think Tammad had forgotten about our date later, and that in itself would be enough to hold my interest for a while. If I had let myself think about it I would have shivered at the prospect, but I wasn't letting myself think about it. Instead, I went to Loddar's *camtah* and got started.

It was almost too hot to move around, but I got a lot done before a *l'lenda* came by to tell me it was my turn at the stream. The only break I'd had was when Loddar had come by shortly after I'd started, not to inspect but to bring me something to eat. The hot spiced meat chunks would have gone better on a cooler day, but I didn't have much choice about eating them. Loddar let me know immediately that the alternative to the chunks was the thick cereal grain I'd eaten that morning, fed to me by a number of women who weren't known for their patience with stubbornness. I ate the chunks under his watchful eye, shared some water with him, then watched him leave, and only at that point discovered that Tammad had been staring at us from the entrance to his pavilion. The barbarian's mind had been filled with its usual calm, but there'd been something behind the calm that I just couldn't get; he was too far away for surface probing. I turned my back on him and continued with the job I'd been given, and the next time I'd looked that way he'd disappeared.

I followed the *l'lenda* through the camp toward the forest, carrying Loddar's dirty laundry in the crook of my left arm. It would have been nice having a change of clothes for myself, but the other *imad* and *caldin* were still in Tammad's pavilion and the pavilion had been put off-limits to all females. Every man in camp but the *wenda*-guards was there, listening raptly to Tammad and Garth. Whatever Garth was saying it was certainly making an impression on his audience, but only after his words of wisdom were translated. The system was unwieldy and annoying to both speaker and audience, and I could see where it wouldn't be long before everyone was forbidden to speak to Garth in Centran. The way things had been going with Garth and Len, it couldn't happen too soon to suit me, but it was a shame Len couldn't somehow be included.

Another half-dozen women and three *l'lendaa* were waiting for us on the outskirts of the camp, and as soon as we got close enough to them they turned and started off into the forest. Most of the women had acknowledged no more than the fact of the presence of someone else, their minds saying they wanted nothing to do with the person who had played around with their emotions the day before. They all knew I'd been punished for what I'd done, but they didn't seem to consider the punishment enough. I didn't know how long it would take them to get over their anger – or even if they would – but it didn't seem to matter. Even if they were willing to accept me I'd never really be one of them, and it would be foolish to believe anything else.

The best that can be said about that walk is that it was cooler in the shade of the forest than it had been in the clearing. We walked until we were out of sight and sound of the camp, but the *l'lendaa* seemed to have no intentions of stopping. One walked up ahead leading us, two walked to either side of our semi-column, and the fourth brought up our rear right behind me. Twice the rearguard had put his hand in my back to hurry me closer to the others, but the gesture hadn't worked until he finally lowered his hand. He laughed softly when I turned my head to glare at him from a safe distance, and deliberately moved his eyes over me from head to toe, staring musingly at the bands on my ankles for a short while before returning his attention to the forest around us. I looked away from him and bit my lip as I walked, positive I knew what was on his mind. The last time I was on that world I'd been five-banded, but now I was down to two. Obviously the *denday* was growing tired of me and would soon unband me entirely, putting me up for sale to any *l'lenda* who wanted me. The rearguard did want me, that was clear enough in his mind, and I suppose I should have been pleased. There were a number of men on that world who wanted me for no other reasons than the ones their eyes gave them, but they were the wrong men.

After another couple of minutes one of the female figures up ahead glanced back, looked at the other women in front of her, then stopped where she was to give me a chance to catch up. She'd also been walking alone, and I didn't understand why until I realized she was the blond tripper from the transport who had been appropriated by the *l'lenda* Hannas. She wore a light blue *imad* and dark blue *caldin,* one of the reasons I hadn't recognized her. If I'd looked at her mind I would have known her at once, but I was too involved with my own thoughts to be distracted by the minds of others. She started walking again as soon as I reached her, and looked at me with serious brown eyes.

"Are you okay?" she asked in a low voice, as if afraid someone might overhear the question. "I heard about most of what happened to you, and you don't look so good."

I thought about the dirty, sweat-stained clothing I wore, the way my hair hung in knotted, greasy strands, the smears that must have been on my face, and smiled faintly.

"Couldn't be better," I answered, making sure the dryness stayed out of my tone. "How have you been doing?"

"I never believed anything could be this good." she answered, her mind verifying the truth of the statement. I looked at her quickly anyway, as though she might be joking after all, and she blushed and looked down at the *haddinn* she was carrying. "Okay, okay, I know you don't look at it that way, but you never lived my kind of life. Hannas is more man than I ever thought I'd find, let alone get for my own, and whatever he wants is fine by me. I'll do it his way as long as he lets me."

"In other words you love him," I said, going back to watching the forest we moved through. "If my good wishes mean anything to you, you have them."

"Why do you sound so dead inside?" she demanded, and I could feel her looking at my face. "Hannas said Tammad really gave it to you for what you did, but that was because he really cares for you and wouldn't let anybody else do it. Don't it matter to you that he did it because he cares?"

My vision of the forest grew momentarily blurry, but I blinked the blur away.

"Don't you think you'd be doing yourself more good by walking with the other women?" I asked without turning to look at her. "They're not very fond of me right now, and you could get the same treatment simply because they saw you talking to me."

"I do my own deciding on who I talk to," she snorted, totally unworried. "Besides, I don't think they're that kind. I can't say more than four words they understand, but they all took turns coming over with a hello and a helping hand. Sure they're mad at you now, but they'll get over it. Probably a lot sooner than you will. Why didn't you answer what I asked?"

"About his caring?" I sighed, realizing there was no decent way out of the conversation. "Don't you think I'd know if a man really cared about me? Caring is hard to hide even from a non-empath."

"What makes you think he don't?" she asked. "Hannas says everybody knows how much he wants you, that's why he went after you."

I opened my mouth to say something else, but my voice was gone, not even a whisper left. My throat burned as if it were on fire, and the tears had started with no warning at all. I tried to push it all away, to keep the grief from shattering me, but the truth was I already had been shattered. I pushed Loddar's dirty *haddinn* up to my mouth to keep the tortured sounds from coming out, and the girl beside me quickly put her arm around my shoulders.

"Damn it, you're not even letting yourself cry!" she raged, furious for no apparent reason. "I used to do that too, to keep it from hurting more than I could stand, but it's wrong! In a place like this you shouldn't have to do that!"

The pain was so great I slipped away from her arm and fell to my knees, sobbing into the *haddinn*. My mind was all feeling and no thought, a small girl lost in the wilderness alone, finally out of the forced courage that had kept her dry-eyed till then. She was so badly lost that no one in the entire universe would ever find her, not even if she continued to live out a very long life. I was unaware of everything around me until many minds came close, their voices soothing, their hands comforting. One set of hands pulled the *haddinn* away from me and another set pulled me to a sympathetic breast, giving me a sheltered place to cry. The voices were speaking the language of Rimilia, and I finally understood that it was the other women of the group, the ones who had ignored me, the ones who had been so angry. For obvious reasons, that fact made me cry harder.

Surprisingly enough, the crying didn't last very long. I suppose I was more than tired of feeling sorry for myself, and I was tired in other ways, too. Every one of those women was genuinely willing to help if she could, and I let them feel my gratitude before I assured them I was all right. There was nothing anyone else could do for me, just what I could do for myself. The only problem I had just then was in figuring out what that was going to be.

We continued on through the forest, but our semi-column had become a tight knot, all of it centering around me. The blond-haired tripper – renamed Findra by Hannas from whatever her name had been originally – took turns with the Rimilian women in giving me advice. I was saved from having to discuss the advice by the need to translate, one way or the other, everything that was said. Findra wanted to know if I intended staying on Rimilia – if I did, then I'd have to do what she did. The Rimilian women laughed at that and asked if the *denday* intended keeping me on Rimilia. If he did, then I'd have to do what the rest of them did. They argued back and forth, not realizing they were all saying the same thing, but the four *l'lendaa* listening in realized it. The men grinned to themselves after exchanging knowing glances, then let the women continue counseling me. I was being told what the men themselves would have told me, so there was no need to interfere.

I found out almost immediately that the entire camp knew I about my disagreement with Tammad that morning. They all agreed I'd been an idiot for defying him, but their suggestions for repairing the damage varied from woman to woman. None of them doubted that Tammad would do as he'd said he would, and all of the suggestions were designed to either minimize the damage or make sure the offense wasn't repeated. It didn't surprise me that none of them, Findra included, asked if I'd had a reason for refusing to obey. Reasons didn't matter on that world, only obedience did, and I'd failed to keep that basic rule clearly in mind. They made sure I knew exactly what would happen to me if I failed again.

We moved on through the forest as we talked, the four *l'lendaa* surrounding us, the heat of midafternoon reaching us even under the deep green of the forest shade. Our noise had chased most of the usual forest dwellers away from our area, leaving only the minds of the humans to chatter and echo along our trail. We strolled along, more involved with talking than walking, the *l'lendaa* letting us do pretty much as we pleased. We were the last group going to the stream that afternoon, and it was still early enough to let us take our time.

The skies fell in with no warning whatsoever. One minute everything was usual and unexciting, possibly even dull; the next minute the *l'lendaa* ahead of us were falling to the ground, arrows in their backs or throats or chests, blood gouting and covering the ground, bodies already lifeless, minds knowing only shocked pain before blackness. We turned in the sudden, dead, unnatural silence, turned as if in a dream, seeing the fourth body on the ground some distance behind us. The dream bubble burst then with the first scream, shattering the silence and calm, touching the outer edge of the shock. More screams followed, sending us running in all directions, running from the blood and death and toward some uncertain safety. I stumbled back and to one side, reaching the bushes and trying to hide in them, choking on the panic from the other female minds around me. I needed to be safe, desperately needed to be safe, but the grin on the face of the giant man who suddenly appeared in front of me said it wasn't to be. His skin was dyed orange from head to foot, white paint marking the orange here and there, his mind numbed with the drug all savages used. He screamed a high-pitched indication of his delight, the sound freezing me with terror, then he moved forward quickly to seize me. The feel of his hands on my arms made me struggle automatically, causing him to hit me hard across the face, sending me to the ground at his feet. I wasn't supposed to struggle, his mind said, but he was too numbed by the drug to be annoyed. He merely crouched down, stuffed a rag in my mouth, then tied the rag in place with a strip of wet cloth. I raised my hand toward the gag, hoping to pull it away, and then the thick, sweet fumes from the wet strip of cloth reached me. My head whirled, making me feel sick and very light and very weak. I folded back down to the ground, sure I would float away, but I never knew if I did. The savage laughed, a half-insane laugh, and then the world melted away to black.

## NINE

The next space of time was sporadically blurred, punctuated with bars of black and hazed with nightmare. I was briefly aware of being carried somewhere over someone's shoulder, then of trying to cry out when my wrists were tied painfully behind me, then of being held face down across someone's saddle. The saddle was moving hard and frantically, as if an animal sped beneath it, but the movement had no meaning, only the extreme discomfort. The thought of protest crossed my mind, but then movement, thought and consciousness were gone again.

The next noticeable thing was motionlessness, but not an empty one. Water poured on me in an endless stream, soaking my hair and body, running into my ears and eyes. Only my mouth was protected from it by the gag – even my back and arms were wet from the ground I lay on. I didn't know why I lay bound and gagged on the ground in the pouring rain, and I didn't know how I had gotten there; all I knew was how stiff and achy my body felt. I was tired and I hurt and I didn't feel well and I was very thirsty. There was water all around me, but I couldn't get any of it into my mouth. I tossed my head in the stream of mud I lay in, burning for the water, and then there were hands at the gag and it was pulled away, the cloth as well as the wadding in my mouth. My eyes closed as the water poured into my mouth instead, taking away the taste of the gag and the dryness it had left. I coughed once or twice, nearly choking, then finally stopped drinking, but the water continued to pour over my face and body.

My thoughts were incomplete and disjointed, and I don't know how long it took before the idea came that I ought to try to get out of the rain. My wrists were still tied tightly behind my back, but I ought to be able to get to my feet even so. I moved my head and tried to move my feet – and only then discovered that my feet were also tied, but not to each other. My right ankle was tied to the ankle of the woman lying on my right, my left ankle to the woman on my left, our ankle bands pushed high to allow the leather access to our ankles. I tried to pull against the leather, to see how tight it was, but movement was impossible. The women beside me were barely conscious, cooperative movement entirely beyond them. I didn't have all that much control over myself yet, but they were even worse off than I was.

Thought became distant again then, as though the residue of some powerful drug were reasserting itself, and when the blurriness abruptly gave way to clarity again, something had been added. A large form loomed over the woman to my left, crouched above her, doing something to her. My left leg had been forced to bend when her right had been raised, and her semi-conscious moans of pain suddenly told me what was being done to her. Fear flashed through me and turned my bowels weak, but that didn't stop the figures that appeared silently out of the dark and rain from coming closer. One of them crouched over the woman on my right, but I had no time to notice what was done to her. Another one was right above me, throwing my sodden *caldin* back to my waist, reaching out with two hands to rip my *imad* open, grasping my thighs to pull me closer. The fear was a living thing, eating at me from the inside, forcing mewling sounds out of my throat and then a cry of pain when I was entered. A vague sense of satisfaction touched the man who had me, and his hands came to my breasts to squeeze hard as his hips pounded against me. Again a cry of pain was forced out of me and again I felt his pleasure, and the realization of what was happening made my blood run cold. The savages could feel very little through the drug they numbed themselves with, needing pain and fear even to feel pleasure from sex. They would hurt us all to find their release, and there was nothing we could do about it.

The ordeal went on for a ghastly long time, the only respite coming from drug-induced blank periods. I never knew how many of them there were, but there had to be more than twice the number of women. When it was finally over and we were left to lie alone in the mud and rain, the pain in my body was more than enough to make me cry. Others cried along with me, sending their misery and pain and shame to me with their sobs, but the reception of their emotions was as blurred as my thinking. Among everything that had happened, that was the only blessing.

At daybreak we were roused from exhausted sleep when our ankles were untied, and then the cloth wadding and wetted strips were brought again. It was a matter of minutes before the drug had me again, blotting out the sight of orange men moving beneath darkly threatening skies. Flashes of pelting rain came a few times along with knowledge of being held face down in front of a rider, and then the darkness was the darkness of night again, and the drug-soaked rags had again been removed. We went through the same hell a second time, and the second time hurt more than the first. I felt myself moaning even when there were no hands squeezing pain into my flesh, even when there was nothing battering against my body, even while I choked and coughed in the rain. Each movement was pain without the drug, pain and intense fear, and then the rain was gone and the sun grew very bright, and the heat increased even beyond what it had been before the rain. This went on for a very long timeless period, and then I awoke to find myself being carried away from the orange men, the gag gone, my clothes hanging in filthy strips, my wrists still bound behind me. The man who carried me wore long robes, the sun was still very bright, and I could barely remember how to breathe. I tried to move, to say something, but the return of the darkness made the entire effort futile.

*TEN*

Dimly aware of some sense of movement, but movement less rapid than it had been, I awoke to the taste of meat broth in my mouth, coughed out some of it, then swallowed the rest. It was warm and tasty, but the presence of it in my stomach sent pains shooting through me, as though I hadn't eaten anything in days. I moaned and gulped at the next swallow fed to me, but whoever was doing the feeding refused to be rushed. The sips came as slowly as the return of full consciousness, making it a long time before I lost most of the hollow feeling and was able to open my eyes and look around.

I was being fed by a woman who held me up with one arm, her free hand holding a wooden bowl which came to my lips only slowly and deliberately. Her thoughts showed her to be undeniably female, but all I could see of the rest of her was her eyes and hands. Her body was covered by a long, full, light-brown robe, the hood of which also covered her hair. Most of her face was hidden by a thick cloth veil, leaving only her blue eyes and tanned forehead visible. Across her forehead a section of bronze chain could be seen, but whether it was secured to either side of her hood or circled her head entirely was impossible to tell. She made soothing, comforting noises at me while I looked at her, then finally let me finish the meat soup. With the soup gone she let me go, rose gracefully to her feet, and walked away. Sitting up alone was something of an effort, but it did let me look around more completely at where I was.

Above and around me was the striped material of a large square tent, holding off the glare of the very bright sun which could be seen through the missing front wall. I sat on hot, clean white sand, more of which could be seen outside, surrounding a relatively small area of grass and trees and cool-looking blue water. It was hot in the tent, hot enough to make me sweat, and I wasn't the only one. Five of the women who had been captured with me also sat or lay sweating on the sand, their hair and bodies filthy and mud-caked, their clothing torn and stained, their flesh marked with bruises. I looked down at myself and saw the same that I saw on them, then looked up again to join in the exchange of strengthless, hopeless glances. We were free of the orange-painted savages, but we were still a long way from anything that might be considered home.

A few minutes later six men entered, large, broad men wearing black *haddinn* on their tanned bodies. They wore nothing in the way of swordbelts or daggers, and around their necks gleamed bright bronze chains. I found myself shrinking back from the one who came to stand over me, and his mind was contemptuous as he crouched down and began pulling away the shreds of what clothing was left to me. My sounds of protest were joined by similar sounds coming from the other women, but none of the men paid any attention to them. We were. all stripped naked in a matter of minutes, then each of us was lifted in the arms of a man and carried outside.

The sun was a blazing hot disc in the sky, too bright by far to be looked at directly. The man carrying me moved across the sand and away from the open tent, bearing left toward a pool of water separated from the main body of water, the others walking beside or behind us. It seemed that we were going to be allowed to bathe, and the pleasure brought by that prospect nearly drowned out the extreme embarrassment I felt over being carried around naked. There seemed to be few men around aside from those who carried us, but I still disliked the idea of being displayed so openly.

When we reached the pool of water I expected to be put down on the bank, but the expected failed to occur. The man carrying me stepped down and waded into the water, moving forward until the water was knee-deep on him. Only then did he put me down, and not to let me begin bathing. He held me by the arms and dunked me completely under the water, kept me under for a moment, then pulled me erect again. The water was only thigh deep when I stood up, but thigh deep is still deep enough to get you good and wet. I stood sputtering and wiping cool, life-giving water out of my eyes, and therefore failed to see where the small oblong of sandy, soapy material came from. I suspect it came from the man's *haddin,* but the first I knew of it was the touch of it and his hand against my skin. I jumped and tried to move away, mortified that I was being bathed by someone else – and a man at that – but evasion wasn't possible. Big fingers clamped around my arm, holding me where I was wanted, and the bathing proceeded according to the wishes of the man with the soap. His mind was still contemptuous, and he took considerable pleasure from the embarrassment he gave me.

By the time the baths were over, none of us were even hoping any longer that we'd been "saved" from the savages. Exactly what our positions were we didn't yet know, but honored guests are rarely bathed all over by strange men, up to and including places usually considered intimate. I'd blushed and cried out, and tried to protect myself, but nothing had kept the big man in the black *haddin* from doing exactly as he pleased. I wasn't the only one burning in furious embarrassment, but the other women kept their consternation to themselves, not even struggling with the men who bathed them. The one odd note in the entire thing was the complete lack of interest in all six of the men. They could have been bathing *seetarr* for all they seemed to care, but I didn't have much time to dwell on the oddity. Two robed, veiled women carrying thick bundles came to stand on the bank of the pond, and their amusement at what was being done to us was too obvious to ignore.

When I was finally released I waded to the bank, cleaner in body but not happier in mind. The two robed women had spread cloths on the bank, and it was to these cloths that we were directed. We were handed other cloths to dry our hair with, and it quickly became apparent why we didn't need to dry our bodies. Within minutes the sun itself had dried us, and was already beginning to take the dampness from our hair. We were given wooden combs to see to the tangles, then we were given dark brown robes and leather sandals, all without a word being spoken. The silence bothered me, but I didn't break it; the minds of the women told me they would not have answered even if spoken to. A wall held their emotions tightly in place, and they worked quickly to get the job over and done with.

When we all wore sandals and robes, one of the veiled women led us toward a large tent while the other stayed behind to gather up the wet, used cloths. The men had disappeared while we were drying ourselves, but they hadn't gone in the same direction in which we were being led. The tent we were taken to was blue and white striped, square and high, and divided inside into many small rooms. The entrance curtain parted to show us a small area entirely hung about with white silk, the same covering the ground, but we weren't allowed immediate entrance. Our sandals had to be taken off and left beside the entrance, then we were able to follow our guide to the right, deeper into the tent. Findra, the blond tripper, walked close beside me, her mind upset and unhappy, but she hadn't said any more than the rest of us had.

Our final destination was a room of white silk somewhere in the heart of the tent. Our guide led us into it and waved her hand, indicating that we were to stand where we were. She herself stood to one side away from us, her mind held purposely blank, her body field relaxed but ready. I didn't know what she was ready for, and I was sure I didn't want to find out. The four Rimilian women with me knew more than I did about what was going on, and the misery in their minds told a good deal of the story. They were trying to hold back on their fear, but it increased in each of them despite everything they could do.

The mystery was solved for me in a shorter time than I had expected. We had been in the room for no more than ten or fifteen minutes, nervous but enjoying the strangely cooler temperature, when a man suddenly appeared from behind one of the silk hangings. He wore white robes over his massive frame, a white veil over his features, and sandals on his feet. Around his waist was a swordbelt, from which hung a sword to the left and a long, terrible-looking dagger to the right, and his mind reacted very little when he looked at us. The veiled woman immediately knelt when she saw him, putting her fists to her forehead as she bowed. The newcomer ignored the gesture as he looked at us, then slowly came forward to the woman nearest him. He crouched in front of her and removed her ankle bands, then stood straight and moved to the next woman in line. In another five minutes the bands – of whatever number – were gone from all of us, and the man moved back to a place where he could look us over again.

"Remove the robes," he suddenly ordered, his voice flat and authoritative. My first thought was to refuse and then demand release, but the waves of fear coming from the other women almost knocked me over. This was not a man to refuse or argue with, their minds said, and they made me believe it as much as they did. I fumbled and pulled at the robe I wore, aware that Findra was doing just as the rest of us were even though she hadn't understood the command. In seconds we were as bare as we'd been in the bath, but the man in front of us wasn't as unaffected as the men in black *haddinn* had been. He examined each of us in turn with his blue eyes, his mind and body humming with approval and pleasure, his amusement clear when he saw the blush covering me. Maybe it was the blush, but his eyes rested on me longer than they did on any of the others, his interest evident and totally unconcealed. I know I blushed deeper then, increasing his amusement, and was almost relieved when he spoke again.

"Kneel before me," he commanded, expecting and getting instant obedience. We knelt on the white silk floor and looked up at him, our fear so strong it must have blazed from our eyes. "It is good you obey so promptly," he said, nodding his head as he looked from one to the other of us. "You are now *bedinn* of our tribe, bound to obey us in all things. Should we feel you do not obey promptly and properly, we will see you taught the lesson of failure. All men here are *hizah* to you, save for those who wear the mark of *bedin* themselves. You will be taught the proper manner by those who have been *bedin* longer than you. Learn quickly, for their lessons are not as sharp as those from *hizahh*. *Bedin*, attend me."

He had gestured toward the robed and veiled woman who knelt to one side, and she quickly stripped off the robe, rose to her feet, and hurried to kneel again in front of the man who had called her. She was naked under the robe she had worn, her veil secured to her long blond hair, the slender bronze chain previously visible only across her forehead now clearly banding her brow and the entire top of her head. Once she was on her knees, she bent forward with her forehead to the silken floor, her arms place gracefully behind her and crossed at the wrists, her mind quivering with fear even as she fought to relax her body. The man stared down at her a moment, vaguely dissatisfied with something, then abruptly pulled a leather string from his swordbelt and crouched to tie her wrists behind her. I thought for a minute that the tying was some sort of ritual, not actually meant to hold her, but her mind winced at the tightness of her bonds, proving they were no mere frill or technicality. When she was bound tight she raised her head from the floor, kissed the man's hand and whispered, *"Hizah,* I beg to be allowed the honor of serving you."

The man straightened and gestured her erect without answering her, then looked at us again.

"You will remain here till another comes to guide you," he said, then turned and left with the veiled woman close on his heels. As soon as the curtain had settled, we were as completely alone as it's possible to be in the midst of a campful of strangers.

"What did he say?" Findra whispered almost immediately, her voice shaky. "Where are we and what's going to happen to us?"

I shrugged and translated what the man had said, ending with, *"Hizah* translates roughly as, 'Lord of one's every breath' or 'Shaper of one's destiny.' '*Bedin*' means nothing less than slave, and that's what's been done to us. We've been made their slaves."

Findra's mind tried to reject the concept, but she was a good deal more practical than that. She settled back on her heels and closed her eyes, then searched inside herself for acceptance of the situation. She, like the other four women with us, was trying to adjust to something she'd never considered having to adjust to, something that came as a considerable shock. I could feel the shock they felt, that and their, attempts at adjustment, but couldn't reach the necessary level for adjustment in my own mind. I wrapped my arms around myself, hearing again how glibly I'd spoken of being made a slave; the words were right and the tone was proper, but the requisite acceptance to go along with them just wasn't where it should be.

Some of the women were whispering to one another, so when I detected the approach of a mind I gestured them to silence. A veiled woman slipped into the room, possibly the same one we'd left at the pool, but it was almost impossible to tell. Her mind read just the same as the mind of the woman who had followed the man out, except for the lack of active fear. Our robes were gestured to, showing that we were to bring them with us, and then we were hurried out of the tent.

After putting on our sandals and slipping into our robes, we followed our new guide to a smaller, plainer tent close to the center of the camp. A brown cloth covered the entrance of this tent, and after taking off our sandals again we followed our new guide inside. Behind the hanging was a single-room tent, the cloth of the walls and floor a plain brown. Women sat or lay all over the tent, one or two sleeping, the rest either tending to chores like sewing or polishing, or seeing to their own bodies. They all tensed when we entered – even the sleepers stirring in sudden discomfort – but seeing who we were put them at ease again. They were all blond, veiled and completely naked, and all wore small-linked bronze bands around their heads.

"Fold your robes and lay them there," our guide said, pointing to a neat pile of robes of various browns before slipping out of her own robe. "When you leave this tent, you are to wear robes of the darkest brown, for you have not yet been favored. When you have finished, I will instruct you further."

"Why do they all wear veils and nothing of clothing?" I asked, taking off my robe reluctantly. I didn't like the idea of sitting or walking around in nothing at all, but it seemed to be the prevailing style there.

"It is the wish of our *hizahh*," the woman answered, watching the robe-folding with a critical eye. "Lay the robes gently but firmly, so that they will neither crease nor slide from the others. Should any portion of our tent be found in disarray, we will all face the lesson."

Her tone was so ominous I wouldn't have had to pass on the emotions behind it even if I'd intended to. After I translated for Findra we all took care finishing up with the robes, then followed the woman to a corner of the tent where we could sit down.

"At darkness, all *hizahh* in the camp will see you veiled and banded," the woman said, looking around at us. "These things you must remember above all others: no word may be spoken in the presence of *hizahh*, save at their command, and all *bedinn* must kneel immediately in the presence of *hizahh*. Should either of these rules be broken, you will immediately face the lesson for failure."

"What does such a lesson consist of?" one of the women asked, her voice hesitant but the intention to know firm in her mind. We *had* to know, even if we didn't want to.

"The girl who fails is whipped," the woman whispered. "The pain is so great one is unable to breathe beneath it, the lash so cruel one's flesh is cut to nothing by it. And yet, this is not the greatest fear of the lesson. The greatest fear is that one may be whipped many times and sent to the *bedin* tent to heal – or one may be whipped to death upon the instant. It is impossible for one to know beforehand, for all proceeds at the whim of the *hizah*. We are nothing, and easily replaced. You yourselves, all of you, cost far less than a simple pack *seetar*, and will not be treated as well as the beast save you are chosen to bear young to the *hizahh*. To be chosen so is highly unlikely, for this tribe boasts many child-bearers born to it, none of whom have been *bedin*. They are kept far from the eyes of all, and never is a *bedin* allowed in their presence. Our service is solely for the use of *hizahh*, our lives theirs to direct forever."

A shudder passed through me at the finality of that statement, a shudder that wasn't felt by myself alone. But the present situation was something I couldn't seem to come to terms with under any circumstances, real or not, caring or not. I just wanted to turn away and ignore it all, all the while telling myself that doing that couldn't really cause my death. My world had never been that way, and I didn't want it to be that way now.

"And – what of the last of us, the girl Alsim," one of the women asked, her mind sick with fear over what answer she would get. "I have not seen her since we awoke, and none has mentioned her. Has she also been made – *bedin* – or has she somehow escaped our lot?"

"She – remained with the savages," the woman answered heavily, her eyes filled with pity above her veil. "The *hizahh* attempted to buy her as well, yet the savages wished to retain one female for their own use. Her suffering will not continue overlong, sister, for the savages do not care for the captives they take. She will soon die from lack of food and the continued use of the stupor drug, therefore must you take heart and rejoice in her coming freedom."

"Freedom," the woman sobbed, then buried her face in her hands. She felt the loss of one very close, more than a friend, most likely a blood relative. The women nearest her put their arms around her shoulders, attempting to soothe and comfort, but the woman was crying harder and harder, rapidly reaching the point of hysteria. I caught a flash of fear from the veiled woman as she glanced at the tent entrance just before adding her own whispered comments of warning; apparently the *hizahh* disliked having undue noise coming from the *bedin* tent. The others immediately began urging the crying woman to calm herself, but some grief transcends personal danger. A long set of memory-emotions rolled across the woman's mind, telling me more clearly than words that the missing girl was the woman's daughter, and my wavering uncertainty firmed itself into immediate resolve. The woman couldn't help herself, but I could help her.

When I knelt in front of the crying woman and took her face in my hands, the women to either side of her drew somewhat away in startlement, undecided as to whether or not to interfere in whatever I was going to do. I ignored the other women and gave my complete attention to the one in front of me, the one who so keenly felt the torment her daughter would be forced to endure before death brought her freedom from it. I gently blended in and shared the loss with her, letting the grief tear at me the way it tore at her, tasting the sourness of helplessness with her. The woman's sobs stopped abruptly as her eyes opened wide, her mind fearful before the peace touched her. The pain and loss were still there – as they should be – but the peace softened the colors of her grief until they were brown and gray with age – and bearable. Distance makes all pain more bearable, but attaining that distance is pain in itself. I'd shortened the distance for her and eased the pain, but not before sharing the taste of it to show her I understood. She understood too, and her arms went around my neck as she cried softly against me, gratitude filling her not so much for the peace I'd given her, as for the way in which I'd shared her grief.

Our guide and teacher didn't understand what had gone on between the crying woman and myself, but she didn't much care, either. She waited impatiently for the crying to ease off, then continued with our lessons. I got the impression that she was in danger of being blamed for anything we newcomers did wrong, and I later discovered I wasn't far wrong. It wasn't usual for anyone but the *bedin* concerned to be blamed for any one incident, but the thought could occur to a *hizah* and thereafter it would become usual. We were taught how to kneel, how to bow with our fists pressed to our foreheads, how to put our wrists behind us for binding when a *hizah* indicated desire for us, and how to offer ourselves in the most acceptable manner. It was a very depressing time, most especially when I remembered the instruction I'd once been given by Tammad on the very same subject. He'd been fooling around at the time and enjoying himself with a joke at my expense, but there was no fooling around or joking involved that time. If we didn't learn how to do everything to the best of our ability, our lives might not continue on very long. One of the women made the mistake of asking our teacher's name, and the answer made us all even more depressed. Our teacher had no name, nor did any of the other women who were *bedinn*. They were addressed only as *bedin,* forbidden to address each other by any other name, forbidden even to think of themselves in any other manner. They wore veils at all times to emphasize this lack of individuality, and the *hizahh* bothered telling them apart only for purposes of punishment. It made no difference to a *hizah* which *bedin* served him, as long as he was satisfied in all particulars. I was given to understand that things might be more difficult for me as I was the only dark-haired female among them, and was told I'd be wise to learn the lessons better than anyone else – just to be on the safe side. I was sure the woman was right – but I didn't know if I could do it.

When we'd learned our lessons well enough to partially satisfy our teacher, we were given something to eat. The something was no more than the thick cereal-grain

Loddar had made me eat, but we were instructed to offer our thanks as though we'd been served a feast. After having been starved by the savages for what must have been days, we were really in no shape to eat anything more substantial, but that wasn't why we didn't share the thick meat stew the other women ate. We would be kept on the cereal until the *hizahh* directed otherwise, or forever if they didn't direct otherwise. None of the women there would dare oppose the men in the least matter, and the subject of what we ate was far from least. Blue eyes watched us from above veils with very little sympathy evident; they'd been through the same themselves and they'd survived. Whether or not we did the same was up to us.

We were drilled again after we cleaned up from our meal, then we were allowed to rest. The tent wasn't as hot as the sun outside, but it was still hot enough to drain away the strength we'd managed to recapture. We sat down in one corner of the tent, away from the other women who occupied it, and it wasn't until five or ten minutes had passed that I noticed how quiet it was. None of the women in the tent spoke to one another unless it was necessary, and then they said their piece as quickly and softly as possible. Their minds were like so many closed doors, locked tight to keep themselves safe within. They didn't dare live without permission, their life-breath itself only a gift from others. It was a horrible way to exist, a matter of living only in the strictest sense of the word. Was life itself so precious that it was worth all that?

"How long do you think it'll be before we're found?" Findra whispered from the place she'd chosen beside me. "If that girl told you you'd have trouble because of your dark hair, I'll probably have the same trouble because of my dark eyes. And what happens if one of them talks to me when you're not there to translate? If they take too long finding us, I might not be around anymore."

I turned my head to look at her thin, pretty face, seeing the true depth of her anxiety no place but in her mind. Inwardly she was crying for Hannas, begging him to hurry, missing him desperately and greatly fearful in his absence. Her feelings weren't something she was willing to admit out loud, but that didn't mean she wasn't experiencing them.

"You don't think they will find us," she said, her large brown eyes examining my face. "If they don't find us we're as good as dead, but you won't even let yourself hope. Do you think you're better off here?"

"The term 'better off' doesn't apply anywhere on this planet," I answered, looking away from her again. "And you're right – I don't think they have the faintest chance of finding us. Do you remember all that rain while the savages had us? And how long was it before they even knew we were gone? And how far did we come across all that sand? They'd have to use magic to find us – or very sophisticated technology – and they don't have either. Just what is it that you see worth hoping for?"

"There's always something worth hoping for," she muttered, turning completely away from me. "They're not like Centran or Alderanean men, and I'm betting they find us. The hard part'll be holding on until they do. Maybe if you look hard enough, you'll also find something to hold onto."

She lay down on her side and began clearing her mind for sleep, confident that if she waited long enough she'd be saved. I followed her example about lying down, but didn't bother with the search she'd suggested. The only rescue I could find interest in hoping for was rescue by my own people, and that was even more unlikely than being found by Tammad's group. I didn't know what I would do in that captivity, but hoping for rescue wouldn't be part of it.

Surprisingly enough, we were allowed to sleep undisturbed for quite some time before quiet bustle awoke us. The veiled women were moving around the tent lighting candles, straightening up, and preparing another meal. We were given a pot, water, dried cereal grain and a cooking stand – a tripod affair with fire-ledge and pot-ring raised two feet from the floor – and told to prepare our own meal. After the meal we all helped in the clean-up, then stood by while our teacher inspected our efforts. She passed them without finding fault, but didn't miss the opportunity to tell us that the men might not feel the same if they inspected. If our efforts were found to be unsatisfactory, the only thing we could do would be to suffer our punishment and swear to do better next time.

Darkness had fallen by the time we were sent for by the *hizahh*. We were the only ones left in the tent when the two big men in black *haddinn* and bronze neck chains entered and motioned to us to follow them, and one of the women was so nervous she almost knelt and bowed to the men before realizing her mistake. We'd been told these unveiled men were *bedinn* too, male slaves who were used to do the jobs women weren't strong enough to do. The men were all members of other tribes who had been found guilty of serious crimes. When a tribe decreed a man among them guilty, they stripped the man of his veil and possessions, castrated him, then sold him to another tribe as a slave. That explained their strange lack of interest in us when they'd bathed us; they were no longer capable of feeling interest. If I'd noticed that their bronze neck-chains had been permanently closed around their necks with tools, I might have understood what they were a good deal sooner.

After putting on brown robes and stopping for our sandals, we were led back to the tent we'd been in earlier that day. The air outside was almost cold, so cold we shivered in our robes until we were inside again. The darkness outside had been lit by torches, but the tents were lit by slim candles standing in ornate holders. We were met at the tent entrance by one of the veiled women in a light brown robe, then led deep inside once our sandals were off. I was used to walking barefoot on that planet, but walking on the soft white silk made me feel strange, as though it was a brand-new experience. I didn't particularly care for the feeling, but I wasn't able to rid myself of it until we stepped through hangings into the presence of *hizahh*.

The white robed and veiled men lay at their ease all over the floor, served by their slaves who moved unobtrusively among them. The female *bedinn* all wore their robes as they served, their minds carefully considering every move they made, their suppressed fear so thick it filled the tent like a noxious vapor, transmitting itself to our group of newcomers. We entered hesitantly, in a bunch, clutching our robes to our middles as the attention of the veiled men came to us, appalled to discover that we'd been deserted by our guide. We stood alone in front of all those eyes, not knowing what to do, suddenly having forgotten everything we'd been taught.

"Why must new *bedinn* always be so graceless?" one of the men said, looking us over with less than approval. "Are all men save ourselves incapable of training females? Even the youngest of my daughters has attained more presence than they."

"They will learn, Kadrar," another laughed, glancing at the first man who had spoken. "Should our *bedinn* come to us already trained, where would be the pleasure in teaching them to serve? *Bedinn,* step forward before us and remove your robes."

Slowly, hesitantly, we moved into the midst of the men, then opened our robes and let them fall to the silk at our feet. The minds around us began to hum so suddenly that I closed my eyes, embarrassed and frightened, wishing I could turn and run out of there. I didn't need to guess what those men were feeling, I could feel it myself, that sudden desire accompanied by the knowledge that nothing could stop them from satisfying that desire. It's a feeling a woman has reason to fear, a feeling that turns her helpless with humiliation when she sees it. If she can feel it instead of just seeing it, it becomes ten times worse.

"Ah, I see we have a shy flower," a male voice came, accompanied by a few chuckles. "Perhaps it will be necessary to deny her a robe entirely until the foolishness is forgotten."

"See how she darkens yet further at the suggestion," another laughed as the amusement spread around the tent. "I believe the shade goes well with her coloring. Let us not discourage it."

"You may do with her as you wish when she serves you, Simlal!" snapped the one previously called Kadrar, the only one among them not amused. "Investing new *bedinn* bores me, and I would have it done with as soon as possible! Continue *now,* Kednin."

"Very well, Kadrar," the one called Kednin sighed, and I knew him as the one who had spoken to us earlier in the day. "We will complete the investiture as quickly as possible so that you may take a *bedin* to ease your temper. Perhaps you would care to take one now, and forgo the boredom you so clearly see in store for you? In view of your great need, we will be pleased to excuse you from the proceedings."

"An excellent suggestion," the one named Kadrar said, and I opened my eyes to see him rising to his feet, He gestured to the nearest *bedin* and then turned and strode out through the silken hangings, his white robes billowing behind him, a sickly frightened girl hurrying in his wake. The man was pleased to be getting out of there, but not half as pleased as the rest were to see him gone.

"An excellent suggestion indeed," the veiled Kednin commented once the other man had left, and the rest laughed their agreement. "Now we may continue undisturbed. Approach me, *bedin,* and kneel before me."

Kednin had pointed to the first of us on his right, and the woman, after a trembling hesitation, walked to him slowly and knelt down as ordered. The man's mind was pleased as his eyes moved over the woman, but all he did was affix a veil to her hair to hide her face and band her brow with bronze-colored links. After that she was sent back to the line and another woman was appointed to take her place. One by one every one of us went, and the last one to go was me. Since I hadn't been standing at the end of the line, I couldn't help wondering why I'd been singled out like that.

"And for our last and newest *bedin* we have the shy flower," Kednin said when I'd knelt before him, his eyes intense above his veil. His hands brought the last veil to my face, and then the last bronze-colored band to my head. The veil was heavier than I'd expected and the band lighter, and somehow there was no difficulty in keeping either one in place. When it was all done I was ready to stand up and go back to the line, but Kednin had other ideas.

"I would see what you have learned, *bedin*," he said, his eyes still on me. "First bow to me, then place your wrists behind you."

I hesitated longer than the first woman on line had, longer than was really wise, but there was something in the man's mind I didn't like. When I felt the beginnings of his annoyance start I quickly did as he'd ordered, but was still caught unprepared when I suddenly felt my wrists being tied with leather.

"Have you never been bound so, *bedin*?" he chuckled, amused by the way I struggled against the leather. "I, unlike my brother, find great amusement in investing new *bedinn*. They find their new state difficult to accept till it has been taught them in a proper manner."

"Unbind me!" I snapped, furious to the point of not caring what they wanted. "Unbind me and return my clothing! I am a free woman and will not be treated so!"

"Ah, the spirit of a free woman," he said, a smile of pleased anticipation in his voice. "I see I was correct in believing the foolishness of rebellion would most easily be drawn from our shy flower. You are mistaken in believing yourself a free woman, *bedin*, and this will be proven to you."

His hands flew out and grasped me by the forearms before I could get to my feet as I was trying to do, holding me in place before him as someone else came up behind me. Drawing back away from his grip proved impossible, just as impossible as avoiding the man behind me. The second man pulled my head back by the hair, moved the veil aside, then forced a wad of cloth into my mouth just as I opened it to scream. The scream turned into a gurgle then died altogether as a strip of leather was tied around the wadding to hold it in place. After that the veil was replaced, my hair was released, and the second man stepped back.

"I see that there are tears in your lovely green eyes, *bedin*." The man still holding my forearms chuckled. "Possibly the tears stem from the manner in which you have just been treated. If this is so do not regret them, for they have enabled you to learn the first of your lessons: no *bedin* may speak in the presence of *hizahh*, save at their command,

and then only in the prescribed manner. For this, the time of your learning, you will only be mildly punished. Should the misconduct be repeated, your tongue will be removed."

The shock struck me motionless between his hands, the shock transmitted by the other women lined up behind me and the stronger shock of knowing he spoke with utter conviction. His statement hadn't been a threat, it had been a solemn promise, a vow he had made – and kept – in the past. I shook my head, denying that that could be happening to me, trying to deny everything he'd said, and luckily he misinterpreted the gesture.

"I am pleased to see you attempt to assure me that the error will not be repeated." He laughed. "It is gratifying to know the lesson was as effective as I wished it to be, yet the punishment will be completed to reinforce your memory of the lesson. A *bedin* with her tongue removed is a *bedin* unable to give full pleasure to a man."

The others laughed heartily at the joke, their minds pleased at the way the lesson was going. They enjoyed this part of acquiring new slaves as much as they enjoyed the slaves themselves. I would have preferred being furious at the attitude, but too much fear was hammering at me, mine as well as everyone else's. The veiled *bedinn* knelt in their robes behind their *hizahh,* relieved to be temporarily ignored, but not foolish enough to believe it would last very long.

"You tremble," the man in front of me observed, with pleasure. "A *bedin is* never so lovely as when she kneels trembling before one. *Bedinn* were born to tremble."

His eyes blazed hot above his veil, his desire so close to me I felt smothered in it. It rolled at me in waves from his mind, making me dizzy and ill, until I cringed back against his hands. He laughed at my reaction, enjoying it and letting it feed his desire, sharing it with the other men in the tent.

Most of them were leaning forward, eager to get on with whatever was to happen next, and Kednin wasn't about to make them wait long.

"It is also required of a *bedin* that she speak longingly of her desire to serve," Kednin said, his voice almost a purr. "As you are currently unable to speak in any manner, you must show your eagerness to please your *hizahh* without words. Do you feel yourself able to do this?"

Numbly I shook my head again, slowly, almost pleadingly, knowing he hadn't been expecting any answer but a negative. I could almost see the grin behind his veil, could hear the soft laughter in his throat, could feel the deep amusement from the others. They were going to do something to me, I knew the were, but my wrists strained as futilely against the leather as my throat strained to utter a scream.

"You are unable to show your desire to please," Kednin nodded, a false commiseration in his voice. "Under such restrictive circumstances, it will then be necessary for your *hizahh* to assist you. We would not wish you to be thought unwilling *Bedinn.*"

Two of the robed and veiled women ran to him when he called, kneeling to either side of me and bowing with their fists pressed to their foreheads. Their minds were unsurprised at the summons and their fright was minimal, showing the entire thing had been well planned. My own fright, unvoiced, was evident only in the increased trembling in my body.

"Your sisters now stand by to be of aid to you, *bedin*," Kednin said, releasing my arms as the two robed women straightened from their bow. I immediately tried to back away from the man and get to my feet, but the women turned as one and took hold of my bound arms, keeping me in place. I writhed in their grip, still on my knees, turning my head from side to side to beg them with my eyes. Please let me go, I tried to ask, please let me get away from him, but their eyes were hooded and uncompromising, their minds not even sympathetic. They moved closer to me to get better leverage, obedience to their *hizah* their only concern, their movement underscoring Kednin's chuckle.

"Ah, I see you anxiously beseech their aid," he said, his eyes unmoving from me, his mind knowing the truth his tongue ignored. "It bodes well for your future servitude that you are able to ask the aid of sisters who are clothed while you kneel naked before your *hizah*. I feel sure they will provide the assistance you so earnestly desire."

Then he laughed aloud, unable to contain his mirth any longer in the face of the burning red suddenly covering my body. It was bad enough being unclothed when everyone around you was the same; the shame of being naked among clothed people was more than I could stand. The difference I'd managed to forget had been pointed out for just that reason, to shame me, but I couldn't keep from reacting just the way Kednin wanted me to. I closed my eyes and tried to bend forward, toward my knees, but the two *bedinn* holding my arms refused to allow it.

"Now do I truly see how eager you are to serve me, lovely *bedin*," Kednin's voice came as I nearly choked on a sob. "You wish the waiting to be over, and so it shall be."

His hands touched me then, causing my eyes to fly open even though it was just my ribs he touched. The women on either side of me shifted their grips, one hand still on my arm, the other hand pressing into my back, forcing my upper torso forward toward the veiled man. I was being offered to the man whose blue eyes burned so brightly above a white veil, a man who didn't refuse the invitation. His hands slid from my ribs to my breasts, touching me as though he owned me, touching me as though I alone offered myself. I wanted to die of shame, being thrust at a man like that, but I couldn't even scream.

Before they were through with me, I learned how much it was possible to go through without dying of shame. Kednin touched me all over, slowly, caressingly, the two *bedinn* keeping me from drawing back and refusing his touch, their hands kept carefully out of his way. but always there. It wasn't long before those smaller hands were on my knees, drawing my thighs as wide as possible, offering the *hizah* a clear avenue for the continuance of his exploration. I had no doubt that he would take the avenue, but when he did a number of other *hizahh* rose from their places and came to crouch closer, to more easily see my reaction. As miserable as I felt I was sure there would *be* no reaction – other than an increase in my misery – but I hadn't counted on all those extra minds and the dimly understood way the barbarian had bewitched my body.

Kednin's invasion began as tearful outrage to my senses, an invasion that would have to be endured because it couldn't be escaped. I cringed inwardly against expected pain, wondering how long I could endure it, but shockingly there was no pain, only a slowly demanding sensation of – expectation, I suppose it would have to be called. I didn't understand the sensation, but before I could begin to analyze it there were many minds very close around me, all of them filled with desire or arousal or both. The men who had come closer were feeling desire and beginning to feel arousal; the women who held me could no longer fight the sensation of burning in their own bodies at the sight of my body being touched; Kednin, my chief tormentor, had been radiating desire steadily from the time he first began with me. It was very much like the low, faraway drone of chanting voices that refused to stop, that refused to keep from growing louder and steadier. The beat of the chanting pushed at me, taking me up in its rhythm, forcing me to move in its flow. I couldn't quite make out the words of the chant, but then I realized there were no words, nothing but movement and feeling and fire.

The movement had already begun when the feeling broke through my awareness. I moved to the urging of Kednin's fingers, my body fighting the hands and leather that held me, but not to escape. I needed to get closer to the man before me, needed more than the scant touch he allowed me, needed to do something about the growing fire inside me. The fire was spreading, forcing me to writhe in its flames, building a moan that could not escape my lips. My breathing had grown so heavy I felt suffocated by the gag, but not even a whimper would come through.

"You appear to be aroused, lovely *bedin*," Kednin murmured, his eyes boring into me, his free hand coming to my breast. "Can it mean that you, the shyest of flowers, wish to serve me here, before all these others? Will the shame not touch you more deeply to do such a thing?"

His words rang in my head, showing me all the eyes intent on my degradation, their owners waiting like birds of carrion to feast on their victim. I didn't want to be their victim, I only wanted escape, but want usually comes in a poor second to need. My need had been brought to the surface and was destroying me, but before I died I had to make a final effort. Still writhing, still straining toward him, I shook my head fiercely to show that I preferred death to degradation.

"Ah, you will not feel shamed!" He laughed, deliberately misinterpreting my gesture. His mind knew the truth, and *I* knew he was punishing me for it. "What a lovely, obedient *bedin* you are, to think only of the service due me. Very well, my lovely, you may serve me here."

He gestured to the two veiled women, and suddenly I was thrust to my side and then to my back. My knees and legs hurt from having been knelt so long, but the ache became insignificant. The *hizah* Kednin rose to his feet and stood above me, towering to the tent top, looking down at me from behind his veil. The two robed females held my ankles, one on each side of him, their hands keeping my struggles to a minimum, and then he was bending over me, his hands on my thighs, his body getting closer. I would have screamed as he entered me, from fury if nothing else; the shame was so great I thought I couldn't bear it, but it was destined to grow greater. He not only took me, he forced me to respond, and through the waves of weakness I could feel the laughter of derision. from all the men who watched. I cried as Kednin made himself indisputable *hizah* to me, but the tears were as useless as tears always are.

After that the other women were used, but my horrible example served them well. They submitted to binding with total deference, then did their best to seem cooperative and enthusiastic. Most of the men chose *bedinn* who were already broken in, and the balance of the new *bedinn* were allowed the comfort of being one among many. I lay on the floor where I had been left, my ankles bound after my service, my body placed at the feet of the *hizah* who had taken me. I finally knew that the entire episode had been contrived to make the other women more pliable, but the knowledge didn't do anything to ease the wretchedness I felt. I lay on a silken floor at the feet of a stranger who had shamed me utterly, bound helplessly at his direction, gagged and used, endlessly reluctant to do more than breathe for fear of attracting attention to myself. The veil covering my face felt more than ludicrous, considering the nakedness of the rest of me; the chain around my brow had grown in weight, taking me down to the ground with the massiveness of its symbolism. I had been taught I was no more than one of the herd, marked with symbols of possession impossible to deny: the veil and head chain might be easily removed – if the wearer dared. But I wouldn't have dared, even if I'd been free to do so, for fear of another lesson of the sort which I'd been given. Death itself was fearsome enough and painful death even more so, but far worse than those was the possibility of unending shame and humiliation, heaped upon me before the eyes of others. I wanted to withdraw myself from everything around me, the soft cries of *bedinn* and the louder misery of their minds, the satisfied grunts of *hizahh* and the smirking pleasure of their inner selves, but I simply didn't dare. Another lack of proper response would bring further punishment, and I couldn't face that. So I lay there and watched the women of Tammad's city being used by strangers, their minds crying piteously for rescue, my own mind as distant as possible while still being near. I couldn't bring myself to cry to anyone the way they were doing, and that made it all unbelievably worse.

## ELEVEN

I was kept tied and gagged all the rest of that night and halfway through the next morning. I alone was left untouched the rest of the night, but not out of consideration for what I had gone through. Very few of the *hizahh* left the festivities early and all of those who remained, each at least once and sometimes twice, visited me where I lay on the silk and demanded some indication of subservience from me.

Once I had squirmed an inch or two in their direction and had put my head to their sandaled feet and had done my best to kiss those feet through my gag, I was rewarded – with the partial attention of a *hizah*. Their hands touched me everywhere, over and over again, but none of them even tried to use me. The night became an endless hell filled with forced humiliation and raging need, my forced punishment for having dared to think I might defy *hizahh*. In the early hours of the morning, before they were either sent back to their tent or taken away by individual *hizahh*, the *bedinn* were ranged around me and made witness to the final humiliation of the night. *Hizah* Kednin himself did the honors, crouched beside me, his mind completely aware of how well I'd been prepared. He graciously granted me the relief I'd been denied so long, making sure everyone in the tent witnessed how easily his hands reached my soul, then he called a male *bedin* to carry me back to the female *bedin* tent. As soon as I was put down in a corner of the tent I withdrew deep inside my shield, disassociating the entire outer world and allowing myself to feel nothing of the emotions clawing red streaks on the inside of my mind. No one came near me, and exhausted sleep found me with no trouble at all.

I was awakened in the early afternoon of the new day when the leather was removed from my wrists and ankles and the gag from my mouth. The *bedin* who untied me helped me drink from a water skin before informing me that I'd been forbidden to speak under any circumstances until the *hizahh* decided otherwise. I was then left alone to try to remember how my arms and legs worked, a painful process no matter how careful I tried to be. My limbs went from leaden lumps to blazing, stabbing foci of agony, but it wasn't something that could be avoided by lying still. I'd also been told I'd be summoned later, and if I wasn't able to answer that summons I'd be punished. Balancing between the agony of reawakening muscles and the sort of punishment given by *hizahh*, I found the agony a better bargain.

I lay struggling on the brown cloth for a few minutes before the thought occurred to me that I was being stupid. I had to relax the shield protecting me from the ravage of emotions, but that let me cope with the more immediate demands of pain. Pain control, not being a shield, is difficult to explain; it's more a deep relaxation bringing about the forced dissipation of pain signals, an emotionally linked attitude-experience coupling refusal-to-admit and actual nonexistence where pain is concerned. It requires a certain amount of calm on the part of the practitioner, a calm that isn't always easy to attain. By ignoring everything around me – especially memories – I was able to force the calm, then established the pain control. After that, moving around was considerably less difficult.

It wasn't long before I was up on my feet and walking back and forth swinging my arms, working the final kinks out. Almost everyone in the tent was asleep, curled up alone or in small groups, sharing proximity rather than warmth. The warmth was enough to go around twice over, leaving a light sheen of sweat on my body as I moved through it. I moved and walked softly so as not to awaken the sleepers, and wound up beside the only other waking person in the tent, the woman who had untied me. She knelt before a cooking tripod, her attention solely for what she was doing, the misery in her mind complemented by the silent tears in her eyes. She was heating a small pot of the cereal grain, but since there wasn't the slightest trace of hunger in her I didn't understand why – until I realized she must have been commanded to eat. After a minute she took the pot from the fire and began to eat, reluctantly and distastefully but with no hint of disobedience. As I stopped behind her, the dim light in the tent finally showed the strap marks covering the entire back of her, red, painful-looking welts that would leave scars in her mind rather than on her body. She had been punished by *hizahh* for some reason, possibly for the extreme slenderness of her build. *Hizahh* seemed to prefer well-rounded women, just the same as other men on that world.

"You would do well to do as I do before being ordered to it," she whispered, aware of me where I stood behind her. "New *bedinn* are punished more often than those who are owned longer, to instill a proper obedience in them."

She continued eating the meal then, knowing I wasn't able to answer or argue with her. I stared around at the dim tent heated by the merciless sun blazing down outside, my mind filled with an impotent fury that was difficult to chase away. I didn't want to have anything to eat, let alone a bowl of that cereal, but there wasn't any other choice. Anticipate the wishes of the *hizahh,* or face their punishment. I knelt beside the woman, nearly trembling with fury and fear, and heated my own bowl of cereal grain.

After eating and cleaning up from the meal, I went back to my corner and lay down again. Eating the cereal had not only been distasteful, it had been ridiculously awkward with the veil in place. I'd been tempted to remove the veil until the meal was done, but the other woman hadn't removed hers. Then I'd remembered that it had been put on me by the hand of a *hizah,* and realized that it couldn't be removed by anything less than that same agency. If the meal hadn't already been ruined, it would have been done for with certainty by that time. I finished up quickly, then went to find escape in sleep.

The next time I was awakened it was late afternoon, and opening my eyes showed me the male *bedin* my mind had already detected. He stood over me in his black *haddin* and bronze neck-chain, impatient and disdaining, and ordered me to see to my hair quickly and take a robe. I did as ordered then followed him out of the tent, pausing only for my sandals at the tent entrance. The other women had been awake by then, but only Findra had come over to hug me briefly before I left.

The heat and glare of the setting sun seared me as I followed the broad, bare back of the male *bedin* across the camp but once we reached the tent I'd been in the night before, every consideration but fear faded away. As I left my sandals at the entrance and was led inside, I knew that the greatest aid the *hizahh* had was a *bedin*'s uncertainty. I'd been sent for, but I didn't know *why* I'd been sent for, and the uncertainty was turning my muscles to water and my mind to quivering mud. Was I going to be punished again?

Was I simply going to be used? What if I didn't do well enough to please them and they had me whipped? What if I forgot I wasn't supposed to speak and they had my tongue cut out? What if they knew how angry I'd been earlier and were going to hurt me for it? I trembled terribly as I hurried across the white silk, following my guide through the hangings, afraid to continue ahead to what awaited me but more afraid to attempt running from it.

What awaited me was the *hizah* Kednin, all alone in a small, curtained section of the tent, his robed body relaxing among cushions, his veiled face showing no more than impassive eyes. When the male *bedin* stepped aside to reveal me to the *hizah*, I clutched my robe tighter and immediately fell to my knees, bowing with my fists pressed to my forehead and my head to the white silk. Through the calm of his thoughts, it was impossible telling whether or not the *hizah* was angry, and I continued to tremble even as I held the bow.

"Approach and kneel before me, *bedin*," Kednin ordered, his voice lazy and sounding recently awakened. I rose to my feet and dropped the robe behind me as I'd seen a woman do the other day, then hurried to kneel in front of the *hizah* as I'd been commanded. The male *bedin* was gone, having been immediately dismissed, and I barely felt his mind trace fading with distance. I was too wrapped up in the man before me, a man who was beginning to feel satisfaction.

"I see you tremble, *bedin*," he said, and his hand came to touch my hair. "You are indeed lovely when you tremble, nearly as lovely as when you writhe beneath me. Have you spoken?"

I shook my head vigorously, feeling my eyes widen as my heart thumped louder in the silence. Would he believe me?

"Excellent," he purred, deep amusement filling his mind. "It seems you begin to learn your place. Present your wrists to me and prepare to see to my pleasure."

Filled with relief I bent and twisted, offering him my wrists behind my back, but he didn't accept the offering. I felt his frown of disapproval as he touched the dark bruises on my wrists from the last time I'd been tied, then his hands moved instead to my thumbs. They were quickly lashed together with his leather, the rest of the strip being wound around my hands. I was still tied, but not in a way to increase the bruises already on me. Bruises are ugly, and detract from the beauty of a *bedin*.

Pleasing a robed man with your wrists tied behind you and a veil over your face takes a good deal of knowledge in proper technique. I'd had no chance to learn the technique, but that fact didn't do a thing to sway the *hizah*. When I couldn't reach him he beat me with a broad strap, one that nearly made me scream with pain. Through it all I kept the screams inside, knowing it would go harder for me if I voiced my pain and fright without permission, then worked frantically harder to reach the man when he put the strap aside. Desperation usually provides added incentive, and the second time I managed to work my way under his robe and around my veil. My back hurt and my bottom as well, and the sweat of fear ran in rivers down my body, but I soon had the *hizah* moaning with pleasure, desire flaring from his mind as his flesh swelled and hardened. The thought came that I might escape serving his pleasure any other way by being very good at that way, but Kednin wasn't about to allow that. His fist in my hair stopped me when he wanted me stopped, put me back to the task when he wanted me at it again, and generally played me like a musical instrument, crescendos and rests orchestrated by him alone. When he finally threw me to my back and entered me, he began his pleasure all over again and was a long time in seeing to it. I tried to pretend to helpless submission throughout the ordeal, but apparently some men know the real from the forced. After satisfying himself to the fullest, Kednin took up his strap and beat me again, letting me know that my body was expected to learn true submission to *hizahh*. I was then sent back to the *bedin* tent, to wonder if anything more would come of the incident, I thought, but the *bedin* tent no longer stood where it had been. Camp was being broken and I was set to work with the other *bedinn,* and in a very short time we were on our way out of the oasis and further into the desert. Away from everything we knew and deeper into slavery.

The nighttime desert is a cold place, but exertion usually warms one up fast enough. I stumbled along barefoot through the uneven mounds of sand, my bound wrists tied with a length of leather attached to the back of a large, wagon-like vehicle being pulled by four *seetarr,* my robe held closed with a sash, my wrists protected from the leather by strips of cloth. My sandals had been packed away before the caravan left the oasis, presumably to keep them from being lost. Retrieving a sandal is difficult when you're tied to a moving wagon by the wrists.

The caravan consisted of at least a dozen wagons, twice that number of pack *seetarr,* saddle *seetarr* carrying *hizahh,* herds of animals being driven by male *bedin,* and female *bedinn* being drawn along by the wagons. I'd experienced a stab of jealousy when I'd seen that the male *bedinn* would not be tied the way we females were, but after a long time of walking with nothing to do but think, the truth of the matter finally came to me. Of course the male slaves were left unbound; where in that vast desert would they go even if they managed to escape? And even if they survived the desert, they would just fall slave again to the next tribe they met.

They were shamed and unmanned, put permanently in bronze neck-chains and allowed nothing to wear beyond their black *haddin.* What would they do with their lives even if they escaped? If they'd been the sort to prefer death to slavery, they would have had it long since. We women were not all that much more valuable, and our being tied didn't mean the *hizahh* were afraid we would escape. It's easy to lose yourself in the desert at night, most especially if you can't keep up with the march. The leather leads made sure we would keep up, without needing to waste anyone's time watching us.

Not being used to walking in sand, I soon discovered that going uphill on the dunes was a time for falling down, at least for me. I finally found the trick of holding on to the leather lead for support, but not before I'd gone down too many times to count. After one of those times when I struggled to my feet, sweating beneath my robe and veil, out of breath with the effort, I looked up to see a crack of light showing in the midst of white silk covering the wagon I was following. Nothing but a dark shadow showed beneath that crack of light, but I knew I was being inspected by one of the women or children of the *hizahh*. The wagons were for them alone, and all female *bedinn* had been knelt with their heads to the ground while the wagons had been loaded. We weren't allowed anywhere near their precious women, but I didn't know why. The curiosity of the young female above me – a mate or daughter – was as strong as mine and just as circumspect, and the sliver of light disappeared sooner than I expected it to. It was clear there would be trouble for both of us if we were discovered.

After some hours the march halted, and we women were freed of our tethers to serve cold meat and sacks of wine to the *hizahh*. They had looked frighteningly large and fierce mounted on their *seetarr,* riding beside and behind and before us, their robes and veils billowing as they rode, and their fierceness wasn't much diminished once they'd dismounted. Even during the rest of a meal break their minds were alert and watchful, their eyes moving everywhere, their attitudes distant. Any *bedin* who put herself in the wrong position in relation to their vigilance was struck aside, quickly and harshly, not allowed a single instant in which to put the men at a disadvantage. Little wonder we all crept about, trying to serve and still be out of the way, all at the same time. The desert was a place of danger, and only the fully alert would be able to survive there. The *hizahh* we served intended staying alive, even if a few *bedinn* were lost in the process.

After the *hizahh* had eaten, we were given a literal five minutes to do the same. I stuffed my mouth with the dry, tasteless cheese the way I saw the other *bedinn* doing, and managed to get one sip of water before being dragged back to my wagon by one of the male *bedinn* who reattached me to the tether. The woman who was tied to my left was not the one who had been there earlier, and her mind wasn't as well disciplined as the other's. She stood shivering in the sand with her head down, her fists clenched near the leather, her mind a turmoil of fear and hate and shame and despair. She was waiting for something to happen, dreading it terribly but knowing it would come. I didn't know why the resumption of the march would bother her so, and then a *hizah* rode by to order us to our knees. I knelt more slowly than she did, finally realizing that the journey wasn't yet to resume, then kept myself from looking up only by extreme effort of will. I'd suddenly felt the presence of many minds above me, all of them female minds, all of them paying close attention to me and the woman beside me. No hint of light shone down to show that the silk had been parted at many points, but I knew those minds were watching openly, no longer afraid of being detected. They were being permitted to watch whatever would happen, and the woman beside me, although unaware of the eyes on her, grew wilder and more fearful inside.

We waited an achingly long time before it was our turn. I felt the minds of male *bedinn* approaching before I heard their sandaled steps in the sand, and then there was a fist in my hair, forcing me backward down toward the sand and over my feet. My tethered wrists stayed high in the air, well out of the way, and I heard my companion's suddenly labored breathing as the same was done to her. I could see the *bedin* bending over me, the dark hiding his features, his mind bored with a job he had undoubtedly already done many times over, his free hand moving to something out of my bent-over-backwards line of sight. The woman beside me gasped, muffling a sob, and then there was a hand at my robe, pushing it aside over my thighs and reaching under. My own gasp sounded as fingers entered me, not to tease or pleasure but to insert something that immediately caused a mild burning sensation. I struggled against the leather at my wrists and the fist in my hair, not knowing what was happening but mistrusting anything that was done to me among those people. The *bedin* held me still without effort, his fingers twisting whatever he had put into me, the object persisting in its mild burning sensation. I suddenly felt a terrible flash of need that forced a moan out of me, a need made worse by the same reaction coming from the other woman being done so. I writhed against the hand between my thighs, trying to drive it away, trying to pull it in closer, trying to do anything that would stop that overwhelming sensation, but nothing changed. Uninterested fingers twisted the object around and around, almost as though time was being counted out, oblivious to and uncaring about what the action did to me.

Another ten minutes passing like hours went by before the male *bedinn* were done. The object was slowly withdrawn from me, leaving behind the mild burning and urgent need, and then the two were gone as suddenly as they'd come. I remained kneeling in the sand, my legs coated with it, my neck aching from my head having been held back, my hands twisting in the leather lead in a vain attempt to reach myself. I could feel tears running down my cheeks, tears that were partly humiliation from the satisfaction and amusement in the minds above me. Those minds were withdrawing now, the silk being as silently replaced as it had been removed, and I still didn't know what it all meant.

"They had no right," a soft voice sobbed from my left, part of the misery pouring out of my sister *bedin*'s mind. "The child need not have been considered theirs! It could have been mine, to carry and beat and tend till it grew! What right have they to take it from me so, when it was they who put it within me to begin with? It is my right to have a child, my right, my right!"

She began screaming wildly then, shattering the deep silence of night all around with pain and insanity too long held inside. I tried to reach her mind to calm it, but the shattered sanity pouring out drove me back and away, my mind clanging with shock from even so brief an encounter. I gasped and cringed back against the tether, shaking from having touched so alien a thing as madness, and then the *hizahh* were all about us, two of them dismounting to go to the girl. One of them held her while the other stuffed something in her mouth, silencing her screams; and then her tether was released from the wagon and she was dragged kicking to one of the *seetarr*. Another minute saw her thrown across the saddle and the *hizah* mounted as well, and then the two of them were gone, riding across the dunes and far out of sight. The mental screaming continued for a long time before it stopped, but my shuddering continued even longer.

Not much later the march began again. I moved woodenly in the wake of the wagon, my mind numb to everything but the continuing – and slowly increasing – burning inside me. I now knew what the – treatment – had been for, and also knew why the *hizahh*'s females had been permitted to watch. The object put inside me was a birth control device, something to make sure no *hizah* put a child on me. The women of the tribe, the lawful, legitimate bearers of children to their men, were permitted to see this being done to assure them that their places were not being usurped. The biggest joke of all was that I didn't need their treatment, but they didn't know that. And then I wondered if it would make any difference to them. I would probably still be done the same as any other *bedin,* no matter what the truth was. The only *bedin* given special attention was one who had failed to please her *hizahh;* the rest just faded into the background in their minds, anonymous in their veils and headbands. Individuality was not a trait prized in *bedinn.*

It was still dark when the caravan stopped and camp was made. All *bedinn* were untied to do the small unpacking and the preparing of a hot meal, and being thrust into their midst was literally staggering. Every one of them, the women from Tammad's city included, was burning up in her need, the single object in mind being reaching the men as soon as possible. The only fear they felt was the fear of being left untouched, and that fear made them frantic in their haste. They would do anything demanded of them in order to be satisfied, and that thought alone made me sicker than I had been. They'd been primed like animals for the coming festivities, animals trapped and bought and trained to perform as their owners wished. I stood to one side while I thickened my shield against their emotions, then slowly joined them and began doing my share. I may not have been much on that world, but one thing I wouldn't be was a trained animal.

Dawn wasn't very far away by the time the *hizahh* were ready for their meal. I noticed a definite warming in the air as I helped the others carry the food to the large tent with white silk hangings. Each of the men was offered what had been prepared and brought, and then the men made their selections – but not only among the food. By some prearranged system the men took turns gesturing women to them, and when all the selecting was done the women were made to eat first. We weren't allowed to eat much, only enough to prove that the food was untampered with, and then the *hizahh* took it. I was aware of some of the *bedinn* moaning softly and pleading with their *hizahh* for attention, but no matter how I felt I couldn't bring myself to do the same. The *hizah* I knelt before watched me closely while he ate, his mind suspicious and somehow unsatisfied. When he finished his meal and gestured that I present my wrists, I had the definite feeling that the coming session would not please him. I couldn't possibly have been more right.

The *hizah* who had chosen me was not Kednin, but he reacted the same as the other man had. After he'd satisfied himself he beat me with the same broad strap they all seemed to use, taking no real pleasure in the beating aside from a feeling of seeing to something that had to be done. He hadn't been dissatisfied with me, or I would have felt a whip instead of a strap; my failure had been one of being just under very satisfying. I'd made the man force me into responding – which was something he enjoyed – but my eventual response hadn't been abandoned enough to suit him. He beat me to teach me his preferences in the matter, then sent me back to the *bedin* tent to clean up after the meal. Once the necessary was done, I lay my aching body on the cloth of the tent floor, ignored the extreme heat of the day, and quickly fell asleep.

I was awakened from a bad dream around midday, but not for anything simple like serving or eating. Every female *bedin* in the tent was ordered into a robe and sandals by a male *bedin,* then led out into the hot sun and through the camp. On the outskirts of the camp, near the tethered *seetarr,* a large wooden frame had been set into the sand. The frame was Y-shaped with notches cut into the arms of the Y, and whatever it signified was a source of great fear to the veiled women around me. As soon as we arrived we were ordered to our knees by the only *hizah* present, who looked down at us with a frown of displeasure in his blue eyes.

"One of you has been found to be in need of a lesson for failure," the man announced; looking directly at each of us in turn, which brought some of those kneeling about me to come close to fainting. "Those who are not given the lesson this day must pay close heed to its teachings, to more easily avoid such a lesson themselves in future. *Hizahh* are not long patient with failure."

He gestured behind us then, but not to have his victim chosen from among us; the victim had already been chosen. Two male *bedinn* came forward with a naked woman held between them, a veiled woman with short blond hair and brown eyes. The woman struggled as if trying to break those impossible grips, but no sounds came forth around the gag which was visible only where her veil didn't hide it. Findra was angry and outraged rather than deeply afraid, but that was only because she didn't understand what was going on.

The blond ex-tripper didn't speak the language those around her spoke, and the lack had turned out to be her downfall.

The *hizah* waited until Findra had been tied by the wrists to the notched arms of the Y frame, her toes at least six inches from the sand, then he stepped closer to her and spoke so that only she might bear. His totally incomprehensible words made no impression on her, but he didn't realize that. He turned away from her and walked back toward the tents with one of the male *bedinn* following him, and quickly disappeared. The remaining male *bedin* had been taking his time uncoiling a long, dark-brown whip, but he didn't drag the thing out beyond the time it took the *hizah* to reach his tent. As soon as the veiled man was gone, the large, bronze-chained *bedin,* clad only in a black *haddin,* brought his arm back and then forward, laying the whip across Findra's back with a crack that was close to sensation for those of us watching.

If the sound alone was pain to us, the actual feel of the lash was beyond pain to Findra. Her eyes widened as her throat tried to scream, her head snapped back with the shock of it, and her body twisted six inches above the sand, straining in silence to shriek out the terror and exquisite agony of the stroke. Kneeling in the sand I was forced to feel everything she felt, every spasm of every nerve ending, every degree of disbelief and horror suddenly bursting from her mind. I staggered under the load, feeling close to passing out, and then my shield snapped shut, protecting me from insanity and an overload of too-heightened emotions. I trembled and put a shaky hand to my head as the lash fell on Findra a second time, but it took the sight of a broad red line on her white, writhing body to make me realize what I was doing. I was protecting myself at Findra's expense, happily leaving her there under the lash as long as my own sensibilities were safe and snug. She'd known I was the only one who could translate for her, but she hadn't pressed me to speak when I'd been commanded to silence. She'd accepted her own peril to keep from putting me in a similar one, and I'd abandoned her to a sadistic "lesson" she couldn't possibly have avoided alone.

The decision *wasn't* carefully thought out, but that didn't make it any less definite. I braced myself and opened the shield again, but didn't let Findra's silent hysteria distract me. It was the male *bedin* I wanted to reach, and when I did I found what I'd hoped to find. The man was as bored and uncaring as all of them were, finding no pleasure in whipping the girl before him other than the vague satisfaction of doing a job that needed doing. The third stroke reached Findra even as I entered the man's mind, choosing among his emotions for the ones I needed most. The boredom was perfect, as was the discomfort he felt in the heat of the sun, and the contempt he felt for all women fitted in with the rest like a sword in a warrior's hand. I was trying to work quickly and powerfully, but the strength of my projections surprised even me.

By the time the fourth stroke fell, the man was feeling nothing but what I wanted him to feel. His boredom over the job he was doing was nearly making him yawn, his strength was draining out in sweat from the heat of the sun, and one contemptuous look at the semi-conscious girl hanging in front of him showed that the lesson had been thoroughly taught. He recoiled the whip as he basked in the pleasure of having done such a good job, then turned to the rest of us and gestured at us to be on our way. As I got to my feet I deepened the stupor Findra had fallen into, and walked away from a completely unconscious victim.

Findra wasn't returned to the *bedin* tent for hours, but as soon as the male slave put her down and left, I was immediately by her side. Her back had been cut open by the strokes of the lash, but the beating hadn't been as bad as it could have been. Her wrists were badly bruised from having held her weight so long, and the front of her body showed that she'd been driven into the body of the Y frame by the force of the whip blows, but nothing was broken or irreversibly damaged. As I knelt above her, feeling the way her mind fought against being overwhelmed with pain, another woman joined us and brought what was badly needed: a salve for the wounds and welts the beating had left. I waited until the woman had begun spreading the salve, then adjusted my efforts to hers, easing the pain far more than the salve alone could do. Findra drew in a deep breath and shuddered, then let her eyes close as exhaustion took her, as swiftly and nearly as deeply as unconsciousness had earlier. Her breathing slowed to the pace of sleep, and I was able to sit back and look around.

The woman who had spread the salve had finished her job and was going back to the place where she'd been sleeping, intent on resuming her temporary escape. The other women around her were pretending nothing had happened, but only to keep themselves from picturing their own bodies savagely beaten. I became aware of several minds concentrated on me, and turned my head to see the women of Tammad's city, their minds concerned but also in some manner confident. Their eyes touched Findra, then found my face, and smiles suddenly gleamed in those eyes before their owners lay down to try to sleep again. They knew I'd done – something – to help the girl, and they seemed to be almost as relieved as they would be to be delivered out of that horrible place. I lay down next to Findra and tried to sleep on my own, bitter with the knowledge that I wouldn't be able to help all of them all the time. My ability was considerably stronger than it had been, but it still had its limits – which were all too confining. I needed something more, something totally overwhelming, but I wasn't likely to find it. The only thing I could do was cope with what I had – and pray that none of the *hizahh* found out about it.

That night, after eating and play time, we moved on again. The people around us were a tribe of the Hamarda, nocturnal desert nomads who moved from oasis to oasis for no reason I was able to fathom. Daytime was a time of sleep – and punishment – and nighttime was a time of traveling – and sometimes battle. The third night out our *hizahh* were suddenly attacked by a large band of men who wore the same sort of veils and robes that they did. Swords hung from their sheaths to answer the attack, but the greatest amount of anxiety during the battle came from the minds inside the silk-covered wagons. The women of the *hizahh* would always fear during such battles, for should their men be bested they would then become *bedinn,* to be used and abused by the men of the new tribe. Conversely, the *bedinn* tied behind the wagons felt very little fear; what difference did it make to a slave which man held the whip over her? That third night the men of our tribe won easily, led to victory by none other than *hizah* Kednin, the man who had taken such interest in me at first. I wouldn't have minded seeing him cut down from his *seetar,* but he was much too good with a sword and much too able a leader. They met the attackers, took the lives from some and routed the rest, but didn't pursue them into the desert. They weren't about to leave their caravan unguarded, not even to finish the good work they'd started. We continued on until it was time to camp, then double guardposts were set about our perimeter in case the brigands came back. I would have known nothing about the guardposts if I hadn't been one of the ones sent to serve the men out there. The only positive part about the whole thing was the fact that the men were too keyed up to notice whether or not we were any good.

The first night after the whipping Findra was tied to a narrow platform on the side of one of the wagons, but after that she was put on a tether again. She took the first opportunity she could find to hug me in thanks for what I had done to help her, and she seemed to have a very good idea about what that help had entailed. We made no attempt to discuss the matter between us, but for her part discussion seemed entirely unnecessary. Her gratitude was a strong, real thing, undiminished by the passage of time.

The days and nights passed slowly and unpleasantly, but they gave me ample time to practice my abilities against the mighty *hizahh*. When a man looked at me, he usually found himself totally uninterested, for no reason he could clearly understand. He didn't feel displeased or dissatisfied in the slightest, but he did feel uninterested. I was able to extend the attitude to Findra and the rest of the women who had been taken with us, but not too often and not if there was the slightest chance the ploy would become obvious. The last thing I wanted was to have the *hizahh* find out there was something different about me – and what that difference was. When I did have to let myself be used, the man involved always felt full satisfaction – even if he didn't get it. The one time I was chosen to spend the daylight sleeping hours with a *hizah*, the man experienced such total exhaustion that he spent the time doing nothing other than sleeping. When be awoke I made sure to beg him for his attention, but it was too late in the day for even a token showing. He ignored the tears glistening in my eyes, stretched to show how good he felt, then sent me back to the *bedin* tent with a fond smack on the bottom and an amused laugh. If I needed more than he had time to give me, it was just too bad for me.

Early on the fifth night, we reached another oasis. This one was true, deep sand on only three sides, with the fourth consisting of gravelly, pebbly ground flatting out into the distance. The bathing pool was larger than that at the first oasis, and I couldn't wait to get to it. Water in the desert was too precious to waste on bathing or clothes washing, but there's a limit to what airing out can do for clothing and bodies. I was tired of smelling bad and wearing robes that smelled bad, and wasn't about to let anything keep me from that water.

Getting to the lake took considerably longer than I wanted it to. After the tents were up and we had unpacked everything, it was time to celebrate arriving at the oasis. The other women and I hadn't been in the camp during the last first-day oasis stop, so we were taken by surprise at the way things went. The first hint I had about something being different about the stop was the misery in the minds of the more experienced *bedinn* in the tent. Despite the fact that we were all in real discomfort from the "treatment" given us by the male *bedinn* during the march, none of the *bedinn* were showing frantic haste to get their work done and themselves over to the men. I'd tried doing something to stop those middle-of-the-night treatments, but even after suffering through five nights of it I hadn't been able to get a grip on the problem. There were no emotions short of fear and loathing that would keep those men away from me, and neither of those emotions would have done anything other than get my throat cut.

As I stood wondering why the women were acting so despondent, three of the male *bedinn* entered our tent and began gathering us up. We were all taken to the center of the tent and thrown to our bellies, then one by one our wrists and ankles were tied. Once we were all trussed up to the men's satisfaction, leather ropes were put around our throats and then tied to the legs of one single tripod cooking-stand put up in the middle of the circle our bodies made. The tripod was light and easily knocked down, and was a simple device for finding out if any of us moved from the spot we were put in. It didn't take much imagination to guess what would happen to us if the tripod was down when it came time to untie us, so every one of us made very sure not to move even as much as the tightly tied leather on us allowed. Lying still was hard right then, but moving would have been harder later.

I had almost dozed off when I was brought back awake by the sound of chanting. The sound was composed only of male voices, but beside the mind traces of the men was the clear indication of many women, not to mention children. The chanting continued for a short while, then suddenly began to change from automatic word-speaking to more and more emotional shoutings. Some of the female minds began echoing the mental output of the men, their numbers growing until nearly all of them were a part of the waxing frenzy. The shouting increased to a higher and higher pitch, taking both shouters and listeners along with it, and then it abruptly broke off into dozens of individual groups wrapped up in the wildness of the moment.

It wasn't difficult telling that an orgy was in progress, and one of the older *bedinn* whispered to us newcomers that first-day celebration was for *hizahh* and their women alone, *bedinn* being forbidden to do even so much as watch. After securing us, the male *bedinn* were themselves chained in a tent by the *hizahh*, to make sure the ceremony was undisturbed and unobserved. During the ceremony, both mates and females stripped off their robes, entered the water, and began washing each other as the men chanted. The washing naturally led to other things, and the other things became the ceremonial orgy, the celebration of finding life-giving water in the midst of dead, ever-changing sand. The *bedin* who knew this had once been a tribe-member herself, as had a number of the other *bedinn*. Before the ceremony was over, this became very obvious from the way their bodies squirmed in place and their minds cried. The one realization that kept me from being swept away by their mass reaction and sharing it myself was the fact that while slaves were forbidden to watch the ceremony, children weren't. I could feel their shallow, alien young minds watching avidly and felt myself cringing. To do such a thing in front of children!

Hours went by before the last of the celebrants left the bathing pool and it became possible for the male *bedinn* to be released who would in turn release us. I'd spent most of the time hiding under my shield to keep from rolling all over the cloth of the tent floor, but shielding alone had turned out not to be enough. I could and did close my eyes, but I couldn't find a way to turn my hearing off. Between the sounds of the orgy outside and the moans of deprived women inside, I had more than a little trouble forcing my thoughts to the subject of escape. I couldn't continue in the role of *bedin* and hope to be left with my sanity, so escape had been the one subject I'd thought most about. Escape into the deep desert would be no more than a gesture of suicide, and I'd been stopped cold until we'd reached the present oasis. Far in the distance, beyond the pebbled flats, a mountain range could just be seen. The sight didn't seem to bring any thoughts of freedom to the other women, but to me it was a direction to travel in, an objective to reach, a jumping-off point on the long road home. I knew if I reached those mountains I'd have my freedom back, but thinking about escape was well-nigh impossible while my body screamed out its needs and demands. I could make others feel full satisfaction but I couldn't do the same for myself without leaving my body. The best eye surgeon in the Amalgamation might be able to operate on himself with a complex set of mirrors, but in my case the necessary mirrors didn't exist. I could curse the *hizahh* for decreeing that I be "treated" with the other *bedinn*, but I couldn't do anything to stop the suffering.

By the time the male *bedinn* came around to untie us, I was well past miserable and deeply into sullen. It had to have been close to midday outside, and the stink of sweating, yearning females all around was enough to make anyone ill. I couldn't wait to get to that pool water to bathe, but that wasn't the first item on the agenda as far as the male *bedinn* were concerned. They'd brought heaps of dirty laundry belonging to the *hizahh,* and washing that laundry was the first task given us. At that point I stupidly lost my temper and refused to do a thing until I'd had a bath, and that was when I learned the circumstances under which male *bedinn* had authority over female *bedinn.* The male *bedinn* never gave orders themselves; all they did was carry out and oversee the orders given by *hizahh.* In that instance, however, they were concerned with something that had to be done *for* the *hizahh,* and therefore had the right to punish without waiting for orders to do so.

I hadn't yet reached that level of understanding when I was suddenly taken by the hair and dragged outside into the sun and sand, one *bedin* leading me, two others following. I was shocked and furious and apprehensive and indignant all at the same time, a mixture that usually proves impossible to work through. I paid for not staying calm and level-headed by having those three *bedinn* take turns strapping me, stuffing a gag in my mouth, while my body was held taut across the horizontal trunk of a wide, broad-leafed shade tree, my wrists held by one of the *bedinn* who wasn't at that time wielding the strap. I would have willingly done my share of the laundry long before they were finished, but I never got the chance to say so. Once it was all over I was tied to the trunk, well in the shade to keep my brains from boiling out of my skull, and was allowed to watch the other women do laundry and bathe at the same time. I hurt all over, and I felt abysmally stupid, but worst of all I had to do without a bath. That made me cry more than the beating had, and made me not even want to bother with pain control.

There was little more than an hour left to sundown when the male *bedinn* came back, but they weren't alone. The *hizah* Kednin strolled along with them, his white veil set beneath his eyes, his white robes full and flowing, his mind hard and definitely displeased. As soon as I was released from the tree trunk I knelt in the sand and bowed, very much aware of the feelings passing through the man's mind as he looked at my naked body. I'd been able to see the mountain range more clearly in the daylight, but the man I bowed to had the power to make my escape impossible – or useless. I felt a shiver touch me in the waning heat, and the hum of interest in the man's mind increased.

"This one may do after all," he murmured to the male *bedinn* standing around him, his eyes an almost physical weight on my back. "Bathe her thoroughly, then bring her with the others."

He turned then and strode off without waiting for an answer, and wasn't wrong in believing he didn't need one. The answer the *bedinn* made was immediately obeying his command, the best answer they could have given. I was dragged to the pool and into it, then bathed quickly and very thoroughly by the one who entered the water with me. Having your face washed with a veil over it is a fascinating experience, but not nearly as fascinating as getting a thorough bath from a man who doesn't care what he does to you. I screamed and struggled while the two watching *bedinn* laughed in amusement, then was carried back to the *bedin* tent over the shoulder of the one who had bathed me. If I'd had my sandals or if a *hizah* hadn't commanded that I be satisfactorily clean, I would at least have been allowed to walk.

Dark had fallen and my body and hair were completely dry by the time the food was ready to be carried to the *hizah* tent. There were considerably more dishes prepared than usual, but that only confirmed the suspicion I'd had that something unusual was going on. Dressed in a clean robe and wearing sandals, I moved carefully through the sand with the other *bedinn,* carrying a large wooden bowl of grilled meat strips, thinking again about the possibilities of escape. I wasn't sure how long the tribe would be staying at the oasis, so I couldn't afford to wait too long. Leaving at night would be best, but the Hamarda *hizahh* tended to be awake and about during the night hours. Leaving during the day meant risking running into male *bedinn* who were always up and about, and also meant dying of thirst sooner if water couldn't be found quickly enough. Leaving alone would attract the least amount of attention, but would it be right to desert the women I'd been captured with? And whoever I took whenever I left, how much water and food would be necessary to keep us alive until we reached the mountains? And last but certainly not least, what was the likelihood of being pursued? As I followed the now-familiar route through the white silk hangings of the *hizah* tent, I tried to decide how important *bedinn* were to these men. Would they let one disappear without caring where she went? If so, would the same be true of six? If they did pursue us, how long would they keep at it before they gave up? Worrying about whether they ever would give up kept me from noticing how slowly the women ahead of me were moving, and saved the surprise for when I stepped through the last of the hangings and looked up. Sitting there beside Kednin, an honored guest, without a worry in the world, was Tammad.

## TWELVE

If I didn't drop the bowl of meat slices, it was only because I don't believe in the unreal. My mind told me it was impossible for Tammad to be sitting in that tent, Kednin to his left, Len to his right, Garth to Len's right, Hannas and Loddar and four other of his *l'lendaa* ranged elsewhere around the tent, and I believed that. The only problem was, I could sense the deep calm in Tammad's mind, tinged with the same amusement touching Len and Garth, could feel the heart-thumping excitement in Findra and the other four women, the longing to run to their men's arms. The only thing holding them back seemed to be fear, most likely stemming from the way the *hizahh* outnumbered the *l'lendaa*. If the women acknowledged their men, the *hizahh* might be provoked into defending their property in the most direct manner – which meant swords. Rather than start a fight, the women just stood there quivering; I just stood and stared.

"These are the *bedinn* who will serve us," Kednin said to Tammad, waving a negligent hand in our direction. "Examine them as you will, honored guests, and choose for your own those who offend you the least. My tent holds naught which will not be bettered by your use."

"It is we who are honored by our host," Tammad said, his voice warm and brotherly, his eyes moving over the line of *bedinn*. "We have traveled far and in too great a haste, and have need of relaxation such as this."

"Your needs will be well seen to in this tent," Kednin answered, a matching warmth in his voice. "For this you have my word. *Bedinn*: put aside your burdens and present yourselves to your *hizah*'s guests."

The *bedinn* among us immediately began putting down their bowls and platters and reaching to their robes to remove them, even Findra and the others quickly moving to obey; only I stood as if frozen, still staring at Tammad and the others. Put the bowl aside, remove the robe, kneel and bow? How could I?

"Have you lost your hearing, *bedin*?" Kednin snapped, gazing at me searingly from behind his veil, his mind beginning to be touched by a monstrous shame. "Do you dare to disobey me before my guests?"

I nearly dropped the bowl in my rush to obey, my heart beating wildly from the shadow of murderous rage waiting to settle over Kednin's mind. He would have killed me then and there if I'd continued to ignore him, but even so removing the robe was difficult. The eyes of Len and Garth immediately began moving over me, examining me boldly as I knelt, with distant amusement as I bowed. They enjoyed seeing me like that, helpless before them, and Tammad's mind was hardly different. Pleasure touched him as closely as he allowed it to, pleasure most likely brought about by seeing me humbled so.

"The choice is yours," Kednin said, and I could feel the sweeping gesture he made with his arm. "Which ones will you have?"

"They are all veiled," Len observed, his voice easy and confident. "How is a man to know which is most beautiful when he cannot see their faces?"

"Of what use is beauty in a *bedin*'s face?" Kednin asked, bringing forth a silent chuckle in Tammad. "One may do no more than gaze upon a face. As for other services, you will find the veil no hindrance to their performance. *Bedinn:* raise yourselves so that my guests may see you more easily."

I came up out of the bow slowly, keeping my eyes down on the white silk floor, the blaze of shame burning brighter within me than it had the first time I'd been knelt so. Those weren't strangers sitting there so comfortably, those were men I knew – or thought I knew. The very real comfort they felt was beginning to make me have second thoughts.

"The one with the short hair and dark eyes strikes my fancy," Hannas said in a thoughtful drawl from where he sat. "With my host's permission?"

"Certainly," Kednin said, the warmth back in his tone. "Go to him, *bedin,* and see that you please him."

After being elbowed by the woman next to her, Findra's heart rose when her body did, and she lost no time getting to Hannas. Tammad's other men were choosing the last four women, and Loddar happily made do with one of the other *bedinn*. I still hadn't looked up, but I don't need sight to know when four pairs of eyes rest on me.

"You find this one of interest?" Kednin asked, his voice now skeptical. "I, too, found her of interest at first, but now regard her solely as a curiosity. It has been necessary to punish her often."

"Somehow, I find that unsurprising," Tammad said, his voice dry but his mind unamused. He didn't like hearing that I'd been disobedient, and I could feel my head lowering even farther. "I do, however, continue to also find interest in her. I have never been fully served by a dark-haired, green-eyed *wenda*."

"As you wish," Kednin said casually. He had missed the way Tammad had stressed the word "fully" but I hadn't. "And the others beside you? Which *bedinn* will they have?"

A silence intervened at that point, during which I could feel an exchange going on between Tammad and Len and Garth. Len and Garth asked with their silence, their minds no more than politely requesting a casual favor they would enjoy having, Tammad's mind understanding what they were asking and considering it. His hesitation was only seconds in duration, then he spoke again to Kednin.

"My two brothers will share the service of this – *bedin,*" he said, his voice showing nothing of the hesitation he had felt. "As you say she is disobedient, the punishment of such additional service will be most fitting."

"As is all punishment for disobedient *bedinn*," Kednin chuckled as I raised my eyes quickly in outrage and dismay. My gaze was immediately captured by Tammad's light blue stare, the expression therein telling me the punishment came from himself alone. No matter what anyone else did to me, it was *his* punishment I was to expect if I deviated from his concept of the proper. He had once warned me about insolence and the need for obedience, and he wasn't in the habit of repeating warnings.

Kednin ordered us all to begin serving the food we'd brought, then sat back with his eyes unwaveringly on me. I got to my feet and retrieved the bowl I'd put aside, then went to kneel again in front of the *hizah*. It gave me some small pleasure to ignore the other three in his favor as I was supposed to, but the pleasure was very small and didn't last long. Kednin took a strip of the grilled meat, tore a piece off, then stuffed the piece in my mouth. I chewed it as long as I dared before swallowing, trying not to show the near ecstasy I felt as the rare juices filled my mouth and trickled down my throat. I hadn't been permitted anything but that thick cereal grain to eat, not unless I was tasting something for a *hizah*. I'd tried to find one who was amused at the idea of feeding a *bedin*, but amusement in those men was much too close to interest. To encourage their amusement and discourage their interest turned out to be impossible, and I'd found I had to give up eating meat if I wanted to avoid rape.

Right after that it was necessary to kneel in front of Tammad, holding the bowl out for his selection, and I found myself moving slowly as I did so. I remembered another scene very much like that one, set instead in the barbarian's tent, and he must have seen the memory in my eyes.

"I find it odd that this *wenda* holds no interest for you," he said to Kednin as he helped himself to a strip of meat from the bowl. "It seems odd indeed that the loveliest *bedin* in the tent should affect you so."

"Perhaps." Kednin shrugged while I tried to keep from cringing at Tammad's continued stare. "It is difficult to say what will attract a man's attention, most especially in a female. Have you forgotten the balance of the service required of you, *bedin*?"

I glanced at him quickly, but didn't need the glance to feel the impatience in his mind. He wanted me to move on to Len, but that move was harder than the one to Tammad. I hesitated another instant, found no way to reach his mind and change it, then absolutely had to change position. When I knelt in front of Len and extended the bowl, I found two serious blue eyes staring at me.

"Such a lovely *bedin* should not find herself ignored," he murmured, taking a strip of meat. "Perhaps she *feels* herself undesirable and therefore *appears* undesirable to men. Come, *bedin*. This will show that I find you of interest. Are you not pleased?"

"This" was a torn piece of his meat strip, larger than the one Kednin had given me, but not so large that it was likely to spoil me. Len stuffed it in my mouth the way the *hizah* had done, giving me no choice about accepting it. He let me feel the grim pleasure he experienced while I chewed, knowing full well how great the humiliation was for me. His sending was crisp and clear, unlike the accidental sendings of the untalented, but the strong anger he felt wasn't quite as covered as he wanted it to be. He knew I'd been tampering with minds again, and he was furious over the fact. I felt my own anger rising at the injustice of the outlook, not caring whether or not he felt it. He wasn't the one who had been in constant jeopardy of being raped; how dare he judge?

When I finished with Len I moved on to Garth, who naturally hadn't said a word. Len had been leaning over toward him from time to time, most likely translating, but the situation wasn't one where Garth could afford to comment. As I knelt before him I wondered why he was even there; not speaking the language put him at a considerable disadvantage. I held the bowl of meat strips out to him, but he didn't accept the offer immediately. His gray eyes stared at me intently, almost accusingly, and at last he shook his head in disgust.

"Knowing you, I'll bet I know what you're thinking," he murmured very low, so low no one else could possibly have heard him. "You're a damned fool, Terry, and Len's the one who's right."

He reached into the bowl for a meat strip then, his mind smoldering with an anger I didn't understand. There was no trace of his usual air of superiority; instead, he seemed to have achieved the sort of calm assurance most people don't even know is possible. I didn't agree with his conclusions about Len's position – on any subject I could think of – and he seemed to know that. Once he had his meat strip he moved his hand in a curt gesture, dismissing me from his presence as though I were a slave. I could feel my lips tighten as I rose to my feet, but that was as far as I could let my anger show. Even that, with the veil in place, became a gesture for myself alone.

After that I was required to start the rounds again, but custom and courtesy no longer demanded that the men take only a single meat strip. Once they all had all the meat they wanted, I was sent for the bowls of dark bread and fried vegetables and mixed sweets some of the other women had brought. The men had their hands full with the meat, so I had to feed them whichever of the other items they wanted while they leaned back and took their ease. Kednin waved me away when I approached him, showing he was uninterested in being served further, but his guests weren't that easy to please. Garth insisted on more than one serving of everything, Len made me eat his leftovers, and Tammad – Tammad nodded wordlessly when I offered something, took the proffered offering without moving his eyes from mine, chewed, swallowed, then waited for the next, all the time projecting a faint air of being displeased somehow. For some reason my hand quickly began trembling as I raised the food to his lips, and wouldn't stop even when I told myself I was being stupid. I didn't care in the least whether or not he was pleased, so why was I reacting that way?

When the food was all gone the men shared a large wineskin, brought to them by the *bedin* they'd chosen to serve them. Once I'd handed the thing to Kednin I was supposed to be through for a while, but Garth gestured me to him while Kednin looked in his direction, giving me no chance to pretend I didn't see the gesture. Garth couldn't have called to me, of course, and I would have taken advantage of that fact if I could have. He seemed to sense my impatient anger when I knelt before him, but instead of being amused he was annoyed. I hadn't expected that reaction in him, any more than I expected the way his fist came to my hair to force my head down to the silken floor. I almost gasped at his nerve in bowing me like that, but Kednin was watching too closely.

"It is unusual having guests in our tents," the *hizah* said to Tammad after pulling at the wineskin and passing it on. "Do you merely travel through the sand to some far destination, or have you come to us with purpose?"

"The truth occupies two places," Tammad answered after a drinking pause of his own. "We come to the sands of the Hamarda in search of that which was stolen from us, yet we also come to bring word to our brothers of the desert. We who dwell in cooler lands have found it necessary to begin a life-game with those off-worlders of whom you are already aware. The off-worlders encourage us to make demands upon them, thinking to bind us and separate us with the granting of those demands. We, however, will use our demands to weaken our enemy and strengthen ourselves, to their eventual sorrow. We invite our brothers the Hamarda to join us, both to stand with us against the enemy and to grow strength as we do. It is my, intention to speak more fully of the matter at the next Gathering of the tribes of the Hamarda."

Kednin was silent for a moment, his mind whirling in frenzied thought, and then he said, "You offer to share the new strength which will be yours? Surely you know that should you keep it for yourselves alone, you would soon come to rule our world. Why, then, would you wish to share it?"

"It is not possible to rule a world which has fallen to strangers," Tammad answered, his voice harsh from the bleak sight his inner eye looked upon. "Should we be foolish enough to keep the gift of the off-worlders to ourselves alone, we would soon find ourselves a small island of strength a world of weakness. Once the balance of our world is taken, how much longer are we ourselves likely to stand? In order to survive a battle a man must have his brothers at his back, else his sword, no matter how sharp, will be rendered useless."

"It is as you say," Kednin muttered, his thoughts disturbed. "No man may stand alone against the hordes of his enemies. Are the off-worlders not likely to deny their gifts to some of us, thinking to create a rift between those who receive them and those who are denied?"

"They are sure to do so," Tammad said, his tone having gone grim. "The demands you make will not be presented as yours; instead they will be added to ours as though they were ours. The demands put forward in your own name will be contrived demands, ones which will cost you nothing when they are refused. You will, of course, be highly insulted at the refusal, sending your anger toward my people rather than toward the off-worlders. It will then seem to the off-worlders that we are bound more tightly to them, having incurred the scorn and hatred of our brothers. When the truth is learned by them, it will be far too late to save them."

"I believe I see the target of your arrow," Kednin said, and then he chuckled. "The hunt itself will be worthy of the effort, even should the quarry not be taken I am eager to speak further of the matter, yet such things are best discussed far from the distraction of *bedinn*. As you are my guests I insist that you first pleasure yourselves; serious words may spoken later. *Bedin:* present yourself to the guest you bow to."

I heard Kednin's words through my confusion, and for a minute they didn't make any sense. I was too busy wondering what Tammad was up to this time to remember what my position there was – until I felt the instantly gathering fury in the *hizah's* mind. I quickly put my wrists behind me, offering them for binding – and only then realized who I was offering myself to. Garth was the one who sat above me, a man who probably knew less of the customs of the tribe than he did of the language, a man who would undoubtedly shame himself by failing to act as the Hamarda expected. I can't say I was disappointed at the thought not after the way he'd been treating me – but I wasn't given much of a chance to gloat.

No more than a lazy minute passed before I felt leather at my wrists, looped and tied tight by the large hands holding it before I had a chance to resist. I didn't want to be tied by Garth, but it was over with and I was pulled to the silk beside him before I could struggle more than slightly.

"You seem disappointed, Terry," he murmured as softly as he had earlier. "Were you hoping I wouldn't know what to do with a slave? It's a shame to dash your hopes, but Tammad briefed us thoroughly before we entered camp. Are you ready to serve me?"

He looked down at me where I lay on my right side between him and Len, his gray eyes showing nothing of hesitation, his mind showing nothing of uncertainty. All around us the evening festivities were well under way, but I wasn't about to be a part of them. Furiously I reached toward his mind with every intention of hitting with fear or disgust or grief or anything that would dent that thick calm he'd developed – but was instead hit so hard myself by a bolt of anger that my mind felt numbed. I moaned as my head rang from the attack, and then Len's lips were at my ear.

"That's just a taste of what you'll get if you ever try that again," he whispered, no trace of that vast anger in his voice. "In order to launch an attack you have to open your mind wide, which renders you immediately vulnerable. The next time I'll hit you with fear."

After saying his piece he drew away again, putting his anger back under control, but that didn't mean there was no anger left. Garth's eyes and mind were filled with it, showing he knew what had happened even if he hadn't heard Len. I twisted against the leather on my wrists, trying to loosen it, fear beginning to fill me even without Len's efforts. These were men of my own civilization; why weren't they acting like it?

"I think you're just about ready to act the proper slave," Garth murmured, putting a big hand on my shoulder to rub gently. "That Hamarda is mostly involved with talking to Tammad, but he isn't ignoring you. Let me hear you ask nicely to be of service to me."

"Garth, please don't go through with this," I whispered, finding it impossible not to squirm under the gentle rubbing of his hand. "You're not a barbarian and you won't be able to forget your...."

"Silence," he interrupted, his voice cold with anger even in the lowered tones he was using, his eyes as angry and cold as his voice. "You were given an order and I expect to see it obeyed. After that shot you took at me a minute ago, any sympathy you had coming is wiped off the books. Now, let me hear that request or I'll force it out of you."

Under the veil I was biting my lip, indecision tearing at me. If I refused to do as Garth said, Kednin would surely notice, and that would mean more trouble than I cared to face. On the other hand, how could I bring myself to say such a thing to Garth R'hem Solohr, a man I'd known under vastly different circumstances? It was terribly wrong, somehow, and I couldn't see myself –

"All right, don't say you didn't ask for it," Garth said, the impatience in his mind unwilling to wait any longer. In the midst of the laughter and low-key conversation going on around us, his hand slid down from my shoulder, caressed my breast, then continued on its way to my thigh. My breath drew in in a mortified gasp, but in another minute I didn't have the breath for a gasp. His touch on me was like a flash of lightning, reawakening and intensifying all the frustrations I'd suffered through that day. I writhed and moaned in low, mindless need, but the humiliation was still blazingly there.

"If you think I'll be feeling guilty about this later, you're crazy," Garth murmured, stretching out on one elbow on the silk beside me to kiss my throat below the veil. "Your skin is softer than Dacrian velvet, woman, and I fully intend experiencing all of it. Speak the way you were ordered to speak, or I'll have you screaming instead."

I moaned again as I looked up into the gray of his eyes, knowing the truth of the words he spoke; if he didn't stop touching me like that I would be screaming soon. I shuddered, miserable to think he was able to do that to me, then let the words come tumbling out when the pressure of his fingers increased.

"No, don't!" I begged, choking in the effort to keep my voice down. "I'll say it if you'll just take your hand away ... Oh! Garth ... All right, all right, I'll obey you! *Hizah,* I beg to be allowed the honor. of serving you! I beg it! Please, no more!"

"There are tears in your eyes, slave," he observed, for some reason not hearing the words he'd demanded. "Is being made to know the needs of your body so painful then? Or is it the man who touches you that's the painful part? I will readily admit I am not yet *l'lenda,* but neither am I *darayse.* And no, *wenda,* I will not grant you the honor you beg so reluctantly. I want nothing of willing service from you – merely the service itself."

He took me in his arms then, ignoring my whispered pleas, and not much later he took even more. I think I was in shock then, especially when I responded to him with very little effort on his part. I didn't know what had happened to Garth, and once he had let me go I was even less sure about what had happened to me. I lay on the silk where he had left me, my body relaxed rather than ravaged, my emotions serene rather than scandalized. I had never before felt that way after being with a man of my worlds, and it was almost frightening.

"That pleasure in your mind feels out of place," Len said softly from my left. "Has it really been that long since you found pleasure in anything?"

I turned my head to him quickly, my mind immediately cringing and begging, and he winced as though I'd slapped him.

"Don't do that," he muttered, shaking his head hard to rid himself of the feelings he'd picked up from me. "Despite your very obvious opinions to the contrary, there are women in this Amalgamation who have been used by me without losing their lunches. If you exert superhuman control, you might even be able to number yourself among them."

His blue eyes looked down at me soberly, showing nothing of the faint hurt he'd felt at my reaction. But they also showed nothing of the calm determination he was filled with. I suddenly felt terribly confused and unsure, but those emotions did nothing to alter my reluctance. I pulled futilely at the leather on my wrists, and thought that maybe if I spoke to Len –

"No, don't say anything," Len interrupted, not the words but the thought. "I don't care to allow you the right to speak to me. The only thing you ever talk about is why everything should be done your way. It's about time you learned you can't back up that attitude – at least not on this world. And it's time you learned not to push people around."

His hand came to stroke my arm then, but his mind also came to mine to let me know the pleasure he felt at the contact. I'd had no idea what it would be like to be used by a male empath, but I soon found out. He fed me every emotion he felt, sharply, intensely, making me feel it despite my struggles. I'd always been stronger than Len and I still was, but I could no more force him out of my mind than away from my body. In order to strike at him I had to open my mind wide, and as soon as I did he was immediately inside, flooding me with emotions that turned me weak and helpless. I whimpered at the touch of his hands to my body as his mind invaded mine, writhed and moaned as he demanded I do, wept and begged in a way that pleased him. He let me suffer a very long time before he took me, but when he did the feeling was indescribably satisfying, almost as good as the best times with Tammad. The fact that Len was forcing me to feel that way diminished some of the pleasure, but after he had left me I came to understand that he could have used the darker emotions to obtain his satisfaction if he'd wanted to. Both he and Garth had given me pleasure instead of fear, satisfaction instead of pain. On that world they could have done anything to me that they pleased, but it had pleased them to do nothing more than share some pleasure. I closed my eyes against the tears flowing out, feeling terribly ashamed, and not only for the way I'd treated them. The shame ran deeper than that, but the reason for it was lost in a welter of confusion.

"I believe the *bedin*'s use is now yours," Kednin's voice came, undoubtedly speaking to Tammad. "On your knees, *bedin*, and present yourself in a proper manner to my guest."

I opened my eyes again at the command, and after a few minutes of struggle managed to kneel in front of Tammad. The barbarian had watched my struggle silently, his mind held by its usual, rigid calm, his broad face impassive. I finally raised my eyes to his, slowly and reluctantly, then immediately looked down at the silk again. That same sense of faint dissatisfaction was touching him, coupled with a sudden surge of hurt that made me cry inside. He was disappointed in me, and whether it was still or again made no real difference. I needed so desperately to be held in his arms, but who would want to hold a disappointment?

"A female is ever more beautiful for having been used," Kednin said, his voice husky. "See how her body trembles even as she displays herself for your inspection. You may now speak, *bedin*, and see that your words please us."

I raised my eyes again to look at Tammad, and it was just as though he alone sat in the tent. That same look was still in his eyes, and I had to do something to get rid of it.

"I beg you, *hizah*, allow me the honor of serving you fully," I whispered, trembling even more. "A lowly *bedin* begs the favor of her *hizah*."

I waited for those mighty arms to come and draw me close to him, but a flash of disgust came from his mind instead, short in duration but so strong it nearly knocked me over. I knelt frozen in shock, unable to understand what was happening even when Tammad turned his head to Kednin.

"I thank my host, but this *bedin* no longer interests me," he said, his voice lazy but impassive. "Should it not inconvenience you, I would much prefer finding a quiet place where we may continue discussing the strangers."

"As you wish," Kednin agreed with a shrug as he rose to his feet. "If you will follow me, I will show you to such a place."

Tammad rose, beckoning Len and Garth up with him, and the three of them followed Kednin through one of the silk hangings. I knelt where I'd been left on the silken floor, my head down, feeling so ashamed I was ready to curl up and die. Not only didn't he want me, he felt disgusted by me, so disgusted he couldn't bring himself to touch me. Maybe it was because I'd been used by so many men, and had not only been used but had been made to enjoy it. Maybe he didn't know how terrible it was to be owned by those Hamarda, maybe he thought I enjoyed all of it. Under those circumstances I could understand why he no longer even pretended to want me; I just couldn't live with the thought. All I'd ever wanted was to have his love and please him in everything, but now that was even more impossible than it had been. I bent lower over my knees, too defeated even to moan, and wished I were dead.

A minute later a fist was in my hair, drawing me to my feet and then stumblingly out through the hangings. I didn't know what that strange *hizah* wanted of me, but couldn't scrape together enough concern to care even when he took me out of the tent into the dark, silent night. I was pulled across the sand, shivering from the coolness of the night, until the bulk of a male *bedin* suddenly appeared in front of us. The *hizah* stopped, threw me to the sand at the *bedin*'s feet, then looked down at me coldly.

"It is the wish of the *hizah* Kednin that this miserable *bedin* be whipped," he said, shocking me even further with the words. "She has failed to please the *hizah's* guests, and will therefore forfeit her life. You are to whip her now, but only in punishment. The *hizah* wishes to be present at her death, but will not be free for some time."

The *bedin* grunted his acknowledgment of the orders, dragged me from the sand by one arm, then started away toward the Y frame. The *hizah* was already retracing his steps toward the tent we had come from, his mind grimly pleased that his chore had been seen to. I struggled along beside the *bedin,* my arm blazing with pain from his grip, almost ready to scream out my fear of what awaited me. I wanted to scream – I needed desperately to scream – but there was no one on that world who wanted to hear me.

## THIRTEEN

I hung slackly from the Y frame, so deeply into shock that I no longer felt the pain. My arms and wrists and shoulders were as numb as my back, but somehow I was aware of the blood trickling down toward the backs of my legs, blood drawn by the whip the *bedin* had wielded. How many strokes I'd had I didn't think I'd ever know, but there had been enough to make me be sick all over myself, enough to make me draw my shield in tight to keep from projecting the agony. My body had sweated into the cool desert night even more than the *bedin's* had.

Suddenly I shivered, and the soul-searing pain that flashed with the shiver seemed to somehow clear my mind. It wasn't all over, it had barely begun, and I couldn't make myself understand that it would be my life that was over. Slowly, straining in an effort that was almost too great to make, I forced the shield back to nothingness. The night flared into new being with the minds that inhabited it, animal minds, human minds – and any combination of the two. I was even more aware of my own labored breathing and the way it forced an echo from my body's reawakened pain.

But the pain had to be ignored if it wasn't going to be added to. I cast my sensing ability around to all sides, making sure no one was watching me even from a distance, and then turned my attention to the *seetarr* tied nearby. Most of them were half asleep, pleased to be allowed to do nothing more than drowse, but one or two were wide awake and aware of what had happened near them. They knew someone had been given pain, but none of them seemed to care – until I reached the mind of Tammad's big male. Weakened though I was, the *seetar* recognized my mind touch immediately, a rumbling anger coming from his throat when he realized it was I who had been hurt. The big male had cared for me almost from the first, and he didn't hesitate when he understood I needed him. His large, sharp teeth clamped onto the lead tying him to the line with the rest of the *seetarr,* the lead parted with a snap as he backed away from the line, and then he was moving toward me, determined to do what he could to help me.

*Seetarr* are very intelligent animals, but that intelligence doesn't make them more than animals. Tammad's *seetar* was completely willing to help me, but I couldn't seem to get through to him with the idea of what sort of help I needed. After a few minutes of trying I was sweating again, and what the sweat felt like on my back is better left unsaid. The problem came down to the fact that the *seetar* didn't understand that I couldn't free myself and needed him to do it for me. What emotions could be used to convey such an idea was beyond me to conceive of, it being all I could do to keep the *seetar* from bellowing aloud at his own frustration and the mounting pain I was feeling. The dizzier I got the more his rage increased, his huge black body stamping in the sand in front of me, his eyes blazing, his nostrils flaring; then, completely out of patience, his massive head shot down, his teeth closed on one of the arms of the Y, and I was suddenly ripped up out of the sand and hurled with the frame into the air. The gesture was so violent and caused me so much pain, I was unconscious before I hit the sand again.

I awoke to a large sandpapery tongue licking at my left arm. I tried to move away from that raspy show of concern, but my body screamed at the first attempt, nearly sending me back into darkness. I forced vision back into my eyes to confirm the fact that I was lying face up in the sand, a heavy wooden something lying on top of me. As soon as I understood the something was the Y frame, everything else came back – including the *seetar*'s violent gesture. I decided I had to move again just to see if something was broken, but I didn't really want to move, and that made it more than difficult. Then my eyes focused on the left arm of the Y frame, really seeing it instead of just looking in its direction. It was raggedly cracked in half, most likely from the *seetar*'s bite, and just a little strength ought to break it the rest of the way and free me.

I was so wild at the thought of being free that it was a good thing nothing on me *had* been broken. I pulled with all my strength against the wood holding me prisoner, setting the various cuts and bruises on me to smarting again, but after a minute the wood cracked through, loosening the leather that had held me tight to the notched arm. I snaked my wrist out of the loops, undoubtedly leaving blood smears behind, then began working on the leather holding my right wrist. It took so long getting it loose that I had to rest when I was done, but I couldn't afford to rest too long. I had no idea when they would be coming back to finish me, and I had to be gone by then.

Slipping out from under the Y frame was harder than I thought it would be. I was totally incapable of lifting it off me, leaving sliding through the sand my only other option. With the help of pain control I was able to do the sliding, but if I hadn't had adrenalin pouring through me I'm sure I would have collapsed. Once I was out from under I lay on my side in the sand, fighting to control the gasping my breathing had become, fighting to keep the darkness from closing in on me. Being untied was only the first step to freedom, and the next had to be taken to make the first meaningful.

I fought my way to my knees as soon as I could, then pulled myself erect by holding onto the *seetar*'s bridle. He had been hovering over me in concern, and when I put my arms around his head and hugged him in gratitude, his rumble very nearly became a purr. He was feeling pleased that he'd managed to do the right thing after all the difficulty we'd had understanding each other, but he didn't seem ready to go on from there. I needed to get to the other side of the oasis, where the beginning of the pebbled flats could be found, but running away on foot wouldn't have been possible even if I hadn't been aching head to toe with pain. I needed a *seetar* to ride and the barbarian's mount would have been perfect; the only trouble was, he was the barbarian's mount. I tugged at his bridle, trying to get him moving, but he wasn't interested in going anywhere. He'd helped me willingly, and would let me ride him when I sat behind the barbarian, but my riding him alone wasn't something he could accept. His mind automatically rejected the idea of going *anywhere* without his saddle being *properly* filled.

I withdrew from his mind with a weary sigh, knowing when I was beaten. I'd be wasting time I didn't have trying to work on the intractable beast. The only thing to do was check out the rest of the mounts, but I needed to lean on the big male beside me until I reached the line the others were tied to. I worked as fast as I could, but I had to go through seven uninterested minds before I found one with enough curiosity to try something new. The *seetar* was a young male, either not yet wedded to the idea of a single rider or not so fond of his owner that he couldn't bear to be parted from him. I stumbled over to the beast, managed to get it to kneel by projecting some of my own weariness, then pulled myself into the saddle. Somehow I was able to stay mounted while the beast stood again, and was also able to take a large, nearly empty waterskin from the next *seetar* over once my mount was standing straight. A gentle flick of the reins got us moving, and I turned to send a final good-bye to the barbarian's large male, who seemed vaguely unsatisfied about something. But unsatisfied or not he stayed where he was, and we moved away, off into the night.

I circled the tents of the camp carefully and quietly, alert for any human presence, giving thanks that an oasis was a place where sentries didn't seem to be required. I meant to stop at the drinking pond only long enough to fill the waterskin, but an experimental easing up of pain control showed me how badly sand does in open wounds. I was forced to take a quick bath in the bathing pool as well, an action which set me shivering and throbbing in the cool night air. Once I was in the saddle again, the *seetar* standing erect, I discovered a rolled up set of sleeping furs tied behind the saddle. I worked one of the furs out with trembling hands, retied the rest, then wrapped the fur around me. As soft as the fur was it still added to the touch of pain, but that didn't keep me from urging my mount out across the flats I'd been so anxious to reach. Even though I hurried, I knew there was no real reason to hurry; one escaped slave would hardly be chased after, even if she *had* stolen a *seetar*. Aside from that there was no one who would be interested in me or what happened to me; that had been made abundantly clear. I was on my own on a strange, savage world, a world I had never really wanted to have anything to do with. I'd work at trying to survive because something inside me insisted that I do so, but if I failed it would be no great loss. Even I didn't care about me any more.

The sun was merciless as it beat down on me, but I kept going until I felt the *seetar* too tired to go on. We were on sand again, long beyond the stretch of pebbled flats we'd started out on, but at least we had the distant mountains to guide us. I sweated terribly under the fur I had covering me, endlessly glad that I'd left the veil and headband behind in the bathing pool, continuously telling myself that sweating was better than broiling alive. I had nothing but the furs to cover myself with, and had even draped the second fur over the saddle so that I might sit on it. It kept my flesh from being rubbed raw by hard leather and burned by sun-baked metal parts, but it also increased the sensation of being buried alive in a soft, awakening volcano.

Once the *seetar* had let me down, I gave him some water and took a drink for myself, then arranged the furs on the sand so that I might lie on them. The *seetar* had fed well enough at the oasis to keep him from being hungry yet, and I was too ill to feel any hunger. My body ached and flared even through the pain control, and I wasn't at all sure I wouldn't be sick all over myself again. I lay down on the fur, burying myself under the top one, the carrying strap of the waterskin under the furs with me. I had given the *seetar* the impression that we would stay where we were until we were rested, but I wasn't strong enough to make the suggestion a command. If my mount happened to wander off before I woke again, I didn't want the water going with him.

Sleep found me almost at once, a sleep heavy enough to be drugged. It lasted until I awoke with a moan, throwing the covering fur off me, still dream-convinced that I'd wander through sand forever, beyond the time when my water gave out, beyond the time when life fled from my body. The sun was just disappearing behind the distant mountains, leaving a twilight zone of cool between it and the cold of night. My *seetar* lowered his massive head to nuzzle me, concern clear in his thoughts. I quickly assured him everything was all right, gave each of us some water, then reembarked upon the torture of moving on.

We came within sight of the end of true desert before nightfall was complete. A stretch of flats appeared again, but this time low, sickly bushes could be seen beyond the flats. We moved into the area of bushes and continued on for hours, but it was growing more and more difficult for me to tell what was around me. My body shivered in the cold darkness even with the furs, my mind wandered from real to unreal so often I was beginning to be unable to distinguish between them, and the pain brought by the sway and bounce of the *seetar* was threatening to grow beyond all control. After a long time I realized we were moving over grass, and even longer after that there were suddenly trees all around. How long we'd been among the trees I didn't know, but the sun was just beginning to pink the sky and my right hand was stiff from having held so tightly to the *seetar*'s short, bristly mane. My mount was hungry and wanted to stop for something to eat, but I laughed weakly and projected a feeling of patience at him. The embassy I'd been searching for was just beyond the trees, and it would have been silly to stop before we reached it.

The sun was well up before we found the embassy in a clearing, but for some reason the building's style had been changed. Instead of still being a wide, two-story affair, it had become a dozen or more small tents with one large tent in the center. The large tent was of red, had a high, pointed roof with pennants at the top, and seemed to be at least hexagonal in shape if not octagonal. The smaller tents were of every other color but red, had lower roofs and smaller pennants, and were only square. I didn't really understand about the arrangement, but moved forward again without waiting for understanding to come. I badly needed one of those tents for myself, and the soft bed it would contain. I didn't feel well, and I wanted to lie down on a bed instead of on hot, blistering sand.

As we reached the tents and began moving among them, I tried to figure out which one would be mine. The last time I'd been at the embassy I'd had a yellow room – tent – whatever it was; if I took another yellow I couldn't be too far off. I directed the *seetar* toward the nearest yellow room, standing about twenty feet away, hoping I'd be able to find the strength to walk into it on my own. Embassy people didn't like having animals in their rooms, and Denny would be angry if I rode in. I realized I should have left the *seetar* parked on the lowest level –

The two men in belted, baggy pants and wide-sleeved shirts came at me silently but swiftly, one grabbing the reins of my mount, the second reaching up to pull me from the saddle. I tried to scream from a dry, aching throat as his hands took my arms and pulled, but the effort was too great. Instead I found myself projecting hatred and fear, lashing out with my mind as I couldn't do with my body. The man holding me screamed and dropped me to the ground, his hands going to his ears in an effort to block off the projection, the man at the *seetar*'s bridle groaning and doing the same. I hit the ground hard as yells and screams came from all over the place, then darkness came in answer to the screams, and I saw no more.

## FOURTEEN

I expected waking up to be painful, but it wasn't. I took a deep breath as I opened my eyes, trying to identify the sweet, pleasant odor of wherever I was, but seeing my surroundings made me forget all about how they smelled. I lay in a large, ornate room, expensive silks in silver and blue adorning the walls, cushions of blue piled on silver-furred carpeting, small, beautifully carved tables of blue-painted wood standing here and there, wide, lightly curtained windows showing late afternoon. What I lay on was not a bed but a pile of furs two feet high, soft but firm, lined with silk and covered with another soft, luxurious fur. I didn't know where I was, but if that was the way whoever my captors were treated their prisoners, I didn't expect to be in too much of a hurry to escape.

Remembering the thoughts I'd had before falling unconscious, I quickly looked around again to make sure I wasn't hallucinating, but if my mind was playing tricks they were tricks I couldn't penetrate. In looking around the second time I discovered one of those small, carved tables right near my bed, holding a half-filled metal goblet. I reached for it carefully, expecting a protest from my body, but no more than faint echoes of pain accompanied the movement. The goblet appeared to contain a still-warm meat broth with a sweet taste to it, the sort of taste that said the broth was medicated. I seemed to remember swallowing that broth another time, before I had regained full consciousness, when someone else had been holding the goblet. I didn't remember who that someone else was, but there had been the feeling of concern. I replaced the now-empty goblet on the table, got comfortable under the covering fur, and fell asleep again.

The next time I awoke it was early morning and I wasn't alone. The delicious aroma of fresh-cooked food had brought me back to the ornate room, and I'd opened my eyes to see a man putting a laden wooden tray down on the small table beside my bed. He was as large as all Rimilian males are, tall and well muscled and blond, but instead of wearing a *haddin* or robes, he wore trousers of red-dyed leather, tight and form-fitting, especially around the ankles. His feet were bare of everything including sandals, and his waist had no weapons hanging from it, but when he turned from the tray to look at me, I drew back with a small gasp.

"Are you in need of aid, *dendaya*?" he asked at once, concern flooding his mind. "Shall I send for the healer to attend you?"

"No," I answered in a rusty voice, surprised beyond anything I cared to show. "I have no need of a healer. Who are you?"

"Your loyal servant, *dendaya*," he said, bowing deferentially in my direction. "I have brought you foods which will return the strength to your body after your great ordeal. Allow me to assist you in partaking of them."

He turned then and went to fetch pillows, which he brought back to put behind me. I was shocked by the title he kept using when he addressed me, a title which translated as the female equivalent of "leader." Were these people mistaking me for someone else, someone who was high-born and important on their world? If that was so, what would they do when they discovered their mistake? The thought was hardly a pleasant one, but I discovered myself to be too hungry to worry over what would happen at some time in the future. If that was going to be my last meal before discovery, I wasn't about to let anything ruin my appetite.

The food turned out to be as delicious as it smelled. The man who had called himself my servant brought me slices of thinly cut, lightly salted meat, fresh-baked yellowish bread, tangy vegetables, and a warm, heavily sweetened brown drink in a goblet. I ate as much of what was offered as possible, finding my capacity considerably below what it once had been, but being treated this well was nevertheless a too-long-absent pleasure. I basked in the solicitous attention the man showed, examining him covertly while I ate and made sure the fur continued to cover my bareness. He was broad-shouldered and deep-chested, as good-looking as most Rimilians were, and his smile of interest was backed by a carefully controlled desire in his mind. I wasn't used to seeing a Rimilian male controlling himself where a patently unclaimed female was involved, and the idea disturbed me. Was I being foolish in believing I was as unclaimed as I thought I was, or was something deeper involved?

When I'd eaten as much as my depleted body could hold, the man put the serving plates back on the wooden tray. I was expecting him to take the tray away again, but the hesitation in his mind suddenly became determination, and he turned away from the tray to look at me once more. A shadow of pain blinked in his eyes, echoing briefly at the back of his mind, and then he was on his knees beside me, his blue eyes filled with such calm, cool attraction that someone else would have sworn no other emotion had ever glistened there.

"Forgive me, *dendaya,* for disturbing you with requests, yet there is something I must ask," he murmured, leaning somewhat toward me. "Later, when you are stronger and desire for me comes to you, I would not wish to be anything less than completely satisfying. Therefore do I ask the honor of being allowed your leavings, so that I will not fail to meet your expectations. Have I your permission for this?"

He was trying hard to look more attractive than hungry, and it came to me with a new shock that he wasn't a servant but a slave. No servant would have to beg someone's leavings, and no servant would accept the idea of being used so I calmly. I didn't know what had happened that made me important enough to be given a slave to serve me, but the idea both repelled and attracted me. Having been a slave myself made me uncomfortable with the entire concept of slavery, but having been treated so badly by men made me pleased at the thought of evening the score a bit. My ego had been badly bruised of late, and it needed as much care and feeding as my body did.

"Very well," I said at last, keeping my voice cool and the least bit haughty. "As the action would be in my own best interests, you may have my leavings."

His mind winced as his face smiled with gratitude, but he didn't let humiliation keep him from the nourishment he needed. He rose immediately and went back to the tray, then began stuffing food in his mouth. He didn't finish anything on any of the plates, which was probably very wise of him. Most slaves aren't permitted the food of their masters, and he'd be buying trouble by advertising the fact that he'd had some. After the last of it he wiped his mouth on the back of his hand, but still didn't get to take the tray out. The wide double doors of the room opened suddenly, and a woman entered between the two men who had opened the doors. The men wore baggy cloth trousers, wide-sleeved, colorful shirts, heavy sandals, and weapons hanging from their leather belts, but the woman, although weaponless, was a much more imposing sight. She wore a long, butterfly-sleeved gown of bright red, V-necked in front, tight below her breasts then flowing unimpeded down to her ankles, matching soft-leather sandals, and a red-dyed band of leather tied around her forehead. Her blond hair was very long and floating free, billowing out behind her along with her sleeves as she walked across the room. She was a very beautiful woman, and her mind and bearing showed how completely she knew her own importance. The male slave turned and immediately went to his knees, but the woman never even glanced in his direction.

"Excellent," the woman said, coming up to my bed to look down at me with satisfaction. "You are awake and have eaten. I trust you are also nearly recovered from your ordeal?"

"So it seems." I nodded, caution keeping my tone neutral. "To whom do I owe my thanks for such timely assistance?"

"I am Aesnil, *Chama* of all Grelana," she announced, her head raising with pride as her green-flecked blue eyes made the statement a challenge. "It was my hunting camp you chanced upon in so strange a manner. I would know who you are and what befell you."

"I am called Terril," I answered, wondering if I was translating the word *"Chama"* correctly. *"Chamd"* was the word meaning "absolute ruler of all"; if *"Chama"* was its female equivalent, the woman before me had reason to be proud. "I am from a land far distant from here, one where little is known of those who dwell here. I was brought to this land by a *l'lenda* who wished to possess me, was then captured by savages, and was finally made *bedin* to Hamarda. The Hamarda grew angry with me and whipped me, intending to ultimately end my life, yet I was able to escape into the desert. After traveling a considerable distance, in much pain and without food, I found myself in your camp. My memory of the arrival is none too clear; should I have caused you distress, you have my apologies."

"Totally unnecessary," Aesnil said, waving away the need for apology as quickly as her mind dismissed the topic. "I was caused no distress by your arrival. So you were taken unwillingly by one of those swinish *l'lendaa,* were you? We here in Grelana have little liking for such practices, and take great pleasure in teaching those backward males their proper place. How is it your power did not protect you from being taken?"

The question was so legitimately offhand and casual that it caught me completely off balance. I could see from Aesnil's mind that she wasn't guessing; somehow she knew about my abilities.

"I do not understand your question," I hedged, feeling my heart begin to beat faster. When they were sure I could do what they thought I could, what would their reaction be?

"When you arrived in my camp, two of my guards attempted to halt you," the woman said, a faint impatience clear in her tone and mind. "You struck at them in some manner which was not physical, with a power which was felt by many in the camp. When you fell unconscious the attack ceased, yet my guards, who were closest to you, did not recover for some time. They have always proven fearless in my defense, yet they cowered in fear upon the ground till they had recovered. It was clear to me then that you possess some great power, and I would know why you failed to use it to protect yourself from the one who took you."

To say I was stunned would be abysmal understatement, especially since I didn't remember the incident. After being so careful for so long, how could I have done such a thing?

"The – power – is not always so strong," I murmured. "Its use requires a good deal of effort on my part, and quickly drains what strength I have. Had your guards been aware of my ability to attack, they would not have been so completely overwhelmed. They would merely have resisted till my strength was gone, and then have done as they wished."

"So the one who took you knew of the power." She nodded, her pretty face thoughtful. "Perhaps it is possible to increase your strength, and thereby increase the power as well. We shall soon see. I would now have you dress so that you might accompany me on a short walk. Continuing to lie abed will do little to increase your strength. I will await you in the corridor."

She turned then and swept out of the room, drawing her guards out behind her. When the doors were closed again I slumped back against the pillows, afraid to ask what I was in the middle of that time. Aesnil had a lot of plans perking around in her mind, and I couldn't quite believe any of them would be to my benefit.

"Allow me to assist you, *dendaya*," the male slave's voice came, and I turned my head to see him holding a filmy, nearly backless gown of bright yellow, the same sort of gown Aesnil had worn in red. Behind him, on the fur carpeting, stood a pair of soft leather sandals, obviously part of the wardrobe left for my use.

"I have no need of assistance," I informed the slave, pulling the fur cover up higher toward my chin. "You may leave those things and go, for I prefer dressing alone."

"Alas, *dendaya*, I may not obey such a command," he said, his voice soft and commiserating, his pretty eyes the least bit sad. "Should you come to harm while dressing alone, the skin would be taken from my body in strips, for I have been made responsible for your safety. Come now and allow me to assist you. You have my word that I will be as gentle as you wish."

He came closer and put the gown on the bed, then crouched to pry the fur out of the double grip I had it in. After all I'd been through with men on that world I wasn't about to trust him, but he gave me no choice at all. He took the cover and threw it off me, then began helping me to my feet. I would have much preferred doing it myself, but it turned out to be a good thing he was there. Standing up made me faintly dizzy, and I suddenly found myself leaning against a broad chest, two strong arms circling me gently. The slave's hands were against my bare back, exceedingly careful of the welts that were still there, his mind bright with deepening interest. I looked up slowly and found his eyes on me, gazing down with the sort of fierceness that made me shiver. Instead of becoming upset the slave smiled, and his hand moved deliberately to stroke my bottom.

"I see you have indeed been a slave to men," he murmured, desire growing ever stronger in his mind. "Should the *Chama* Aesnil learn how deeply you were touched, she will feel great insult and have you returned immediately to the position of slave. That you fled slavery at the peril of your life was clear to her the moment she saw you; as she believes she would do the same, she has given you a place of honor in her palace. Do not allow her to know the depths of your feelings, for understanding of the state comes only with experiencing such slavery. It would be to no one's benefit were you to fall from her good graces."

His free hand came to my face and his lips lowered to touch mine gently, and then he was reaching past me to retrieve the pretty yellow gown, his mind once again controlling the desire he felt. I wasn't dizzy any longer but my head still whirled, mostly from what the man had said. I thought "man" rather than "slave," and the contention was beyond doubt; the man was free no matter what his physical condition, finding no need to drag others down to the level that had been forced on him. We were busy for the next couple of minutes getting me into the gown, but once it was on and he had brought the sandals over to me, I put a hand on his arm.

"Thank you," I said quietly, trying to let him know I meant it. "I do not even know your name, yet you have my sincere thanks."

"Thanks are unnecessary." He smiled, then knelt to put the sandals on my feet. "Here I am called Daldrin, servant to those who hold me captive. It would be idle to speak of that which I was called elsewhere."

"A man is a man by whatever name," I said, finding the words trite but the sentiment nevertheless true. "No matter how little their worth, my thanks remain yours, Daldrin."

"You had best join the *Chama* now," Daldrin said, rising to look down at me. "Are you able to walk without assistance?"

"Easily," I assured him, and proved the point by starting for the wide double doors. He walked beside me until we got there, then opened one of the doors to let me pass through. I walked out without looking back or acknowledging the courtesy, for I'd felt Aesnil's presence close by and there was no need to look for trouble. Just as I'd suspected, the *Chama* was watching me closely from a large, carved-wood chair in the wide corridor beyond my door. She smiled faintly at the snub I'd given Daldrin, and rose to her feet as I approached.

"We will talk together as I show you this wing of my palace," she said, a smile on her face as she touched my arm to indicate the direction in which we would be going. "My time is limited, yet this conversation must be had."

We moved off along the corridor to the left of my room, but "corridor" would not have been my choice of word as a description of the area. Beyond my room and two or three others like it on both sides of the area was a section of balcony or breezeway, open on both sides to the warmth of the sun and the fresh, lively air. My gown and Aesnil's rippled gently in the breeze as we walked, and didn't lie still again until we had passed into another area of rooms. Outward to the left was a magnificent view of the mountains I'd been riding toward, tall and regal and still unbelievably far off. I would have died many times over before reaching those incredible peaks, but I'd been too desperate – or too uncaring – to think about that back at the oasis. To the right was an inner – fortress, I suppose it would have to be called, all stone and blank walls and thin, narrow slits that could scarcely be called windows. The wall seemed to go on and on as we walked, and Aesnil caught me staring at it.

"My inner palace," she explained, nodding toward the forbidding blankness. "Only certain of my people are allowed within its walls, and of those, fewer still are allowed to leave. It is the final refuge of my family in times of crisis, and has withstood many a siege in its time. Should you have the wisdom I hope to find in you, you will make every effort to keep from entering it."

I looked at her sharply, feeling the smug satisfaction in her mind at my reaction, then watched her smile grow fangs.

"I wish to have you by my side," she purred, for all the world like a woman trying to attract a man. "The power you possess is fearsome indeed, and few of those who plot against me will find the courage to face attack from within their own minds. Their fear of me will grow truly great, knowing that with a single gesture I might have you send them groveling to their knees. It will increase my power tremendously, and ensure my safety for some time."

We had stopped in another of the breezeways to face one another, our hair and gowns fluttering this way and that, oblivious to the guards who stood ten feet to either side of us. The woman was totally sure of herself, completely convinced that she had the situation well in hand. I had a feeling she wasn't wrong, but there were still questions that had to be asked.

"And if I refuse to do as you ask?" I said, feeling considerably less sure of myself than I sounded. "If I should choose instead to continue on my way?"

"Should you agree to my service your life will be filled with pleasure," she said, brushing at her hair as it fell across her face. "The best of foods, the finest of accommodations, your choice of the male servants to see to your needs. Should you refuse you will be returned to the life of a slave, condemned to give pleasure to my guards, to the *vendraa,* even to slaves should they want you. Under no circumstances will you be allowed to leave my palace alive – and certainly not if you should be foolish enough to attempt attack upon my person. I have archers stationed well hidden from your, sight, who will feather you immediately should I be placed in jeopardy. Is your position now clear to you?"

"Completely," I answered, turning away from her. "I will consider your request and give my decision in due time."

"Ah, you feel you must consider your response," she said, and I could hear the smirk. "You may have until the new sun rises to give me your decision; should you at that time attempt to extend the moment of decision, the decision will then become mine. Now let us continue our walk – to improve your strength."

I glanced at her to see her smile of satisfaction, then continued on in the direction we'd been going without argument. The *Chama* wasn't prepared to hear argument on any subject, so I didn't waste my breath. It was clear Aesnil had drawn certain conclusions about my "power," and incomplete as those conclusions were they had still trapped me. The fact that projection was only a part of my ability meant nothing; I was to be a weapon Aesnil used against her enemies. It would eventually occur to her to ask what else I was capable of doing, but by then the answer might be irrelevant. It would not take long before the *Chama* decided I was too dangerous to have around, and that no matter how cooperative I'd become. Attempting to gain control of her emotions would be useless; it would be impossible to control her every minute of every day, and the decision to end me would come when she was alone. I had very little to look forward to no matter which way it went; my decision would have to be based on how willing I was to be used – and how quickly I wanted to die.

Aesnil continued walking me around for another hour or so, showing me audience rooms and party rooms and guest chambers, all built around the central structure of the fortress. Guards were everywhere, and droves of servants – and countless numbers of slaves. Male slaves, dirty, manacled and naked, were used for heavy repair jobs and for carrying in and out back-breaking sacks and bales of foodstuffs and goods. Guards stood over them with whips, stroking them whenever they seemed to be slacking, bringing red agony to their minds even when no outcry was made.

We were passing an enclosed courtyard when Aesnil paused, whispered to the guard who walked beside her, then redirected our steps so that we entered the courtyard. Inside the area was a workgang of slaves, carrying new stone to the walls so that workmen might repair gaps and increase the height of those walls. At a signal from one of the guards with us the slaves were directed to one side of the courtyard to rest, allowing Aesnil the chance to inspect their work. She walked to the stones to look down at them, then turned to give the slaves the same sort of inspection. The large blond men were sweating and filthy in their heavy chains, worked to the point of exhaustion, denied all vestiges of pride, but when Aesnil turned to look at them, their eyes went to her as well. She smiled faintly as they stirred where they sat or sprawled, but if she could have felt their minds the way I felt them, she wouldn't have smiled. The slaves had been denied a very long time, and showing them a beautiful, desirable woman wasn't kind – or wise. When she finished her inspection and walked back to me, their eyes following her, I felt distinctly uneasy.

"The slaves have done an excellent job," she said, turning again to look at them. "In order to encourage continued excellence, I feel they should be rewarded. Approach them."

I stood frozen at her command, wondering if she really knew what she was saying. The slaves' minds were ablaze with flaming need, shamed at being forced to public display by Aesnil's presence and mine but unable to control themselves. Each of them would have killed for a woman, and each of them would have killed any woman he used. Approaching them was out of the question unless I wanted to be torn apart.

"I said, approach them!" the *Chama* repeated, turning to stare at me coldly. "You have been commanded and will obey!"

"I cannot approach them," I whispered, frightened by the firm decision I could see in her mind. "They would kill me."

"Not immediately," she answered with a sudden smile, then gestured imperiously with her hand. My arms were suddenly gripped by two of the guards, and I found myself being forced toward a line of filthy, desperate beings who had become more animals than men. They growled in pleasure as they rose up in their chains, their hands already reaching for me, their flesh hard and straining, their minds a solid sheet of red-hot lust. I screamed as I was dragged closer and closer, so close my gown was caught and ripped, panic and horror filling me so completely I couldn't breathe. I screamed again and struggled insanely, and suddenly I was free of the restraining hands, free to run from the pack of slavering minds. I fled in absolute terror, all the way back to the corridor and up against a smooth, stone wall, my shield snapping shut when my mind discovered it couldn't run far enough. I was cowering against the wall and breathing in gasps when Aesnil came to stand over me.

"There you see one of the possible results of your decision," she said, purring as she looked down at me. "It would be well to remember the incident at the end of your deliberations. Ah, how unfortunate! Your gown has been torn. You may return to your chamber now, and I will have another sent to you. Our conversation may be continued at another time."

She turned and walked away then, accompanied by most of her guards, leaving three of them there to pull me to my feet and head me back to my room. Behind us was the sound of whips striking flesh as the slaves were forced out of their frenzy by the most direct means possible – the infliction of terrible pain. I could hear their screams and snarls and could imagine how savage their minds must be, and shivered inside my shield.

After a few minutes of walking, I had calmed down enough to understand an important point. Aesnil had arranged her little scene to show me what could happen if I refused her, but that hadn't been her only purpose in forcing me near the slaves. She'd also proven to her own satisfaction that I couldn't defend myself from something like that, proving beyond doubt how vulnerable I was despite my "power."

It had been a test to see how dangerous to herself her personal weapon would be, but I wasn't sure how she had read the results. Had the decided I was vulnerable and therefore controllable, or had she decided I hadn't attempted to use my power because I knew she must be bluffing? My terror had certainly been real enough to me, but how had it looked to her? If I hadn't had my shield closed tight I would have known enough to make a reliable guess, but as it was…. When I got back to my room and the guards closed the doors behind me, I threw myself down on the fur layered bed and began to brood.

I was left alone for a few hour, long enough to fall asleep for a while and wake up on my own. I went to the wide, lightly curtained windows to look out at a pretty day that was just past noon, but admiring the lovely day was all I could do there. There were no bars on the windows, no guards just outside – nothing but a sheer drop going down at least a hundred feet into a ravine of some sort. I'd wondered about the openness of this side of the building, but didn't have to wonder any longer. The palace was protected by a natural barrier that kept strangers out and prisoners in, an effective arrangement even without the central fortress. I banged a fist of frustration into the wall by the window, but all that that accomplished was to bruise the side of my hand on the stone under the silk hangings.

A minute later I heard the sound of a door opening, and turned to see Daldrin coming in. He carried a tray full of fresh food and what looked like a white gown over one arm, but that didn't explain why the guard who pulled the door closed behind him was grinning. The guard had been amused, but Daldrin was more angry than amused, which he proved as soon as he'd put the tray down on the table by my bed. He pulled the gown off his arm and tossed it into a corner, then turned to look at me where I still stood by the windows.

"It was my impression that you had agreed not to anger the *Chama*," he said, his voice cold as he put his fists on his hips. "What have you done to have incurred her displeasure?"

"I have not truly incurred her displeasure as yet," I answered with a shrug and turned back to the window. "She merely awaits my decision on a matter discussed between us."

"The *Chama* is not one to merely await a decision," he ground out, coming to stand behind me. "Agree to her command whatever it may be."

"The decision is mine to make, not yours!" I snapped without turning to look at him. "You know nothing of the matter and therefore cannot presume to..."

"I know more than you believe!" he interrupted, grabbing my arm to pull me around to face his now obvious anger. "Call the guard and beg them to take your agreement to the *Chama*!"

"Beg them?" I blurted in outrage, staring up into the angry blue of his eyes. "For no reason other than that you command it? Am I now the loyal servant and you the *denday*? Has this chamber now become yours?"

"In a manner of speaking, it has indeed." He nodded, letting go of my arm to lean his hand on the wall above me. "You may either call the guard and do as I suggest, or prepare yourself for a time of humiliation and degradation which will be known to all those about you. It is, of course, the *Chama's* concept of humiliation and degradation, however it may also be yours. What is your choice?"

"How may I make a choice when I know not what the options are?" I demanded, putting my fists on my hips as he had done earlier. "You speak in circles, Daldrin, and then demand that I listen in a straight line! It cannot be done!"

"Very well, then I shall speak more plainly," he said, but before going on he turned away from me, walked to my bed of furs, and stretched himself out on it. "The

*Chama* has given me leave to use you," he said, turning his head to stare in my direction. "I have said, 'given me leave,' and yet the truth is more that I have been commanded to do so. I, a servant who is used by others, am now to use you as though you were vastly lower than I. Is the concept of humiliation and degradation not exquisite?"

His bitterness cut at me so deeply that I flinched inwardly, feeling all anger and impatience with him drain away. Aesnil was trying to help me with my deliberations again – and undoubtedly testing again – and she didn't care who she hurt as long as she got what she wanted.

"Do not allow her the pleasure of your pain, Daldrin," I urged, taking a step toward him. "She is unworthy of it – and seeks to shame only me."

"Such is not the complete truth of the matter," he denied with a headshake, staring at me soberly. "There is a thing between Aesnil and myself – which is of no moment here. Perhaps you will now be so good as to speak with the guards."

"There is nothing I wish to say to the guards," I informed him, feeling my chin rise. "Aesnil will have no satisfaction from me through high-handedness."

"Then the satisfaction is to be mine," he nodded. "Very well, come here."

"For what purpose?" I shrugged, reaching out to him with my mind. "You feel no desire for me."

He snorted and was about to argue the point, but the sort of disinterest I'd fed him is hard to argue with. A frown creased his forehead as his mind registered surprise, and then, oddly enough, outrage.

"By the Sword of Gerleth, woman, what have you done to me?" he demanded, sitting up straight on the furs. "I am a man, and will not be treated so!"

"What might I have done?" I asked with wide-eyed innocence, reflecting that it was considerably easier using projections than waiting for the proper emotion to come by on its own in the subject's mind and then enlarging on it. "I have not even approached you."

"It is apparent you need not approach," he said, his tone grim. "I now understand the power referred to by Aesnil – and understand, too, why another awaits you behind me."

"Another?" I frowned, immediately suspicious. "Who might this other be?"

"The one who waits behind me is a full slave," he said, lying back on the bed again with his hands tucked behind his head. "He is one who must be bound in chains in order to be kept in Aesnil's service. There are others of us bound in other ways, yet he is not one such. He, like the others enchained, has become less than a man in the pain and labor and denial forced upon him. You will undoubtedly be able to do to him as you have done to me."

I turned away without answering, closing my eyes as my insides curled up. It might turn out to be possible to control one of those wild men, but I didn't want to be the empath to try it. Their minds were too full of ravening self-interest to make the attempt a likely candidate for success. Damn Aesnil and her back-ups!

"You tremble," Daldrin observed from right behind me. "Am I correct in assuming your power is not of sufficient strength to cope with the desires of a slave?"

I nodded jerkily, frustrated but unable to do anything about it. I wasn't strong enough, and that was that.

"Then you will now speak to the guards as I suggested earlier," he said, a gentleness having entered his tone.

I shook my head violently, up to *here* with being forced to do things everyone else's way. If Aesnil didn't like it, she could lump it!

"Why do you continue to refuse?" Daldrin demanded in a roar, pulling me around so that he might shake me with two hands. "Are you pleased by the thought of being taken by a slave? Do you wish to be thrown to a chain of them? Do you wish to spend another two days in pain-filled unconsciousness?"

"For what reason would it matter?" I shouted back, struggling against his grip but unable to break it. "Perhaps good fortune will be mine and the slave will slay me! A chain of them would surely do so! I would be foolish indeed to seek avoidance of so desirable a thing!"

Daldrin stared down at me in silence for a moment, his fingers still locked tight around my arms, then he nodded slowly.

"You have no slightest hope of rescue, then," he said, his mind pitying me. "What of the warrior who took you from your own land? Surely he will come seeking you, demanding your release and promising vengeance for any harm done you? A *l'lenda* is not easily brushed aside."

"The *l'lenda* no longer finds interest in me," I said, just as though the words meant nothing. "'There are more urgent tasks to his hand than the seeking of an unwanted *wenda*."

"The life dies in you when you look so." He frowned, taking my face in his hand to raise it higher. "Speak to me of this *l'lenda* who no longer finds interest in you."

"Speak to me first of who and what you were before you came here," I countered, holding his penetrating gaze. "What name were you called by and – which were the glories you made your own?"

"Your point is taken," he said, releasing my face and stepping back away from me. "The two matters are hardly the same, yet – your point is taken. You had best take your meal now. The slave will hardly be likely to allow you time to heal your hunger."

"I have no hunger," I said, gesturing a dismissal of the idea. "How are they to know you have not used me? Are they likely to torture the truth from you?"

"Torture would be unnecessary." He shrugged, sitting down on the fur carpeting in front of my bed and leaning back against it. "I am scarcely used so often by the *Chama*'s female guests that my needs are seen to. When I leave your chamber I will be taken to a slave room and chained by guards, and then those guards will attempt to arouse me. Should they succeed, it will prove I have not had my fill of a woman."

"Will they succeed?" I asked, feeling my face grow warm at the direction the conversation had taken. "Are you not able to resist the – attempts of another man?"

"The – attempts will be more than successful." He grinned, amused by my blush – which naturally made me blush even more deeply. "I have not had a woman in so long, a *seetar* would be successful with me. The gown I fetched should have been pink. The color suits you."

"I hate you!" I suddenly shouted, moving forward with fists clenched to scream down at him. "You, and every man ever born! If not for men I would not be trapped so, desperate yet knowing not what to do!"

His amusement didn't leave him, but he moved like lightning to wrap his arms around my legs and pull me down to his lap. I yelped and tried to fight my way free, but a man doesn't have a call himself *l'lenda* to be built like one.

"Your problem is scarcely a problem," he laughed, pinning my arms behind me to keep me from battering at his face. "The truth you must face is that you will be used, by another if not by me. The source of your difficulty lies not in the presence of men, but in having incurred the displeasure of another female. Now: though I may force your use with none to deny me, I will not do so for you are not banded as mine. Lost freedom does not equate with lost honor. As you refuse to send word to Aesnil, which will you have: a slave in chains – or a loyal servant?"

He gazed at me levelly, a faint smile still on his lips, but inwardly he was holding his breath and trying to ignore the signals his body was sending him. His long denied need kept flaring up like fireworks in a barrel, almost bright enough to see as well as feel, but he hadn't been lying when he'd said he wouldn't force me. Daldrin seemed to be a man of honor in many ways, but I couldn't make the choice he was hoping for.

"I – cannot have either," I told him heavily. "There is yet a third choice, which I will take as soon as you release me. As you are familiar with the concept of honor, perhaps you will understand when I say I cannot allow myself to be used by any man. It would not be… honorable."

"Your statement on honor is unclear." He frowned, his mind honestly puzzled. "No woman may be held accountable for that which is done to her by a man. Is the man not larger and stronger than she, made to take whatever he wishes? To say a woman may not allow herself to be used else she faces dishonor is foolishness."

"It is a concept firmly believed in by my people," I told him stiffly, upset by the scorn I could feel in his mind. "No man of my people would wish to have a woman used by many others. No man – of any people – would wish such a one."

"Ahhh, I believe I begin to see," he said slowly as I looked down from his stare. "It is the belief of your people that a woman may not allow herself to be used, and yet you have been *bedin* to the Hamarda. Is this the reason you feel yourself unwanted by the *l'lenda* who took you from your land? From the beliefs of a people not his?"

"I believe so from the last words he spoke," I whispered, prodded by the scorn he continued to feel. "'I no longer find this *bedin* of interest,' he said, and how might I deny his choice? Was I not proven a slave before his very eyes? Did I not heap dishonor upon him with my weakness? I cannot fault him for the disgust he felt, yet I cannot bear it. Release me, Daldrin, I beg you! Release me!"

I began struggling again so suddenly I caught him unawares, pulling loose before he had a chance to tighten his grip. Throwing myself to one side put me beyond his grab, and then I was pulling the gown's skirt to one side and scrambling to my feet, heading for the windows and the waiting crevasse below them. I knew then that I hadn't been trying to save my life by running from the Hamarda's camp; I'd been trying to end it in more anonymity than the Hamarda would have allowed me. Right then anonymity was unnecessary; the deed alone was enough.

I reached the windows and flung the curtains aside, put one knee over the sill – but was taken around the waist before I could throw myself out. I screamed hoarsely and kicked with all my strength, trying to make him let go, but frenzy is nothing when matched against brawn. Daldrin pulled me away from the windows, carried me to the other side of the room, put me down on the floor, then knelt across me.

"To take your own life is a waste!" he said harshly, holding my wrists above my tossing head. "It is also the act of a coward! Are you such a coward, then?"

"Yes!" I rasped, still struggling uselessly. "A coward and worse! Let me do what I must!"

"For what reason must it be done?" he countered, scowling down at me. "For the foolish beliefs of a foolish *wenda*? For the beliefs of a people no longer yours?"

"I lied!" I spat, glaring at him wildly. "My people may believe what I said, yet I had never done so! Not once, with all the men I had, did it ever seem wrong! And then I met another man, a different man, one I wished desperately to belong to! Yet that man wished only the use of my power, speaking of love only to keep me beside him. He gave me to many men, when it was his touch alone that I died for. And then I was taken by the Hamarda, and he said – he – he – "

I couldn't go on with the tears choking me, and it hurt too much even to think about. Daldrin let my wrists go and sat beside me on the carpet fur, then gathered me to him and held me while I cried. I don't know exactly when I began talking again, but I ended up telling him everything – about how Tammad had lied when he said he wanted me, how he had watched me being used by other men and it hadn't bothered him, how disgusted he had felt when I'd begged to be taken in his arms. At Daldrin's gentle prodding, I admitted how ashamed I'd felt when I responded to other men with Tammad watching. I had no real reason to be loyal to the barbarian, but I'd still felt as though I were betraying him.

"I fail to understand how such a thing might be thought of as betrayal," Daldrin said, smoothing my hair away from my face. "Are you not a woman, and were you not being used by men? How else is a woman to reply if not with her inner being? Do you think yourself stone rather than flesh?"

"If I were truly his, I would not be taken so by any touch other than his," I explained unevenly, still leaning against his chest. "Although he cares nothing for me, he must surely have been hurt by my failure."

"Only if he were a fool," Daldrin snorted. "No man of this world takes a woman but with the expectation that she will respond to him. Should she fail to do so, it is certain that either she is ill or he is clumsy and incapable. Some women may not wish to respond, perhaps due to anger at the man, yet such an attitude is scarcely unknown among free women. All men are aware of it, and most have learned what must be done to overcome it."

"And yet it was possible to resist a number of the Hamarda," I maintained, staring at the upper part of one of the arms that held me. "If it is possible with some men, it should be possible with all. The fault was obviously mine, for not having been determined enough."

"Too many of the Hamarda have allowed themselves to become dependent upon *bedinn*," he snorted in derision. "With females who must please you or forfeit their lives, a man quickly comes to believe no effort on his part is necessary. The Hamarda are not fit representatives of the men of this world."

"To one of determination, all things are possible," I repeated, really believing it. "Had I had the determination I have now, I would not have shamed myself."

"*Wendaa!*" he muttered, the annoyed frustration growing in his mind. "Such foolishness is impossible to any save them. Hear me, woman: there is no shame to be found of the sort you speak of, for determination would be useless with any true man. Should you doubt the truth of this, I am prepared to prove it."

"It cannot be proven," I mumbled, feeling his heartbeat through his chest. "The choice is mine, and I will not allow myself to be used again."

"The choice is yours only with a man of honor," he said and I could feel him looking down at me. "No matter how great its strength, should your determination be put to the test, it will fail."

"It will not fail," I said, knowing, really *knowing* I was right. "Had I the wish to increase your frustrations, I would invite your efforts."

"I thank you for your consideration of my feelings," he said, suddenly amused. "I, however, prefer accepting your invitation."

I jumped when his hand came to the bottom of my gown, but I settled back against his chest again without protesting. He was determined to try wearing me down, and the best thing I could do would be to let him find out how wrong he was. Once he knew the truth he would leave, and then I'd be able to get on with settling my problems permanently.

Daldrin first untied my sandals and tossed them away, then returned his attention to my leg under the gown. With a man in his condition of need I didn't think it would take long proving I was right, but the servant-slave of the *Chama* didn't do anything I expected him to. He acted as though he had all the time and patience in the world, trailing his fingers over my flesh in long caresses, closing his hand around my calf or ankle, running his palm all the way up my side and then down again with no attempt to touch my breast. I didn't understand what he was doing, and that was probably what quickly began making me uncomfortable. I stirred in his arms and put my head back to frown up at him, and was greeted by his grin before his lips lowered to touch mine. His kiss was gentle and undemanding, as though he were merely continuing a faintly interesting investigation, and my confusion grew even greater.

Not long after that my torn gown was removed, but it didn't seem very important. Despite the extreme satisfaction in his mind, I was so sure he wasn't getting anywhere I even helped get the gown off. The pleasure in his mind grew vastly greater when he placed me flat on the carpet fur and began looking at me, and again I didn't understand why I should be so uncomfortable. It was true he hadn't yet removed his leather pants while I lay there naked, so possibly that had something to do with it. Then he stretched out beside me to take me in his arms and kiss me again, and I forgot all about what was being worn by whom.

I couldn't say exactly when it was that I discovered I was gritting my teeth. Daldrin's hands had been all over me for some time, when I suddenly discovered I couldn't stand anymore. I quickly decided we'd been experimenting long enough and opened my mouth to say so, but his lips interrupted the words with a kiss that had more heat in it than any of the I others he had given me. I moved feebly against him, trying to protest, and then nearly choked on a moan when he touched me deeply and possessively, sending a scream of fire through my body. All at once it was as though I were being consumed alive, as though the screaming flames had been brought just to the surface and held there until Daldrin decided it was time to release them. Now they were free to ravage me – and so was the man. The thought of resisting didn't even cross my mind; resistance was impossible with a man like that, and my body knew it even if my mind hadn't. Daldrin laughed as he rid himself of clothing, and then I was his without question.

A very long time later I lay on my side on the carpet fur, staring at the blue and silver silk on the walls, trying to coax some strength back into my body. I felt totally exhausted, but the feeling wasn't anywhere near as unpleasant as it should have been.

"Your silence does not seem to be filled with pleasure," Daldrin observed from his place on the carpet fur behind me. "Why are you disturbed?"

I moved my cheek slightly against the carpet fur, but didn't answer him. All I'd managed to do with words that day was talk myself deeper into self-hatred.

"Ah, now do I recall our discussion before we merged," he said, chuckling as he put a hand out to touch my hip. "The truth of my words has been proven beyond doubt, and you now feel the foolishness of your contention. Do not concern yourself with it, *wenda*. Such foolishness is best left behind you."

He put his arms around me and gathered me to him, but his grin faded when he saw the tears in my eyes. Even with the tears I wasn't really crying, and he seemed to know that. He stroked my hair gently until I lay my head on his chest, and then waited in silence for the words he knew would be coming.

"I feel so shamed I cannot bear it," I whispered at last, putting my arms around his broad, powerful body to keep myself from trembling. "I must truly be a slave to respond so to every man who touches me. It is now no wonder that he gave me so often to others. He wished to show me how slave-like I am, and how unworthy of him I am. Should he ever look upon me again, I will die of the shame."

"Ah, *wenda*, why must you give yourself such unnecessary pain?" he sighed, tightening his arms around me. "It is as I told you earlier: no woman will fail to respond to a man who has learned the ways of women. Why have you not mentioned the battles fought by your *l'lenda* with the men to whom you were given?"

"Battles?" I frowned, somehow distracted by the oddness of the question. "There were no battles fought. The men were his friends, his brothers, with deep feeling shared between them."

"Then your beliefs concerning his attitudes cannot be true," Daldrin said, pleased. "For one *l'lenda* to give a slave to another is deep insult, as *l'lendaa* consider the ownership of slaves to be beneath them. In another light, there is nothing more precious a man may share with his brother than the use of the woman of his heart, for what other thing may be as valuable? Should a man wish to show the love he holds for another man, it is most easily done by permitting him the use of one who will give him great pleasure. Had you been cold and unresponsive, he would not have allowed your use by others, for he would not have wished to be shamed. Do you see now how far from the mark your thoughts have been?"

"The concept is too far beyond me." I struggled, shaking my head to try to stop the whirling of my thoughts. "Even were I able to accept your words, they would not explain the reason for his coldness and disgust when last I saw him."

"There is no knowing his reason short of asking him," Daldrin said, dismissing the importance of the question. "Perhaps it was the Hamarda and their practices which displeased him. When he comes for you, you will then be able to ask."

"Ah, Daldrin, you know as well as I that he will not come," I sighed, somehow feeling better even though I was still miserable. "That he found me once is unbelievable enough; to follow a second time, across rock and sand, would not be possible. Even were his love truth rather than lie, it would not be possible."

"Tell me," Daldrin mused, toying idly with my hair. "Were you banded by your *l'lenda*?" At my surprised nod he asked, "How far?"

"I was two-banded," I answered, wondering what he was getting at. "What has that to do with…"

"It has much to do with all you have said." He laughed, pulling gently on my hair to make me look up at him. "It has been your contention that the *l'lenda* who took you cares nothing for you, only for your power. It is now clear to me that you are as mistaken in this belief as you were in your others. How well did you obey your *l'lenda*? How pleased was he with you?"

"He – was not well pleased at all," I admitted, then raised my chin defiantly. "My unhappiness was great, and I disobeyed him whenever I might."

"And added insolence to disobedience as well, I warrant." He grinned, tugging harder at my hair. "Had it been your power alone that he coveted, *wenda*, you would have worn five bands – and the welts of many beatings. Do you doubt that this *l'lenda* has the ability to exact perfect obedience from you?"

I stared silently at the amusement in his blue eyes for a moment, then shook my head.

"No," I grudged with a good deal of idiotic embarrassment. "The ability is his without doubt."

"Then you will admit that true feelings must surely have stayed his hand," Daldrin pressed, triumph in his mind. "Your punishment lay in the shame of being allowed no more than two bands, that and what strappings he could not in all good conscience let by."

"You overlook one point you are not aware of," I said, puncturing his triumph somewhat by refusing to acknowledge it. "The *l'lenda* is well aware of the fact that I cannot be forced to use my power if he would rely on it. Too, great pain puts the power beyond my ability to control it. This, also, is part of his knowledge. How, then, am I to conclude that true feelings stayed his hand? Might it not have been awareness of the delicately balanced game he played?"

"It might have indeed," Daldrin nodded, his mind and eyes suddenly sober. "Just as it may have been as I suggested. Your power must surely be a terrible possession, to breed such doubts about those who may care for you. Does it bring joy as great as the pain it engenders?"

Again I stared at him silently, having just heard the same question I'd asked myself a thousand times. There was no true, final answer to the question; there was only the partial response I'd been able to come up with.

"The power did not come to me as a result of my desiring it," I shrugged, then lay down flat on the carpet fur beside him. "Whatever it brings must be accepted, just as the power itself must be accepted. Just as you accept the commands of the *Chama*."

The expression changed in his light eyes, sharpening to match the surge of fury that caught him unawares, twisting his insides as it tightened his jaw muscles. Then he had control of himself again, and a bitter smile came down to me with his stare.

"You strike at me as I struck at you," he said, reaching over to run his thumb down my cheek. "The action is fitting in a *l'lenda*, foolhardy in a *wenda*. And yet I will answer you more fully than you have answered me. It is true I bring pain upon myself, yet there is little else I might do. The *Chama* Aesnil holds my brother prisoner as well, his well-being the bond for my behavior, mine the bond for his. He is bound as *vendra* in Aesnil's arena, I as a servant-slave in her halls. We each of us do what we must to preserve the life of the other."

"What is a *vendra*?" I asked, sure I'd heard the word before, but not from him.

"A *vendra* is a warrior enchained." He sighed, moving his finger from my cheek to my collarbone. "The *vendraa* fight upon the sands of the arena, at times with beasts hungry for their flesh, at times with each other for the privilege of retaining life. We each of us accounted for enough of the *Chama*'s guard upon being captured to qualify of the arena, yet we knew the dangers of accepting such an arrangement. It was inevitable that the *Chama* would have us face one another for her amusement, and this we would not do. Therefore did we draw lots, the winner to go to the arena, the loser to become a slave without visible chains. I have cursed the draw many times since we were separated."

"But, why?" I asked, unable to suppress a small shudder. "In the arena your life would be in constant jeopardy, a living nightmare. These halls, though unpleasant, at least are safe. Why would you wish instead for the arena?"

"In the arena, I would be free to raise a sword to any who would attempt mockery of me," he answered, his mind straining to control the fury of shaming memories flashing across the back of his unfocused eyes. "In the arena I would be free to be a man, to stand rather than kneel, to fight rather than crawl, to wipe insult from me with the edge of a blade!" His voice had been tight and harsh, but suddenly he took a deep breath, broke the tension, and managed to send me a grin. "And also would I be free to reap the benefits of a victorious *vendra,* benefits which make life much the sweeter."

"I do not believe I would care to hear of such benefits," I said, disliking his grin as much as his previous distraction. "They are undoubtedly as grim as the balance of a *vendra*'s doings."

"Hardly grim." He laughed, unexpectedly sweeping his hand over my body. "Each victorious *vendra* is given a number of female slaves to tend him, the number depending upon whether it was man or beast he slew, slave or other *vendra.* For slaying another *vendra* a man is given four slaves, each lovelier than the last, each naked and eager to please him. A servant-slave in these halls is given nothing of female slaves, nothing of females at all lest there be one who displeases the *Chama.* Have you yet seen the wisdom in quickly acceding to her demands, or must you first be given to one who will not take the bother of seeing to your comfort and pleasure before using you?"

I began to point out that my doings were still none of his business when the doors to the room opened suddenly, making both of us twist around to see who it was. Unsurprisingly it was Aesnil sweeping into the room, her guards at her heels, her red gown clinging to her body as she moved; her blond hair spreading around her lovely face in a way that made her look young and very innocent. I was incensed that she'd just barge in like that without any warning and was about to say so, but her gesture to Daldrin came before I could get the words put together.

"You need not kneel to me now, slave," she purred, looking him over with amusement and scorn clear in her eyes. "A man not long out of his pleasure is a man who does not care to be disturbed, I am told. Was she worth the taking?"

"Indeed," the man beside me drawled, putting his hand possessively on my backside. "I found the woman as eager to please and serve as all women are."

"Hardly *all* women," Aesnil corrected with a sniff, then shifted her haughty look to me. "Those women weak enough to fall victim to men deserve no better than to be made to serve them. Have you found that being put to your back suits you, girl? Should your answer to me be the incorrect one, you may well find yourself *chained* to your back in a corridor, available for use to any man who chances by. Think of the constant pleasure you would then be given."

"It would undoubtedly be greater pleasure than that found in this chamber!" I spat, pushing Daldrin's hand away from me. His answer to Aesnil had annoyed me, almost as much as the threats the woman kept coming up with. "You will have ample opportunity to judge my answer for yourself – in the morning! For now, I believe this chamber remains mine! I invite you to take your guards – and your loyal servants – and go!"

Daldrin's flash of frustrated anger was fierce, and strangely enough it was almost the same emotion Aesnil felt. The woman's hands curled into fists at her sides as she stared down at me, but she was undoubtedly realizing that there was only so much she might do to me if she hoped to have me working for her. I would have been happier standing on my feet to face her, but I didn't want to feel the eyes of her guards on me any more than I already did. Lying on my stomach in the carpet fur wasn't as good as being dressed, but it was better than standing upright.

Aesnil tore her eyes away after a minute of silent staring, then sent them around the room in an effort to calm her temper before speaking. She was boiling mad inside, but seemed to consider showing her anger an indication of weakness. Her wandering gaze eventually found the small table with the tray on it, and she frowned as she walked over to examine it.

"This food has not been touched," she announced angrily, turning to glare at Daldrin. "Were you so desperate to take her that you jeopardized her health by keeping sustenance from her? Have you any idea what your lot would be if she should die before I am able to make use of her power? You were specifically instructed to bring her food before using her!"

"And so I did," Daldrin pointed out, gesturing toward the tray as he sat up. "I had not been told it was your intention that I force her to a meal. Twice I had her refusal in the matter, and thereafter let it slip from my mind. There were other things afoot of greater concern to me."

"Such as her use," Aesnil snorted in disgust, then turned her attention back to me. "You will not escape my service through starvation. The healer directed that you are to eat well, and so you shall. A fresh tray will be brought you and that you will eat from, else you will be given pain. I know you are no stranger to the whip; disobey me, and you will be taught other ways of punishment."

Her attention went back to Daldrin, and her head cocked to one side. "This woman is my honored guest, one I thought to give pleasure to by sending you to her, and yet her displeasure is so great that she angrily orders me from her chamber. Are you so untalented then, that you are unable to give pleasure to a woman? Does the blood run so thinly in you that you find difficulty in serving a single female?"

The abrupt turnabout of Aesnil's speech brought confusion to all of us, her guards included, and not excepting Daldrin. We all stared at her as though she were crazy, but Daldrin also flushed with annoyance and insult.

"I was instructed to see to a matter for you," he said, his voice tight with anger. "The matter was seen to to the best of my ability. I had thought, *Chama,* that you were pleased with my efforts."

"I had not realized how *dis*pleased my honored guest was." She shrugged, then sat herself on the end of my bed. "I am told by those more interested than I that you are well enough endowed to make any woman writhe. Any woman, that is, foolish enough to find herself in your arms. If this is so, I cannot fathom the reason for my guest's dissatisfaction. As it cannot be she who is at fault, the error must be yours. The only thing for it is that you repeat your performance here and now, and my guards will remain alert for what mistakes you make. You may proceed."

She settled herself more comfortably on the bed, while I stared at her in disbelief. The guards were guffawing where they stood in front of the doors, finally understanding that they were in for some fun. Daldrin was still angry, but he was also groaning inwardly and furious with me for causing the mess. Aesnil hadn't liked my previous attitude toward her, and she'd found a way of getting even – or at least she thought she had. *I* thought it was high time she found out what she was fooling with.

Slowly and deliberately I rose to my knees on the carpeting, then climbed to my feet. Aesnil's eight guards were staring directly at me, their minds growling with interest, their eyes saying they wouldn't have minded if they were the ones to use me instead of Daldrin. They weren't expecting me to stare back at them, so when I did a faint shadow of doubt ghosted across their minds, the sort of shadow that leaves a perfect opening behind. Into that opening in each of their minds my projection went, comprised of repugnance and horror and backed with the strength of anger. The eight men were standing close to one another, bunched up in a way that seemed purposely set for the needs of projection. Their faces twisted when they felt the repugnance, but when the horror followed quickly in its turn the experience was too much for them. They backed away almost as one, slowly at first and then more and more quickly, falling over one another and shoving at one another in their haste to get to the doors and out. Nothing but gasps and grunts came from them, showing they were brave men, and once they were gone and the doors slammed closed behind them, I turned off the projection and turned to look at Aesnil.

The *Chama* still sat at the edge of my bed, but her body was no longer relaxed. She sat bolt upright with a tense, unnatural stiffness all through her, her face pale, her eyes wide, her mind filled with ice-tinged fear. When she saw my eyes on her her breath caught in her throat, but she'd been too important for too long a time to easily conceive of the concept of personal harm.

"Your power will be of more use to me than I had at first thought," she said in a scratchy voice, looking up at me with distinct evidence of triumph beginning to enter her mind. "I will have the fearful obedience of every *denday* in my country, especially those who now laugh at me as nothing more than a mere female."

She took a deep breath and got to her feet, then turned her head to look at a silent Daldrin.

"See that she eats well of the fresh food sent to her," she told him, the snap of command back in her voice. "Also see that her body is well pleased, else you will lose what you fail to make acceptable use of. I will not have her in a foul temper from bodily demands she has grown used to having tended."

She gave Daldrin a final glare, sent me a radiant smile filled with much warmth, then took herself off toward the doors, her mind already twisting and spinning with plans and ideas. I frowned as I watched her go, not quite believing she could dismiss me that easily, but once the doors closed the question of belief became secondary to the overwhelming weariness I'd been holding off while Aesnil was there. The strength needed for the projection sent to her guards had completely drained me, but I hadn't wanted Aesnil to know that. I'd wanted her to think of herself as threatened, but all she'd seen was a demonstration of how valuable I could be to her. I let myself sink back down onto the carpeting with a silent groan, stretching out flat as Daldrin made a sound of annoyance.

"It is she who needs her bodily demands seen to," he muttered, his eyes still on the doors. "It is whispered among the serving slaves that the *Chama* has never been taken by a man, thus the reason for her constant intemperate behavior. You took a foolish chance, girl, and nearly saw yourself used for the amusement of Aesnil and her guard. Were you mine, you would now face punishment for such foolishness."

I glanced up to see him staring down at me, the annoyance in his eyes as strong as it was in his mind.

"Leave me be," I groaned, turning my face away from him. "I no longer have the strength to argue male evaluation of my behavior. Let me rest."

"So you need to rest, do you?" he mused, reaching over to turn my face back to him. "What would have occurred had others come to replace the guard you sent scurrying? Would you have been able to do the same to them had they meant you harm?"

I didn't answer him, but he didn't need an answer; I could see in his eyes that he knew I hadn't particularly cared what happened to me, as long as it was fast and clean.

"The death of one who attempts harm to the *Chama is* designed to be neither swift nor easy," he told me harshly, his light eyes angrier than they had been. "Should you continue as you do now, you will soon learn the truth of the matter. Take your rest now, but think upon my words, for they may save you a good deal of agony."

He let go of my face and got to his feet, but the churning in his mind didn't stop beating at me until he had walked to the other side of the room. I was too played out to do the sort of thinking he wanted me to do, and didn't think it wise to mention the archers Aesnil had warned me of. He would have pointed out that they weren't close enough to do me much good, and I didn't need him to point out the obvious.

A short while later a discreet tap came at the doors, and Daldrin opened one to reveal a female slave carrying a tray. The naked girl hurried inside, put the tray down on the first available table, then turned and knelt to Daldrin, putting her forehead to the floor at his feet. As neither one of us had dressed again, the girl had taken it upon herself to assume that Daldrin was the proper inhabitant of the room, I no more than another slave sent to entertain him. Daldrin grinned at me over the girl's body before sending her on her way, but I saw nothing amusing in the situation. That, on top of everything else, was almost enough to make me a supporter of Aesnil's cause.

I felt too washed out to be interested in eating, but Daldrin refused to take no for an answer. He insisted he'd been commanded to see me well fed, then proceeded to stuff me with whatever the tray contained. It takes a certain amount of strength to fight off a man with food in his hands, but when brawn is lacking, brain is sometimes a superior substitute. When I reached the point of being just short of exploding, I took advantage of a momentary lull and suggested that Daldrin help finish the stuff off. The servant-slave hadn't been fed anywhere near well enough to resist an offer like that, and went at it with abandon after no more than a token hesitation. I could tell he was wondering whether I'd had enough, but the amount he'd stuffed into me plus the demands of his own needs worked together to overcome his doubts. This time he finished the food to the last bite, and I managed to have my revenge for the way he'd pushed me around. A light wine had been included with the meal, but all he got to do was taste it. I finished the rest of it myself while he glowered at me over my insistence that I needed it to build up my strength again. For some reason, I don't think he believed me.

By the time the meal was completely over, the sun was getting ready to go down outside. The wine had relaxed me to the point of dozing, but it had also worked on me in another way – which I didn't find out about until Daldrin took me in his arms. I opened my eyes in the late afternoon dimness to discover that I really wanted that man, and that was all Daldrin needed to know. He laughed softly as I pressed my body up against his, kissing him gently but lingeringly wherever I could reach, moving against his hands wherever they touched me, stroking his body as he stroked mine. The blaze of desire grew quickly in his mind to a point beyond his control, a raging storm that swept me up willingly and took me with it, deeply into the storm of my own mind. The winds blew a very long time, and when they blew themselves out all that was left was the darkness of night surrounding the darkness of sleep.


## FIFTEEN


My escort to Aesnil was a full dozen guards, walking me down the corridor in a direction I hadn't taken before. I wore the new white gown and the leather sandals I'd worn the day before, but as far as I could tell from the minds of the guards around me, I might as well have been walking around naked. Their eyes grew hungry when they looked at me, and I had the feeling they'd been promised something if my interview with Aesnil didn't turn out the way she wanted it to. After the night I'd had with Daldrin, that little extra put me into a worse mood than I'd been in to begin with.

I'd awakened very early in the morning, held in Daldrin's arms, one fur beneath us, another covering us, feeling as though I'd done something stupid. Since most of the night had been spent in pleasure I didn't understand why I felt that way, but then Daldrin woke up and pulled me closer, and I began understanding exactly what I'd done.

At some point or other I'd projected my feelings to him, giving him something he'd never had before – but now wanted many times again. I'd tried talking my way out of it, but he'd refused to listen, instead going to work on me with all the knowledge of women he'd accumulated in his years of manhood. I'd had one lesson in how badly I did trying to resist him; the second lesson was worse than the first. I managed to keep from giving him the projection he wanted, but I was little more than a rag when he finally let me go. I know I expected him to be annoyed if not angry, but apparently he was a believer in the saying, "A thing worth having is a thing worth working for." He chuckled in amusement over how close he'd come, kissed me deeply to reinforce the lesson he'd taught, then went to take the breakfast tray from the slave who had entered without my hearing her. I didn't know how long the girl had been standing there, but there was very little for me to be embarrassed about. Her wide-eyed stare and trembling body were for Daldrin alone, his completely if he cared to take them. Daldrin laughed and kissed the girl before sending her away, giving me the impression that he never took advantage of sitting ducks – or slaves in need. The freer the woman, the freer he felt to take advantage.

Breakfast was a battle – at least on my part – but I rarely win battles with men on that world. I ended up eating considerably more than I wanted, and I refuse to say what Daldrin did to make me obey him. He grinned all the while he watched me eat, then he punished me further by making me feed him whatever I'd left over. Our relationship had under gone a considerable change since the day before, and I was more than relieved to dress and leave the room with my escort. The only thing that bothered me about the dressing part was the fact that Daldrin had tied my sandals – in a way that made me feel more as though I were being banded than having my sandals tied. I would have told myself I was imagining things if there hadn't been such extreme satisfaction in his mind.

The walk down the corridor would have been long enough to give me the jitters if I hadn't had other things on my mind. Up until the afternoon before I'd been dead set against giving Aesnil her way, but what had happened with her guards had made me stop and think. Every time I got mad, I managed to do something with my talent that I'd never done before. Just a few months earlier I'd had trouble splitting a projection five ways, but the night before I'd split one eight ways without noticing anything but the fatigue from holding the projection so long. And as far as holding it went, I was doing that a lot better, too. It seemed that unrestricted use and practice was making my talent considerably stronger than I'd been led to believe it could be. It was more than possible I'd been lied to about my potential, which meant I'd also been heavily conditioned without my knowing about it. The more unthinking my reaction, the better my talent worked; if I stopped to think about it, I usually didn't use it. For an empath that was like not using eyesight or hearing or any other natural ability. Someone had gone to a lot of trouble to half-cripple me, but I'd been learning to use my limbs again without realizing it. How much more could I accomplish if I worked knowingly against what had been done?

Which didn't mean I'd decided on wholehearted cooperation with Aesnil. I didn't like being blackmailed, and I didn't like the plans Aesnil had all blocked out. She would use me ruthlessly to get what she wanted, and as soon as she had it she would let herself realize how really dangerous I could be to her. What she did after that would depend on her mood, but it wasn't likely to be anything I'd enjoy. The only real chance I had to stay alive and healthy was to go along with Aesnil, pretend to be on her side, and then see what I could do to work myself free. It wasn't much of a chance, and I'd probably never survive on my own even if I did get away, but I was desperate enough to try just about anything. I couldn't face the idea of being made a slave again, and if nothing else, the world of Rimilia would see to taking my life even if I couldn't find the nerve to do it on my own.

The corridor finally led to a set of immense double doors, which two of my guard escort opened in front of me. Behind the doors lay a very large room, empty now except for Aesnil and her personal guard. The *Chama* lay in the middle of dozens of red pillows piled on the top of a very wide two-step platform that looked out into the rest of the room, and it was to the foot of this platform that I was taken. Aesnil looked down at me with a sweet, friendly smile, but her mind held no friendliness. There was something she wanted very badly, and if she didn't get it she would allow her temper free rein.

"I bid you a good morning, my honored guest who is called Terril," she purred, surprising me by remembering my name. "It is now time for your decision, which I eagerly await."

"So it is," I drawled, looking idly around me before bringing my attention back to her. "I would, however, like to ask one question before I reveal my decision. When last we spoke, you mentioned *dendayy* who treated you as though you were no more than any other woman. Should I agree to assist you, how greatly would I be restrained in dealing with these – males."

The venom I put into the last word brought the light of triumph to Aesnil's eyes, just as I knew it would. Her mind surged with happiness and strong belief that I was on her side, a belief I had no trouble bolstering without her knowing about it. Aesnil had only limited understanding of my abilities, an advantage for me if I used it right. As long as she thought I couldn't touch her without her knowing about it, I could do almost anything.

"It is my intention to teach these – males – that I am a woman to be reckoned with," she assured me, with a good deal of warmth. "Should your efforts make them appear more foolish than I had intended, it will please me no end. Am I to understand that it is now your decision to join me?"

"Your understanding is correct." I nodded. "If I am not to be restrained, I will gladly join you."

"Excellent." She laughed softly, throwing a number of pillows down to the step below her. "You may sit yourself there, and we will discuss what comforts you wish in return for your assistance. I must soon begin the day's audiences, yet there is ample time for us to talk."

I made myself comfortable in the spot she'd indicated, and the *Chama* and I discussed my price for helping out. I asked for everything I could think of that she would be willing to give, and the more I asked for, the happier Aesnil became. The *Chama* was well acquainted with and very much approving of the mercenary attitude, feeling as many others did that a person who couldn't be bought couldn't be trusted. The more she gave me the greater the hold she had over me, and the more there was that could be taken away if I became troublesome. I asked for larger quarters and more clothing and better food – and my good friend Daldrin. I asked for something special for him, explaining that he'd been too keen on following orders for my taste, and Aesnil had laughed and agreed immediately. She didn't mind knifing a loyal slave if it made me happy; slaves weren't worth anything and I was. As long as what I wanted wasn't unreasonable, I would get it.

When our talk was finished, Aesnil gave the order to open a different set of doors than the ones I'd come in by. People immediately began streaming inside, the hum of their voice breaking off as they saw me, only to resume again at a different pitch. They all bowed in Aesnil's directions as they found their places on the floor, but it was fairly obvious I was drawing more attention than the *Chama*. Aesnil noticed their stares with a good deal of amusement, and her eagerness to show me off was childlike: she couldn't wait to see their reactions to what I could do, but was determined to drag the thing out as long as possible to torture everyone. I put a satisfied look on my face and kept it there, and made sure not to think about anything but the possibility of escape.

It took a while for all the people to get themselves inside, and after a time I noticed that there were considerably more women in the crowd than men. The women strutted around with contempt in their minds for any man they saw, and the few men among them frowned in distinct discomfort and disapproval, while looking totally out of place. They looked as though they'd been ordered to appear, and the fact that they wore *haddinn* while the women wore gowns, added to their out-of-place look. No man wore weapons but Aesnil's guard, which compounded and underscored all the rest.

Once the people – who, I suspected, were regular members of the court – had settled down, Aesnil began the audience. The first to be presented was a big woman with very short hair, leather pants and shirt, and a sword at her hip. She introduced herself as the ambassador from some place called Vediaster, then began showing the gifts she had brought. Female slaves trotted in priceless furs and magnificent cloth, spices and leathers, wine and weapons – and at the end of it all, a matched pair of male slaves. The men were twins, and it was painful to feel the outpourings of their fearful minds, the confusion, the hesitancy, the agonized worry over what would become of them. They were large, magnificent males, splendid to look at – but they'd been raised as slaves and would be slaves till the day they died. When the ambassador bowed herself out and took the slaves with her, I was finally able to unclamp my jaws.

After the ambassador came a long string of people with quarrels, mostly female people quarreling with male people. In almost every instance the *Chama* decided in favor of the female complainant; the only exception was when she found against both sides in the argument and confiscated the land involved in the dispute. The woman she found against was shocked, and quickly left the audience room with her mind in a turmoil. She didn't know whether the *Chama* was angry with her, or simply had wanted the land. If the truth lay in the former supposition, her troubles were just starting.

The first of my victims didn't show up until the petty squabbles had been taken care of. The first I knew of it was when I felt a heightening in the hostility of the women of the court, and looked up to see a large man in a green *haddin* standing with folded arms as he stared at Aesnil. The *Chama* was busy selecting a tidbit from a tray held by a slave and didn't notice the man, so he shifted his gaze to me while he waited. I could feel the approval in his mind when he looked at me, but that was the only approval he felt over anything in the room. He hadn't come there willingly, and he didn't enjoy being kept waiting.

"So, Lerran, you have finally answered my summons," Aesnil said, bringing his attention back to her. "Where are the fighters and hunters your city was supposed to have supplied? Why have they not yet reported to my guard captain?"

"My city is unable to supply the levy you demand, Aesnil," the man Lerran answered, his voice flat and final. "The savages harass us from all sides, stealing our women and children, killing our game, attacking us whenever they might. You find it unnecessary to send your guardsmen to deal with these savages; very well, we accept having to see to our own safety. We refuse, however, to further sap our strength by filling your levy. Our *l'lendaa* are needed and will remain with us."

"*L'lendaa!*" Aesnil spat, straightening in the cushions to glare at Lerran. "*Darayse* would be a truer term! Your hunters and fighters fear leaving the streets of their city, knowing how poor a showing they will make among my guard! You, their leader, pamper their fears, yet they must grow to manhood at some time! Send them immediately, or suffer the consequences!"

"And what consequences do you speak of, *wenda*?" the man asked very softly, the fury in his mind adding thick menace to his tone. "Do you forget that it is we, the *dendayy* of your cities, who have allowed the extension of the law you so earnestly requested? Do you wish us to revoke the extension? It may be done quickly, should there be cause, and attack upon one of your own cities would be cause enough. Walk carefully, *wenda*, lest a misstep cause your downfall."

"How dare you speak to me so!" Aesnil hissed, her mind in a frenzy of madness. "How dare you address me so! I will have you flogged and mutilated and hanged from my palace walls! I will send you to face the best of my *vendraa!* I will have you carved slowly into pieces! I will – will – ”

The woman was nearly frothing at the mouth, so furious was she and so shaken by the threat the man had uttered. I didn't know what the threat entailed, but whatever it was, the idiot was likely to lose his life for having put it into words. Aesnil had forgotten all about me, but I still had a chance to do something to make her forget the promises she was making.

A quick check of Lerran's mind showed the man totally unimpressed by the fury he'd caused in Aesnil. Happily, though, not everyone in the room felt the same way; the women watching and listening had become alarmed, some even downright frightened. I took the strongest apprehension I could find and shunted it through to Lerran, hitting the man hard but expending no energy on my part other than the minimal effort it took to pass emotions on. Lerran paled and almost staggered under the load, suddenly finding himself filled with worry and fear that grew stronger as the seconds passed. His mind automatically tried rejecting the load, then tried controlling it, but I was there to see that his usual control-of-self didn't take over and get him killed. I let the flow of fear increase almost to its peak, then hit the *l'lenda* with remorse and contrition. His broad face twisted with soul-hurting pain, and then he was taking a step forward and putting his hand out toward Aesnil.

“*Chama,* forgive me!” he blurted, confusion roughening his voice. “It was not my intention to cause you such agitation! I regret the pain and the – the – ”

He stopped in total confusion, shaking his head hard in an effort to clear the mud of his thoughts, but he'd said enough. After a brief experience of shock, Aesnil was flooded with delight and triumph – enhanced only slightly by me. The *Chama* had the victory she'd wanted over a *denday,* and his death was now absolutely unnecessary.

“At last you come to your senses, Lerran!” she crowed, a laugh bubbling in her, words. “I, your *Chama,* accept your apology, and direct you to return to your city and obey my commands. Guards! Show him out.”

Two guardsmen came to move Lerran toward the doors, and he needed the assistance. He was having trouble understanding where he was and what was happening, but the confusion wasn't likely to last very much longer. Once he was out of my area of influence, his mind would begin to clear itself. As soon as he was out of sight a hubbub of excited conversation broke out in the room, and Aesnil leaned down to put a hand on my arm.

“His apology was your doing,” she said, looking at me with all the pleasure and happiness in her mind. “You are magnificent, and worth whatever I have given you. You may be sure there will be other gifts as well.”

“The *Chama* is more than kind,” I smirked, letting smugness come through in my voice. “Her pleasure is my pleasure.”

Aesnil laughed at the triteness of the remark, then went back to listening to complaints. The court people hadn't heard the exchange between us, but they were still looking at me in a very odd way. I was glad Aesnil hadn't made any general announcements about what I could do, and I'd have to try to convince her to continue the silence. It would help neither one of us if her people attacked me as a witch or something.

Another couple of hours dragged by in boredom, and then there was a sudden stir all around as a man pushed his way through the people waiting and watching, and made his way toward the platform Aesnil and I sat on. He was a really big man, well made and completely confident, dressed in *haddin* and swordbelt and, strangely enough, still wearing his sword. The guardsmen around the room hesitated in an odd way and looked toward Aesnil, who was radiating waves of fear and frustration despite the brightly interested smile on her face. The big man stopped about ten feet away from us, gave Aesnil a cursory glance of approval, then shifted his eyes to me.

"Ah, how thoughtful of you, Aesnil," the big man said, his voice deep and carrying despite the fact that he spoke softly. "You have found a *rella wenda* for me, to console me till you wear my bands. Shall I take her now?"

"Terril is *mine!*" Aesnil snapped, rising to the bait the big man had dangled. "Never would I find a woman for you. Never!"

"For the reason that you wish me for yourself." The man grinned, pleased he'd gotten a rise out of the *Chama*. It had faintly surprised him that I hadn't gotten huffy over his comment, but he couldn't know that I was able to tell he wasn't serious. "As you are so eager to have me, let us dispense with the delay granted you by the council of *dendayy* and see to the matter now. I, too, am eager."

"Eagerness for you is a flaw I do not suffer from," Aesnil told him with a grating purr designed to annoy the man. "And now that I think on it, I fail to see any reason for allowing the council of *dendayy* a say in whose bands I shall wear and when. The decision in such a matter should be mine alone. For what reason are you here, Cinnan? Merely to bedevil me as always?"

"I need no reason to visit with she who will soon be my belonging," the man Cinnan answered, his easy grin still in place. "That the Council of *dendayy* is disturbed is not yet my concern – though it soon shall be. As it happens, I heard of the deep agitation Lerran suffered from when he left your presence, and thought I might inquire as to what was done to him. There is little wisdom in antagonizing one's supporters, Aesnil."

"I need no words of advice from one such as you, Cinnan," the *Chama* answered coldly, looking down at the man imperiously. "Lerran was taught a lesson which you and the other *dendayy* would do well to learn as well: I am not a woman to be trifled with. And as for the rest of your babble – by what right do you speak of me as one who will soon be your belonging?"

"By right of council law, *wenda,*" Cinnan sighed, sounding as though he had gone through all that many times before. "A *Chama* will always rule in our land, yet her decisions must be tempered with the advice of one chosen by the council to band her. I am he chosen to band our present *Chama,* therefore do I speak as I do."

"Chosen, perhaps, yet not chosen by me," Aesnil said, leaning back among her pillows again. "I do not care for the choice made by the council. Leave here, Cinnan, and do not return, for I shall have no part of you."

"The choice is not yours to make, *wenda*." He shrugged, more than a touch of compassion in his mind. "I will do my utmost to see that you do not regret the council's choice, yet you may not deny me."

"I *do* deny you," Aesnil came back, a flash of anger in her mind. "I have commanded that you leave. Will you obey?"

Cinnan shrugged again as he folded his arms, then clearly shook his head, refusing the command. I got the impression that his refusal was required by his position, that is, that the *Chama* commanded all but the man who was to band her. Even I expected Aesnil to grow angrier, but instead she just smiled.

"You refuse my command," she purred, her mind filled with satisfaction. "Excellent. Guards, arrest this man and place him in chains! Should he prove himself worthy, I may allow him to become a *vendra*. Now, arrest him!"

The snap in her voice sent the spectators in all directions to get out of the way and brought the guard from their places around the room and toward Cinnan, causing the big *l'lenda* to stare around him in disbelief. I could see his disbelief would not be lasting very long, but I could also see how determined the guardsmen were. They would try to arrest Cinnan, he would resist, and the floors of the audience room would be stained with blood. As his hand began moving toward the sword he wore, I grabbed the faint trace of disbelief in his mind, brought it back to its original intensity, then quickly increase it. His mind wobbled from the dual pressure of belief/disbelief, but belief didn't have an empath backing it. His hand fell away from the sword in confusion just as the guardsmen reached him, and they were able to take his weapon and tie his wrists behind him with leather before a headshake brought him to the reality of his capture. He tried to struggle then, but it was much too late – as Aesnil's tinkling laughter told him.

"You now know what befell Lerran," she informed him, the purr even thicker in her tone. "As I stated earlier, Terril is mine. Take him away."

The guardsmen pulled him, still struggling, out of the room, but not before his frowning stare had come to me and noticed the faint sheen of sweat on my forehead. Fighting his intentions had been like trying to lift him physically, but happily my mind was on a par with his physical strength. It had been a struggle, but he'd had no real chance against me.

"The morning's audience is now at an end," Aesnil announced once Cinnan was gone, raising herself from her nest of pillows. "Should it be my wish to resume this afternoon, you will all be informed. You may now leave."

There was very little noise as the former spectators took themselves out as commanded, but if Aesnil could have heard the mental static, it would have considerably dimmed her pleasure. The prevailing attitude was shock, even from the women who had felt contempt for the men – or who had pretended to feel contempt. To see men handled that peremptorily had shaken them, as though they now felt themselves in jeopardy. It would be interesting to see how many of them returned, now that Aesnil had proven herself so powerful.

"Terril, your guard will escort you to your new accommodations," Aesnil said as I got to my feet, her face glowing with joy. "There will be many gifts for you for this day's work, you have my word on it. For now, I am sure your new accommodations will give you pleasure. Rest there till I have need of you again."

She squeezed my shoulder with true, deep-down warmth, gestured in the direction I was supposed to go, then left by another door, her guard right behind her. I noticed then how nervous my own guard was, but led them out without letting them know it. I was surrounded by eight big, strapping men, and *they* were just short of being afraid of *me!* It was ludicrous to think I could handle all of them, but as long as they thought I could I was more than halfway there. It was a new experience walking around on that planet without having men's minds humming at me, but at that point I considered it a change for the better.

My new room wasn't far away, but as it turned out it was more an apartment than a room. I was let into the reception room by the guards, and was left alone to examine the pink and white pillows, silks, and carpeting, and take a tentative taste of the fresh food standing on a newly brought tray. Seeing another door made me wonder what was behind it, and opening the door showed me my sleeping room – with an added convenience I'd forgotten I'd asked for. The sleeping room was of silver and blue, fixed up with a wide set of sleeping furs stacked high, large windows letting in sunlight, blue pillows on silver carpeting just like in my old room – but with the one addition I'd asked for.

Daldrin, chained hand and foot to the floor.

"That smirk does not become you," my loyal servant growled, looking up at me from his place on the floor. "As you have now had your amusement at my plight, I would appreciate being released."

"Would you indeed," I murmured, stepping closer to look down at him. "And what has a slave to say on the doings of his *dendaya?*"

Daldrin, annoyed, opened his mouth to snap out an answer, at the same time pulling at the chains on his wrists: As large as he was, the metal had no trouble holding him, and he bit back the words he'd been about to say as a very bad idea. He stared up at me in silence for a moment, fighting his thoughts back under control, then tried again.

"It seems the *dendaya* has won the approval of the *Chama*," he said, his forwardness shrinking back to the level at which it had been when I'd first met him. "Is this the thanks a poor servant receives for having aided both his *Chama* and his *dendaya?*"

"A servant should be grateful that he was allowed to be of assistance," I pointed out as though the idea were no more than reasonable. "Would he dare to expect a reward after receiving such favored treatment? No, I think not – unless he also sought punishment. Does the slave wish to be punished?"

"No, *dendaya*, this slave does not wish to be punished," he assured me in a meek tone while his mind seethed. "This slave wishes only to give pleasure. Release me, *dendaya*, so that I might give you pleasure."

"Perhaps later." I yawned, pretending I was actually considering it. "What has become of your clothing?"

"It was taken from me," he answered, practically through his teeth until he unclamped his jaw. "Perhaps the *dendaya* knows something regarding the reason?"

"Ah, yes, I do seem to recall now," I said, tapping my lips with one finger. "It pleases me to look upon a body as lovely as yours, therefore have I had your clothing taken. For what reason should I have deprived myself?"

"Lovely," he choked, pulling at the chains again. "You now have the power to do as you wish with me, therefore do you see no reason to deprive yourself. Perhaps I, in your place, would have seen a reason."

"Perhaps you only believe you would have," I said, looking down at him. "What difference is there between chains holding a man and the strength of a man holding a woman? Should it please me to take you, as it pleased you to take me, what difference would there be?"

"If no other," he said, trying to smile, "there would be the difference between man and woman. A man learns the ways of a woman's body so that he may use her as she was meant to be used. A man was not made to be used. So you do this to me in revenge for what was done to you earlier. Was the experience so unpleasant, then, that it called for revenge?"

"Pleasant or unpleasant, it was not my choice," I said. "Should pleasure be given you against your will, does the sweetness take the sour taste away?"

"Perhaps it would in part." He grinned, and then the grin softened. "To wish to use a highly desirable woman is no more than natural in a man. Should the action have given you distress, you have my apologies – yet not my regret."

"And without regret, the action would happily be repeated at first opportunity," I summed up with a nod. "I see you need to be left in chains – or perhaps to be taken so after all."

"*Wenda*, do not leave me chained." He laughed, unable to put the desperation he wanted into his voice. "Should you leave me so, there will be pleasure for neither of us. I must be free if we are to chase the sourness away."

"I do not see the necessity for freeing you." I shrugged. "Should I wish pleasure, I may take it as you have taken it – as easily and with as little regret. I have been taught that among *l'lendaa*, the ability to do gives the right."

"Among *l'lendaa*, yes," he agreed, no longer laughing. "You, however, are not *l'lenda*, nor shall you ever be. You are *wenda*, subject to *l'lenda*, to his desires and de- mands. I am a man and cannot be used as a woman is. Release me, else your pleasure will be an elusive thing."

His light blue gaze had become sober and very determined, downright stubborn if you included the indications in his mind. He was convinced he could and I couldn't, and argument on the subject was a waste of time. I shrugged as if conceding the point, then turned and left the room.

A minute later I was back with the tray of food, but it wasn't my intention to torture him by eating in front of him, as the wary look in his eye seemed to assume. I put the tray down near him, took my sandals off, slipped out of the gown, then sat down to feed him.

Knowing how people feel about things does quite a lot to help you deal with those people, but very often empathy is unnecessary when dealing with certain people and specific actions. Daldrin had had me feed him earlier that day, and I would have had to have been entirely without senses not to know how much he had enjoyed it. I tasted the food first, as I'd been taught to do with the Hamarda, then I fed him as much as he would take, silently, gently, as though *he* were the important one. I used my lap to hold his head up as he ate, and he was very much aware of it; his eyes moved over me as if he had never seen me before, and his hands closed to fists beneath the cuffs of his chains.

After I had finished eating my portion of the meal, I moved the tray away and slid out from under his head. I could feel his reluctance to let me go, and I'd been careful to keep out of range of those big hands of his. If he had gotten a grip on me, I would have been caught until I unchained him – and probably a good deal longer. I moved around to his right side and knelt beside him, then leaned forward to kiss him very lightly without touching him. Without looking I could feel his hands fold into fists again as he gritted his teeth, determined not to react to anything I did to him. He was rested and well fed and had worked out his needs earlier that morning; that was probably why he was so sure he could resist me, but I knew better. The men of that world rarely denied themselves anything, and even having been a slave hadn't changed Daldrin's basic outlook on life. The initial kissing had been a warning of my intentions, but not a warning that would benefit him. He was very much aware of what I was doing, and his trying to dull his senses automatically heightened them. That was when I began on him in earnest.

A man of the Amalgamation would have had no trouble resisting me, but Daldrin was a Rimilian and didn't stand a chance. In a very short time he was writhing on the carpet fur, his broad body twisting, his muscles corded as he strained to break loose from the fetters that held him, sweat glistening all over and teeth clenched with effort. I felt weak and breathless myself, but I raised my lips from his body and reached over to kiss his face softly.

"A woman may pretend disinterest even while she writhes," I whispered, spreading my hands out on his chest. "Do you, a man, wish to claim disinterest?"

"I will beat you for this, *wenda,* you have my word!" He gasped, chest rising and falling with the effort of speech "Unchain me now! I demand it!"

"Oh, do not beat me, *hizah*, I beg you," I wheedled, kissing more and more at his face. "Forgive a poor *bedin* and do not beat her. Allow her instead to soothe you in your misery."

"Do not speak so!" he screamed, his mind burning as high as his body. "Release me *now, wenda*, now, now!"

"Forgive a poor *bedin, hizah*," I pleaded, pressing myself to him as I put my arms around his body. "This *bedin* may not release you, yet she may bring you release. Allow her to bring you release, *hizah*, command her to your pleasure."

"By the Sword of Gerleth, I cannot bear it," he groaned, actually quivering beneath me. "You have used your power, and now I am done."

"I have used no power on you save the power of a woman," I told him, sitting up to look down into his eyes. "You are a man, and born to have such feelings for a woman. Will you be pleasured as you are, as helpless as I found myself to be in your arms, or must I taste the bitterness of defeat alone? I find, you see, that I must seek a proper ending to those feelings begun by the touching of a man. Should you refuse to take your pleasure in chains, should you refuse to learn the helplessness I was taught, I will then find it necessary to release you and allow you your way with me. I must have your word, *l'lenda*; which will it be?"

He stared up at me silently, his face shiny with sweat, his expression serious, his eyes troubled. I could feel how much he wanted to be freed, how desperately he needed to exercise his usual masculinity, and his words, when they came, were a surprise.

"It is impossible – to know – the depths of slavery till one has been a slave," he got out, regretting every word even as he said it. "A wise man learns all things so that he may grow wiser still. Let us taste the bitterness of defeat together."

I smiled very faintly, admiring his courage, then began helping him to grow wiser. He and I both found that although his body had been forced to readiness despite his wishes, his mind didn't share that readiness and couldn't be made to feel the sort of pleasure it should have. He did try, I'll give him that, but the humiliation and frustration were too great to overcome. After an unsatisfying time of trying I finally gave up and unchained him, thinking my experiment was over, but I was only half right. Daldrin had a lot of frustration and forced need to get rid of, and the minute the last shackle was open I found myself seized and thrown beneath him, to reap what I had sown, so to speak. After what I'd done he wasn't concerned with being gentle with me, but he wasn't unnecessary brutal, either. When it was all over he let himself drop to the carpeting beside me and sighed deeply.

"I find it difficult to believe a woman has so little pleasure from being taken through a man's desire," he said, his voice sounding tired. "Never before have my *wendaa* seemed other than pleased, yet never before have I had such a thing done to me."

"A woman's feelings are not those which you experienced," I admitted, sitting up slowly to rub at my arms where his fingers had dug so deep. "For me the shame shows itself afterward, when I am able to realize what I have been forced to. Perhaps other women feel no shame; I know only that I felt no pleasure treating you so, no more than satisfaction in vengeance achieved and little even of that."

"Perhaps we have both grown in wisdom," he chuckled, putting his hand on my calf to squeeze gently. "It is said that to a wise man all experiences are worthy in that one may learn from each of them and thereby grow to be wiser still. Go now and search for a strap, *wenda,* and bring it to me here."

"For what reason do you require a strap?" I asked, turning my head to look down at him. "A strap alone, without clothing, would appear foolish to any who saw you."

"I do not intend wearing it," he said with a snort of derision. "Though I be chained here through my loyalty to my brother, I will not allow a *wenda* to chain me in reality and afterward go unpunished. My word was given you on the matter earlier; now you will have the beating."

"You jest," I said, searching his mind with a frown to find the emotion that would show he was joking. "You, yourself, agreed to remain chained – and I would not fetch a strap that I was to be beaten with."

"I did indeed agree to remain chained," he said, the look in his eyes harder than it had been. "I did not, however, agree to be chained to begin with. And you will most certainly fetch the strap you are to be beaten with, else will the beating be sharpened to cover the disobedience. You may now do as you have been ordered to do."

"I shall do no such thing," I said, rising stiffly to my feet. "I am no longer a slave, therefore do I refuse to be treated as one. You, however, remain a slave – and need not have been unfettered so quickly. Do you think me your belonging, to be treated as you wish? Even were I to allow such a thing, one in your position would hardly be permitted a belonging."

"My position will not forever remain what it is," he growled, standing up to look down at me. "Should I wish a belonging I will take her, defending my right to her, if necessary, with a sword. Are you familiar with the use of a sword, *wenda,* that you would attempt to deny me my choice?"

He looked down at me coldly, shoulders stiff with anger, his body large and menacing. He was having more and more difficulty in keeping himself from reverting to *l'lenda* status in my presence, and that wasn't a good sign. He hadn't claimed me openly because he was, technically, still a slave, but waiting for it to happen would just be asking for trouble.

"I have no knowledge of the use of a sword," I said with a headshake, not happy about what I would have to do. "Daldrin, you forget I have no need of a sword. I, myself, am spawn of the dagger, not to be gripped with no regard for my edges. Do not force me to hurt you."

"I fear no woman," he rasped, and reached a hand out toward my arm. He honestly felt no fear of what I might do to him; after all, hadn't I been used by him more than once with nothing untoward happening? I hoped that one day my ability would be a reflex action coming into play the first time I was threatened, to make future scenes like that unnecessary. It was painful for me, but I took one step back and defended myself.

Doubt can be an agonizing emotion, especially when it's strong and especially when you're not used to it. Daldrin's hand froze in midair, a sudden worry in his eyes, but he didn't have much time for worry. The guilt hit him fast, a soul-shriveling guilt that put every ill in the world on his shoulders, bowing his head and sending him to his knees even as he sobbed once in an effort to ease the pain. His brawny body shook, wracked with self-accusation, and then the pain of guilt was gone, leaving behind a knowledge of how humbly grateful a man must be to find himself rid of such a burden. I strengthened the humility and gratitude, made sure they had a good hold on him, then went and got my gown and slipped it on. If I'd had any real inner strength I would have been able to stay and look at what I'd done, but the sight of Daldrin on his knees weeping was too much for me. I picked up my sandals and carried them to the next room, put them on, then called the door guards and told them I wanted a different room for that afternoon. They were still too edgy to ask me why, which was just as well. I followed them to a different empty room, closed the door, then lay down among the pillows and fell asleep.

When I was awakened by a female slave, I discovered that it was still early afternoon. The poor cringing little slave apologized for waking me, but she'd been sent by Aesnil to say that the *Chama* wanted me. I couldn't have been asleep more than a few hours, but I felt rested in both body and mind, enough so that I could face Aesnil again without flinching. I stretched into the pillows until I had yawned away the last of the sleep, then followed the slave out.

Aesnil was waiting for me in the corridor outside of the audience room, but we didn't go in. We turned, instead, in another direction I'd never walked in, and I was curious as to where we were going. Aesnil was smugly happy, and still filled with warm approval of me.

"You seem pleased to have me here," I said to her as we walked down the corridor escorted by our guards. "Do we go to tend to further matters where my power will be required?"

"Your power will not this time be required." She laughed, enormously pleased with the secret she had. "And yet, should you wish to use it, you may feel free to do so. I have promised you gifts for your service to me, and the first of them now awaits you. It is sure to please you as much as your service has pleased me, perhaps even more so."

Her cryptic comments made me even more curious – and wary – but I couldn't get another thing out of her but wait and see. She was anxious to give me the gift and really believed I'd like it, so I gave up prying and just followed along. We went down the corridor only halfway, then left the palace by what was obviously not a main entrance. We descended the steps to a wide, well-worn path, and followed the path about three hundred yards to a structure of very high stone walls that stretched away to either side of a heavy wooden gate fully as high as the walls. There was a beautiful day all around us, but the high stone walls seemed to echo with the stronger, more violent emotions, pushing at me harder the closer we got. I narrowed my sensing down to the dead, unechoing wood of the gate, and that way was able to continue on as if nothing bothered me.

We had to wait for the gate to be unbarred from the inside, and then we were able to enter. There seemed to be an awful lot of guards around, all dressed in the baggy pants, loose shirts and heavy sandals of the guards we'd brought with us. The inside guards were armed in the same way our escort was, but they also carried heavy whips, either in their left hands or coiled over their sword hilts. Aesnil's pleasure was very great as we were greeted by a man who seemed to be the head guard of the structure, causing her to smile warmly when the man bowed.

"Has everything been prepared according to my instructions?" she asked, looking around at the bustle. "They have not yet been returned to their cells?"

"They await your inspection, *Chama*," the man answered, and then he grinned. "The one sent us this morning is a wild beast, requiring many chains and men to subdue him. He will make an excellent *vendra,* surely surviving as long as that other new one. Perhaps on the next feast day they may be made to face one another to the death. It will be a spectacle long remembered by the people."

"An excellent suggestion," Aesnil laughed. "I will consider it carefully. You may now show us to where they are being held."

"At once, *Chama*." The man bowed in acknowledgment, then led us away from the wide-spaced entrance area to a narrower alleyway between the high outer wall and an inner wall that was almost as high. It was warm with the sun shining down on us and all the men with us were sweating in their long, bulky clothes, but none of them mentioned their discomfort to the *Chama*. I hadn't understood why the guards wore more than *haddinn* and swordbelts, but Aesnil undoubtedly had had something to do with it. She seemed to equate clothing with freedom; the less clothing, the less freedom. I wondered if the attitude was personal, or had something to do with tradition.

The alleyway continued on for at least fifty feet, then abruptly opened on another wide area. This area, unlike the first, had no outer gate that could be opened and closed. It was all high stone wall with one or two doorways in the inner wall, both stretches of stone brooding down even in the bright sunshine, penning in even further the chained men it contained. There must have been twenty or thirty of them, all very large and well-muscled, all heavily chained to strong wooden stakes, all of them naked. Every one of them in sight was covered with sweat, many of them also covered with welts from the whips carried by the guards. and they stirred when we appeared.

"The newest one is here, *Chama*," our guide said, directing us to the first post on the right. "He is much quieter now, having learned the kiss of the whip. Would you have him able to speak to you?"

"No," Aesnil smiled, staring up at the broad face of Cinnan, the *l'lenda* I'd helped her capture that morning. He was heavily gagged with cloth and leather, but his eyes spoke volumes on the fury he was filled with. Aesnil's eyes moved down to inspect his body, seeing the many welts he was covered with – as well as other things – and his mind surged higher with the frustration and shame of helplessness. He struggled in the chains, his muscles straining with the effort, and Aesnil's tinkling laugh rang out.

"You are beautifully made, Cinnan," she jibed, posing as though inspecting him in great detail. "Should you win what matches you are given, you will undoubtedly give great pleasure to the slaves sent for your use. And yet it seems unfitting that one slave should be used by another, no matter that the second has earned the privilege. Perhaps I shall direct that you be denied slave-flesh for your lusts, and be made to suffer while the others pleasure themselves. It may teach you to speak more carefully to your *Chama* when next you stand before her. I shall decide when I see how well you fight."

She turned her back on his anger with another laugh, stood for a minute looking around at the other *vendraa*, then slowly began moving down the right-hand row of posts, inspecting each man chained in place as she passed him. The fourth one in line made me pause briefly because of how familiar he looked, and then I saw the connection. Although the face in front of me was fractionally older, it was undoubtedly Daldrin's face I looked at, or at least that of his brother. His body was scarred here and there and marked with welts but other than that he seemed to be all right. His eyes looked at me without interest and his mind was bored, but he had still survived as a warrior in chains.

I moved down the line again after Aesnil, wondering who she was standing and inspecting now. She stood looking up at the man, her face composed but her mind filled with glee, her glance in my direction showing she was waiting for me. I increased my pace just a little, reaching her in a matter of seconds – then stopped dead in shock when I saw who was chained to the post.

"You did not suspect, and my surprise is a success!" Aesnil crowed, clapping her hands in delight over what must have been a stunned expression on my face. Standing there chained to the post, anger and confusion all through him, was no one other than Tammad. How he had gotten there I had no idea, but Aesnil was anxious to give me what details she had.

"He appears quite tame now," she laughed, "yet his great body was filled with insolence when he came before me two days ago. He spoke of 'his' woman having been taken to my palace, and cheekily demanded that I give you to him immediately. I naturally had him subdued by my guards – he and his two companions – yet only he proved worthy of a place as *vendra*. He has fought twice and won twice, and provided my people with great sport. I intend fighting him again with the new sun, when I will be able to witness the spectacle, and invite you now to join me. Are you not delighted to see him done so, without covering and in chains?"

"You have not the least idea how great a delight," I said slowly, knowing I had to go along with her if I was to do anything for either Tammad or myself. "I had never thought to see him so, the one who so arrogantly took me from my people to serve his base desires. So you have fallen slave, eh, *l'lenda*? How demeaning for you – and how deliciously proper."

My laugh put a darkening on his skin and a scowl on his face, but that was nothing compared to what it did to his mind. Reading him made me want to close my eyes and swallow hard, but I didn't dare; all I could do was continue to laugh, and hope the chains holding his wrists to the post above his head didn't snap. The way he was straining at them there was no guarantee they wouldn't, and that despite the ugly welts all over him. He wasn't a good, obedient slave, that was for sure, and I couldn't even ease his pain. His mind was so wild with outrage and indignation that I couldn't get through the barrier he was inadvertently projecting. I let the laughter die away and turned to Aesnil.

"I will happily join you come the new sun to watch this – beast – provide a spectacle for our pleasure," I told her. "You are indeed generous to a guest beneath your roof, and I will not forget how much is owed you for this gesture. Let us leave this place now – the smell of their sweat sickens me."

Aesnil smiled and nodded and began to turn away with me, but the sound of Tammad's voice stopped us.

"*Wenda*, you are not yet done with me," he growled, causing us to turn back to look at him. "Do not come to see me fight, else your pleasure will be considerably diminished when I reclaim you. Run, instead, and attempt to hide from me – and learn for the final time that I will find you wherever you go. You will not escape the reckoning due between us."

He stood there glaring down at me, all self-righteous pride. The stiff-necked fool refused to entertain the least possible idea that the helpless female might be trying to give the mighty warrior a hand in getting free, and that made me mad. As far as he was concerned I was useless, fit only for standing around and waiting until *he* did something. He didn't deserve my help, but he would get it anyway – as well as a little something extra.

"I rarely find it necessary to run from a chained slave," I told his anger, deliberately looking him up and down. "Slavery becomes you, and will undoubtedly be your lot for quite some time. Tell me, *Chama*: has he yet been given a slave for the latest of his victories?"

"The slaves await the victors now, chained by the neck in their cells," Aesnil told me. "These *vendraa* would already have been returned there had I not ordered that they be made to await my pleasure. Do you wish the slave given him removed again?"

"No," I answered, still staring at Tammad. His anger was just as strong as it had been all along, but my own anger gave me the added strength I needed to break through hit iron defenses. I fought with his definitely opposed will, the sweat breaking out on my forehead, only partially aware of seeing him bare his clenched teeth, and then I was through deep inside his unprotected mind. He struggled in his chains at the post, as though physical movement would help repel mental invasion, but he was much too late even if he'd been tight. I poured my suggestion into his mind, strengthening it and underscoring it, and then withdrew slowly and deliberately, showing him I could come and go at will. Blazing fury followed me out of his mind, but the heat of the blaze couldn't touch me.

"No," I repeated to Aesnil, taking a deep breath. "Leave the slave as she is. He will continue to feel desire for her, and will need to attempt her use before proving to himself that he is now incapable of using a female. A sudden feeling of inadequacy will come to him each time he attempts it, so strong a feeling that it will overcome his desire. The sight should be quite amusing."

"Excellent." Aesnil laughed. "Exquisitely fitting. How clever you are, Terril. Let us leave them now to their own devices and return to my palace."

"A lovely idea," I agreed, turning away from Tammad, who was struggling so hard to get loose that the post was groaning. He was absolutely livid with rage and humiliation, and it was a considerable relief to walk away from him. He would not enjoy his next few hours of life, but my position with Aesnil had become much more secure. With a little luck, I'd never have to do anything like that to him again – not that he didn't deserve it. If he'd had a little faith in me, it wouldn't have had to happen in the first place.

Once we got back to the palace I found it necessary to join Aesnil in the royal suite for a glass of wine, but was able to put the time to good use. Through casual questioning I discovered that the other two men taken with Tammad – one a "normal" blond and one unusually dark-haired like me – had been brought to the palace to be servant-slaves when it was discovered that they weren't *vendra* quality. Aesnil was curious about the dark-haired one, and grew indignant when I told her he was a man of my own land who had betrayed me to Tammad. I added that I would like to have that one in particular as a servant right after seeing Tammad fight for his life the next day, and she agreed immediately then asked what I had in mind for the turncoat. I painted a picture of humiliation and degradation that set her chuckling with pleasure, then excused myself to return to my rooms. Aesnil had told me a bath would be available any time I wanted it, and I was quick to say I wanted it immediately.

By the time I got back to my rooms a slave was already there, waiting to take me to the bath chamber. I found a closet filled with gowns, chose one in a cool ice blue, then let the slave carry it as she led me and my guards through the corridors. I'd looked in both rooms before leaving in hopes of finding Daldrin, but the man hadn't been anywhere around. I'd chewed my lip over his disappearance, but hadn't let myself worry the question long. I needed his help desperately to free Garth and Len from the palace, and couldn't consider trying it without him. If something had happened to cause his permanent disappearance, I'd find myself with plenty of time for worrying then.

My guards were left outside a single door which led to a small area with another single door in it. The slave opened the second door to reveal what looked like a candle-lit, furred and pillowed resting area, and after closing the door behind us she carefully set my gown in one corner, then gestured me after her to the third and final door. The resting area had been warmer than the entrance area and corridor, but behind the third door lay a large tub below floor level and more heat than I'd already experienced. I entered slowly, looking around at the windowless walls hung with silks and large candles, seeing two other slaves jump to their feet as the third closed the door behind us. All three of the slaves were naked, and in that room it was a good idea.

"Allow us to assist you, *dendaya*," one of the slaves murmured, coming closer with the other two to help me out of my gown. I didn't particularly want their help, but the sudden heat was making me drowsy, adding to the tiredness I already felt from my battle with Tammad. It was easier letting the slaves have their way, and before another minute had gone by my sandals were also gone and I was being directed into the water. I sank down in the tub with a sigh and put my head back, then let all my worries and aches soak out of me into the warm, soothing water.

The slaves let me relax a while, then slowly and gently began washing me. It felt wonderfully good to be taken care of that way, and by the time my hair was also done I was ready for a nap. I let myself be urged out of the water and into a thick, soft cloth being used as a towel, then followed one of the slaves into the resting area. I had my eye on a comfortable-looking pile of gold and white pillows, but the slave asked me to stretch out on the carpet fur so that lotions could be massaged into my skin. I agreed with a sigh, loosening the towel as I lay down, telling myself the massage would be worth the loss of the pillows. I got as comfortable as possible on the carpet, letting my eyes close as the slave left, probably to get the lotions.

I know I dropped off for a short time; I awoke to the delightful aroma of flower petals and felt the touch of hands on my body, spreading something warm and thick over my back. It felt so good I almost fell asleep again, but when the hands reached my behind and thighs I got a shock that woke me all the way. The mind behind the hands hummed, and the hum belonged to Daldrin.

"Lie still, *dendaya*," his voice came as I tried to turn over and sit up. "I am ordered to tend your body and shall do so. The lotion must be used before it cools."

The back of his arm shoved me face down again even as his mind chuckled; he was nothing but an innocent servant-slave, following the orders of his masters. I gasped as his hands did more than massage me and tried to crawl out from under his too-close attention, but one of his arms circled my waist while the other continued the ministrations.

"Daldrin, release me!" I hissed, trying to keep my voice down while still putting a snap into it. "There are important matters to be discussed between us. There is no time for this foolishness!"

"How might this insignificant slave discuss matters of import with a *dendaya*?" he murmured, tightening his hold around my waist. "I must do as I was ordered to do, else I shall be beaten. I do not wish to be beaten, *dendaya*."

"You misbegotten son of a lame *seetar*, release me!" I snarled, trying to squirm loose with the oily help of the lotion on me. "Have you no sense in that thick blond head? Have you no desire for escape? Why will you not list – oh!"

"There is need for the lotion even there," he commented while I kicked and struggled and tried to make him stop. "Somehow I feel that that place will require a good deal of lotion. Why do you not force me to release you as you did earlier in the day?"

"I cannot," I gasped, dizzy from what he was doing to me. I needed tight control of my emotions for a projection, but his touch on me was producing the mental equivalent of an earthquake – and I was sure he knew it.

"Just as I thought," he said with a good deal of satisfaction without stopping what he was doing. "Now, what is this about escape? I thought you understood my reasons for remaining here."

"Your escape – will assist in your brother's escape – as well," I panted, barely aware of the fistfuls of carpet fur I held to. "Daldrin – I cannot think when being done so! You must release me!"

"I need do nothing of the kind," he denied, his mind hard with decision. "Should you wish to speak to me, I will listen for a short while. After I have listened I will then decide what must be done. In any event, you are sure to figure prominently in whatever the results come to be."

I didn't like the ominous sound of that, but I had very little choice. I had to get it said while I could still talk.

"There are two men confined in this palace who are close to me," I got out, the words spilling over one another in the rush. "Should you help them to escape they will surely take you with them to find the others who await them nearby – and who will return to attack the place where the *vendraa* are held. In such a way will you be able to free your brother. Now, release me."

"There seems little reason for them to return, not to mention launching an attack against the *vendra ralle*," he mused, ignoring my last words. "Perhaps there is some point you have neglected to mention – such as the presence of another of their number in the *vendra ralle*?"

"Yes, yes, of course!" I raged, struggling. "The third of them has been declared *vendra,* and they will not desert him. They *cannot* desert him. Daldrin, please! I cannot bear it!"

"I shall consider your proposal," he said in a very neutral way, then finally stopped torturing me. "Lie still now, for there is lotion which still must be used upon you."

I shuddered as he resumed spreading lotion, from relief as much as from dread. What would I do if he refused to help? What *could* I do? And more to the immediate point, what was he going to do to me? What I'd done to him earlier in the day hadn't been pleasant; would he see that I'd only been defending myself, or was he out for revenge? His mind was calm and his emotions were completely under control, and I couldn't see a damned thing one way or the other to help me out.

When the lotion had been spread down to my ankles, I was ordered to turn to my back. I obeyed with reluctance, then watched his big, hulking form as he began spreading lotion up the front of my legs. I finally noticed that he was working automatically, his eyes seeing and his hands doing without the supervision of his mind. His intellect worked at another job, turning here, twisting there, poking and prodding. It almost seemed as though he'd already made his decision, but his mind still hadn't stopped working. When he reached my ribs his hands finally stopped spreading lotion, and his eyes came to my face.

"The two you speak of," he said, holding my gaze. "I believe I know which ones they are. They were brought to the servants quarters not long after your arrival, badly beaten by the whips of the guard. They have been toiling in the kitchens ever since, for there are no other female guests to tend at the moment."

"Will you help them to escape and go with them?" I asked, needing to know which way he had decided.

"This third one, the one who has been made *vendra,*" he said, ignoring my question, "is undoubtedly the *l'lenda* who took you from your own land, the one who could not follow you even had he wanted to – which he did not. It is obvious you wish to free him so that he might rescue you."

I suddenly found it very difficult meeting that steady blue gaze. I turned my head to the side to stare at a nearby pile of orange and yellow cushions, but Daldrin's hand came to my face and turned it back to him.

"You would not be so foolish as to run from him once his freedom was assured," he stated in a flat voice, staring at me narrowly. "Not even a *wenda* such as you could be so foolish as to refuse rescue."

"I will rescue myself once his *l'lenda* have attacked," I said, trying to ignore the flush I could feel on my cheeks. "The diversion will be enough to take all eyes from me, so that I may go my own way. There is little hope for me if I remain to be – rescued."

"You have done something to anger him," he said in exasperation, for some reason annoyed. "What have you done, *wenda*, and how badly will you be punished for it?"

"I will not be punished at all for I will no longer be here," I told him, pushing at his hand to make him let my face go. "As for what was done, that does not concern you. Will you assist me, or do you prefer rotting here the while I assist myself? I will make the attempt with or without you, no matter the consequences."

"I do believe you would," he said, shaking his head as he continued to stare at me. "Never before have I seen so stubborn a *wenda* – and one so badly in need of a strong hand to guide her. I will assist you in freeing your *l'lenda*, for I, too, wish to see him free – and myself as well. Let us finish with this lotion so that the task may be done."

"I wish no further lotion," I said, taking the opportunity to roll away and sit up when he turned to reach for the lotion jug. "And I would know why you wish to see Tammad free. That you wish freedom for yourself is easily understood, yet not so the other. Why should his freedom be of interest to you?"

"My reasons are not your concern," he answered, his mind as calm as his gaze. "Return yourself to me so that this lotion may be applied."

"I know not why that misbegotten lotion concerns you so!" I snapped; bothered by his answer – or lack of one. "Give it here and I will apply it myself."

I reached my hand out for the jug, but all he did was shake his head and continue to stare at me. After a minute I took my hand back, and admitted to myself that I had no choice. I needed his help no matter what I'd said, and he knew it as well as I did. I moved forward again to where he was sitting, and watched a faint grin appear on his face.

"When one cannot use a weapon, one may as well not have it," he observed, tilting the jug over his hand to let the lotion flow out. "You are willful and disobedient to a large degree, undoubtedly because of your power, and yet any woman may be taught to obey him to whom she belongs, should the matter be pursued strongly enough. We cannot begin your quest till darkness has fallen, therefore may we concern ourselves with other matters for the time."

He rubbed his hands together to spread the lotion on both of them, then proceeded to cover the areas of me he hadn't yet touched. I'd never before thought of myself as easy, but Daldrin was almost as bad as Tammad when it came to resisting him. I'd been able to accept most of what he'd done to me earlier, but he brought the memory of that back and added to it so thoroughly that I soon found myself in his lap, kissing at him and trying to talk him into taking off those red leather slave pants he had on. He laughed softly as he ran his hands all over me, making me squirm against his chest as I kissed him, making me willing to do anything if only he would satisfy me. Once we reached that point he took me in his arms and kissed me deeply, then began making me pay for what I wanted. His price was unreasonably high but he still took all of it, and it was a long time before I could think coherently again.

When I left the bath chamber, dressed in my new blue gown, Daldrin followed after me with his head down and a tight-lipped expression on his face. I didn't know why he had chosen to look that way until the members of my guard began ragging him, telling him how delicately lovely and well-used he looked, and how satisfied his *dendaya* looked. It then came to me that the guardsmen might have grown suspicious if he hadn't looked that way – after all, we'd been in the bath chamber alone together an awfully long time, and if he hadn't satisfied me in all that time, he'd be in for replacement and punishment. I put a smug, self-satisfied look on my face to match the hang-dog one on Daldrin, and kept it there until we got back to my rooms.

Once we were inside with the doors closed, Daldrin patted my bottom in approval and went to check the other room to make sure we were alone. I felt very impatient over the fact that it was only just sundown, and prowled around the reception room while Daldrin lighted the candles. We couldn't begin our escape attempt until well after dark, when most of the people in the palace would be settled down for the night, and even the tray of food brought by a slave a few minutes later didn't distract me. I was ready to ignore it completely, but Daldrin had other ideas. He forced me to sit down and eat what he gave me, keeping the strap he had found well in view while I did so. He grinned at the way I glared at him between bites, but there was nothing I could do to wipe that grin off his face. If I started raking him over the coals by twisting his emotions, he'd be useless when I needed him the most.

The minutes and hours dragged by so slowly I was ready to scream, but Daldrin was entirely untouched by tension of any sort. His big body lay stretched out on the carpet fur, his blond head propped up on a cushion, his eyes closed and his mind dozing lightly. I sat down in one corner and tried to match his calm, but without using self-hypnosis I couldn't do it. So many things could go wrong that night, so many little things – and so many big things. I was up and pacing again before I knew it, but not before Daldrin knew it. It was the third or fourth time my pacing had broken into his doze, and he was finally annoyed enough to do something about it. Against my will I was forced to lie down next to him, held tightly in his arms so that I couldn't pace and he could sleep. I was tempted to sink my teeth into one of those massive, ridiculously strong arms that held me prisoner, but Daldrin still had that strap and was annoyed enough to use it on me, leaving me no choice but to grit my teeth and lie still. I don't know how it happened, but in a very few minutes I was asleep, too.

I woke up when Daldrin did, and it was clear from the alertness in his mind that it was time for us to be moving. We spent a couple of minutes going over our plans one last time, then I went to the doors to my room while Daldrin stood well back. I didn't need to open the doors to know there were four guards out there, but the guards were an expected presence. What I was checking for was unexpected presences, up and down the corridor as far as I could reach. A quick, thorough search revealed no living mind within my range, and that was all I'd been waiting to learn. The guards were the only ones to be taken care of, and that was my job.

Slowly, gently, I reached out to the four minds, finding the boredom that filled them all, increasing it carefully before injecting sleepiness. I heard a yawn through the doors, and then another, and then the sounds of men sitting down to get comfortable on a dull, routine job. They weren't supposed to be sitting down, of course, but the dash of indifference I'd fed them made it all not worth worrying about. Their indifference and boredom increased, and then their sleepiness, and in another few minutes they were all snoring softly, asleep and likely to stay that way.

I turned to Daldrin and gestured him closer, glad he'd had the sense not to argue when I'd told him I wanted him well out of range of any stray projections. He was at the doors in an instant and opening one of them carefully, then both of us were out in the corridor with the door closed behind us, tiptoeing past the sleeping guards. We were on our way to the servant quarters, where Len and Garth were being held, and that was what I'd needed Daldrin for. I didn't know the way to the place they were being kept, and without Daldrin I could have wandered all night without coming anywhere near them.

Daldrin led me down the corridor a long way before he stopped at a single closed door and opened it carefully. Behind the door was a stairway leading down, and we took it without anyone showing up to wonder why a servant-slave was sneaking around in the middle of the night with an important-looking female trotting along behind him. We had argued about that point, Daldrin and I, back in the bathing chamber when I'd been able to argue again. Daldrin had insisted that I couldn't wander around the servant-slave area in a gown and not attract the sort of attention we didn't need. He'd wanted me to go naked, pretending to be a female slave either on her way to or coming back from being raped, but I didn't like his grin. I wouldn't have put it past him to arrange a false alarm, and then rape me himself just to make our act look good. Happily, all I'd had to do was ask him how many dark-haired slaves the palace boasted of, and he'd had to concede the point. Anyone seeing me would know who I was, naked or clothed to the teeth. The only thing for it was to make sure no one saw me.

There was no door at the bottom of the stairway, only an arch that opened onto a narrow corridor cut into the dirt and rock walls. Torches sputtered in rusty iron holders on the walls, illuminating the worn, dirty stone floor just enough to let us see where we were going. The air smelled stale and rancid, from old cooking odors and sweat and pain. Pain has its own smell when you live in a world of emotions, but I'd never realized that until I'd come to Rimilia.

Daldrin moved along the corridor to the left, his mind eager to leap ahead despite the restraining hand I had on his arm. I was letting my mind pull ahead of both of us, searching for anyone still awake, but the only traces I touched were the exhausted minds of slaves, deep in a sleep of escape. We passed archway after archway, some of them slaves' quarters, some of them punishment rooms, some of them eating rooms or training rooms, all of them smaller than the one Daldrin pointed out as the kitchen. All the cooking for the palace was done there, and it seemed large enough for fifty people to work in and still have room to spare, but fascinating as it was, we weren't there on a guided tour. We passed the four kitchen entrances quickly, and went on to the area that quartered the kitchen slaves.

"Their cell is one of those," Daldrin whispered in my ear, pointing to a series of barred doors across from a bunch of the usual archways. "They are chained to their work places during work time and locked away during the darkness, for they were caught trying to escape shortly after they were brought here. They were whipped for the attempt, of course, yet to give them another opportunity would be foolish."

I nodded without saying anything, then quickly grabbed for Daldrin's arm before he could slide open the peek hole on the first of the cells. I didn't need to look inside to know if Garth and Len were there, but Daldrin was having trouble understanding that. I checked the first cell my own way, shook my head to show it wasn't them, then moved on to the next.

It wasn't until we reached the fifth cell that I found what I was looking for. I tried to slide the bolt back on the cell door myself, but it took Daldrin's strength before the heavy bar would move. He also pulled the cell door open, but I was inside first to quickly kneel beside the two still forms. Their minds and bodies were so – untenanted –

that I thought at first they were dead, but a closer look in the harsh torchlight of their cell showed they were only in a deep, exhausted sleep. Their bodies, above the ever-present red leather pants, were covered with the mark of the whip – and bruised besides – but they couldn't be considered child-slender. They were full-grown men with men's forms, and I couldn't understand why my old thought-picture of them considered them children. I shook my head to dismiss the idiocy of the idea, then began rousing them.

It took a few minutes to get them awake, and once I did I had to convince them they weren't dreaming. I explained the plan to them in a whisper while they listened intently, and the three of us were so wrapped up in the briefing that the interruption came as a cold-water-down-the-back shock.

"What do you do in here with these miserable slaves, girl?" a raspy voice demanded, causing me to twist quickly around where I knelt. A guardsman stood in the open doorway, a guardsman who was neither sleepy nor drunk, a guardsman who was looking at me critically – and liking what he was seeing. Len and Garth stirred where they sat, but the guardsman's hand was immediately on his hilt.

"None of that," he growled at the two men, his mind so cold and empty of emotion that I shivered. "Should I find it necessary to spit you two wretches, no one other than the kitchen master will take notice. And you, girl. If I am not mistaken, you are the one so cozy with the *Chama* that she sends you trays of the best foods, and servant-slaves to tend your needs. I doubt she would be pleased to hear of your consorting with slaves not given to you – if she should hear of it. Once I have taken you to my quarters and we have discussed the matter, I will likely forget all about your presence here. Up on your feet now and come with me. The stink of these slave quarters turns my stomach."

He kept his eyes on me as I rose slowly to my feet, my mind racing frantically as it searched for a way out. I could stop the guardsman as easily as I'd stopped anyone else, but whatever treatment I gave him it wouldn't be permanent. Once he recovered he would remember everything, and right after that Aesnil would find out about it. If I went with him at least Garth and Len would still have their chance, they and Daldrin. Three slaves being gone would cause only a small stir – until they came back with the rest of Tammad's *l'lendaa*.

I was three feet away from the guardsman when the dark shadow appeared behind him and the massive arm circled his throat, squeezing tight with the speed of thought. The guardsman made a choking sound and scratched at the arm cutting off his air, tried to reach behind to claw at a face, then tried again to move the arm across his throat. His efforts did no more than make the arm tighten further, and then head and arm moved abruptly backward, a sickening snap accompanying the jerk. The guardsman's mind exploded into shock as his body sagged, and them his life-trace began thinning and fading, disappearing into nothingness. I didn't realize I had backed away in deep shock of my own until I felt Len and Garth to either side of me, their presence meant as comfort – and protection.

"I will dispose of this carcass and then we may leave here," Daldrin's soft voice came as he hefted the dead body higher off the floor. "It will take no more than a moment."

He dragged the body out of the doorway, moving further away from the direction in which we had come, and Len drew a deep breath then let it out slowly.

"Nice friends you have, Terry," he said, patting my arm to calm the jumping shivers he could still feel in my mind.

"Just be glad he's on our side," Garth commented as he tried to stretch the aches out of his back. "What did that first joker want, anyway?"

"He wanted Terry," Len said, turning to look at me in the flickering light. "And she was ready to go with him to give us our chance to get out of here. I don't think I know any other woman who would be willing to do that for me."

"I *know* I don't," Garth said, adding his part to what had become a general stare. "Why would you do a thing like that, Terry?"

"I hate to see a good plan go to waste," I told them, taking my own deep breath. "I went through a lot to get this thing moving, so don't go wandering off once you're out of here. Find Tammad's *l'lendaa* and get them over to the *vendra ralle* before it becomes a wasted effort."

"So we're supposed to believe you're doing this for no one other than Tammad," Len said, narrowing his eyes. "If all you were interested in was launching an attack against that arena, you could have sent your friend out there to find the *l'lendaa*. There was no reason to include us in on the escape plan."

"And good reason not to," Garth put his oar in. "Getting us loose from here had to make the plan three times more dangerous and five times more likely to fail."

"You forget that Tammad's men don't know Daldrin," I said in exasperation, glaring at the two geniuses. "What if they didn't believe him? What if he got into a fight with some of them before he could explain why he was there? If you two don't know how to think, that doesn't mean I don't either. And if you're so bothered about getting out of here, I can always leave you behind after all. Maybe just sending a note with Daldrin will do it."

"Totally unnecessary," Garth said quickly, holding his hands up. "Much as I love this place, I'm willing to tear myself away. We're right behind you."

"But we're not right behind her," Len said, his mind still disturbed. "In case you've forgotten, she isn't going. What's to keep you from going with us, Terry? If three can get out, four shouldn't be that much harder."

"Len, if I go with you Aesnil will have every guard in the place chasing after us," I sighed. "She – accidentally found out about some of what I can do, and has made me her – enforcer, I guess you could call it. You three can make it without notice. I can't."

"All right, let's not start an argument over that," Garth said quickly when he saw the expression on Len's face. Len's expression matched his mind perfectly, and I didn't want to look at either one. "All we can do now is get out quickly and get back even faster. Once we get Tammad loose and tell him what's going on, he'll …"

"No," I interrupted quickly, looking up at Garth. "I don't want Tammad to know anything about my part in this. Just tell him you talked Daldrin into helping you escape, and I never came anywhere near you. This is important to me, Garth, and I want your promise."

Garth exchanged looks with Len, who was still more than angry, but the two of them nodded the way I wanted them to.

"All right, we'll keep your secret," Garth agreed. "Why it has to be a secret I don't know, but we'll keep it anyway. What are you going to.…"

"We may now leave," Daldrin said, suddenly reappearing in the doorway. "Come quickly but silently, and we may yet live to see the new light."

No one had to be told that twice, but we made sure to close and bar the cell door again before moving back up the corridor. We reached the stairway without incident, climbed to ground level, then hurried up the corridor that led to the exit they would use. The air was so much fresher up there that I was able to breathe normally again, not having realized that I'd been breathing in small gasps the entire time I'd been below ground. When we were almost to the exit Daldrin and the others stopped, letting me go on alone. The guard at the small door went to sleep the same way the guards at my door had, and the three men were able to join me.

"Care for yourself until our return," Daldrin told me, looking down at me with reluctance in his mind. "I do not care to leave you unprotected, yet I may do no other thing. And curb your foolishness, *wenda*. It will not prove profitable."

He pulled me to him then and kissed me deeply, and then he had gestured to the other two men and led them off. Len and Garth looked at me strangely as they passed, but I was more concerned with Daldrin's strangeness. Why had be kissed me like that? The question bothered me all the way back to my rooms, but I hadn't found an answer even when I'd undressed and gotten into bed. I was tired enough to fall asleep immediately, but to add another strangeness, it took quite some time before sleep came.

## SIXTEEN

A female slave brought my breakfast tray the next morning, and also found it necessary to wake me. I had been just as well wrapped in the sleep of the innocent when a guardsman had burst into my sleeping room in the small hours of the morning, thinking to find me dead or gone. The guardsmen outside my door had been found to be fast asleep when their reliefs had arrived, and all that had saved their hides had been my presence and safety, and the fact that the relieving guardsmen were friends of theirs. Nothing of a reason for disturbing me was mentioned, and I went back to sleep secure in the knowledge that Aesnil would not be told about my guards' dereliction.

The girl slave served me my meal and helped me get dressed, but none of it was my idea. I would have been happier being left alone, but without Daldrin there *someone* had to do it, and the girl considered herself elected. I ate food I didn't want, and had my hair brushed and combed, and then was dressed in a pale tan gown and a new pair of sandals. The sun was bright and strong outside my windows, the warmth of the air showing it was going to be another hot day. Once I was dressed I sent the slave to find out if Aesnil needed me, then walked back and forth until the girl returned. The *Chama* had sent word that she was almost ready to leave for the *vendra ralle,* and that I was to await her outside the royal suite. My guards had to jump to it to catch up with me when I left my rooms, but I didn't care how odd it looked. I had the best excuse in the world – that I was going to see the man who had kidnapped me put his life on the line – and I intended milking it for everything it was worth.

Aesnil didn't keep me waiting long, but we made a procession of it to the arena. Surrounded by a couple of dozen court women and men, we strolled out the main palace entrance, walked a wide flowered path to the *vendra ralle,* then entered through a wide stone archway. We weren't anywhere near the high wooden gate we had used on our last visit; this entrance led to the stands of the arena, where we could sit on cushioned stone benches eight feet above the glaring white sand of the vast arena circle, with nothing to obscure our view of what went on down there. Aesnil gestured me down beside her with a smile as our guards moved to positions behind us, and we were finally ready to start.

A trumpet blared a warning, and the surprisingly large arena crowd cheered as a *vendra* appeared from a barred archway and slogged his way through the sand to stand in the middle of the circle. I saw immediately that the *vendra* was Daldrin's brother, but he had changed from when I had seen him last. No longer chained or naked, he stood in a *haddin* as red as Aesnil's gown and gripped a sword in his fist, his mind alert as his head swiveled around to keep the entire circle of wall in view. I gathered from that that his opponent could come from any of the numerous barred gates around the wall perimeter, and that he stood in the center of the wide circle to protect himself, not to show himself off for the crowd's edification.

Suddenly a *fazee* came racing out across the sand from one of the archways, its mind wild with hunger and madder than a *fazee's* mind normally is. The beast is horrendously large, taller than I am and equipped with claws and fangs, but the *vendra* did no more than turn calmly to meet it, his sword up and his body poised. The beast came charging in, but all it got for its trouble was a slash across the chest as the man jumped quickly to one side, avoiding the charge. The beast wheeled and came in again, sending the sand flying in all directions in its haste to reach a meal, its mind barely aware of the wound it had gotten. I glanced at Aesnil as Daldrin's brother avoided the charge a second time, but the *Chama* was too wrapped up in enjoying the spectacle to notice my glance. Her mind was excited and happy at seeing a man forced into fighting for his life, and I could feel the emotion but not understand it. It was pleasant looking at a well-made man, yes; it was not pleasant seeing that same well-made man ripped to bloody shreds by an insane beast. Possibly one needs to be closer to the fangs and claws before one can learn how unpleasant the situation really is.

It took a while, but Daldrin's brother finally killed the *fazee*. He stood over the bloody corpse while the spectators screamed out their delight, his chest heaving from the exertion, his body covered with sweat, his flesh cut and bleeding along his left side where the *fazee* had raked him with its claws. His gory sword was still firmly gripped in his fist, but then two barred archways opened to admit a dozen guards with swords held high and ready, their eyes on the *vendra* as one of them gestured to him. He stared at them a long moment, weighing the sword he held, and then he threw the weapon down to the sand in a disgusted way, glared up at Aesnil where she sat beside me, then slogged his way back across the sand to the waiting guards. They kept him under their weapons as they herded him out, and the crowd roared, again in derision and delight. The guards hadn't been willing to face the *vendra* on a one-to-one basis, but they really couldn't be blamed for that. Considering the man's ability as a fighter, there wouldn't have been many of them left afterward to take him back to his chains.

Once the *vendra* was safely out of the way, male slaves with a *seetar* came in to remove the *fazee* carcass, and the next spectacle was begun. The time moved by rather slowly for, me, and I was glad when an awning was put up over Aesnil and me to cut down the glare of the sun. Even with male servant-slaves to fan us and female slaves to bring us cool drinks and tidbits to nibble on, the day was becoming too hot to be enjoyable. *Vendraa* came and went on the glaring white sand, their bodies covered with sweat even before they began fighting, and the crowds continued to yell and scream and demand more and more.

Most of the *vendraa* won against the beasts they were put up against, but one of them was so badly clawed and bitten that he collapsed as soon as the large silver animal did. The guards hurried out to carry him off the sand to the screaming and stomping of the crowd, and no one bothered to ask if he was still alive or likely to stay that way. The next match was between two men, and everyone seemed to know it and look forward to it.

I suppose no four-legged animal can match the ferocity of the two-legged kind, that's why the crowd was so eager. The two *vendraa* were very well matched, each seeming to know that only one of them would be walking away from the fight. They cut each other to bloody bits before one was able to gut the other, and the only way I was able to watch without changing expression was with my shield firmly in place. The sight was still enough to turn someone's stomach, but at least I didn't have to feel another mind die. As far as everyone else was concerned, the day was going beautifully.

As soon as the dead *vendra* was gone from the sand, a guard appeared from one of the archways, walked to the center of the arena, and plunged two swords into the sand, hilts up. I'd been wondering and wondering where Tammad's *l'lendaa* could be, at the same time imagining every horrible thing that could have happened to Len, Garth and Daldrin to keep them from reaching the *l'lendaa,* but that unusual gesture by the guard captured my attention. Swords had not been left like that at any other time during the morning, and the rumble from the crowd showed they were as perplexed as I. Opening my shield showed Aesnil ready to bounce in her seat in excitement despite the tranquil expression on her face, but that was no clue at all as to what was going on. Something was about to happen – but what?

The guard in the center of the arena made sure the two swords would stand upright in the sand as he'd placed them, then he turned away and walked back to the archway he'd come out of, grinning at the shouted demands from some members of the audience but not answering any of them. As soon as he was gone a near hush fell over the arena, the result of almost every mind in the place straining to catch the first glimpse of what was about to happen. And then, from opposite sides of the arena two large forms appeared, clad in the red *haddinn* of *vendraa* but totally unarmed. One was Cinnan, the *l'lenda* Aesnil had declared *vendra,* and the other, somehow unsurprisingly, was Tammad. The two men looked around cautiously, looked at each other in passing at they looked around again, and then both started slowly toward the swords they could see in the middle of the sand.

"They do not truly understand," Aesnil giggled, wriggling around on her cushion. "When two *vendraa* are set weaponless upon one another, there is never more than a single weapon put in the sand for them to battle over. They believe they are to face one another, yet the time is not right for such a glorious battle. They must first survive my little game."

She laughed softly at the two men on the sand, being entirely correct in everything she'd said. Their alert minds *were* confused, and they *were* looking at each other as potential adversaries. The two swords in the sand worried them, but they weren't going to let that worry make them do something stupid.

They were both about halfway to the swords when two archways opened to admit gray and black forms, animals that stood almost waist high on the men. The beasts blinked an instant at the glare of sun on white sand, pulled their muzzles back to snarl savagely, then leaped after the two men on the sand. The men, having seen the appearance of the beasts, immediately began running toward the swords left for them, now thinking they understood what was happening. Reaching a weapon was the only way to survive, but they'd been made to hesitate through suspicion of one another. Their minds crackled with self-disgusted cursing as their feet were slowed by the hot, shifting sands, and Aesnil bounced up and down as she clapped her hands. her laughter ringing out.

"Run, Cinnan, run as you never have!" she shouted, her words drowned out by the crowd roar. "Run from them as I wished to run from you, and find as much good in the running as I did!"

I must have been the only one to hear her, and my blood ran cold as I looked quickly back to the arena. The two men were almost to the swords, the beasts no more than three jumps behind them, when arrows whizzed to the sand just in front of the men, making them dodge away from those sweetly beckoning weapons. More arrows sang and thudded into the sand, making the men dive and, roll to keep from being hit, and the crowd went crazy as it screamed out its shock.

"And now what will you do, Cinnan?" Aesnil sang out, like one of the arrows seeking a target. "Will you brave the shafts to reach the sword, or will you fight the *remdaa* with your bare hands? Come, you two mighty *l'lendaa*! Why do you not command the beasts as you attempted to command me?"

The lean, gray-and-black *remdaa* had been thrown off their attack by the arrows flying past the contortions of the two men, but not for long. They each had their victim marked and they returned to stalking them with slavering fangs, moving more slowly now but nevertheless moving. Tammad and Cinnan rose from the sand they had rolled through, their minds ignoring the way the sand had burned them in order to concentrate more fully on the animals. The two men spoke briefly, coming to some sort of immediate agreement, and then Tammad jumped forward to attract the two *remdaa* while Cinnan darted toward the swords. The whine and ping! of an arrow bouncing off a hilt came to force Cinnan to throw himself to one side with a curse, just as the *remdaa* jumped for Tammad. Everything was happening so fast that I didn't know where to look first let alone what to do about it, but seeing those beasts go for Tammad forced me to act without thinking. Savagely, I hurled a bolt of terror at the beasts just as Tammad hurled two fistfuls of sand at their eyes before diving out of their way, and the beasts reacted to both attacks with howls and shaking heads and a skidding through the sand. Cinnan had come immediately back to Tammad once he saw the swords were still beyond his reach, and the two *l'lendaa* stood talking in low, rapid tones while the animals cleared their eyes and regathered their courage.

The large crowd in the arena had grown unbelievably quiet during the brief lull, but not because they didn't want to break the spell of the moment. Aesnil was sure they were enjoying the sight as much as she was, but she couldn't feel the overpowering swell of anger and disappointment the way I could. The people watching enjoyed a good fight between equals – whether man against beast or man against man – but they didn't enjoy the sight of slaughter and that's what the bout was turning out to be. The two men would be helplessly slaughtered without those swords, but they weren't being allowed to touch them.

In the arena the action was starting again, but this time only one of the *remdaa* was coming forward. The other was cowering back despite its hunger, unwilling to move in for the attack after what had happened. I felt the shuddering fear in its mind and knew my projection had hit it hard; it was too bad the other beast hadn't been affected the same. The second *remda* was racing toward Tammad and Cinnan again, not caring which man it took down as long as it could eat. The two *l'lendaa* had been standing together, but suddenly they separated, forcing the beast to choose between them. The beast hesitated no more than a fraction of an instant before going in Tammad's direction, and before I could even think about sending a projection, Tammad had dodged its leap and thrown his mighty arms around the *remda*'s throat from behind, squeezing tight as he forced the *remda*'s head back and it's body up on two legs. The *remda* screamed in fury and clawed the air, trying to dislodge the man and free itself to turn and rend, but Cinnan hadn't just been standing around watching. As soon as the *remda* turned for Tammad, Cinnan turned and snatched up two of the arrows almost buried in the sand, and ran back to where Tammad struggled with the *remda*. Tammad was straining terribly to keep the beast from breaking loose, and Cinnan didn't waste a second. Just barely avoiding the thrashing claws of the beast, he took the two arrows and stabbed into its body with all his strength, driving the arrows deep and causing the *remda* to scream as though its soul were being violated. The *remda* spasmed so forcefully it tore loose from the hold Tammad had it in, but it was done too late to do the beast any good. It rolled in the sand, screaming and clawing at its own body, and then the final spasm took it, ending its screams and pain forever.

The two *l'lendaa* raised themselves from the sand to the shrieks and yells from a thousand throats, the claps and bangs from a thousand hands, the stomps and jumps from a thousand feet. They had won after all, despite their lack of weapons, and the people were going crazy.

"He is magnificent," Aesnil breathed, staring wide-eyed at the two *vendraa* clothed in her color. "I had never thought to see a man so magnificent. He braved those claws with no more than arrows in his hand, plunging them into the beast without regard for his safety. Such strength and such courage! Should he survive this day, I may well hold him in my dungeons for the time I will wish a child."

"He has survived," I said, seeing the second *remda* slink back on its belly, its mind filled with fear of the two men, of the smell of blood, and of the deafening crowd noise.

"Not quite yet," Aesnil said very softly, and again I felt that thrill of fear run through me. I twisted back toward the sands just in time to see two more archways opening, this time admitting a total of four *remdaa*. The cheering crowd noise immediately changed to a concerted scream of rage, unbelievably heightening in volume when three more arrows snicked into the sands, stopped the two *vendraa* short in their reflexive start toward the weapons. Insane fury blazed from the minds all around us, coming at me in wall-high waves that tried to crush me down. I gasped under the onslaught, unwilling to raise my shield while there was still a chance I might be able to stop the four new beasts, but after no more than seconds was forced to admit the truth: even if I could keep from collapsing under the wave, I could never work through it. I quickly let the shield form around my mind, a sensation very much like donning sound deadeners in a high-tech processing area, and the pressure eased up immediately – just in time for the next thing to happen.

In the midst of the bedlam of yelling, screaming and gesturing people, knots of men with drawn swords appeared, moving purposefully toward what seemed to be prearranged positions. Some of the positions were guard stations spotted here and there around the arena, where fighting broke out immediately between the newcomers and Aesnil's guard. The sounds of battle were lost in the still-present crowd roar, and the roar rose to cloud-breaking strength when arrows flew once more – to strike the four *remdaa* as they came within ten feet of the unarmed, double-braced *vendraa*. Tammad and Cinnan stared at the kicking, howling – dying – beasts for a brief instant, then jumped as one for the swords they had been unable to touch until then. The hilts were already in their hands when it became clear that fighting was also going on behind most of the barred archways, between Aesnil's *vendra ralle* guardsmen and others in the *haddinn* of free men.

"Who are those men?" Aesnil demanded, standing up to glare around her. "How dare they raise weapons against my guardsmen?"

"*Chama*, the two *vendraa* …!" a woman behind us squeaked in alarm, pointing down toward the sand. We turned back to see Tammad and Cinnan, figurative blood in their light eyes, trotting across the sand in our direction, swords held ready in their fists. It seemed clear they intended scaling the eight-foot wall to reach us, though how they intended doing that with Aesnil's guards and mine to bar their way I didn't know.

"Stop them!" Aesnil screamed, pulling at her guardsmen's sleeves and then pushing them toward the wall. "Protect your *Chama* as you are sworn to do!"

"We shall, *Chama*," the head guardsman said, stepping out in front of his men to order them into position. "It would be best, however, if you were to retire now, with those guardsmen assigned to escort you. It is dangerous for you to remain longer."

Aesnil looked around wildly, saw the six men with drawn swords waiting for her, and immediately began climbing the tiers up to them. I hesitated a bare moment longer to look around, then began climbing after her. The fighting had spread closer and closer to us in the stands, and if I'd tried getting through on my own I never would have made it. I'd have to stay with the *Chama* until we were in the clear, and then I'd be able to pick my own direction.

The guardsmen formed a protective semicircle, then began pushing their way through the crowds, fighting only when necessary. They were heading us toward the archway we had come in by, but once we reached it we weren't able to go through. The fighting was so thick and heavy there that we were forced to the right, past a heavy wooden door, into a torch-lit corridor that seemed to circle the arena from beneath, losing two of our guardsmen in the process. They weren't dead, just so hardpressed by some of the attackers that they couldn't break free. The remaining four men hurried us along the corridor, one holding Aesnil's arm, one holding mine, all of them deaf to the fact that I didn't want to go in that direction. I'd intended waiting behind the door in the side corridor until the fighting had stopped or flowed away in a different direction, but the hand on my arm hadn't allowed me a choice. By the time I tried opening my shield and found that I could, it would have been worse than a waste of effort to feed the man holding me a dose of indifference. I could hear the sounds of fighting following behind us in the corridor, and could do no more than run with everyone else.

We were all breathing heavily and sweating from the heat in little more than a few minutes, but all we could do was keep going. We rounded a curve in the corridor and nearly went sprawling over the blood-spattered bodies of five or six guardsmen lying in front of one of the barred archways, a set of empty chains on a post hanging like a marker over their lifeless forms. Aesnil gasped in shock and the men gripped their swords more tightly, and I flinched at the fear flowing out of all of them toward me. That's not to say I wasn't feeling fear of my own, but my own was enough; I didn't need theirs to add to it.

Once past the bodies we ran more cautiously, expecting to catch up to the fighting at any time. We passed more bodies, two of them men in plain *haddinn,* and then, from around the next curve, came the din of metal striking metal or stone, and the thud of metal striking flesh. Men shouted and cursed and screamed, and my shield snapped back into place just as the melee came rolling toward us. The guardsmen with us hesitated, too long as it turned out; the mass spread out and enveloped us all, drawing the guardsmen into it and pressing Aesnil and myself back up against the stone of the wall. A minute later the attackers appeared from the end of the corridor from which we'd come, hemming us in completely and adding their own screams and shouts to the din.

Aesnil and I edged along the wall to the left, behind the backs of the giant men fighting for their lives, Aesnil whimpering and hanging onto my right arm with a death grip. I could feel her terror even with my shield in place, as though the emotion went through her skin and into mine, increasing with every added minute of contact. I could taste the terror in the sourness in my mouth and feel it in the heavy thudding in my chest, but there was no escape for us in that rough-walled, doorless corridor. We hadn't passed a single place where we could stop and hide, and now it was too late. One of those men would swing his sword at the wrong time – or the right time – and we would go down without a hope of defending ourselves.

And then the massed bodies parted for a brief instant, leaving us clearly in view to the men farther down the corridor to the left and out toward a barred archway. They weren't guardsmen and they weren't of the attackers in plain-colored *haddinn;* they were red-clad *vendraa,* men with hate etched in their faces, and when they saw Aesnil they started toward us.

If the fighters hadn't moved back to close the opening again, I think Aesnil would have fainted. The *vendraa* were fighting like madmen on the edge of the mob, trying to back their way through to us, and it was only a matter of time before they did. I felt as paralyzed by shock as she did, and could do no more than stand and stare.

"Quickly, *Chama,* in here!" a hoarse voice called, and I jerked my head around to see one of our guardsmen only five feet away, pointing into a gap in the stone. The man had no choice but to turn back to the fight in order to stay alive, but his few words were enough. With Aesnil still clutching my arm, I edged toward the gap he had pointed out.

It took an age to get there, but we finally reached the gap to discover a doorway in the stone wall, one which led to a large room with other doorways. It was a way out, it had to be a way out, and Aesnil and I fell through the doorway in frantic haste, then turned to close the door. The heavy wooden door closed more easily than we'd expected, as if the door hinges were kept well oiled, but when we searched for the metal bar that would slide across the door and lock us in, it was nowhere in sight.

Aesnil walked woodenly to the middle of the room and crouched down to sob into her hands, but there were still the other doors to check before I could – or would – join her in despair. The torchlit room was large but nearly bare, with nothing to decorate the walls but chains hanging high above the floor on the left, separated by about three feet of empty stone between each set. On the right, beyond the farther door and halfway to the door straight ahead, was a bench carved out of the rock, with no cushions set on it to make it more comfortable. The floor was swept rock as well, but smoothed over as though by the passage of many feet.

I started with the closer door on the right, but pushing it open showed nothing but a smaller room carved into the rock beside the first room. It had carpet fur on the floor and cushions scattered about, but no entrance or exit other than the one I stood at. Strangely enough it also had two or three thin chains and collars attached low down on the silk-covered walls, but I was in too much of a hurry to wonder what they meant.

The farther door in the right-hand wall was large and heavy, with a metal bar set into the stone beside it that closed it tight. I paused at it briefly before going toward the last door, quickly deciding to leave it for a last-ditch effort. The heavy wood and metal would take more than my strength to move, and there was no sense in trying to get Aesnil's help if it wasn't necessary.

The third door was unbarred even though it could be barred, but I was glad I opened it only a crack to look out. I recognized the area where Aesnil and I had seen the chained *vendraa* by the chain-hung posts in sight, but the posts weren't the only things in sight. Dozens of men fought with swords in the area, some of them clearly guardsmen and some of them recognizably Tammad's *l'lendaa*. There was no way out that way, especially not for me, and I closed the door again with a sinking feeling inside me.

"Aesnil, come and help me here," I said as I turned back to the only barred door. "Do you by any chance know where this might lead?"

"No," the girl answered, standing erect with defeat stamped on her features. "This room is for use of the guardsmen, and I have little knowledge of the inner workings of the *ralle*. Do you feel we might escape if we should succeed in opening it?"

"It is highly unlikely," I told her, putting my shield down to study her more closely. She was still as upset as I was, but she was no longer giving up. "To leave this room we must go either back as we came, or forward to the courtyard area. As men fight in both places we may do neither, yet perhaps another corridor may lie behind this door, to lead us eventually to a way out."

"We must try," she said, putting her hands on the metal bar near mine. "The *Chama* must not be found cowering in a corner. If she is to die, she must die with some semblance of dignity."

Good girl, I thought as the two of us began pushing at the bar. Aesnil had quite a few bad points, but at least she wasn't a quitter. We strained at the bar, forcing it to slide free of the brackets it was seated in, then started on the door itself. It opened more easily than we thought it would, but there was nothing behind it we could use.

"A stairway," Aesnil observed, pushing sweat-soaked hair back away from her face.

"Leading downward into darkness," I added to the obvious, wiping at my forehead with the back of my hand. "Perhaps it comes out again elsewhere."

"I fear not," she sighed, moving to the stone wall to lean against it. "It is undoubtedly the dungeon of the *ralle*, where the cells of the *vendraa* are located. There is but one entrance for security's sake, and this...."

Her words were cut off as the door to the corridor was opened with a crash, admitting three figures in *vendra* red. The men's swords dripped red with blood, and their minds growled with anger and a need for vengeance. Aesnil and I backed up against the wall as the three advanced slowly, their swords held in front of them, anticipation and grim pleasure on their faces. The corridor behind them seemed empty of life, no more than savagely slashed bodies to be seen on its floor, unliving bodies we would soon resemble. My heartbeat thundered in my ears as loudly as the swirling in Aesnil's mind beat in my head, and I was shocked when Aesnil stepped away from the wall to stand in front of me.

"I am the *Chama*," she announced to the three men, trying to stand proud and straight despite the trembling of her body. "Slay me if you will, yet you must not harm my companion. She had no hand in causing your trials."

"She accompanies you of her own free will," one of the men said in a flat, uninterested voice. "She may also accompany you in death."

"That is not so!" Aesnil protested, but the men weren't listening any longer. They were coming toward us again with sword points raised; I grabbed her shoulder and quickly pulled her back against the wall – as though it would do some good. They came another step closer, two steps closer –

"Hold!" a deep voice rang out, causing the three big *vendraa* to wheel around in instant readiness. Incredibly, unbelievably, Tammad and Cinnan stood just inside the doorway, their giant bodies braced as they stood with swords up, their entire manner shouting battle-readiness. It was Cinnan who had spoken, but the eyes of the three nearer men moved to Tammad.

"You cannot take this pleasure as your own!" the one on the extreme left protested to the barbarian. "You have been *vendra* no more than a short while, he beside you an even shorter time. It is we who have suffered the longest, *we* who strove so long for survival that this day might somehow come to be! We must have her life in payment for what was done to us!"

"Enough lives have been lost in this insanity of guiltless *vendraa*!" Cinnan interrupted harshly, bringing their attention to him. "No others save criminals were to have been declared *vendra,* yet it is now clear that too many others have fallen so. Should you wish one to blame you may take me, for I have been unforgivably remiss in my duty. It was my place to band the *Chama* at the proper time, not give heed to her pleas for delays. There will now be no further delays, for this you have my word."

"You are the one meant to band her?" the same *vendra* asked, outraged disbelief in his voice. "And you, too, were made *vendra?*"

"As easily as the merest child," Cinnan growled in self-disgust. "I could not believe she would dare do such a thing. There will be payment enough for that doing to satisfy each and every one of you. Death would be too easy."

"Indeed." The *vendra* nodded, turning to look at Aesnil with a snort. "Death would indeed be much the easier. Should my brothers agree, her life is yours."

"What of the other?" a second *vendra* asked, the same one who had spoken to Aesnil. He turned to look at me, and his eyes were deadly cold.

"The other is mine," Tammad said very quietly, with his usual calm. "That one must answer to me."

The second man turned back to look at Tammad, his mind measuring the barbarian and his own chances for winning against him, but he had seen the larger man fight and knew himself no equal to him. His teetering emotions indicated indecision and discretion.

"Very well," he said, finally lowering his weapon. "The second one is yours. We will, however, seek others of the guard of this place, to see if their swords are as quick as their whips. Have either of you any further objections?"

"None." Tammad laughed as Cinnan grinned agreement. "Should you find any still among the living, speak to them of our own displeasure with them."

"The pleasure will be ours, brothers," the man answered, but his mind was still too grim to find amusement in anything. Tammad and Cinnan each stepped to one side of the door and the three men passed between them, turning left when they were in the corridor. Cinnan waited a moment before leaning out into the corridor to make sure they were gone, then came back in to nod at Tammad and close the door behind him. With all the preliminaries taken care of they turned to look at us, and their expressions were friendly when compared to their minds.

"So you mean to torture me!" Aesnil suddenly blurted into Cinnan's lowering stare, her back hard against the wall beside me. "Do as you will, beast of a man! I am the *Chama,* and will not beg for my freedom!"

"Do you hear the foolish *wenda,* Tammad?" Cinnan asked without taking his eyes from Aesnil. "She would have us believe she is *Chama,* when it is clear to any with eyes that she can be no more than a common *wenda,* one who has undoubtedly come to the *vendra ralle* without her father's permission. Would the *Chama* be clad in a torn and dirt-stained gown, with hair so fly-about in disarray? Would the *Chama* be found without her guard, foolishly alone in a place where her life might be lost in a trice?"

"Certainly not," Tammad said, regarding Aesnil as Cinnan spoke. Until then he had been staring at me, and it was all I could do to keep from trembling.

"Therefore she must indeed be no more than a common *wenda,* her presence here an obvious disobedience," Cinnan said, tossing his sword to the floor beside the wall with the hanging chains. "I feel it my duty to correct the disobedience, to insure that it will not be repeated. She must have a good strapping."

"Cinnan, no!" Aesnil whispered, paling as she shook her head at the slowly advancing man. "It is not permitted to treat the *Chama* so! You know this as well as I!"

"That dictum will soon be changed," Cinnan said grimly, stopping in front of us to look down at an Aesnil who was trying to crawl into the rock wall behind me. "Had you been properly seen to before this, much grief would have been avoided. Perhaps I will strap you each morning before you hold audience, to allow the ache in your body to remind you that punishment must often be tempered with moderation. Come here."

He put his hand out to take Aesnil's arm, but her trembling fear affected me so strongly that I began beating at Cinnan with my fists, to drive him away from her. A faint annoyance flashed briefly in Cinnan's mind, and then I was being taken by the arms and pulled out of the way, to be pushed slightly before being released. The push sent me stumbling backward, but instead of falling I found myself crashing into another hard male body.

"There has been enough interference from you," Tammad said, taking a fistful of my hair with such force that I cried out in pain. "So you would run others' lives to suit your own comfort, eh, *wenda*? It pleased you to betray me, to take amusement from me as you have done other times in the past. You will regret having done so, *wenda,* for this time punishment will not be withheld from you."

The bitterness in him cut at me deeply, but unlike Aesnil I had nothing to say. He no longer held his sword, but he had no more use for it than Cinnan did. Aesnil yelled and cursed as Cinnan dragged her around by one arm, looking for a strap, but I made no sound at all when Tammad took me by the hair and headed for the stairs into darkness, pausing only to take a torch from the wall.

The stairway leading downward was rough-cut stone, but smoothed by the passage of many feet. I stumbled down the stairs in Tammad's grip, the torch in his other hand throwing shadows all around, desperate to know what he was going to do with me but unwilling to ask. The air temperature lowered the farther down we went; by the time we reached the bottom it must have been twenty degrees cooler. The flickering torch bounced glares of light off the damp stone walls and floor, illuminating the beginning of a long row of cells stretching left and right away into the darkness. The area before the immediate set of cells was wide enough for a number of people to stand abreast, and didn't narrow until one walked right or left away from that area. Tammad turned right into the narrowing, continued on at least twenty feet, then stopped in front of one cell to put the torch in a sconce on the wall.

"You may have the cell that was mine," he said, swinging the slatted metal door wide and propelling me through. "Though you cannot hope to open a door I was unable to open from within, I have another gift for you. Here."

He forced me down to the stone floor at the rear of the tiny cell, then crouched to reach beside me and lift something metallic that flashed dully in the dim glow from the torch across the corridor. The metallic something turned out to be a collar with a short chain let into the wall down near the floor, and he closed it about my neck with a good deal of satisfaction.

"This trinket is used upon whatever female slave a *vendra* earns," he told me, standing straight again, to stare down at me. "Should the *vendra* earn more than one slave, he must use them only one at a time and before the guardsmen for their amusement. This indignity, however, was not mine to suffer; I am *l'lenda,* and do not use slaves. You will remain here till I see fit to release you, to think upon what you have done and what further punishments I shall find for you. May you find the joy here that I did."

He turned away then and left the cell, closed the door and slid the locking bar across, then took the torch and went back the way we had come. As feeble as the torch-light had been, it had been better than nothing, a fact proven to me as soon as the darkness closed in. My hands went to the narrow metal collar around my throat, but there was no removing the thin, stubborn band. I was locked in place and locked in the cell, in the empty, damp darkness where I had been left. I leaned back against the stone of the wall with a shiver, trying to tell myself I was lucky just to be left like that. When dealing with Rimilian barbarians, there are worse things than just being left alone in the dark.

And then I sat straight again, suddenly realizing that I *wasn't* alone. With the darkness had come the approach of half a dozen tiny minds, simple minds filled with simple desires, like roaming and procreating – and eating. That last seemed to be the major mover, the one that made the other desires possible. Each of those small minds shouted with hunger, needing food, wanting it, desiring it with all their might. They were very cautious in their approach, sensing danger surrounding the food they wanted, but their approach was nevertheless sure and steady, not to be denied by anything less than an actual attack against their lives.

I shivered again from the damp, wrapping my arms about myself, wishing I could believe those creatures were no more than company in the darkness. I knew, though, that they would attack me if they got the chance, using my flesh and blood to sustain them and their desires. I sighed shakily with the necessary decision to protect myself, then reached toward their minds – only to recoil again in shock. The fear I'd projected had done nothing more than ripple through their minds, passing like water through a net but with considerably less effect. A net is wet by the water that touches it, but those small, hungry minds had been totally untouched by the emotion of fear, not recognizing it *as* an emotion! Fear, love, hate, lust, greed, kindness, generosity – all were unknown to those tiny beings, and all were therefore useless against them. Numbly I tried again by projecting satiety as though they'd just finished the best meal of their lives, but that, too, was unknown to them. They had no concept of being full and satisfied, indeed would probably eat themselves to death if ever given the opportunity to do so. They advanced again even as my mind tried to fend them off, totally untouchable, totally unstoppable.

My heart thumped loud in the all-enveloping darkness, a counterpoint to the roughness of my breathing. I backed along the floor until I was right up against the wall, knowing I was trapped with a sureness that turned my muscles to water. Those creatures would come closer and closer, testing my defenses, growing bolder with every successful encroachment, until they leapt upon me, biting and tearing in a frenzy of eating. The trembling I hadn't been aware of grew more violent as I stared about in the pitch black-ness, seeing more clearly in my enforced blindness than an untalented person would in full daylight. They were coming for me, those six small minds motivated by hunger, closing slowly but surely, their lines of advance lit by their life-traces blazing in the dark. I twisted to the wall with a sob and a clink of chain, shaking with fear, closing my eyes and shield tight as I put my hands over my ears to stop the sounds of tiny, scrapings. They would have me no matter what I did, and I couldn't bear to see – or hear it coming.

I tried desperately, though terrified, to understand what happened next. One minute I was cringing against the wall, fighting to keep from screaming, and the next I was being pulled against a broad, warm chest, held in arms that circled me with protec-tion and lent me strength. I shook terribly in those large, strong arms and they tight-ened immediately to hold me closer yet, soothing sounds coming from the throat above them. I didn't understand what was happening and tried to say so, but the words refused to come past the tightness in my throat.

"Hush," Tammad said, moving one big hand to stroke my hair. "I thought I would find myself able to do this to you, but I find instead that I would rather return to this place myself than abandon you here. You have earned punishment many times over, yet this will not be it. Come, let us leave this place."

He paused to open the collar he had put around my throat, then urged me to my feet and out the cell door. It wasn't until he took the torch from the sconce on the wall that I realized there was light again, but there are things to have more precious than light. I clung to his body and presence as we walked, and slowly let my shield fade away, admitting the true sounds of the world again. The small creatures were well behind me, and Tammad's mind hummed with a contentment I hadn't felt in quite some time. Calm dominated his mind as usual, but the contentment was too obvious to miss. It was difficult knowing what he could be content about, but there was no mistaking the emo-tion.

We had climbed almost to the top of the stairs before I heard the crying, but by the time we were back in the room I already knew exactly what was happening. Tammad left me in the middle of the floor while he returned the torch to its original place by the door, and from that position I could see directly into the small room that had probably been used by the guardsmen when they took their pleasure. Cinnan had evidently found the strap he had been searching for; he sat cross-legged on the carpet fur of the room with Aesnil draped over his lap, the skirt of her once-pretty red gown thrown back to her shoulders. The strap in his hand struck Aesnil's bottom with a terrible, even rhythm, punishing her as though she were a child, bringing tears pouring from her eyes and wailing screams from her throat as she kicked and struggled uselessly. I could feel her deep humiliation as well as the awful blaze of pain given by the strap, and turned quickly away as I closed my shield again. I didn't need to share her punishment to know what pain and humiliation were like.

"Perhaps that should be your punishment as well," Tammad mused, seeing how I felt as he stared down at me. "Cinnan has deduced that his capture was somehow due to your efforts, and would be pleased to see you done the same. It will soon be his word which rules this country; his good will would not be without benefit."

"Then by all means give him his pleasure," I said, turning away from the blue eyes staring down at me. "What else is a *wenda* for, than to give pleasure to a man?"

"Terril, you will speak to me," he growled, grabbing my arms to turn me back to him. "I will know all that goes through that head of yours, and we will settle each point *now*, before further time passes. This has too long been...."

He was interrupted by the heavy door to the courtyard bursting open, but before he did more than jerk toward the sword he had tossed to the floor, he discovered defense was unnecessary.

"Tammad, you are here and safe." Loddar smiled, striding in with others of the barbarian's *l'lendaa* behind him. They all carried bloody swords in their fists, including Garth who walked to the back of the group. Len came right behind Garth, trying not to look haggard, but I could imagine what he'd gone through being in the middle of a battle where men died one after the other. He didn't have a sword of his own, but I wasn't sure he'd be able to use it. He and Garth both wore *haddinn* instead of red leather pants, and both looked happier for the change.

"I see you have Terry," Garth said, coming forward with Len to stand beside Tammad. That makes me feel considerably better. I was afraid something would happen to her in that war we just went through."

"Where do you come from?" Tammad demanded, frowning at Loddar and the rest. "Where do all of you come from? The last I knew, my *l'lendaa* were left encamped with orders to await my return, and my new brothers were being taken to a captivity different from mine. How is it you are all now here, armed and aware of what difficulty I faced?"

"Our new allies were much involved in that." Len grinned, speaking so that Loddar and the others were able to understand him. That left Garth out of the conversation, but Tammad's question, in Rimilian, had already done that.

"We were approached when we came to storm the *vendra ralle,*" Len continued. "A force much larger than ours already waited here, and their leaders convinced us that we would do well to wait with them. They came to free one of their own number, a *denday* named Cinnan, who had been declared *vendra* just the previous day. They awaited the time when all *vendraa* were removed from their cells and chained to posts in anticipation of their turn upon the sands. We immediately saw the wisdom in this course of action and joined them, only later to discover with them what was planned for you and Cinnan. We thought it best to await the time weapons would be available to the two of you, yet nearly misjudged the time. The guardsmen fought well and bravely, delaying us all in our advance until it was nearly too late. That we came when we did was fortuitous indeed."

"Cinnan and I remarked upon the very same thing." Tammad grinned, clapping Loddar on the shoulder as he looked at his men in approval. "That his people also saw to the guardsmen set to keep us from scaling the wall to the stands was of equal good fortune. The sands are not a pleasant place to be in the heat of the day."

All the men laughed heartily at that and Tammad laughed with them, relief making the comment more amusing for them than it would normally have been. The barbarian had had his back to me as he had spoken to the others, so I had taken the opportunity of moving slowly but steadily away toward the door to the corridor. When the laughter began I turned and walked the rest of the way, intending to go through and lose myself in the confusion of battle's end, but just as I opened the door the first crack, a hand came over my right shoulder to push it shut again.

"You don't really want to do that, Terry," Garth said, leaning his weight on the hand that kept the door closed despite my furious tugging. "Daldrin warned us you would probably try something like this, but you'd be a fool to go ahead with it. A woman alone on this world doesn't stand much of a chance of surviving."

"And I don't see much of a chance if I stay here," I retorted without turning to look at him. "If I want to be a fool that's my business. Let go of the door."

"There is no need for him to release the door," another voice came, making me close my eyes and lower my head to mourn the passing of what would probably be my last chance to get out of there. "Do you again seek to escape earned punishment, *wenda*? I have told you that this time the punishment will be yours, and I have not lied."

His hand came to my hair to pull my head back with a jerk, and Garth frowned at the gasp forced out of me.

"Tammad, what are you doing?" he demanded, his gray eyes showing confusion. "Hasn't anyone told you how much we owe her?"

"Garth, you promised!" I whispered intensely, tears in my eyes from the hold on my hair. "Please, you promised!"

"What is this of a promise?" Tammad asked, the same confusion touching Garth reaching for him. "What was to be told to me that this *wenda* does not wish me to know?"

"It was a promise made to be broken," Garth answered, looking at me with gentle regret. "Len and I would still be chained slaves in the palace kitchen if Terry hadn't gotten us out. She even supplied a guide and protector, another palace slave named Daldrin, to go with us and make sure we reached camp in one piece. She told us where you were being held so your men might free you, not realizing there was another attack being planned. If Cinnan's men hadn't been there, you'd be owing your life and freedom to her right now."

"I see," Tammad said heavily, his hand opening slowly to release my hair. "And yet she aided the one called *Chama,* walking beside her as a valued friend."

"Daldrin told us all about that." Garth snorted out his disdain for the idea. "That Aesnil female threatened to throw her to the male work slaves if she refused to cooperate. She pretended to be a willing worker just to get enough elbow room to do what had to be done. Like freeing us to arrange for your rescue and staying behind to make sure we weren't chased down."

"And doing what she could against the beasts of the arena," Len put in from somewhere behind Tammad. "I saw those two animals coming for you when Cinnan tried to reach the swords. You threw sand in their eyes, but it was the deep fear Terry projected at the same time that kept one of the things from attacking again. I was only on the fringes of the projection, but it almost knocked me over. If not for that, our rescue might have come a little too late to do you and Cinnan any good."

There was suddenly a lot of silence all around, most of it coming from Tammad, but I still didn't look up or open my shield. I was too wrapped up in my own emotions to worry about what anyone else was feeling.

"Terril, you said nothing of any of this when I accused you," Tammad said at last, his voice sounding tired. "Why did you not tell me of what you had done on my behalf? Did you think I would disbelieve you?"

"What does it matter?" I whispered, closing my eyes. "It doesn't even matter whether or not I helped you. All that matters is that I'm still here instead of gone."

"*Hama,* why do you speak so?" he sighed, coming closer to fold me in his arms: "It matters a great deal that your thoughts were for me. It is an action that speaks more clearly than words of your love for me. A love I had almost begun to doubt."

He held me strongly but gently against his chest, bringing me closer to the familiar smell of him, holding me the way I'd needed to be held for so long. It didn't make saying the words any easier, but they still had to be said.

"I can't stay on this world," I whispered, rubbing my cheek on his chest despite the sweat covering him. "I don't understand it and I don't fit in, and I'm sick to death of being used. I'm going back to Central, where I belong."

"I see it is indeed necessary that we talk," he murmured, stroking my hair, then raised his voice as he switched languages. "Loddar, gather our *l'lendaa* together and prepare them. We return to camp immediately."

"Tammad, I will not hear of your leaving so soon," Cinnan's voice broke in, causing the barbarian to turn to him. He stood in front of the now-closed door to the small pleasure room, much of the anger gone from his light eyes. "You must remain a time as my guest, to allow me to thank you properly for your assistance. And to allow us both to see to that female you hold."

"We were mistaken, Cinnan," Tammad said quietly, tightening his arms about me. "My men have told me of her assistance to both them and us, without which we would have found attaining freedom much more difficult. You are done with punishing that – common girl – you found?"

"For now," Cinnan murmured with a faint grin. "I took the time to add something of additional pain to the strapping given her, teaching her the power of a man. When next I touch her there will be no pain, only the helplessness of a woman in the arms of a man. She will quickly learn to crave it as all women do."

I pushed out of Tammad's arms in disgust, wishing I could open my shield and blast every man in that room for the smug agreement I could see on their faces. Instead I turned away from them, hating them and their world even more than I had.

"I must speak to my woman privately," Tammad told Cinnan as he put a big hand on my shoulder to keep me from moving any farther. "I will be pleased to accept your hospitality, provided there will not be a great deal of delay. These words have spent too long a time unspoken."

"It will take but a moment to gather my men," he said, walking toward the sword he had put down earlier. "Once we have shown our strength and determination to the palace guard, they will not long oppose us. All matters will be righted this day, for they have already been paid for in blood. Remain here till my return, and we will enter the palace together."

Tammad nodded and Cinnan left, and we began our wait in silence.

## SEVENTEEN

In less than an hour Tammad and I were walking into my rooms at the palace, led there by a female slave. The girl cringed away from the barbarian in wide-eyed fear, knowing him for a *vendra* by the red *haddin* he still wore, obviously worried that the palace was being invaded. The palace guard had made no attempt to stop Cinnan when he marched Aesnil in in front of him, her body now clasped in five bronze bands, the tears still falling from her eyes. I had reluctantly lifted my shield to help her with her pain, and had discovered something I hadn't expected. Unless I was interpreting her wrong, Aesnil was all through with being *Chama*. If she couldn't direct her country and her own life completely alone, she was determined not to do it at all. She was too proud to play puppet for anyone, no matter what they did to her. Her worst fears had already been realized, and she was prepared to give up her life if necessary. Cinnan would find himself with more trouble than he'd bargained for in the days ahead; the laws of the country demanded a *Chama* on the throne, and he'd ruined the only one they had. I took my mind away from Aesnil's and let her be, hoping she was strong enough to keep to her resolve. She may have been ruthless as a *Chama*, but at least she'd been free.

"Go to my men and tell them to fetch me a *haddin* from our camp, girl," Tammad told the trembling slave, keeping his voice soft and soothing despite the disgust he felt. He was completely repelled by the sight of the slave, notwithstanding the fact that she was attractive and very available. "This color does nothing to calm my memories of the unpleasantness now past."

"At once, *denday*," the girl whispered, edging toward the door he held open for her. Her relief flashed strong when she darted through and escaped without being grabbed, and Tammad closed the door behind her with a grimace.

"I cannot bear such slavey cringing," he muttered, putting his palm on the hilt of the sword he now wore scabbarded at his side. "How could a man put children on such a one and expect to receive strong sons and courageous daughters from the effort? When the spirits dies in a woman, even her offspring are tainted with the loss."

"Some time you might try asking yourself what killed her spirit," I commented, walking toward the room's windows. "How many times do you think you can rape and beat a woman before she cringes at the very sight of a male? Until you've had a taste of being treated like that, you can't afford to sneer."

"You are mistaken in thinking I sneer," he said, following me over to the windows and stopping behind me. "I merely find myself furious that any man would produce such a state in a woman, believing her attractiveness to be thereby increased. If one is a man, one need not beat a woman to the ground and put a sword point to her throat to obtain obedience from – Why is your back marked, as though you were beaten with a whip? Why was I not told that someone had dared to treat you so?"

He had moved my hair aside to get a better look at the welts still covering me, his mind exploding with a near-insane anger. He had kept his voice down with effort, so as not to frighten me, but I had never seen him so close to being out of control. I stared at the thin curtains covering the sunlit windows, not knowing what to say, and he turned me gently, then put his hand beneath my chin.

"*Hama*, do not fear to speak to me," he urged, raising his face so that I must look up at him. "You are my beloved, my chosen. What other has greater right than I to avenge harm done you? Tell me who is responsible for having given you such pain."

"This world is responsible," I told him, trying to make him believe it as much as I did. "If I'd been on Central it never would have happened. I'm going back with your help or without it."

"Had I kept you beside me, none of this would have occurred," he sighed, a knowledge of guilt touching him briefly. "You have my word it will not happen again, no matter the need for traveling about. You will accompany me where I go, standing always beneath my protection. No other will touch you so long as I live."

"But after that all bets are off," I said, pulling my face out of his hand. "As if I'd care what happened to me if you were killed. And how long is your guarantee good for, O *denday*? A week, a month, a year? On this world, how could I know? And what would I have to do to please my next owner? I'm tired of being used in all senses of the word, and I want to go home!"

"To be used by those who named you Prime." His eyes narrowed as he let me go. "I found little difficulty in buying you from your people, *wenda,* people who profess to be above the purchase and sale of others. They use your talent in whatever way best serves their purpose, at the same time selling your body to any man who is able to meet their price. You fear my world and with good reason, yet here my protection is yours for the taking. Who is there who will protect you upon your own world?"

"Murdock will protect me," I choked, turning away from that remorseless blue gaze. "Even if it were as bad as you say, Murdock would protect me. You saw how he stood up to you when we landed."

"The Murdock McKenzie is a true man," he agreed, but only to that one point. "He attempted to take you from my side when he believed you no longer cared for me, yet his power upon his own world comes from those you would have him oppose. He would make the attempt, of that I have no doubt, and would go down beneath their heels when they saw he stood in the way of their desires. What then, *hama*? What would become of you then?"

I shook my head without answering, and put my face into my hands in defeat. Everything he said was true, and I felt more trapped than I had in his cell beneath the *vendra ralle.* I couldn't stay on Rimilia, but returning to Central would be a wasted effort; if I didn't want to be used again, I'd have to find something else to do.

"There are planets other than Central in the Amalgamation," I said at last, taking my hands away from my face. "I'll find one where no one knows me and start a new life. I'll get a job doing anything at all, and never let anyone find out what I am. I'll just — damn!"

I pulled myself away from the window and went to stand in the middle of the room, my hands in my hair and wild frustration in my mind. How could I live a life where I would have to give up using a part of myself in order to be safe and blend in with everyone else? And what would happen if I slipped and accidentally used my ability with witnesses around? I'd be pursued all over again, wanted for nothing more than my ability again, made to run and hide to keep from being captured and used again. And if I managed to get away, where would I go then? Where would I find a place where the same would not happen all over again? Where, in the entire universe, would I ever find peace?

"It is fortunate the decision of what is to become of you is not yours to make," Tammad remarked, coming up behind me again to put his hands on my arms. "'The agony of such a decision would be great indeed, too great for the small shoulders of a *wenda* to bear the burden of. I will not ask you to accept my word on the matter of your safety, for words are easily spoken. You will see for yourself how matters go. Now tell me: who is to blame for the whip marks on you? I will not rest till I have learned his name, therefore would you be wise to speak now."

"So you want me to speak, do you?" I growled, pulling from his hands to turn and face him. I was furious at what he'd said, and wanted him to know it. "The name of the man responsible is Tammad. Now go ahead and take that wonderful vengeance that's so rightfully yours!"

"What do you say, *wenda*?" he frowned, staring down at me. "Never have I touched you with a whip."

"You didn't have to," I answered grimly. "Back there in the desert, with the Hamarda, you refused to touch me because I'd been beaten down too far for your tastes. I reminded you too much of those slaves you so despise, so you told your good brother Kednin that you were no longer interested in me. I needed your arms so much then, but all you did was let other men use me and then get up and walk out, too good to contaminate yourself by touching a slave. That's why Kednin had me whipped, because I'd failed to please you, and that's why I would have been whipped to death once Kednin had the chance to watch the fun. I was an idiot to get loose and run away; if I hadn't, I would have been out of this long ago."

I turned away from the stunned expression on his face and in his mind and ran toward my sleeping room, needing to be alone for a while. I closed the door and leaned against it, blinking away the blurry vision I'd suddenly developed. It seemed impossibly hard for some men to understand how tiring being brave all the time tended to be; all they could see was how easy it was for them to do. I wasn't proud of what I'd done in the Hamarda camp, but all the time I'd been condemning myself for what I'd thought had repelled him, he was being self-righteous and particular. I walked to the pile of cushions the room held and lowered myself down among them, then simply closed my eyes.

I was nearly asleep when I heard the door opening, and Tammad come walking in. His mind had tried to recapture the calm that was so much a part of him, but this time he hadn't made it. He was furious with himself, and was having trouble keeping that fury from lashing out all around him. He came over to me where I lay among the cushions, and crouched down to touch my face.

"Terril, I have come to offer my apologies," he said, his voice tight with the anger he held inside. "I searched for other words which would speak of the stupidity I have been guilty of, yet words come poorly to my tongue when they are most needed. I have too often depended upon my sword to speak for me, a practice which avails me naught in these circumstances. Were it possible for me to suffer the pain you were given, I would do so gladly."

"But it is possible," I murmured sleepily, looking up at him. "I can recreate every-thing I felt and give it to you just the way it was given to me. Would you like me to do that?"

He hesitated a very long time, seconds at least, his mind trying to adapt to the alienness of the concept. Then, very solemnly, he nodded his head.

"Should that make the pain more bearable for you, you may do that very thing. It was my place to protect you, to take you in my arms no matter the consequences, to demand your release or die in attempting to free you. Give me the pain you were given, *hama*, so that I may share it with you and thereby lighten its hold on you."

He continued to stare at me, the calm in complete possession of him again, his mind open and waiting for whatever would come. He spoke the truth when he said he would welcome sharing the pain, and I could feel the tears returning to my eyes. Deep down beneath the anger which had nearly dissolved was his own pain, a self-condemna-tion so great it made mine pale and wraithlike in comparison. I sobbed once before I could stop myself, and then I was clawing my way out of the nest of cushions to throw myself into his arms. He held me to him while I nearly strangled him with the hold I had around his neck, but nearly strangling didn't bother him. He immediately radiated such contentment and pleasure that *I* was nearly drowned.

"It still won't work," I moaned, trying to defend myself from the assault of his mind. "I won't work for you and I won't obey you, and I won't stop being what I am. Rimilia isn't the world for me!"

"It is the only world for you for it is my world," he murmured, pressing me back into the cushions. "This world is mine and you are mine, and no man will ever take either from me. I have missed you sorely, *hama*, and have spent many empty nights dreaming of once again holding you in my arms. Now I need no longer be content with dreams."

He twisted around to put his lips on mine, cutting off the rest of my protests; my head began whirling immediately, and didn't stop for a long, long time.

It was nearly dark by the time food was brought to us, but somehow we didn't miss it any sooner. I wrapped a piece of silk around myself to go into the next room for the meal, and it turned out to be a good thing I did. just as we were finishing the meal, a knock on the door preceded the appearance of Len and Garth.

"Here's the *haddin* you wanted, Tammad," Garth said, coming forward with the dark green cloth. "There was a time when I would have preferred red to dark green, but those days were before my time in the kitchens."

"You would have disliked it even more if you'd ended up in the *vendra ralle*," Len told him, closing the door before following him farther into the room. "It was all I could do to keep that from happening."

"It was all you could do?" Garth frowned, stopping to turn back to him. "You mean you manipulated someone to get that to happen? Why?"

"I decided I needed you more wherever *I* was going than Tammad would need you where *he* was going," Len shrugged. "I'm not used to the adventurous life like you rugged types. If I was going to have my throat cut, I wanted someone around to say good-bye to."

"And you complain about Terry," Garth said in disgust, looking Len up and down. "All this time I thought I'd been sent to the kitchens because I wasn't good enough to be a *vendra*."

"You were more than good enough," Len assured him, actually looking ashamed. "If I'd known it would mean that much to you, I would have explained a good deal sooner. I'm sorry, Garth. I should have gone alone after all."

"I don't believe this," I said, talking to the empty air. "One of them is complaining about not having had to risk his life in the arena, and the other is apologizing for having saved him from it. They must both be crazy."

"They are men," Tammad chuckled, rising from his place on the floor beside me as Len and Garth both laughed. "It is not possible for a woman to know the mind of a man even with a talent such as yours, *hama*. The thoughts of each are too alien for the other."

"That doesn't change the fact that they're crazy," I returned, watching Tammad take the *haddin* from Garth and turn toward the sleeping room with it. They were all amused by my comment, but I noticed that none of them denied the charge.

While Tammad was in getting rid of the trappings of a *vendra*, Len and Garth explained how they'd managed to track me down each time. In the first instance, the dead *l'lenda* had been found much sooner than they normally would have been when someone was sent to hurry us in our bathing and clothes washing so our guards could join the other men in listening to Garth. Tammad took most of his *l'lendaa* and chased after us, finding that the savages were moving in a straight enough line to be followed even in the pouring rain. The *l'lendaa* caught up to the savages right after they'd sold us, rescued the last woman who hadn't been sold, then set about "questioning" the savages with Len's help. As soon as the drugs wore off the savages were easy to reach, and once Tammad learned where the rest of us had been taken the savages were put out of their misery and the Hamarda were run down. None of them knew what had been done to me by the Hamarda, but when I had turned up missing along with a *seetar*, Tammad noticed that his own *seetar* had broken its tether. After buying the other women and sending them back with two of the men, Tammad had had Len ask the *seetar* if he knew where I had gone. Len had had a hard time making himself understood, but finally managed to convey the question. The *seetar* did indeed know which way I had gone, having followed me with his mind as far as he could, and he didn't mind taking Tammad and the rest in the same direction. He'd been worrying about me since I'd left, and was anxious to find out if I was all right. Amazingly enough, a *seetar's* ability to follow someone is greater than that of the *zang*, used in olden times on Central to track down criminals. Tammad and his men turned out to be just as amazed, especially when they were led to Aesnil's palace, but they were too anxious to end the chase to remember to be cautious. Aesnil had the three chasers arrested, then started her campaign on me.

Tammad came back just as the story was finishing, but before he could comment another knock came at the door. This time it was Cinnan, who entered with a small roll of the sort of parchment Rimilians used to write on. He nodded to Len and Garth, eyed me with a directness I still found disturbing even after so much time on Rimilia, then turned to Tammad.

"This was given to one of my men earlier this day," he said, handing over the roll. "He was directed to give it to the *vendra* Tammad as soon as possible, yet found his duties in the aftermath of the battle too weighty to put aside. It was brought to me no more than a few moments ago, and I now bring it to you."

Tammad accepted the roll with a frown of curiosity, opened the thing, then began reading. I could feel his anger grow greater the farther he went, and at last he looked up and threw the roll from him.

"Who is this Daldrin?" he demanded, staring at Len and Garth. "Am I mistaken in believing his name was mentioned by the two of you?"

"Daldrin was the slave Terril brought to guide us back to camp when our escape was accomplished," Len said, answering in Rimilian because the question had been put in that language. "He seemed disturbed over leaving Terril unprotected, yet otherwise did exactly what was required of him. He even returned with us to attack the *ralle*."

"So his concern was for Terril, was it?" Tammad growled, still glaring at Len and Garth. "It seems he intends to continue concerning himself with Terril."

"What do you mean?" Cinnan asked as I stared in shock. "What word does the message contain?"

"See for yourself," Tammad said, gesturing toward the roll he had thrown away before pacing to the windows. Cinnan retrieved the roll and opened it, then began reading aloud.

"'To the *l'lenda* known as Tammad,'" Cinnan read with a frown. "'Accept the greetings of one called Daldrin, a man who is less of a fool than you. When one finds a *wenda* worth banding, one bands her to the limit of his desire, not considerably less as a punishment for her. The *wenda* Terril will wear five bands when she is mine, which will occur as soon as I am able to return from bringing my brother to our home, where his wounds will be carefully tended. Should Terril no longer be in your possession, I will find her wherever she has fled; should you be less of a fool than I believe you and retain possession of her, we will face one another as men. My home lies higher in the mountains, north of that place known as Grelana. A true man might come to seek me out, yet I have little doubt that I shall find it necessary to seek you. Till the time we face one another, I shall remain – Daldrin.'"

"He doesn't mince words, does he?" Len muttered, turning to stare down at me where I sat frozen in place. "How many conquests do you have to make, Terry?"

"He can't be serious," I choked, shaking my head back and forth. "He hardly knows me – and I never even pretended to love him."

"A woman may be taught to love the man to whom she belongs," Tammad said, turning back from the windows. "Did this Daldrin use you?"

"We used each other," I answered, suddenly feeling defensive. "He was the slave Aesnil assigned to me, sent here with orders to rape me – which he refused to do. Why are you feeling so put out? You've never hesitated in giving me to other men."

He started to snap out an answer, then thought better of it and forced himself to calm.

"It is my right to give my *wenda* to any man who proves himself worthy of her use," he explained, trying not to sound as though he were stating the obvious. "For a man to take her use without my permission is an insult in itself; for that same man to then challenge me to battle is to call for a fight to the death. Had he not known my feelings for you, he would have attempted to buy you rather than tell me you were not adequately banded. We must meet, this Daldrin and I, and settle the matter between us."

"You can't mean you intend going along with this insanity?" I asked incredulously, rising to my feet with the blue silk still held around me. "I won't let myself be fought for, do you hear? I won't have it! And what about the rest of your plans, and the dealings you have with the Amalgamation? Do you intend just letting them …?"

"Hush, *wenda*," he said, coming close to take my face in his hand. "The matter is not yours to discuss nor decide. Was it not you who once pointed out that my love for my people was greater than my love for you? I now find that I cannot turn away from one who would challenge me for you, no matter that other matters, weighty matters, await my attention. You are mine, *hama*, and I will not allow another to claim you."

He leaned down to kiss me, then turned to Cinnan to explain what we'd been talking about. I let myself fold slowly back down to the carpet fur, stunned by what had happened. We'd been through a lot of back-and-forth about our feelings for one another, but now, because of me, he was going to face another man to the death. He was determined to go through with it, but I became just as determined that he wouldn't. I'd have to stop him – and stop Daldrin – without either one knowing I was interfering. I could do it easily enough but – without letting them know it was happening? With two overgrown, stubborn beasts who both knew what I could do?

How would I ever accomplish that – and resolve the rest of my problems at the same time?

How?

# IF YOU LIKED *THE WARRIOR ENCHAINED,*
# YOU MIGHT ENJOY:

## OTHER BOOKS BY SHARON GREEN

**Haughty Spirit**
Sharon Green $11.95

**The Warrior Within**
Sharon Green $11.95

### FICTION FROM GRASS STAIN PRESS

**The 43rd Mistress: A Sensual Odyssey**
Grant Antrews $11.95

**Justice and Other Short Erotic Tales**
Tammy Jo Eckhart $11.95

**Love, Sal: letters from a boy in The City**
Sal Iacopelli $11.95

**Murder At Roissy**
John Warren $11.95

### BDSM/KINK

**The Bottoming Book: How To Get Terrible Things Done To You By Wonderful People**
D. Easton & C.A. Liszt, ill. Fish $11.95

**The Bullwhip Book**
Andrew Conway $11.95

**A Charm School for Sissy Maids**
Mistress Lorelei $11.95

**The Compleat Spanker**
Lady Green $11.95

**Flogging**
Joseph Bean $11.95

**Jay Wiseman's Erotic Bondage Handbook**
Jay Wiseman $15.95

**KinkyCrafts: 99 Do-It-Yourself S/M Toys**
Lady Green with Jaymes Easton $15.95

**The Loving Dominant**
John Warren $15.95

**Miss Abernathy's Concise Slave Training Manual**
Christina Abernathy $11.95

**The Mistress Manual: A Good Girl's Guide to Female Dominance**
Mistress Lorelei $15.95

**The Sexually Dominant Woman: A Workbook for Nervous Beginners**
Lady Green $11.95

**SM 101: A Realistic Introduction**
Jay Wiseman $24.95

**The Topping Book: Or, Getting Good At Being Bad**
D. Easton & C.A. Liszt, ill. Fish $11.95

**Training With Miss Abernathy: A Workbook for Erotic Slaves and Their Owners**
Christina Abernathy $11.95

**When Someone You Love Is Kinky**
Dossie Easton & Catherine A. Liszt $15.95

### GENERAL SEXUALITY

**Big Big Love: A Sourcebook on Sex for People of Size and Those Who Love Them**
Hanne Blank $15.95

**The Bride Wore Black Leather... And He Looked Fabulous!: An Etiquette Guide for the Rest of Us**
Drew Campbell $11.95

**The Ethical Slut: A Guide to Infinite Sexual Possibilities**
Dossie Easton & Catherine A. Liszt $15.95

**A Hand in the Bush: The Fine Art of Vaginal Fisting**
Deborah Addington $11.95

**Health Care Without Shame: A Handbook for the Sexually Diverse & Their Caregivers**
Charles Moser, Ph.D., M.D. $11.95

**Sex Toy Tricks: More than 125 Ways to Accessorize Good Sex**
Jay Wiseman $11.95

**The Strap-On Book**
A.H. Dion, ill. Donna Barr $11.95

**Supermarket Tricks: More than 125 Ways to Improvise Good Sex**
Jay Wiseman $11.95

**Tricks: More than 125 Ways to Make Good Sex Better**
Jay Wiseman $11.95

*Please include $3 for first book and $1 for each additional book with your order to cover shipping and handling costs, plus $10 for overseas orders. VISA/MC accepted. Order from:*

 greenery press

*1447 Park St., Emeryville, CA 94608*
*toll-free 888/944-4434   www.greenerypress.com*